THE BIG FINISH

THE BIG FINISH

BROOKE FOSSEY

THORNDIKE PRESS
A part of Gale, a Cengage Company

WITHDRAWN

Thorndike Press® Large Print Basic.
The text of this Large Print edition is unabridged.
Other aspects of the book may vary from the original edition.
Set in 16 pt. Plantin.

LIBRARY OF CONGRESS CIP DATA ON FILE.
CATALOGUING IN PUBLICATION FOR THIS BOOK
IS AVAILABLE FROM THE LIBRARY OF CONGRESS

ISBN-13: 978-1-4328-7867-2 (hardcover alk. paper)

Published in 2020 by arrangement with Berkley, an imprint of Penguin
Publishing Group, a division of Penguin Random House, LLC

Printed in Mexico
Print Number: 01   Print Year: 2020

For Chris Markos:
May his memory be eternal.

EVACUATION PLAN

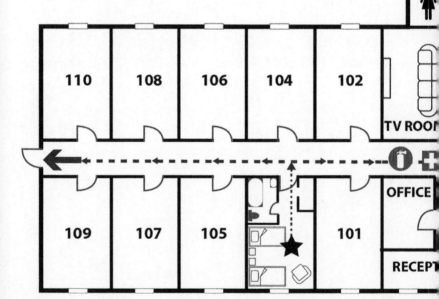

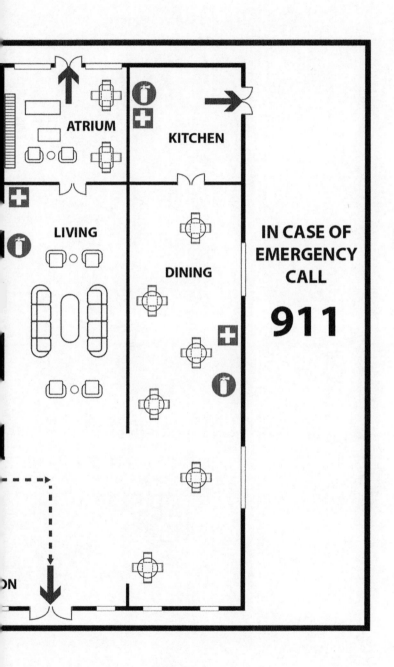

ATRIUM

KITCHEN

LIVING

DINING

IN CASE OF
EMERGENCY
CALL

911

ON

THE CENTENNIAL SCHEDULE
August 26 — Saturday

8:00	Breakfast
9:00	Sit and Be Fit, Atrium
10:00	Bus Trip to Walmart
12:00	Lunch
3:00	Name That Tune, Atrium
5:00	Dinner
6:00	Movie, TV Room

1

The morning started like always, with Nurse Nora rapping on my door, and me hollering at Carl to get his sorry ass out of bed so we didn't miss breakfast. And then there was Nora again, with her coffee breath and her hum of gospel songs, helping me stand and pulling up my trousers and shushing me and winking at me and telling me to let sleeping dogs lie, and *Why can't you be nicer, Mr. Duffy,* and me telling her if I were both nice and handsome, people wouldn't want to be friends with me.

And then, sure as the sunrise, Nora smiled despite herself, because I have that effect on people, and said, "Who went and told you that you're handsome?"

"A man simply knows these things," I said, sliding my shoes on, using her shoulder as leverage. "Hey, Carl, did you hear Nora calling you a dog?"

"I heard her call you ugly." Carl's walker

11

squeaked on the green linoleum floor as he made his way around his bed, smoothing the wrinkles out of the covers. "She's right too. I've said before that I can't tell the difference between you and Margaret Thatcher, but I think you take it as a compliment."

"I do," I said. "Old Maggie had bigger balls than me."

"Who doesn't?" Carl said, snickering at his own little joke.

Oh, how I loved our daily spar. There was no better way to sharpen the knives and start the day. "Those are fighting words, sir. If the lady of the house wasn't here, I'd set you straight."

"Boys," Nora reprimanded, or rather, as I called her, *my* Nora — my beautiful honey-skinned, big-breasted, long-nailed, hard-nosed Nora. She was a songbird built like a spark plug, like any good nurse should be.

She said, "The scrambled eggs go cold fast, and I know it's gonna take you a good ten minutes to get down that hall —"

"We move faster than that," I said.

"Mm-hmm. Not if you squeeze in your social hour on the way." She ran a hand over my cowlick and floated over to Carl to dust off his shoulders, where he kept a never-ending collection of dandruff.

"You are simply the best, Nora," he said, chin tucked so she didn't miss a spot. "Do you want to take another one of my books? Or maybe some saltines? I saved them from yesterday."

"What've I been telling you, Mr. Carl? If you keep on giving things away, you're gonna go broke." She knelt to Velcro his shoes, then wiped her hands on her pants and stood. "Listen now. I'll be seeing you boys down there. I'm gonna help Mrs. Zimmerman bathe this morning."

Carl let out a low catcalling whistle while I pretended to gag.

"You're awful," Nora said to me on her way out, which was true.

I turned to Carl and regarded him, with his spindly legs and his cardigan hanging on him like he was a little kid who had borrowed the sweater from his old man. "Why on earth are you whistling? You have something going with Mrs. Zimmerman I don't know about?"

Carl fidgeted some, then fixed his watery eyes on me. They were set deep, no lashes; he always looked half-surprised.

"Well?" I said.

"Of course not, and you shouldn't make fun of her like that."

I waved off the suggestion and set about

closing all the half-open dresser drawers. In the meantime, I could feel Carl's gaze boring into my back. He was trying to force his sense of decorum onto me, because he knew my tasteless impersonation of Mrs. Zimmerman was brewing. He never did like when I pretended to have a bout of dementia, which required me to holler obscenities in my falsetto while following him around like he was my long-lost love.

After slamming the last drawer shut, I turned to find Carl's face pinched up in worry. Like he thought I might eternally doom myself if I didn't behave.

"Relax already," I said. "I won't clown around today."

"Thank you."

"But perhaps you shouldn't have started it with your whistling."

"You're right," he said. "No more jokes at her expense."

"Fine."

"Especially since she has no idea where she is most days," he added, as if I hadn't already obliged him.

"Right."

"Have you heard her yelling out her daughter's name?"

"Yep."

"She sounds possessed. It's such a shame."

"It is."

"She has no clue what's about to happen to her either. Imagine what it would be like if she realized that she's headed to —"

"Christ, Carl," I said. "Would you shut the hell up?"

Silence followed, cold and injured.

For a second, I regretted being an ass, but the moment passed, like it does. And anyway, he'd made the mistake, not me. He knew better. He knew we never talked about what it meant to be put out to pasture. Not that or being put in a box.

Yes, Mrs. Zimmerman was on the tail end of her thirty-day notice, and, yes, she was fixing to be dumped at that infernal nursing home I refuse to name, and, yes, I felt bad for her. But I sure as hell didn't want to make it part of my morning chin-wag. I preferred sleeping tonight in lieu of staring at the ceiling, imagining the wasteland beyond this place. Remembering the little peek my uncle had given me while rotting away in his piss-smelling bed. It would take me days to recover from the thought, to shove it back into its dark corner, where it would bide its time, waiting for the next opportunity to eat its way out and keep me wide-eyed and wrestling with my sheets in the middle of the goddamn night.

15

So, no, we would not discuss Mrs. Zimmerman's fate. Living it would do.

Carl straightened up. Cleared his throat. "Shall we go eat?"

"As if you need to ask," I said, relieved.

Together, we turned to the door and prepared to meet our constituents for breakfast. And this is not an overstatement. Carl and I, we were the benevolent rulers of Centennial, crowned because we were able-bodied for the most part, intellectually sound, and, as I point out to my Nora whenever I see her, movie-star handsome. Never mind that Carl's face was back-end ugly when he didn't have his dentures in; he always remembered them, and that's what was important. And truthfully, between the two of us, Carl preferred to be the brains in the background while I served as the bullhorn. Which is how come I wanted him to get his ass into gear. Our people needed to hear from us, lest they think us dead.

I motioned impatiently for him to go in front of me, on account of him having a tendency to throw his walker into my heels if I didn't keep pace. He motioned back, equally annoyed, then made his way by.

In between his walker squeaking on the linoleum and me saying, "Any day now," there came a rapping on the outside of our bedroom window — an inquiring *tap, tap, tap.* Jorge, probably. The lawn care man. He and I had a long-standing relationship through that window — pounded hellos in either direction, exchanged waves between my newspaper and his weed whacker, and occasionally if I was bored, a handwritten *Gracias,* which I taped up for him to read. As for right now, I was closer to the door than not, so we'd have to catch up some other time.

But that knocking came again, and this time it was not Jorge-like at all. It was harder, sharper. It left the air quivering and stopped me in my slow tracks. I tugged on Carl's shirttail and pointed to where the mini blinds were drawn.

As Carl fumbled his walker back around, the window's sash squealed against the sill. Metal on metal. Carl cringed and cupped his hearing aids. I started toward the noise but froze when somebody's shadow overtook the whisker-thin slices of sun wrapping our bedroom walls.

Carl slowly dropped his hands from his ears and looked at me, mouthing, *Who's that?* I shook my head and put my pointer finger to my lips. We waited, listening. Everything went dead quiet, except for a sparrow calling through the open window.

And then, all at once, the dusty aluminum blinds went off like live wires. They clanked and rocked and flapped, and from under this ruckus came a foot — one bare pink-toenailed foot with a sole black as tar. Another foot entered to match, followed by legs with turnip-looking knees. And then more: smooth thighs, cutoff jeans, a cocktail apron, a bare belly, a cropped shirt, a neck, and a mess of straight black hair. So came a girl, no more than twenty years old, slithering from the opening as if the window had birthed her.

Once through, she landed like a sack of taters, though everything else she brought in scattered like marbles. She must've been punch-drunk from the fall too, because without even looking up, she got on all fours to chase down her bits and bobs and shove them back into her apron pockets. She stopped only when she reached for a half-eaten candy bar lying near the toe of my shoe. Her gaze crept up my leg and eventually landed on my face. I stared back, mainly at the shiner that had swollen one of her eyes shut.

"Shit," she croaked.

"The hell?" I said, having found my voice.

"I'll get Nora," Carl stammered.

18

She struggled to her feet. "Nonononono. Don't do that."

It sounded like something between a plea and an order, and it confused Carl enough that he paused.

"Go," I said to him, exasperated. "We're getting robbed."

He started moving again.

"Whoa, whoa. Hold up," she said. "I'm not robbing you. This is just a little misunderstanding. I thought the room was empty."

"Don't you move," I warned her.

"Chill." She had her hands up, her good eye on me, her chin cocked like *I* was the crazy one. "I'm not trying to jack anything from you guys. Promise. I'm just looking for somebody —"

"Of course you are."

"— named Carl."

I paused. Cupped an ear, even though I'd heard her just fine. "Say again?"

Carl, who'd made it to the doorway, stopped with his back to us and pivoted only his head.

"Carl Thomas Upton," she said.

Without looking away from her, I crept my hand toward the emergency call button hanging around my neck. I'd forgotten about it because I spent so much time pretending I didn't have one, though I'd make an exception for this. I was just about to press it too, when Carl shifted in my periphery, inching his walker back into the room and easing the door shut.

During the next heartbeat, I rewound the morning, trying to understand how exactly a young barmaid had landed here with Carl's given name on her lips. For whatever morbid reason, it occurred to me that maybe Death didn't come on a pale-ass horse, waving a scythe around. Maybe instead, he arrived like this, looking like her.

"He's Carl Thomas Upton," I blurted with a finger point, because ratting him out right then made a whole lot of sense.

The girl tensed. My hands turned to fists, ready for anything. We all spent some time looking at one another.

Finally, she said, "For real?"

Carl's lips parted, and he stuttered out something. Might've been a yes, though if so, it was loaded with enough doubt you'd think he was lying.

"No way," she said, just above a whisper and mostly to herself, before stepping forward, arms open to him. "I'm Josie."

He recoiled. "Who?"

She stopped midstride, dropped her hands, and made a funny punched-in-the-gut sort of noise. "It's me . . . Josie."

"Josie?" Carl turned his walker around, folded down the built-in seat, and sat to look at her.

I waited for something more from either one of them. Nothing came.

"Well?" I blustered. "The hell?"

"I'm his granddaughter," she said, like I should've already known this.

"Nice try." I smiled shrewdly. "But Carl and Jenny never had any kids. Did you, Carl? Tell her."

His eyes flickered before glazing back over. To the uninformed, he looked a tad vacant. I knew he was thinking through things, albeit a little slower than me. Josie glanced between us. Comparing, contrasting. Then she leaned in to whisper in my ear, smelling like bubble gum and hair spray and all sorts of youthful, girlish pastel things. "Has he got Alzheimer's?"

"No," I said.

"Dementia?"

Carl piped up. "I'm surprised, that's all."

I said, "I bet you are, seeing how you don't have any kids."

"My mom is his *kid,*" she corrected, glaring at Carl. He stared at the worn, impaled tennis balls at the bottom of his walker. She said, "Seriously? Are we doing this?"

I glared at him too, wanting to ask the same damn thing. All he had to do was open his mouth to shut her down, but instead he had me wondering which one of them was a liar, which was stupid. Carl didn't even cheat at solitaire. This was a clever ruse by her: dropping in on old, lonely seniors, claiming to be long-lost blood. It probably netted her some serious cash. On looks alone, she might could've had us too, with that Carl Upton complexion and birdlike build. But her disposition was clearly all sorts of wrong.

When she caught me checking out her black eye, her hand came to hover near the deepest hue of the bruise.

I tipped my head. "What's your story there?"

"What's it to you?"

"Oh," I said. "Excuse me. Let me rephrase that. Why have you come through our window on a Saturday morning looking like a failed featherweight?"

She drew a deep, patient breath. The kind that came from people who thought they needed to talk slow and loud to the elderly. I drew the same kind, to indicate I was neither stupid nor hard of hearing.

As I held my lungful of air in an asinine attempt to prove my acuity, she sighed and gathered the rest of her garbage off the floor, pocketing a men's deodorant, a few charcoal pencils, some scattered coins, and an order pad. Then she walked to a folded piece of paper lying near the base of the window. She sat on her heels to pick it up, and didn't smash it into her apron like the rest of her junk. She slid it into her back pocket instead, careful not to crumple it.

I exhaled, frustrated, and asked no one in particular, "Is breaking and entering a felony?"

She ignored me and strolled around the room, running her fingers along the dresser, pausing to look at Carl's old wedding photo, taped to the mirror. She leaned in a little closer, her nose inches from it.

"Please don't touch that," Carl said.

I said to him, "And so now, finally, he speaks."

She turned to Carl, jaw set. "Look. I came because I wanted to see you."

I said, "Nice try again, but visitors usually come through the front door."

"No joke," she said to me, "but I'm pretty sure I'm not on the visitors' list."

"There's no *list*. Where do you think you are? A federal prison? This is our home. We have a coat check, even."

"Super, but today I didn't feel like mess-ing with some welcome-desk bullshit, so I walked around back, looking for another door in, and then I saw that note on your window."

"What the hell are you talking about?"

"When I saw his name on the little sign —"

"There's no sign."

She smirked. "Stop it."

"You stop it." I marched to the window and ripped the blind cord down, ready to point to nothing. The room flooded with light and blinded me, but, sure enough, when colors started bleeding back into my sight line, there, tucked in the corner of the windowpane, was a forgotten sun-bleached index card meant for Jorge. It read *Carl is napping. Keep it down! (Por favor.)*

Her smile widened. "So I let myself in."

I snatched the card and balled it in my fist. My voice dropped into a timbre I hadn't needed to use in years. "Enough. Why are you here, you little piece of —"

"Duffy," Carl chided, poised to stand, though knowing him, it was only a threat.

She met his eyes, looking downright earnest. The girl was a pro, all right. She said, "I really thought you'd be happy to see me. I planned on spending the week here with you."

24

"Nuh-uh. Nope. No way," I said, and went for the door.

I was nearly there when Carl yelled frantically, "Wait!" He looked as surprised as me at his outburst. Nevertheless, he followed it up with an emphatic whispered, "Wait."

"For what?" I said. "She's hustling you."

His Adam's apple bobbed, and he opened his mouth, but nothing came out.

I blinked at him, hardly able to speak myself. "It *is* a hustle . . . Right?"

Another hard swallow, then finally: "She's telling the truth."

"Christ almighty," I breathed.

"Thank you," Josie said to him. And then to me, "See?"

For a moment, I got dizzy. Maybe from the surprise of it all. Maybe from the knife in my back. When everything finally straightened out around me, I heard Nora singing. We all did. The hymn filtered into the room from somewhere in the hall, growing closer and louder.

I swore a few times and walked in a circle. Carl stood, his legs bowing like they do, and wrestled his walker forward to brace the door from opening. Locking it did no good; Nora had the key and never hesitated to use it if she had cause for concern.

Josie watched us, confused. "What are you

guys doing?"

"You shouldn't be here like this," Carl said.

"Can't. She *can't* be here like this. This is worse than Milton sneaking in his cat and his cigarettes, and think of what happened to him." When Josie didn't move, I stopped pacing. "Well? Hide already."

"Fine. God. So much for this being your home." She swept past us into the bathroom, hopped into the shower, and whirled the curtain closed.

Nora's voice came to hover right outside our door. Carl's walker hiccupped as she tried to let herself in. "You boys okay? Why aren't you at breakfast yet?"

"We're coming," I yelled, then hissed at Carl, "That girl's not staying here."

Carl whispered back. "Let's talk about it."

"There's nothing to talk about."

He tottered around to look at me with this horrid mix of desperation and pain. *"Please."*

The walker skidded back as Nora forced her way in. "What *is* going on in here?"

A suspended second followed with all of us standing there, and during it I had an odd feeling — one I couldn't quite place. It tugged just below my heart, near my gut. Made it hard to breathe, and it got even

26

worse when I looked at Carl, with his forehead pleated all the way to the crown of his balding head.

I nudged the bathroom door shut and slapped Carl on the back. "We're talking, is all."

Nora crossed her thick brown arms, propping up her big bosom.

I looked back at her, dopey-eyed, hoping it would disguise the flush creeping up my neck. Carl fussed with his sweater, checking the buttonholes to make sure he hadn't missed one. We went on like this until she hummed an unconvinced *mm-hmm,* and backed into our bedroom door to open it.

"I tell them," she said to the empty hallway as if it held an audience, "don't be acting like you're blessed special, because you're not, but still they're walking around misbehaving, huffing Janelle Pratt's oxygen —"

"That was so long ago," Carl protested.

"And it was a joke," I said. "We were just trying to have some fun."

She wagged her finger, her voice quiet. "You know Miss Sharon calls an ace a spade if it gives her a reason to sell your spot for twice the price. And for you, Mr. Duffy, she might even consider taking a cut." She added a dramatic pause, then went back to hollering into the hall. "I tell them all the time, but do they listen?"

She smiled then, teasing me. Warning me. She had a nose for our mischief, and thank God too, because it kept us from doing things that could get us booted. Things like this.

"We listen," I said after a beat.

"Well, good then. Let's be getting a move on the day. Time's a-wastin'."

"Always is."

She opened the door wider yet. Carl shuffled forward, paused, and glanced over his shoulder into the room. I did too, and though there was nothing to see, I could feel it — a supernova energy, the kind from the wild blue yonder, the sort that came from sinking stars and gravitational collapses.

It pulsed from within our shower, the one with handicap grab bars and an emergency-call pull string, and it radiated to my fingertips, plagued me with ear ringing, and gave me gooseflesh, all of which made me certain of one thing: This energy needed a new solar system — somewhere far, far away from here — and assuming Nora hadn't already, I intended to make that point to Carl after I had my fill of coffee and cold powdered eggs.

"And now they're quiet. Who do I have to thank for that?" Nora said as she escorted us to our table in the corner of the dining hall.

Carl pointed at me, while I pointed at him. She laughed her belly laugh, tucked us into our chairs, and scrutinized our nutritious, portion-controlled, diabetic-friendly breakfasts. It looked and smelled no better than the C rations from my army days, but still she hummed an *mmm, mmm, mmm* before leaving us to it.

I kept an eye on her as she zigzagged between the mismatched tables dotting the room. Ours was an old Shaker-style four-top cozied up next to a window. I liked it because I could look outside and watch the world go by. Carl liked it because he could see visitors come in through the front door. But right now, we had something to do besides lounge around, keeping Centennial under surveillance. Right now, we needed to undo the nooses we'd tied for ourselves.

When I felt no one was in earshot, which didn't take much considering our present company, I leaned over my plate and said, "We've got to get that child out of here before somebody notices."

Carl tucked his napkin into the front of his collar. "Act normal, will you."

"Normal," I repeated, making it sound as ridiculous as it was.

He responded by slowly stripping the wrapper away from his straw.

I said, "I think you've confused acting normal with acting like an idiot."

"Nora doesn't think so." His eyes darted in her direction.

I peeked over my shoulder, and she met my gaze from across the way as she listened to blue-haired, big-mouthed Connie Salas yap. That old woman could beat her gums for an hour straight about the state of her health without even breathing. I forced myself to wink at both of them, turned back around, and, like Carl, paid extra-special attention to my fork, my milk carton, my cold eggs.

"That's more like it," Carl said.

I faked a smile and added a singsong lilt to my voice. "How could you keep something like having a daughter and grand-daughter from me?"

"We don't have time to talk about that, Duffy."

I shelved the happy-day routine and pointed my fork at him. "Three years we've lived together, and you never once mentioned them."

Carl stared into his coffee, then reached for the creamer and poured.

I huffed and started stabbing things on my plate without reason. I couldn't decide if I was more mad or hurt, like we had *time* for either. It's just that we'd itemized our entire lives for each other, starting with the days we were born. Nothing was secreted, not our stories of losing our virginity, not our shared complaints of persistent hemorrhoids, not our madcap ideas about God and heaven. We'd shared it all. Except for, I guess, we hadn't.

Carl finished stirring his coffee and tapped his spoon on the edge of the mug. Set it aside. "Let's talk about what to do."

"Easy," I said. "Call your daughter so she can come pick up her runaway."

"Well, I would, but . . ."

"But what? We can find you a phone right now if you don't want to walk back to the room. People carry those things around in their pockets nowadays."

When he didn't respond, I stopped assaulting my eggs for a moment and stared at him.

"I don't have her number," he said.

"And why not?"

His smile faltered. He stretched it back quick, though it didn't carry through to his eyes. "I think you're talking too loud," he said, then took a bite of turkey bacon and chewed it like cud.

I set my fork down, so that I didn't accidently stab him, and lowered my voice. "Her father then. Phone him."

After a sour-faced swallow, Carl said, "He's absentee."

"Oh? That sounds fancy. Is it a nice way of saying Josie's a bastard?"

"Duffy," Carl reprimanded, as if our biggest problem at the moment was my lack of civility.

I said, "Fine. He's *absentee.* So who else can return her to wherever she came from?"

Carl sipped his coffee and gave bald, Bible-beating Sherri Linley a wave from afar with his spare hand. He then plucked a sugar packet from the holder and raised it up as an offering to her, even though she had her own.

I banged the table with my palm. All the

dishes clattered, and the conversations nearest us quieted. The outburst was stupid of
me, I realize, but I'd had it. This was not
something to be trifled with. He'd heard
Nora, same as me. If borrowing a little
oxygen therapy from Janelle Pratt was
borderline cause for eviction, then running
a hostel from inside Centennial seemed like
a surefire bet.

I waited for the ripple in my water glass to
settle before daring to look up. Thankfully,
Nora had disappeared on some unknown
errand. My next-door neighbor Charles, sitting one table over, stared at me.

"Something wrong?" I barked at him. The
man was stone-deaf, narcoleptic, obese, and
destructive with his motor scooter. We'd
never gotten on, because I spent most of
my time yelling at him, either to wake him
up or so he could hear.

He turned back to his meal without answering.

I whispered at Carl, "I nearly solved this
problem ten minutes ago, but you told me
to wait. *'Wait,'* you said. So I did, thinking
we'd have an intelligent conversation, and
now here you are, acting as if . . . as if . . ."

Carl set his coffee cup down, taking care
that his shaking hand didn't cause it to spill.
He wiped the corners of his mouth with his

napkin, pushed his plate away, and looked at me hard. "I want to keep her."

I snorted. "She's not a pet, Carl."

"I want her to stay here for the week, like she planned. She looks like she might be in between places right now."

I readjusted in my chair, glanced around, then leaned in. "Have you had a stroke?"

"Why would you say something like that?"

"Maybe your hearing aids are broken."

"I can hear you just fine."

"Really? Then did you hear Nora this morning talking about Sharon? Remember that lady? She kind of looks like a hornet. Been around for a few months. Keeps busy by handing out pink slips to anyone who coughs wrong. Sound familiar?"

After a reluctant pause, his chin dipped. I'd left out some of the more choice adjectives I had for Centennial's new owner, but he could fill them in on his own.

I said, "Well, that's good news. You must just have low blood sugar then. Why don't you eat something, and when Nora gets back we'll tell her what's happened. I'm sure she'll —"

"You don't understand," Carl said.

"No, you don't understand." My pointer was suddenly at the tip of his nose, and my next words roiled in my throat like bile before I spat them out. "I don't care if your granddaughter's homeless. I don't care if her name's Josie or Jesus. I'll be damned if one of your handouts lands me in *Simmons.*"

My voice cracked open and bled on that last word, like always. That's why I tried to never say it. Simmons Home for the Aged was the only other old folks' home in Everton, Texas, and the moment its name passed my lips, I saw the hellhole in detail. There was my uncle, lying in that bed, looking up at me like he was a dog I'd accidently clipped on the highway.

This was the same man who'd helped build my father's farm, who'd taught me how to fly-fish and whistle, and the very last time I saw him, I ran from him. I ran from that place. He died there a week later, surrounded by nothing except the moans coming from the hallways, and at the time, the news gave me a cool blue feeling: *Thank God I don't have to go back.* Three decades later, and that feeling had turned blacker than the inside of a casket.

I swapped my coffee for ice water and took a sip, confident I'd made my point by merely naming the dump out loud, but, just in case, I added, "You got savings for some other place that I don't know about? Because I sure don't."

He shrugged, like it didn't matter, and sat there for a while, fingering the dull wedding band stuck forever on his finger by his arthritic knuckle. I watched for a bit, then decided this must be about Jenny, his late wife. They were married for fifty-two years, no children to show for it, yet here we were. So he'd obviously messed up at some point, and now he wanted to pay his penance.

Personally, I've never really subscribed to that stuff. Too much work. Carl, however, believed in heaven and hell, and at present he thought he had horns instead of a halo. Maybe he was right; I don't know. A man like me couldn't get all square with God this late in his life no matter what he did, so why bother trying. But Carl hadn't been born sorry like me, even counting this mess, so I guess I didn't bemoan the effort. Thing was, Josie staying here was a horseshit idea, soul-saving or not, so we had to think up a better way.

I said, "How about you set Josie up at the Como Motel? It's only sixty-nine dollars a night."

"That fleabag?" Carl said.

"It's a roof."

"I wouldn't let my dog sleep there."

"Okay then. The hotel in town."

He gave me a give-me-a-break look. "A week there would be almost" — he paused to calculate — "two thousand dollars."

We both went quiet at the number. It sounded like a lot because it was a lot. More than we could afford.

Finally, I said, "Wait until she gets settled somewhere and invite her to visit later, like a normal person."

"There is no *later,*" he snapped.

"Easy now. How can you be so sure? You haven't even offered —"

"I *have.* There are shoeboxes in my closet full of —" He caught himself with a sharp breath and met my eyes.

After a moment, I ventured, "Not shoes."

He shook his head and said quietly, "No. They have all the letters I wrote to my daughter after Jenny died, begging her to meet with me."

"I see," I said, my voice wilting with the realization that he'd lied to me while hiding the truth right inside *our* room. I'd passed by those dusty boxes on the top shelf of his closet a thousand times and never once gave them a second thought. Didn't have a reason to. I would've never pegged Carl for the kind of man who would piss on your leg and tell you it's raining. Yet here I was, drenched.

He cleared his throat. "I wrote her every week for ten years straight, but the letters always came back unopened. When I moved here, I didn't have room to store any more, so I gave it up." He paused, shaking his head. "For *fifteen* years, I've prayed for some kind of response — a note, a call, anything — and now my granddaughter is at my doorstep —"

"Windowsill."

"— and I know if I turn her away, then that's it. It could be fifteen more years before I hear from any of my flesh and blood again, and by then . . ." He looked at me, his spine bowing. His chin trembling. "This is it, Duffy."

I had to look away; seeing him break like that cored me out. It almost moved me.

Almost.

He grabbed my forearm. "We always said if we could change anything —"

"I'd swap my roommate," I said, hoping like hell to lighten the mood.

"— anything at all in the world, it would be to have some family left."

"We can't go back in time." I spoke reflexively; it was my standard answer for regrets, especially this one.

"I don't have to," he said softly, carefully, taking his hand away.

I stared at him while it registered — how different we suddenly were from each other. Yesterday, we were a pack of lone wolves. Today, we were nothing.

"At least let Josie stay here the night," he said. "One night."

"We have nowhere to hide her," I said, feeling suddenly desperate. "Look around you."

He complied, even though he didn't have to; we could walk around Centennial blindfolded. His slow inspection started with the hall, where our room was the second door on the left. There were nine others just like it down there, all double-occupied except for the last, which Sharon was fixing to renovate for some new highfalutin, high-paying resident. Next, he looked to the living area, and beyond that, the TV room, which we shared with everyone, just like we did the dining hall, and the foyer, and the atrium. The glossy trifold brochure said the building was a retired bed-and-breakfast, but I likened it to an oversize wardrobe. And we shared it with two nurses on duty, one front desk manager, one life enhancement coordinator, one cook who doubled as the muscle when needed, and sixteen other senior citizens.

Hiding a girl here — especially a girl like

Josie — would be about as easy as pissing up a rope.

Yet once Carl had looked at it all, he turned his gaze on me and said, "I'll make it work."

"You can't do —"

"It's what I want," he said with some strength in his voice.

I opened my mouth to argue more, but Chef Anderson had come to fetch our plates. He slid them onto his tattooed forearm and stood there, waiting for me to harass him, because that's how I usually spent the first thirty minutes after breakfast. Today, I kept my mouth shut and my head down.

He nudged my chair and said, "What's up, chief?" in a deliberate way, like a challenge.

I didn't answer.

Anderson set the plates down and squatted, so that his head was table-high and impossible to ignore. He'd recently had a haircut and shave, effectively carving out his square jaw and his round head. The only thing that offset his symmetry were his thick eyebrows, which never synced up — even now, as they pinched together in concern. "Is it the food? Because you know I wish Sharon would let me stock my own kitchen like I used to, but . . . ."

I glanced at him. His chef's shirt, rolled carelessly at the elbows, bore our last three years together in stains. Seemed wise to act like this was any other day, and the only thing that ever changed about our post-breakfast natter was what I bothered him about. If he got a new tattoo, I'd find something wrong with it. If he flexed, I'd wave my bingo wings in the air and tell him not to get too attached. If he talked about getting laid, I'd talk about the clap. He always came back for more too, like a stray cat to scraps, and I fed him because I liked the kid.

I said, "Anderson, who was the seventeenth president of the United States? We're trying to remember." Trivia was a staple in my ball-busting toolbox, because it allowed me to passively shame him into going back to college. In my humble opinion, he was a hard worker who was working hard on the wrong thing.

He studied me. "Weren't you there for the inauguration?"

"Andrew Johnson," Carl blurted, taking my lead.

I said, "Right, well, good. That's settled. We can get on with our day now. Carl, should we head to exercise?"

41

I moved to stand, using the tabletop as a guide. Carl did too, while Anderson hopped up to place his walker in the best position. But before he'd angled it just right, he froze and stared past us at the front door, and then his big-eyed ogle tracked toward the welcome desk, prompting me to look with him.

"Anderson, move it a little closer," Carl said. "I can't reach —"

The way Carl's voice hiccupped to a stop, I could only guess we were all seeing the same thing now: our dear Josie, backside to us. She was bent over the counter to reach the desk bell, all legs past the fray of her cutoff jeans.

She waited a moment, and once it became clear no one would come, she turned toward us. She no longer had on her apron, and the daylight flooding through the window lit her up in such a way that you couldn't tell she had a black eye. Sun-drenched like this, she was an unquestionable beauty. A beauty who wore a pair of Carl's shoes.

"Jesus Christ," I said.

Carl dropped back into his chair.

Anderson instinctually, and without taking his eyes off Josie, grabbed Carl's arm to soften the fall. "Look at you two. Especially after all that talk about your glory days."

42

We stared at him, silent.

"Don't get me wrong, guys. She's hot. But you need to play it cool if you want to get some. Watch and learn."

He ducked out of his apron and left it in a ball on our table, then walked to Josie with a stride reserved for men with motorcycles who refused to wear helmets. The kind of men who meant all sorts of trouble, and the kind we all, at some point, were.

"Oh God," Carl said, as if just now realizing he hadn't thought this through. "What now?"

"Smile," I advised, doing the same myself. "You have a visitor."

3

I'd no sooner blinked and there Josie stood, leaning over our table with her hand extended, introducing herself to me as Carl's "grandbaby." I shook it because I didn't know what else to do. Her cropped T-shirt had fallen off one shoulder and given me an eyeful of more cleavage than I'd seen in decades, and it was distracting enough that Anderson took a long look at it instead of her black eye. Carl just stared at the ceiling.

"Nice to meet you," I managed.

Anderson joined us, swinging a chair around and straddling it backward. "Carl, you don't look old enough to be a grandpa."

"I'm eighty-six," he said, thrilled and chagrined at the number all at once.

I snuck one last bite of breakfast from Carl's plate while they were talking, since it was still around and it'd be easier keeping my mouth shut if it was full.

Josie took the seat next to me. "I call him

44

Peepaw."

"Peepaw?" I sputtered before it could be helped. What a hustler she was, granddaughter or not. I opened my mouth to say so, but somehow a chunk of reconstituted egg lodged itself in my throat. All of a sudden, it felt like I was sucking air through a plastic Stop-N-Shop sack. After a few failed attempts to draw a breath, I looked to Anderson, who gave me an unaware smile until I made this noise — this horrible noise — that sounded like a scream in reverse.

Immediately, Anderson jumped to, pushed his chair out of the way, and raised my arms high above my head. It hardly helped, and I started thinking — very briefly, as Nora hightailed it across the room and my eyes watered past the point of seeing — that this was how it would end for me. Not with heroics. Not with dignity. No. I would leave this world as an old coot who couldn't clear his own goddamn throat during breakfast. Maybe it didn't sound as bad as passing away in a piss puddle like my uncle, but that was a sliding scale I preferred not be on.

As my vision gave way, someone, from somewhere, gave my back one meaningful crack on just the right spot. And that was it. I coughed proper, and the offending chunk of egg, no bigger than a damn corn kernel, popped onto the tablecloth.

Crisis averted.

Though in the seconds that followed, while staring down the tiny morsel that almost took me out, I experienced an entirely different crisis. The existential kind. What good did it do me to die here, among my best pals like I dreamed of, if I went out with all the fanfare of an emptying balloon — which started its exit with a shrill wheeze and had a grand finale that sounded like a flatulence?

I frowned and looked up, only to find Josie standing over me, her hand poised for another karate chop. Valencia, our resident buttinsky, sat a few tables over with her fake-chinchilla-fur stole clutched near her ears. Nora leaned on Anderson, catching her breath.

"I'm fine," I announced to the crowd, though mostly to Nora, who had to report to Sharon anytime a resident required "excessive" care. That was all I needed.

I raised my glass to her and took a sip to demonstrate my fineness. I smiled. I sipped some more.

Valencia released her stole and petted it back into place on her narrow shoulders. She'd penciled in her eyebrows as inverted

46

Vs today, so even though she sounded fully recovered from the incident, she didn't look it. "I say you should chew your food better next time, Duffy," she said. "And you should thank that quick-thinking young lady for saving you."

"It's not a big deal," Josie mumbled, slipping back into her seat. It was clear I'd scared the shit out of her. Her voice had a tremble in it. So did her fingers. For a moment, I felt moved to reach out and hold her hands to keep them from shaking. But she tucked them away in her lap when she caught me noticing, adding, "You can get me back later."

It's no wonder what she had in mind. I straightened my shirt collar and tried to reset. "What were we talking about?"

"Peepaw," Anderson said.

I gave Carl my straightest face.

Nora patted my shoulder and turned to speak to Josie for the first time, but paused when she saw the black eye. "Girl . . ."

"I know, right? I caught the corner of a kitchen cabinet," Josie said quickly, which sounded like pure bullshit to me, unless her cupboard had a great left hook.

Anderson said, "Welcome to my world. Once a week, at least. Let me see the damage."

47

"No, that's cool. You don't —"

He crouched down and closed in. Josie held fast in her seat, trying to act casual. Looking everywhere but at him. As for Anderson, he studied her bruise for a hot second, but then his gaze grew imprecise too, and before either of them knew it, they were both looking at me as their safe point of focus.

I flipped them a friendly bird.

Anderson stood with a smirk, saying to Josie, "I'll get you an ice pack."

"Ice pack?" I said. "Whatever happened to a cold cut of beef?"

"They don't do that anymore," Anderson called as he sauntered off with our dirty dishes. "Meat carries E. coli."

I leaned back in my chair. "Christ, how did we ever survive?"

Nora chuckled as she took her turn inspecting Josie's injury, but the laugh turned into a cluck as she pivoted Josie's face by the chin. "You got yourself good. I'll bring you some over-the-counter for the swelling."

"Thanks."

"Mm-hmm." Nora straightened up, moving her narrowed-eyed, tender gaze to the whole of Josie. Looked like she smelled trouble, but, same as me, she couldn't decide if Josie was giving it or taking it. In the end, all she said was, "While you're here visiting, make sure these boys treat you *real* nice."

"That's the plan," Carl declared.

Nora gave him a satisfied nod and checked her watch. "Lord, this day is moving." She looked at me, shaking that pointer finger again like earlier. "You behave now. Don't be putting on any more shows."

"I have a matinee in store," I mumbled as she faded away to her drug cart for the midmorning pill distribution. The room slowly emptied behind her.

The moment we were alone, Carl blurted, "We'd love if you'd stay the week."

My eyes went wide. "We barely agreed to one night."

Carl put his hand up to silence me. "But you have to understand that we're a little worried —"

"Try *terrified,*" I said.

"Concerned," Carl amended, like this was an improvement, "because we're not allowed to have overnight guests."

Josie propped her elbows on the table, cutting me out of the negotiations as best she could. "Totally get it. But I know we can figure it out, Peepaw. I mean, do they check on you at night? Like, after the lights go out?"

Carl suppressed a smile at hearing his name like that. "Not really, not unless we push our help buttons."

"Okay. So . . . it's easy. Why don't I just come for breakfast like this, hang out, leave after dinner, then I'll pop in your window to crash. In the morning, I'll pop back out and come for breakfast again. No one will ever know. What do you think?"

"I think it's stupid," I said.

Carl took a break from nodding and hunched forward so he could see me better around Josie. "What's wrong with it?"

"Besides *everything*," I said, "where the hell is she going to sleep?"

Finally, Josie regarded me. "You guys have that recliner in the corner of your room."

"You're not sleeping on a daggone recliner," Carl said.

"Why not?" I asked.

"She's a lady."

"So what?" I blustered, though really I was thinking she hardly qualified.

Carl squared his shoulders, jutted his chin. For a moment, he looked like the man in the black-and-white picture taped to our mirror — the man from fifty years ago with the smart haircut and the tight neck and his arm hooked for his new bride's hand. A real gentleman, that man.

"She'll sleep in my bed, and I'll sleep in the recliner," he said.

And so this is how he shamed me. By being like he is.

"Now wait a minute," I said. "You know your hip won't let you walk for days if you spend any amount of time in that chair."

Carl shrugged. Josie appeared unmoved, which gave me yet another reason to find her distasteful. But that was beside the point. It looked like Carl had no intention of turning her to the streets, and I had no intention of letting Carl be more disabled than he already was. I got sore as a boil on the days I had to push him around in a wheelchair to get him to wherever we were going.

"Oh, fine," I said, crossing my arms. "I'll sleep in the damn chair. It makes more sense."

This offer quieted Josie and prompted Carl to look at me with this unrestricted delight that was both a thank-you and a holy-shit-we're-going-to-do-this glee. And despite myself, I joined him in it, because how could you deny that breaking the rules was just a little bit fun.

Truth be told, I'd only really given up

entertaining myself that way when I got to Centennial. I'd never forget the very first time I toured the place. It was colder than blue-belly hell that day, and the sky was dropping swollen raindrops that would've been snow had the temperature given up another degree or two. The overcast afternoon and water-streaked windows lent the inside of the building a distinct snugness — a warm gray without the grimness. They'd turned the fireplace on, and there were board games and soft music and people shuffling this way and that with convincing purpose.

After suffering some serious consternation about the money and the necessity and everything else that goes along with admitting you can't — shouldn't — do it on your own anymore, I decided I needed this exact sort of hug at the end of my life. Especially considering that Simmons was my only alternative.

When I finally arrived, I promised myself I'd behave. I wouldn't give this place up. Not for anything. Not for anybody.

And I couldn't let myself forget that. Sure, our little scheme gave me a fun skydiving buzz, but I reserved the right to pull my chute at any time, and I wouldn't forget where I had to land in the end. And it was here.

There was no other place but here.

Carl had settled in, pert as a cricket, covering everything for Josie, from the week's schedule to the weather, like we were going on a goddamn cruise. The way he ran his mouth made me worried to leave him unattended, so I stayed put to supervise — even as the music from Sit and Be Fit trickled out of the atrium and into the dining hall, reminding me that I was missing the opportunity to exercise next to my favorite resident, Alice Roda. She was my Jane Fonda replacement, but even better, since I didn't have to watch her through the boob tube.

"Hopefully, it doesn't rain this week like the forecast says," Carl told Josie, like we didn't spend every waking second inside.

"When have we ever given two shits?" I said.

Carl didn't even pause to tell me to mind my manners. He pointed to the sunshine outside the window. "I want it to be nice like this while you're in town."

Anderson, perched on the nearest table, regarded Josie, who had the ice pack squashed to her face. "Where you from?"

53

I held my breath.

"Minneapolis," she said.

"Minnesota, huh?" Anderson studied her. "How'd you skip out on the accent?"

A shrug. "Just . . . did."

"You a Gopher?"

"A what?"

"She's not," I declared in an exhale, because that girl had probably never been north of the Mason-Dixon Line, let alone gone to college. Building a cover required fibbing, but there was no need to lose our heads about it.

Anderson shot me a glance. "You're not planning on giving her one of your higher-education talks, are you?"

"I save those special for you."

"Right." He eyed the foyer, where the entrance's automatic doors were stuck open. Big Charles had parked his scooter there and fallen asleep. This elicited a half smile from Anderson. "I better move Chucky over and start lunch prep." The other side of his smile appeared when he looked down at Josie. "Am I setting an extra place?"

"Absolutely," Carl said.

"Great. I'll make sure to stick it on Duffy's tab," he said with a wink in his voice, "as a thank-you to Josie for saving his life."

I waved him off, annoyed at him for bringing that up, but he was right happy with himself as he disappeared behind the swinging door to the kitchen. Carl immediately started back up with his nonsense — something about game night — while I sank farther down in my seat and tried not to listen.

The tempo from the muffled music changed shapes, smoothing out, so it had to be time for weights. I craned my neck to see who'd taken my workout spot, and there Alice sat, framed by one of the beveled glass panes in the atrium's door. She was curling two-pounders, bringing them to her snowy white pinned-up hair, then back down to the lace collar of her blouse. She turned right then and spotted me spotting her. And, like always, I suddenly felt like being a gentleman. I straightened up, cleared my throat. Alice did this to me. Maybe because she smelled like rosewater perfume, or because she had the most delicate little nose, or maybe it was her eyes, which were the color of barrel-aged whiskey. Whatever it was, there was something to it.

I raised my hand in greeting, and she lifted her little dumbbell shoulder high to return the favor. Even after she fixed her attention away from me, I kept watching her, and it left me stirring in my seat. A week from now, if things went south, I could be packing my bags with only one place to go: Simmons. And this moment — me admiring Alice Roda — it didn't exist there. Carl and I, we didn't exist either. Nothing really did.

The more I thought about it, the more my excitement for our adventure turned into revulsion. I could hardly sit still. It didn't help that Carl's voice droned in my ear, talking about ice cream and art projects and sing-alongs. I couldn't take any more.

"Enough already," I exclaimed.

Carl stopped midsentence. "Excuse me?"

"Enough of this bullshit."

Josie smirked. "What? You're not a fan of canasta on Tuesdays?"

I waved my hand erratically in her direction. "You need to call your mama."

Josie's smile wilted.

"I'm sure she'll be glad to hear from you, and then we can all sit down and talk about a better way to do this little reunion tour."

Carl's voice went suddenly shaky and tentative. "I'm sorry, Duffy, but this isn't the time."

"When is, pray tell?" I spoke the words like a dare, cupping his shoulder like a big bully. It felt stiff and bony in my palm, but I didn't let go. "Maybe you'd like to talk to her too, seeing how you lost her number. How long has it —"

"Stop it," Carl said, shaking off my hand.

We looked at each other, both breathing unreasonably hard.

"Don't you have something to do besides sit here with us?" Josie asked me.

"No," I said simply.

"Go find something, then," Carl said, with feeling.

He'd never declined my company before, and even though I didn't necessarily blame him right then, it still stung. The hurt actually slowed me down, made me grab a breath. When I spoke again, I tried to make my appeal as a friend, because that's what we were: friends. First and always. "Don't you want to talk to your daughter though?" I said.

The parts of Carl's face that were tied up in anger let out a bit, giving way to something that looked closer to an ache. In time, that turned into a meek nod.

"See now?" I said. "That'd make everybody happy. Josie, why don't you give your mama a call to come pick you up."

Her brow knitted. "I . . . I can't."

"Oh, sure you can. You got one of those phones, don't you?"

"Yeah, but —"

"Then don't be difficult," I said. "If you two are having a row, eating a little humble pie and making a two-minute call is a lot easier than sneaking around here forever. Just pick up the phone, take your bitty finger, and —"

"She's dead," Josie blurted in two stubborn syllables.

Her words echoed in the empty dining hall and registered slowly. All the hope of neatly solving this problem leached from my chest at about the same rate.

"She's dead," she said again, her voice barely a whisper and curdling with hurt.

Carl wheezed out a painful little burst of air. I sank into my chair, not sure what to feel about him losing a daughter I'd never once heard him speak of.

But before I could decide how best to console him, his huff warped into a strangled word. "When?"

Josie held her head in her hands, and the tremors I'd spotted earlier in her fingertips were now quakes. "God, I don't know. A couple of weeks?"

His eyes went wild. "How?"

"She was sick."

"Sick?" Carl said, baffled. "Of what?"

Her head popped up, and she snapped,

"You want the gory details?"

"Please, no," Carl said, the words knotted together. "I want you to tell me it's not true. Tell me —"

"Tell you what? You want me to pretend like she's going to walk in and say, 'Hey, *Dad.* Long time no see. Where you been?' "

At first, this lashing stunned Carl, but once the pain registered, he let loose a single cry, then covered his mouth to keep the rest inside.

"Mom wouldn't have come here anyway," Josie muttered.

"Oh my word," he blubbered, turning in his chair, looking like he wanted to run away. Out of the room. Out of Centennial. As fast and far as possible. But physically, he could only stand in place, gripping the edge of the tabletop with one hand while reaching for his walker with the other.

"Help him get it," I commanded, expecting Josie to jump. But she didn't move. Didn't even blink.

I wrestled my chair back, but by the time I'd stood, Carl had already taken an unassisted step and was leaning into his next unsteady stride. It was only by the grace of God that he landed in the arms of his walker, and he stood there for a second, head hung, white-knuckled, crying without making a sound. And then he started moving, jerking the walker forward with every heaving breath, all the way to the edge of the dining hall.

He clearly needed help, but I didn't move and I didn't dare call for it. I knew him too well. Knew him like I knew myself. And in these moments, we were the same. When weighted down with a sorrow so large it didn't fit inside me, I had to be alone with it until it shrank or I grew.

So as he struggled on, I caught my breath and leaned my weight on Josie's chair, where she sat vacantly watching him go. At some point, she got tired of the sorry sight of him shuffling toward the hall and closed her eyes. But not me. No. I kept guard, with my thumb hovering over that damn call button hanging from my neck — but only because Carl was the one exception I would always make.

4

It was unbelievable that a tiny thing like Josie, who was hardly big enough to cast a shadow, had done so much damage in so little time. We'd have been better off housing a tornado, though you wouldn't have guessed it by the looks of her now. She'd come out of her stupor enough to quietly tend to her nails, alternating between biting them and picking at them. And with me staring her down, there seemed no end to the amount of manicuring that suddenly needed doing.

When I couldn't watch her go at it anymore, I clapped the armrests of my chair and said with lawyerlike authority, "Are you telling the truth?"

She edged out a glare over her knuckles. "Are you for real?"

"Are *you*?" My heartbeat ticked up a notch. "You barge in here, barefoot as a yard dog, dump a load, and expect us to buy it.

How do we even know that you're Carl's granddaughter, or that his daughter's really dead?"

She locked eyes with me, like I'd offered her truth or dare and she'd picked both, and leaned forward to dig into her tight back pocket. She drew close enough for a moment that her breath feathered across my face, and the sharp smell of it sliced right through her bubble-gum coating. It hooked my attention, jogged my memory. It suddenly became the most important thing in the entire room, even more so than the paper she fished out and tossed onto the table.

I cut the distance between us in half, my nose twitching. "What is that?"

"That," she said, holding her ground and tipping her head to the page, "is your proof, though I didn't bring it along to show some random asshole."

The smell on her breath bloomed with every word she spoke, building on itself, germinating, until it was a dense, distinct cloud that could be made from only one damn thing: *alcohol.*

I reared back as it registered, but by then it was already too late. Everything in me had seized up: my brain, my blood. It all stopped to make way for an old, well-known want that spread with the quiet efficiency of a gasoline fire.

Between gritted teeth, I said, "There's no way in hell you're staying here. I don't care what that thing says."

"Actually," she said with a smile, nodding to the paper, "that's my reservation."

I hardly heard her. I grabbed the paper and fanned my face to clear the air, which took a dozen wafts, plus a dozen more to really collect myself.

"Be careful with that. It's old," she said, prompting me to finally stop and take a look. As it turned out, my fan was actually a birth certificate for a baby girl whose name I didn't recognize: Kaiya Mori. Eight pounds, six ounces. Eighteen inches long. I rolled the name around in my head a few times like you would a magic spell, hoping it would conjure up a memory. *Kaiya Mori, Kaiya Mori, Kaiya Mori.* It jangled nothing, meant nothing. But suddenly Carl's full name came into focus, written with poised pen strokes on the line reserved for the proud father. And that, I recognized.

When I peered up from the sheet, Josie had her chin propped up in both palms, and her feet were rattling the entire table. Her shakes from earlier had moved south to her toes and picked up steam.

"I have my mom's death certificate too, in my apron back at the room, if you want it," she offered casually, but there was a hitch in her voice that gave her away.

I ignored the flutter of pity in my gut and snatched the table edge to keep her from vibrating it. "Fine," I said reluctantly. "But for your information, this little piece of paper doesn't somehow turn Centennial into the Biltmore."

She leaned across the table and pinched the top of the paper. Gave it a deft yank. Refolded it and slipped it back into her pocket. "Whatever. I'm not asking for too much."

"You don't even know what you're asking for. It is too much."

"Yeah, well, lucky for me I'm not asking you."

Maddening. I wanted to knock her upside the head. Instead, I thought it better to knock some sense into Carl. Somehow he'd created this mess, and somehow he had to fix it. I pressed my knuckles to the table and stood. "I think it's time I go talk with your *peepaw*."

She twirled her hair and studied the split ends. "Tell him I'm waiting for him."

I marched to our room, grumbling all the way. When I opened our bedroom door, my to-do came to a stop. Inside, Carl was perched at the end of his bed, looking about as sorry as I'd ever seen him. And the air in there — God, it was awful. It was laced with grief so thick it felt muggy. Reminded me of a funeral home. Odd, seeing how I hadn't patronized one in eighty years, not since we buried my ten-year-old brother, Cormac.

I forced myself into the gloom out of necessity, because I didn't want to leave Josie out there too long, saying God knows what to God knows who. We needed to giddyup this pity party, and fast. But once I sat next to Carl, shoulder to shoulder, I realized my ambitions exceeded my talents. I'd always been the kind of man who went out of his way to avoid needing this sort of comfort, and consequently I'd become the kind of man incapable of giving it. I felt a visceral need to shake him and tell him to dry it up, just like my father did to me back in the day. Trouble was: I wasn't my father, and Carl sure as hell wasn't me.

I resorted to my collection of hackneyed sympathy sayings — all bullshit, really — and settled on "Carl, I'm sure your daughter is looking down at you from heaven."

Like it made things different.

Like I believed it.

A sigh shuddered through him — a soundless scale playing down his thin body. I gave him a minute, then peeked in his direction to gauge our progress. He had his red-rimmed eyes fixed on his old wedding photo, taped to the mirror. He revered that picture like my mother did her crucifix. It was the only thing in his possession that he acted tight as a tick with.

I waited for him to say something, but after a minute of sitting there doing nothing but getting crushed by the blue in the room, I spoke up. "How about I open a window?"

He stopped me by grabbing my arm, his clutch weak except for his fingertips, which dug into me like little meat hooks.

"Come on now. A little air will do us some good."

"You don't understand what it's like to lose a child." His grip tightened. "To lose your *children*."

I instinctually bristled at this. It sounded too much like an accusation, and there was a plurality about it that didn't make a damn bit of sense. I shrugged off his grip and leveled myself on the bed. Tried to keep my voice as even as possible. "Exactly how many *children* have you had?"

His slack-jawed sorrow gathered up in anger.

"I'm just asking," I said, indignant. "Excuse me for losing track today."

He stared hard at me and pointed with a shaking hand out the bedroom door — counting Kaiya Mori, I suppose. Then he raised his other hand and pointed to the picture, and that's when I remembered entirely too late: He'd had a child with Jenny too. A stillbirth. I'd forgotten because he mentioned it only once, and afterward I didn't pry and never asked about it again.

I swallowed past the knot in my throat, cursing myself. "I'm sorry. I didn't mean to —"

"How could you forget *that*?"

"I remember," I said, franticlike, hoping to keep him from recounting it. When it came to talk about using a coffin for a crib, once would do me.

Carl shook his head and turned silent for a long time — long enough for the angry furrows in his face to unfold back to misery. "He was a perfect baby boy, Duffy. Perfect nose. Perfect lips. Everything perfect except —"

"Don't do this to yourself," I pleaded.

"— except for he wasn't breathing. But I still held him like he was. I kissed him like he was. I remember thinking everyone was wrong. I looked at him and thought, 'No, they're mistaken. They've lost their minds.

He's just quiet like his daddy is sometimes.'" His voice faltered. "But when the nurse took him and handed him to Jenny, and I saw her face . . ."

I wanted him so badly to shut up. "Carl, please —"

He balled his fist and dug it into the center of his chest. "It broke me, Duffy. I didn't know what to do. I rushed home before they released her so I could drag the cradle to the curb and pack up all those little clothes for charity, because I thought it'd be easier if . . ." His reedy voice gave way to a sob, and he covered his face.

I put a hesitant hand on his back and patted, trying to calm him.

"I couldn't fix it," he bawled before coming up for air. "So you know what I did? I stopped trying. I stopped coming home from the pharmacy. I'd hide out in a corner booth at the Biddy Board Diner every single night."

Somehow, I'd gotten to where I was hitting him too hard on the back, like I was trying to excise everything he was making me feel by beating the shit out of him. I had to consciously lighten my touch.

"You came around," I offered.

His eyes met mine, but they seemed blank, like he was looking at something playing on the inside of his head. And he stayed like that, saying nothing, until it had me worried.

I stopped patting altogether. "Carl?"

"I came around," he whispered to himself, "because I met Koko."

He blinked a few times and then really looked at me, and somehow it felt like we'd just been introduced. I'd known him to be happily married fifty-two years. I had the number committed to heart, because people around here, they compared the longevity of their marriages like you would baseball stats. I always lost, since I had none of my own, but I'd tout his to compensate. It was a strange source of pride for me: my devoted roommate, my loyal friend. And, yes, I'd had all morning to get used to the idea that he'd cheated on Jenny, but hearing him admit it out loud was like a sucker punch. And even though I had no room to talk when it came to playing women fast and loose — God knows, I had my fun there — I suddenly wanted to send him up the river on account of it.

The thing is, Carl was like my brother — not because we'd grown up together but because we stayed old together — and ever since we'd met, there was one thing I had all sewn up about us: He was the better

69

man. He was a God-fearing, good-natured, well-bred man. He was everything I wasn't, and that's why we made such a good pair. And now what? That bastard had gone and tilted our universe; he'd taken a dump on our enterprise. I wanted to beat the shit out of him for real. Yet I had enough sense to leave my hand on his back and shut up and nod like nothing more needed saying, because there was still Josie to contend with.

"It happened by accident," Carl said, sensing my anger. "She waitressed at the Biddy Board, and I sat in her section because I knew she could use the tips."

"You don't have to explain," I said flatly.

"I never stopped loving Jenny," he said, his voice breaking in a dozen different places. "She was my everything. My every day. But Koko's the one who patched me up. She saved me. And I knew it was wrong while it was happening, but I couldn't get my head on straight. Without her, I didn't feel alive, and without Jenny, I didn't have a reason to be. So I let it go on until the day Koko told me she was pregnant, and then I . . . I . . ."

"I'm sure you did what you had to," I said, disgust seeping out.

"I did what I thought was right," he spat back. "What was I supposed to do? Go be

70

with . . . some other woman? Jenny didn't deserve that." His face pinched up, angry. "And I was a church lector, for God's sake."

I raised my eyebrows and waited.

He shook his head, frustrated, and amended his answer. "I came up short — I know that. I'm not stupid. I missed my daughter's first steps, her graduation. I never even held her like I held my son, and that little girl hated me for it. *Hated.* I don't blame her either, but I meant to make it up later. Then later came, and she wouldn't let me. Those letters kept coming back, and coming back, and . . ." His eyes cut to his closet. "So I decided to will them to her, along with everything I own, because I knew by the time it all arrived, there'd be no place to send it back to."

He turned to me, face wet with tears and red as a blister. "Don't you see, Duffy? She was supposed to forgive me after I went, but now *she's* gone. They're all gone. Jenny, Koko, my . . . my *children.* I did them all wrong, and now they're dead." He tipped his head back to choke down a cry, then said to the ceiling, like it was an actual prayer, "I wish to God I was dead too."

The words hung in the air, and I objected to them with every cell in my body, even as mad as I was at him. Still, I let his wish pass

71

without a word because it fell into all that talk I refused to deal with — being put in a box, being put in the ground. *Later,* I thought, understanding that the vagueness of the promise made it possible to think it. *We'll fix all of this later.*

Eventually, the quiet in the room quieted him. His whimpering tailed off, and the shake in his shoulders settled. But somehow the air seemed worse. Now it was thicker than before, downright engorged, full enough to remind me of the day Cormac died instead of the day we buried him.

I could feel myself turning eight years old again, curled up in the indent of his empty bed at the farmhouse. I could smell him — haystacks and cap guns and sweat. I could hear my mom wailing in the room next door. I could feel myself holding my breath, trying to be soundless, trying to *dry it up.* It was a lifelong skill set that was suddenly failing me.

I withdrew my hand from Carl, but I could still feel the thrum of his pulse radiating from him like heat. Or maybe it was my own blood rushing past my eardrums, pounding behind my eyes.

"Carl," I said, my voice tight, "I think you could use a rest, don't you?"

He wiped his eyes with his sleeve, then

fished a handkerchief from within the cuff and sat there, twisting it tight as a rope. Finally, he let it unwind and offered a listless nod.

"Okay. Okay, good," I said, almost as a reassurance to myself. He could sleep it off. He'd feel better when he woke this afternoon — we both would, like new — and then we'd talk about what to do with Josie. Now wasn't the time.

I stood and put his walker at his feet, then folded down his bedcovers and fluffed his pillow — my normal routine whenever I left him for a nap. I joked that I did it because it took him so much work to get up, all so he could go lie down. But, really, it was a favor turned into habit. "Do you need anything else?"

A listless headshake this time.

When I made for the exit, he spoke up, stopping me at the door. "Tell Josie I'm coming. I just can't quite manage yet. Okay? You'll tell her?"

"I will," I said nice and slow.

"Duffy," Carl said, warning in his voice. "Without her, I think I'm . . . I'm lost. Make sure she stays."

I turned to him, though I regretted it instantly. He seemed small and wilting except for his wide eyes, which made him look crazy as a bullbat. And maybe he was, asking me to risk everything like this for a stranger. I hated the request, and I hated him for making it. The kind of hate that makes the ends of your fingers numb.

He said, "Please promise me."

I stared without answering until he went out of focus and the room appeared oddly empty. It was just me in the hollow of the space, alone — the lights too bright, the floor like quicksand. It took a dozen blinks before he reappeared, before the world was right again, and it's then I realized only one answer would do.

"I promise," I said.

He drew a deep breath of relief and closed his eyes. "Bless you, Duffy. Thank you."

I straightened and tapped the bedroom wall. "Rest up, friend."

"Just a quick nap," he agreed, hands on his walker so he could stand and go on his way.

Meanwhile, with plenty of reluctance, I went on mine.

5

As commanded, Josie hadn't moved, and this would have thrilled me if not for the crowd that had grown around her while I'd been gone. I'd taken a calculated risk by leaving her alone, but all I'd done was give her time to dock and unload her baggage for whoever might want to help with it. And she had plenty of takers.

I was still suffering the side effects of my talk with Carl, but there was no time to recuperate. I loosed my collar and pushed my way into the mob, elbowing through the soft, shapeless bodies of all those senior citizens.

I nudged past Big Charles, who'd driven his scooter over so he could spend one of his few waking hours in Josie's company. Past Alice, who smelled as nice as ever. Past Valencia, who was rubber-necking again like when I'd choked, though since then she'd added rhinestone glasses to her fake-fur getup. And there was Reginald too, the mighty windbag, who I disliked more than anyone here. He was a close talker who thought anyone who didn't graduate from Howard University like him was an ignoramus, and when he wasn't running his mouth an inch from your face, he was smacking his lips, which is exactly how he bided his time now while lurking behind Josie's chair.

Josie sat at the epicenter of this crowd, dining on fresh orange slices. When she saw me, she set down her snack. "How's Peepaw?"

"Not so great." I glanced around at all the expectant cloudy eyes. Here, saying someone wasn't well had heavy implications. "He's having a rest is all," I clarified.

The raised eyebrows settled. Reginald waved his hand in agitation at the false alarm.

Alice wiggled her delicate fingers at me as a hello, a cute crinkle around her eyes. "Join us. We're enjoying Josie here. It's such a treat to have company."

"Valencia invited her to Walmart," Charles croaked.

"I did," Valencia said, "but only because nobody had done it already. That's what I told her. I said, 'You shouldn't have to wait

76

to be invited by *me.*' "

Josie flashed me a shit-eating grin.

I sneered back and sat. With everything going on, I'd forgotten about the planned outing. We'd signed up for it a week ago because I was running low on toothpaste and Carl was running low on Preparation H, though we didn't need a shopping list for an excuse to go out on the town.

"Won't that be nice to have her along?" Valencia prodded. "Tell her that would be nice."

"No room on the bus," I grumbled.

"Don't be a putz," Reginald said. "She can take Carl's spot."

"He's expecting her here when he wakes up."

Josie said, "I'll be back. I just need to grab a few things."

"Oh? Do you have money to shop?" I asked pleasantly.

Her eyes locked with mine from across the table, and we managed to slice through all the noise around us — Reginald's lip smacking, Valencia's discussion with Alice about if it was a Sunday or Monday (even though it was neither), and Charles's heavy breathing, which was more than likely a snore.

She shrugged. "I'll manage. I didn't get a

chance to hit the store on the way here."

"What for? Here we have food, drink, and your dear peepaw. What more does a girl need?"

"Just stuff."

"Name it."

"No."

"I can't imagine what you might need." The nicety in my voice fell away, and I added under my breath, "But if you're here freeloading while you have the means to go off shopping, then, God help me, I'm going to —"

"Tampons," she barked. "I need tampons."

Alice stopped midsentence and put a hand to her chest. "Oh dear."

My jaw, which I'd unlocked to unleash a threat I had no power to enforce, hung open.

"Because I'm on the rag," Josie added, as if there were any confusion. She said to Alice and Valencia, "Do either of you have any feminine hygiene products I can use?"

Alice glanced at me without a word, though the steady red hue marching up her neck and into her cheeks said it all.

Valencia peeked over the rim of her glasses at the men before whispering at a decibel even Anderson could've heard from inside the kitchen, "Oh, sweetheart, it's been thirty-five years."

"I'm sure they have diapers in the supply room," Reginald offered.

"Oh, good," Josie said. "Problem solved."

Everyone chuckled and turned to me, probably wondering what harm there was in having her come with us. How could I even begin to explain?

"Leave a note for Carl," Reginald said in his deepest bass.

Damn him, forever fouling up conversations by blowing his hot air into them. All those curious eyes turned critical, and the very last thing I needed right now was a scene. Especially involving a hormonal woman, which if I recalled correctly was best dealt with by rolling over and playing dead.

I opened my arms to Josie. "Join us, please."

With this said, the older women, free from having to talk any more about their atrophied wombs, did their best to gracefully exit. Valencia declared she needed to get on her walking shoes, and Alice said that was a good idea indeed. Reginald shuffled away too, muttering something about his wallet, and Charles, true to form, slept. Drool had already collected near the breast pocket of his gigantic T-shirt.

Josie and I appraised each other in everyone's absence.

I said, "Say I pay you a hundred dollars to leave and never come back, and another fifty to promise Carl on your way out that you'll visit him soon."

She met my eyes, blank-faced.

The chilly reception prompted me to do some quick accounting of my rawboned bank account. "Fine. One hundred to go, and another hundred to lie, but not a penny more. And at that price, you need to tell him that you love —"

"I don't want your money."

"Would you rather have Carl's? Is that what you're after?"

She paused, then reached for a string hanging from her cutoff jeans and ripped it away with a violent tug. "My mom's been sending that shit back to him for years."

"Perhaps you're more reasonable."

She tore another thread away and chucked it to the ground. "Perhaps you don't get it."

"I understand that she was upset with him."

"You don't understand anything," Josie said, genuinely affronted. "You probably had a dad who taught you how to throw the football in the front yard or whatever."

I made a noncommittal noise. She wasn't exactly right. Not all wrong either. My father hadn't been the nurturing type, but he did teach me how to a shoot a rifle. In the backyard, not the front.

She shrugged, mocking me. "What? Was he horrible? Did he ignore you and then shove some cash in an envelope to make up for it? Or did he split town before you were even born?" Her chin went wobbly, along with her voice, as she said this last bit.

"He was all right," I said finally.

She drew an uneven breath. "Lucky you."

I looked away; crying girls were like kryptonite to me, probably on account of watching my mother boo-hoo plenty, and it appeared things were headed that way. Yet once I steeled my nerves and glanced back, I found Josie lounging with her bare arm carelessly thrown over the neighboring chair like she owned it. Eyes dry as bone. It left me a little off balance.

"Listen," I said, the word drawn out in a long breath. "The bus leaves in fifteen minutes. I'm going to drop Carl a note. Whatever you do, don't get on without me, even if you see the rush."

Her eyebrows perked up. "The *rush*?"

"So to speak," I said, before getting up to trudge to my room. Again. It wasn't even noon, and I'd already beaten my daily step count by a shedload and then some. And damned if I didn't add extra steps once I made it to the hall too, but only because Alice, Valencia, and Reginald were clustered around the very last door on the right, looking at something. Had to be good if they'd risk missing the bus for it.

"Looks like this wagon train fell into a ditch," I said upon arrival as Valencia shifted out of the way, revealing a piece of paper taped to the door. I closed in, and a city construction permit came into focus. Dated and signed. Printed and posted. Like a decree from the king.

"Oh," I said, unimpressed. "So Sharon's renovation finally begins."

Valencia said, "I heard the bathroom's going to have marble countertops and a new skylight, and the bedroom's going to have a TV set on the wall. Didn't we hear that, Alice? I say it's going to be nice."

"It'll be lovely," Alice said, her breath tickling my ear. "But I don't think it's worth paying double the rent. How can Sharon get away with charging that?"

Reginald harrumphed. "She can't charge anything until it's done."

Everyone quietly stewed. Technically, the facility facelift didn't affect us and shouldn't bother us. Unless we died or moved, Sharon was legally bound to honor our contracts. And she had. She was. With fanatical attention to a little clause entitled "Residency Health Requirements." It had cleared this room out, and it's why Mrs. Zimmerman was fixing to hang her wash on Simmons' line. As for the rest of us, all it would take is one fall, one infection, or one misfiring brain wave. And didn't we know it too.

Reginald crossed his arms and leaned into the arch of his back, getting too close to me, like usual. "This won't be done for a while," he declared with authority. "Contractors are lazy. The city bureaucracy is slow. Sharon'll go broke without us around to pay the bills for this money pit."

"We're the money pit," I corrected.

A hush fell. Alice blinked at me with wide eyes. "Us?"

I wished to hold her then. Wrap her up tight and keep her like that, safe. Instead, I nodded. We made Sharon less and cost her more than someone new.

"Oh, phooey," Valencia said, throwing the loose end of her stole over one shoulder. She hooked arms with Alice and gave her a tug down the hall. "I say don't listen to him. What we need is a little retail therapy. Come on. We're going to be late."

Alice gave me one last worried look, then peered glumly down at her pink slippers as Valencia pulled her along.

Reginald sniffed loud, pulled up his britches, and stomped off behind them, muttering, "It won't be done for a while."

Boy, did this day keep on giving. I leaned my forehead against the permit, closed my eyes, and took a breath. I might've never budged from that spot again if not for the whine of Big Charles's scooter. Of all people to get me moving.

He parked in front of Centennial's bulletin board at the other end of the hall, and I schlepped down there and stood beside him. There wasn't really time to fiddle about, but I needed that bulletin board at the moment. Thought if I soaked up all of its colors, it'd take some of the gray away.

I began in earnest with the calendar of events, with its field trips and classes and games. From there, I read Sherri Linley's list of favorites, which was pinned up with her picture because she was the resident of the month. Beside her smiling face was a picture of Anderson dressed up for Halloween like an egg over easy. Another, of Alice after she won the euchre tournament. One more, of Carl and me, him smiling, me shoveling Thanksgiving dinner into my pie-hole. I'd complained when that one went up, but truthfully I didn't mind; this was my life, held up by pushpins. Seeing it made me happy.

It also made me a little depressed. When I looked at it all at once, my existence seemed too small — inside these walls, dictated by this calendar. It was strange to be this old, with your life telescoping to a point, every day worth more but somehow you spent each one doing less.

It could be worse, I thought. *Simmons doesn't even have a bulletin board. Instead it has those dry-erase numbers so the shift change knows your name and what time they need to roll you over.*

Beside me, Big Charles let loose a barky laugh and looked up, pointing his fat finger at a newspaper comic strip someone had hung. "Funny," he said too loud.

"Very," I yelled back. Then with heavy, deliberate steps, I turned to my room and walked toward it. Again.

6

Genetically speaking, Josie had missed out on her peepaw's tidiness. Carl cleaned up every day of the week and twice on Sunday, whereas Josie had been here all of four hours and she'd already crapped out our room. Her apron was flung across my bed, wrinkled up like dirty clothes. I walked to it, grumbling about making her trip to Walmart a one-way, and helped myself to her order pad and a pencil so I could write a note.

In the meantime, Carl slept. He had his head lolled to the side and his mouth hanging wide open. Napping like only he could. I was glad he'd settled after our talk, but it would've been nice if the Josie problem didn't feel like it was all mine.

Irritated, I ripped out a blank order sheet and brought it closer to read the header. Then I rubbed my eyes. Read it again. On every pass, it said the same thing: *Bates Bar*

86

and Lounge. Followed by — would you believe it — a goddamn local phone number.

It sank in slow at first — that Josie had not, in fact, materialized from space. That she was an Everton *townie.* That all I needed to do was make one little call — an anonymous SOS — and someone would scoop her up and return her to wherever she belonged. Once it all hit me, I moved faster than if I'd had the runs, and this was how I came to be at the nightstand between our beds with the telephone to my ear and my heart in my throat.

Carl slept on, and thank God too, because I was dialing. I couldn't help it.

On the first ring, I tried to calm down and reminded myself to whisper. On the second, I realized — given my history — that this wasn't the kind of hot tip I would've necessarily chosen for myself. And on the third, someone answered.

The man's voice was husky, a Midwestern lilt, edges roughed up by tobacco. "This is Bates," he growled.

His gruffness gave me pause. I hadn't quite planned on handing over a little girl with a black eye to a man who sounded like the type to hand them out. I'd imagined, in what little thought I'd put into it, someone more soft-spoken. A woman, maybe. But before I could really sort through that, the mirror across the way caught my eye, and suddenly I had bigger worries. Like where the hell Carl's wedding picture had gone.

"This is Bates," the man said again, peeved. "Hello?"

Damn that Josie, I thought, breathing heavy into the microphone, taking a step to investigate the crime scene. Carl never took that photo off the mirror. Said it caused too many fingerprints. Didn't want to lose it. Insisted it be in the one place he could see from every corner of the room.

On my next step forward, the phone cord ran out of length, causing me to stop hard, causing me to look down. There, I spotted something that made me stop breathing altogether.

Bates said, "Who is this? I can hear you. I swear to God if this is —"

I cupped the receiver to mute his voice and turned in a slow circle. At my feet, bits of photo paper littered the floor, scattered like bird shot. I looked to Carl, stunned, and in his loose grip was what remained: sweet Jenny, looking the same as always — wearing a shapeless two-piece suit, corsage at her breast, smile on her lips — only now she had part of her arm torn off.

I couldn't believe it. He'd lost his damn mind. There was no other explanation. Not for this, or for wishing himself dead. None of this behavior fit him.

But then again, what did I know anymore? He'd kept so much from me. Too much. I had no way to gauge how thin his edge between self-loathing and self-harm was, and I stood there considering it until the off-the-hook howler tone beat against my palm. Then I hung up with only one good option: I had to gauge his edge by imagining it was the same as mine.

With this measuring stick, I had an amended to-do list, and no time to do it. I bent over, sucking in a shriek of pain, and collected every last piece of ripped picture off the floor. Then I walked to the dresser, hands shaking, put the little pile to the side, and set about writing Carl a note. A few scratched words on the back of the order slip: *Walmart. Josie joined. Be back.*

The curled tape from the photo still hung on the mirror, so I pressed my message to it. From there, I pulled my sock drawer open, swept the unmatched ones out of the way, and uncovered the tin cigar box where I kept my dog tags, my fake Rolex, and my father's old Smith & Wesson pocket pistol — a two-inch-barrel .38 hammerless, which shot tried and true as long as the target was no farther than across a poker table.

Firearms were frowned upon here, obviously, but I'd cataloged it as an antique keepsake. People seemed to believe its age devalued its purpose. I witnessed my father shoot it only once, up in the air, when we won World War II, and I'd shot it a few times at a range. He'd called it his "lemon squeezer." Carl called it a memento. I called it my life insurance.

Very funny, Carl had said. And it was, wasn't it? But then again, it wasn't, because he didn't know how many decades I'd hung on to a single cartridge for a single selfish purpose. And he didn't know there was a shameful number of times I really thought about using it — long before this place, before him, before I'd managed to carve out this late-in-life contentment.

Nowadays, notions like that sounded like a foreign language to me. Pure gibberish. Imagining them coming from Carl's head was even more disorienting, like no language at all. More of a banshee scream. It was absurd to think he'd help himself to my gun while I was gone, and yet . . .

The clock above our door ticked away. The bus departed in three minutes — the time it would take me to schlep to the foyer.

I peeked over my shoulder at Carl, then slid the cartridge out of the gun cylinder. The cold metal case chilled my fingertips and sent my heart rate to the sky. It was strange that such a small thing could do so much damage, that we should fear or flaunt it like we do — or that it should be such a relief to have it in my pocket. But it was, and after I slipped the revolver back in the tin, along with the bits of photo, and closed the drawer, I felt safe — which in my opinion was a hell of a lot better than feeling sorry.

So with this assurance, I tapped Carl's reflection in the mirror once before leaving, and I turned the cartridge around and around in my pocket all the way to the front door.

7

Of course, Josie had already boarded the bus. She sat in the front passenger seat right next to Shawn, Centennial's life enhancement coordinator and bus driver. He was a middle-aged man who had a comb-over and entirely too much energy, but we got on well enough because he always saved me shotgun. Except for today. The moment I stepped outside, he started waving at me through the windshield like a lunatic, pointing at his new passenger to make sure I didn't get confused and accidently sit on her lap. I waved back in understanding, sour-faced as all get-out.

Nora's protégé, Luann, waited at the minibus's door for me, one hand jammed in the pocket of her scrubs and the other scrolling through her phone. As per usual, she looked bored. She'd confided in me weeks ago that her heart didn't beat for geriatric care. I told her I didn't blame her;

mine didn't either.

"We waited for you," Alice chirped from inside.

"Appreciate it," I said, pausing to admire her from where I stood. She looked to be made of flowers, with her lily white hair and rosy cheeks. How lucky was I to have springtime, anytime.

"Let's move," Luann said, emotionless.

I sighed and grabbed the interior bar in order to get up the first step. Like Everest, the ascent was the hardest part. Luann took ahold of the back waistband of my pants to help, but all she did was use my underwear to floss between my cheeks. Eventually, I made it inside and took the seat behind Josie, and soon after that the bus was zipping past the nearby prefab homes and fast-food chains at a good clip.

Alice, who sat behind me, hovered over my shoulder. "I can't stop thinking about the renovation. You're right about it, you know?"

I sighed. It hadn't been my intent to burden her. It seemed ungentlemanlike to point out a hole in her fence without the means to mend it. The best I could do at the moment was give her a little hope, even if I didn't share it.

"Don't mind me. Reginald's the one

who's right." I could barely get the words out.

Alice absorbed this quietly. "It's been a busy day, hasn't it?"

"A circus."

"Josie's a nice addition, at least. I can't believe her quick thinking at breakfast. She moved so fast you'd think she did that sort of thing every day."

I nodded agreeably but didn't turn around. My face would've given me away. Instead, I watched the back of Josie's head bounce with each road rut while she charmed Shawn by playing a game of twenty questions with him. She'd even put her hand on the back of his headrest and twisted in her seat to chat him up better.

My gaze settled on that little mitt of hers as it clung to Shawn's chairback, and once again it appeared she had the shakes. Those jitters from earlier were on the move, ping-ponging between her fingers and her toes. So far I'd written it off as nerves, but upon closer inspection I could see her fingertips moving at a hundred beats per minute. Almost like she had a condition.

I looked down at my own hands as a reference. They were lying still and obedient in my lap, but I remembered when that wasn't always the case. I remembered a time when they were on their worst behavior: years ago, in my old apartment, middle of the day, the September sun blotted out by the blinds. The radio — which I'd turned on to hear Oil Can Boyd pitch his last game for the Sox — played nothing but static. And there I sat on the floor in the foyer, next to an empty whiskey bottle and a pile of mail that had come in through the slot, shaking like a shitting dog.

Those shivers went clear into my bones, but they hadn't started like that. They'd started small at first, in my pinky, and the memory of that one quivering digit now replayed in my head until we shimmied to a stop in front of Walmart.

"Land ho," Shawn said cheerfully, pulling his clipboard from the dash.

I stayed put, but the bus turned into a beehive around me. Alice hung her head over the aisle to ask Valencia what they should shop for first. Behind her, Sherri Linley raised her arms, saying her usual blessings over us before we set off, a petition for strong hearts, sharp minds, and good deals, amen.

"Don't forget that we have less time than usual because some moron made us late," Reginald hollered, while Luann wrestled in the back with Clarence Riley's wheelchair.

During all this hubbub, Josie popped out of the passenger seat and skittered to the Walmart entrance like it was a damn fire drill. I tracked her progress from the window, and it drew me to my feet, moved me to the stairs.

Surprised, Shawn set his pen down and unbuckled. "Whoa, there, captain. Do you have your sea legs?"

"I sure do," I lied, every word a pained wince on my way down.

I stepped onto the asphalt, feeling nauseous. Greasy. Panicked. My flashback had caused phantom bottle-aches with no quick fix. For a sick second, I wanted my symptoms to be real, because then at least, like on that fine-looking September day, I could cure myself one of two ways: by either getting drunk or getting clean.

Same way Josie could now.

There seemed no other explanation. She had the shakes, the breath, the attitude. In my experience, that added up to a bout of barrel fever. And it looked like she'd already picked her remedy too.

But I had to know for sure. I commandeered an empty shopping cart in the parking lot and pointed it toward the building. We weren't allowed to be on our own. We had a buddy system, a check-in/check-out

96

system. I walked on anyway, toward the hope of guiltlessly telling Josie to take her drunk ass back to wherever it came from. I could not and would not keep that kind of company, even for Carl's sake — because aside from Simmons, the only other thing I truly feared was sliding back down the interior of a glass bottle and slowly drowning.

The wheels of my cart squeaked as I entered the building, where twenty beeping check-out stations echoed. I scanned the crowds, and there, past check-out number seven: a flash of Josie's pint-size body, her sleek black hair reflecting the fluorescent lights. With purpose, she disappeared between the racks of women's clothing.

So the chase is on, I thought, just as the automatic doors behind me whistled open for the rest of Centennial's crew. They made their way with the help of our two chaperones, who tucked shirts back in, pointed walkers right, and guided clumsy feet over curbs. After watching them for a moment, I decided a shortcut might be good.

I readjusted my grip and squinted at the signs hanging from the rafters. Automotive. Socks and Hosiery. Toys. Boys. Vision Center. Girls. Restrooms. Save money. Live better.

Like hell. Which way to Beer, Wine & Spirits?

"Duffy," Luann called. "Wait for us."

I started moving. Truth was, ever since Walmart began carrying alcohol a few years back, I walked a wide berth around the store to make certain I never went near that section. And this meant I didn't actually need a sign. I knew exactly where it was, because I'd spent so much energy making sure I never went there.

I cut through the baby section, going by rattles, pink rompers, bitty socks, and one runny-nosed young'un in a cart who would've loved for me to pull a penny from behind his ear like I do. But I blew by without so much as a funny face and popped out at the junk food. From there, I took a hard right, passing the canned goods, the toilet paper, the sodas. I slowed enough to glance down the pharmacy aisle, since it had cough syrup, mouthwash, hand sanitizer. Underage hooch. No Josie, though, so I kept going, toward the back of the store, faster now, and my heart raced with me, leaving behind a tender spot at the edge of my rib cage.

An endcap stocked with boxed wines and spritzers came into view, and somewhere nearby I heard footsteps, either coming or going. Couldn't tell which. I plowed on, breathless and bloodless, until I rounded the corner and reared to a stop with a startled "Son of a bitch."

I'd expected Josie, but instead — inexplicably — I'd gotten a battleship. A naval fleet destroyer. It was built to scale in the middle of the aisle with stacks of twenty-four-packs of beer — the main deck made of Coors and the captain's bridge made of Budweiser — and the hollow-tube gun turrets at the bow were aimed directly at my head.

I stood in its crosshairs, motionless and wheezing. It's almost like it knew that I'd been the previously crowned king of getting clean and relapsing, especially on a bad day. And this here, this was a bad day. I could already hear my favorite sounds coming from the shelves: the dull crack of carbonation escaping a newly opened can, the low-pitched pop from an uncorked bottle, the snap of the plastic cap from a handle of alcohol.

But I could take it. No prob. So long as I didn't make direct eye contact.

With head down, I took a cautious step backward, then another, but even with my cart, I realized I had to attack my retreat another way unless I wanted to fall flat on my ass. I decided on a three-point turn and glanced up only to get my bearings. Then I went no farther.

Josie was so quiet at the opposite end of the aisle while perusing the wines. So unassuming. She moved like a little sprite, poised and frantic all at the same time, her basket swaying at her side. She pranced closer, then paused near the aft of the ship, in front of the cheaper wines — the twist-tops — and pulled one from the shelf, gripping the cap as if she intended to open it. Before cracking the seal, she checked down the aisle and startled.

I straightened, trying to sound unmoved. "Hello."

She slid the bottle back onto the shelf and touched the neighboring bottles too, as if tidying up.

"On the hunt for something?" I said.

A shrug. "Thought I'd come see the cool beer boat on my way to the checkout." She gave it a once-over, then casually strolled to me. "What about you? Get anything good?"

"Nope."

A slow nod. "When does the bus leave?"

"Depends. Mine or yours?"

She rolled her eyes, then plucked the box of tampons from her basket and waved it inches from my face. "I'm all done shopping. See you back on the bus."

As she moved to blow by, I grabbed her bicep. We stood so close I saw the tiny broken blood vessels around her black eye, the buttery hue at the edges, the splotched purple near the center. Close enough to sniff the bitterness of her breath one more time. She finally broke away with a quick lash of her arm and stared me down.

"I think we should talk about your drinking problem," I said evenly.

She huffed. Then when she realized I wasn't joking, she pitched her head back and let loose a deliberate, hollow laugh, and carried on even after she began to walk away.

I blurted, "I can help you," then followed this up by slapping a hand over my mouth to stop an offer I hadn't meant to make but couldn't retract. It'd come out before I'd had time to vet it, to consider what it meant, to wonder where it came from. It had been reflexive, impulsive. Stupid.

And it had stopped her. She spun, drew close again, pointing at my nose. "You don't know me."

"I know you better than you think."

"Leave me the fuck alone." In this same breath, she took off with the sort of speed that made it seem like she'd disappeared. One blink and — hey, presto — she's gone.

A baritone voice called on the loudspeaker for a price check. I turned to the shelf and stared at the champagne for some undetermined amount of time. An uncomfortable calm had taken over me, like the eye of a storm. I picked up a bottle and tested its weight, then flipped it over to read. As I did this, a dull twinge throbbed through my back molars, traveled up the nape of my neck, and tickled the dusty parts of my brain.

The following urge was so familiar and came so easily, it felt like putting on an old pair of shoes, the kind with your toeprints already indented in the insoles. The kind that took you somewhere, instead of the other way around. Even now, after stringing together my longest run of sobriety ever, they still fit. But wearing them around meant moving to another home, another life. It meant going to a hell that only looked like heaven. And I had heaven already, didn't I? I had Centennial. I had Carl. I had Alice and Nora and Anderson. I had my health.

As long as this was true, I was determined to continue my hard-fought battle, my ongoing war, even as I held this bottle in my hand, as I pressed it to my liver-spotted cheek, this bottle that contained the one thing I had ever really loved in all of my eighty-eight years of life.

8

Luann found me wandering in the pet section, still pushing my empty cart, still reeling. Something in my face led her to ask me the most basic of questions: What was my name? What year was it? Did I know what time it was?

I answered all correctly, in my opinion. I said, "My name is Duffy Sinclair, it's the Year of the Rooster, and I suspect it's time to go."

And so we went.

"You can't run off without telling us where you'll be, Duffy — you know this. You should've stayed with the group, like always," she said.

"I'm not a child," I grunted as the bus's doors yawned open. I hitched one leg onto the first step. Everyone watched from the windows. Josie sat in the front again and didn't acknowledge me.

"No, you're worse than a child," Luann said.

I turned to her, shouting louder than necessary, "Am I?"

Everyone on the bus quieted, but I ignored them and instead focused on getting inside. When I reached the top landing, Alice gave me a worried look and a tiny headshake. A warning, not a reprimand. My outburst had *internal report* written all over it, and with enough of those, you might as well write your own eviction notice. Still, I sat down in my seat without apologizing to Luann. I didn't care about her or Sharon right now, not when the eye of the storm had shifted and I had the squall of my past life to contend with.

As the bus set off from the parking lot, the bullet in my pocket, which I'd all but forgotten about, began to feel hot against my thigh. I looked around, irrationally panicked that others could see those awful bygone days: me stealing my mother's wedding ring to buy booze while she was in hospice care, me in the back of a cop car, pantsless and puking, me browning out, blacking out, fading out. *Could they see it?* I thought. *Could they see me killing my own dog, smashing him with both sets of wheels before my drunk ass realized I'd hit some-thing?*

Don't be stupid, Duffy. No one knew you then. They were all too busy living their well-lived lives, and now they were button-ing them up with the same aptitude, peace-fully looking out their windows and enjoy-ing one another's company, oblivious, and thank God for that.

Thank God, too, that eventually I got too old to be an addict. I entered my last twelve-step program because it required some ef-fort to get drunk and stay drunk, and I didn't even have a dependable enabler. Every decent addict needs one of those. When I got to Centennial, I was ten solid years sober, reinvented, and there seemed no safer place for the homestretch.

Except now, on account of Josie, it wasn't.

Even with only a slice of her profile and the back of her head, I could tell she was jonesing, and jonesing bad, and as far as I was concerned, she deserved to suffer, same as me.

Shawn, with his eyes on the road but his head inclined my way, said, "Did you get all the goodies you needed from the store?"

With this, I remembered Carl, who had probably woken up by now. I'd planned on picking up his Preparation H as a peace offering and a pick-me-up, but instead here I was, empty-handed and bad-tempered.

"Yes," I mumbled.

Alice, who was sitting behind me again, tapped my shoulder. "Here." Her hand hovered near my cheek, holding two foil-wrapped butterscotches. Her sweet way of trying to defuse me before we got home.

"Oh, no, thank you, Alice. I'm not in the mood," I said.

"Do you have dentures?"

"No, I have my teeth."

"Diabetes?"

"No, I'm diabetes-free."

"Valencia eats these, and they always pull her dentures out."

"Well, maybe she shouldn't eat them then." I crossed my arms and looked out the window. Josie had spoiled this day beyond belief. Typically, I'd enjoy Alice's company, invite her to sit next to me, relish in her perfume and our banal conversation, which, in a former life, might even have been considered flirting.

I closed my eyes tight to the blaring sun, trying to think of something more pleasant than all those days I'd spent commode-hugging, knee-walking drunk. I settled on an imagined scenario: me and Alice going on a date. An evening at an Italian restau-

rant with checkered tablecloths and mando-
lin music and waiters in white aprons, our
table in the corner with a bread basket and
a flickering candle in the middle that we'd
have to talk over.

Wooing Alice at a joint too rich for my
blood would be my final meal, if I had to
pick one, and pretending this way lowered
my heart rate, even though it was nothing
but a wish to be out in the world again, living, doing all the little things I once took
for granted — like asking a girl out, buying
her dinner, holding her hand.

"Alice," I said, my eyes still closed, "tell
me something."

"Anything."

The tension in my shoulders let out even
more. This is how so many of our conversations started, and I settled in for a welcome
diversion. "Do you miss being able to go
out for a night on the town?"

"Sure, I do," she said. "But you know
what's funny? I miss staying in more."

I smiled. "I don't know if you've noticed,
but we do that in spades here."

She snorted an adorable little laugh. "I
mean, I miss ending my days by sitting on
the swing of a covered porch with a good
book."

"Centennial has everything in that sentence but the swing."

"And my nightly zinfandel."

This comment made me want to bang my head against the window. Instead, I held it in my hands.

"I know it sounds silly," she said.

"No . . . no, not at all."

"But I do miss it. You know, that *feeling.* Your supper dishes are done, and your girls are tucked into bed, and you pour yourself a nice glass of wine and go outside where the cicadas are buzzing."

"Sounds nice," I agreed, if only to keep her from talking about it more.

Her presence drew a little closer to my back, as if she'd leaned forward. "It was, and you know what? My girls never bring me any zinfandel, because they think it's bad for my blood pressure, but every once in a while, Anderson will pour me a glass."

I opened my eyes. "Do what?"

"He's a jewel, isn't he? He's done it every year for my birthday."

"I didn't know he could do that."

Her voice fell away. "I thought he did it for everyone's birthday."

I wanted to turn and face her, because this conversation was falling apart and I thought seeing her might fix it. But my hips and my back and my general lack of flexibility made this impossible.

I resorted to pitching my hurt up to the ceiling. "Not mine."

Alice said nothing, and in her silence it dawned on me why Anderson had never offered me a celebratory drink when I'd braved another year. I'd told him during my first week that I didn't touch the stuff, and though I didn't elaborate, the proclamation was delivered in such a way that anyone with a brain could have figured out why.

This meant two things to me. First, Anderson continued to prove he was the cat's pajamas. Second, he'd be a shitty supplier if I needed one.

I couldn't believe I was even thinking this way. I shook my head, like it would help. What was happening today? First, there was Josie climbing through our window; next, Carl was telling me about his secret life; and now, I was thinking about drinking in a way I hadn't in years.

The bus rattled to a stop under Centennial's porte cochere. Carl sat in a rocking chair on the porch, looking only a little calmer than before. He certainly didn't look ready for what I had to tell him, and seeing him pushed everything to the surface. I suddenly became acutely aware of the bullet in my pocket, the picture in my tin, and the

110

chip on my shoulder. I was glad to see him alive, but I also wanted to kill him, so for the time being I resolved to split the difference.

The exiting process for the bus took a while, except for Josie. She jumped out and breezed past Carl, who smiled for the briefest of moments until he realized she wasn't stopping. He looked after her like an abandoned puppy.

By the time I reached him, he was in the midst of trying to pull himself out of the rocker, which he knew better than to sit in.

"What are you doing, Carl?" I held his walker to keep it from skidding.

"I thought we'd sit here."

I glanced at the empty rocker next to him. "I can sit there."

"Not you." He pulled himself up. "Her."

"I know," I said, taking her place anyhow. I gave the chair a few pushes. "But she's not here."

"I'm sure she needed to use the powder room," he said.

I sighed, watching the bedlam that always seemed to go with getting Clarence Riley's wheelchair off the bus.

"Now you're in her seat," Carl complained, "and I'm not in mine."

I motioned next to me. "Sit back down.

I'll move when she gets back."

Carl's brow furrowed. "No. I'll wait in the living room. It's not so hard on my hip. I've been sitting there for over an hour waiting, you know. Why were you all so late?"

I broke my stare from the bus as it pulled away and looked at Carl. "Traffic."

"At this time of day?"

"There was an accident," I said, believing this was not altogether a lie.

"Hmm." He straightened his shirttail. "Well, if somehow I miss Josie and she makes it out here, tell her where to find me. I have something I'd like to give her."

"Of course," I said, watching him shuffle away. Before he made it inside, I called his name.

He turned.

"Feeling better?" I said.

We studied each other, and my normal insight into him was worth spit now. I typically knew when he was skeptical by the way his lips dipped, or pleased by the way his eyes lit. I knew he got slower when he was thinking and mouth-breathed when he wasn't. I knew all these things, but at present, I could tell nothing.

"Better," he said finally, then hobbled inside, head hung, saying with his body something else entirely.

9

The heat and the dead air outside were suffocating, but I rocked for a bit because the quiet helped me think. And I had a lot to think about. Actually, there were so many things going on in my head that most of it amounted to nothing at all. But I did keep wondering why I'd offered to help the very girl who could ruin me. Josie had Carl choking on sorrow by the spoonful, she had me parched and seeing Simmons around every corner, and still I'd thrown out my services like she was some special Sharon-approved project.

Which was ridiculous, because if there was anything harder than hiding a girl at Centennial, it was hiding a vomiting one. And that was coming for her. Soon. Unless, of course, I somehow found her something to drink.

I stopped the rocker short at the idea, then started up again, whispering swear words every time I pushed off the asphalt. I had no business becoming a moonshiner. None at all.

Anderson must've spotted me out there, sweating and mumbling to myself like a mad hatter, because he came outside and took a seat in the spare chair. He didn't say anything, just picked at the splintering paint on his rocker. I felt the vibe coming from him, though: an honest desire to check on my general well-being.

I'm fine, I wanted to say, but I couldn't speak these words with any amount of authenticity. I was out of my depth and knew it. I had a view of the shore and one of the open sea, and I had it in my mind to swim out farther.

"Am I in your spot?" I asked after a while, since he spent his breaks out here, typing on his pocket phone.

He chucked a paint chip onto the sidewalk. "No. I came to see if you were joining us for lunch. It's not like you to miss a meal."

I patted my paunch. "Day's gotten away from me. Been busy around here."

"I made chicken noodle soup."

"Low-sodium?"

He smiled, that bastard, his teeth bleach white and all accounted for. "What else is

114

there," he said.

I tipped my head to the dining hall windows. "Josie and Carl in there?"

He turned and stared at the glass for some time, though you couldn't see inside. The afternoon sun glared off the panes, and they gave away nothing, besides our vague reflections. We were shrunken and warped in them — so really, I looked about the same as I did in real life.

"They're in there." He turned back and squinted at me. "Is that why you're out here?"

"Hmm?"

He shook his head, because he knew better. "What's going on?"

Ode to the question of the day. I shrugged. "I'm just making sure Carl has some time with her, is all."

"That's nice of you . . ." A sly smile crept across his face. "Do you want to make sure I have some time with her too?"

I snorted. "Oh, God help us."

"What? She's good-looking. You don't think?"

"I am not in a position to make a determination like that on a girl more than sixty years my junior who is also my best friend's granddaughter."

He held one brow high, waiting, insinuating that my lack of frankness was out of character. Which it was.

"I'm not saying one way or the other, Anderson."

"Objectively," he urged.

"No."

"Man to man."

"Knock it off."

"She's hot, though, right?"

"I guess," I grumbled, to shut him up. He pumped his fist in victory, so I added, "You're a miserable human being."

"Bullshit. I made you lunch. In fact, you owe me, and you can pay me back by putting a good word in."

"No can do," I said without hesitation. That was all I needed to be doing with my time — helping their fledgling acquaintance become a bona fide relationship.

"Come on. I'll bring a saltshaker to your table."

"You are on your own, sir. Plus, I don't know what you like about this girl besides her looks, and if you can't articulate that, I think you should probably stay away."

Thoughtful, he crossed his arms, his tattoos arching with his biceps.

"This isn't just some random dolly, you realize," I added, hoping he gathered the implication. She was Carl's and she was

116

young and she was vulnerable, and after everything was said and done, she was going.

"Duffy," he said, "do you seriously think I'd play her?"

"Well." I thought of all the things Anderson had ever told me. Happenings at bars and parties, plus a one-time romp with one of his friends' mothers. But then I thought of all the things I'd actually seen him do, the least of which included rubbing Valencia's foul bunion-covered feet just because she'd asked him to.

"Come on," he prodded. "You know I'm not just some guy."

I grumbled, even though he was right. The boy was altruistic, kindhearted, and reliable. Marriage material, I suppose. But I also thought he was stupid, spending all those boons here, serving us. And evidently, he didn't know nothing from nothing when it came to his personal life either, which was such a waste.

Yet when I *really* thought about this misfortunate combination of foolishness and virtuousness, I realized it wasn't all bad. I'd been sitting there trying to solve all the world's problems when one of them already had an answer. Josie needed a drink, and here Anderson was, willing and able. For my part, all I had to do was facilitate.

I asked, "What were the terms again for your deal? A salt-shaker for a nice review?"

"A glowing review."

"Done," I said. "I'm hungry."

"Good." He clapped his knees, stood, and grasped me around the elbow. I returned the grip to his forearm and then, with a grunt, rose.

For whatever reason, he held on to me for longer than necessary. Concern flitted across his lopsided brow, or maybe it was affection. Before I decided which, he let me go and offered to get the door, which required him to merely walk ahead of me.

"I wonder . . ." I said, shuffling in behind him, feeling generous of spirit. "I don't know if Josie ever got that aspirin from Nora, but either way I bet she could use another one for that black eye."

He paused in the foyer. "Kitchen cabinets are a bitch."

It took me a second to respond. "Yes, they are."

"I'll grab her some ibuprofen."

Carl waved at me from our table, where Josie was sitting in my seat. *My* seat. This impropriety suddenly blotted out all the progress I'd made outside, as well as every-thing else around me, because the next thing I knew Anderson was tapping me on the shoulder.

"Hello? Does she need anything else?"

"Forget it," I said, then marched forward to reclaim what was mine. When I arrived at the table, it took a moment to regain my composure.

Carl pushed away his soup bowl and motioned to the empty chair — the one facing the back side of the dining hall, the one looking at the wall with a dime-store watercolor painting hanging crooked in the middle of it. I took the seat but made sure to cause extra ruckus while getting situated.

Carl said, "Look at what I gave Josie. It's one of my old pharmacy lapel pins. You like it?"

I glanced to where she'd stuck it on her T-shirt and nodded. Carl had gifted different versions of those to just about everybody here; I was actually surprised to see he hadn't run out. Before I could say as much, Anderson strode over with my soup and Josie's medicine.

"Hey," he said to her, his voice more low and liquid than when he spoke to us. "Medication time."

God, the way she looked up at him. He might as well have been offering her the moon or, at the very least, something on the rocks. But on second glance, it became apparent she wasn't looking at him at all but at the tiny paper cup in his hand. Aspirin was a hallowed thing to a drunk; it took the edge off. But this got me worried, because who knew what we were taking the edge off of. What kept her motor running? Couple drinks a day? A dozen? More?

I thought of Sal, an old friend of mine . . . well, not really a friend, more of a bar buddy, which is distinctly different, but anyhow, he convulsed when he tried to go cold turkey. Bit a hole through his tongue. Came to the bar a few days later to show it to me while he disinfected it with his usual scotch and water. I imagined what Josie would look like if her eyes suddenly rolled into the back of her head.

With this in mind, I had a moment of inspiration and blurted, "Happy birthday, Josie!"

She had thrown her head back to swallow her pills as I said this, so the announcement hung in the air until she could finally offer a "Huh?"

Anderson said, "Is it really your birthday?"

"Her birthday is in December," Carl said.

"No, it's today." I gave Josie a meaningful look that I hoped she could decipher, which meant I hoped she was clairvoyant.

"December," Carl insisted.

"It's in February," Josie said, unbothered by the confusion, wrapping a plait of hair around her finger. We watched her stupidly.

I gathered my wits. "We should celebrate anyhow, since you've come to visit."

Josie stood abruptly. "Is there a phone charger anywhere?"

I growled in frustration before offering a tight smile. "Reginald has one."

"Kind of," Anderson amended. "Reginald has a flip phone that he wears on a belt clip."

"Oh my God," she said, disgusted.

"Right?" He pointed. "I got you. Front desk. Should already be plugged in."

Without any further pleasantries, she traipsed away.

Which was probably for the best, seeing how she wasn't helping out even a little bit. I picked up my spoon and stirred. "So, what should we do to celebrate? Maybe something special at dinner? A bottle of champagne for a toast? Anderson, I don't suppose . . ."

"I could probably hook you up." He put a hand on my shoulder. "As long as you don't forget our deal, man."

I smiled big. "Not a chance."

Anderson grinned back and wandered off, navigating the table maze to collect abandoned plates.

Boy howdy, did I feel accomplished. I took a hearty bite and said to Carl through a mouthful, "What do you think Josie would make of the tin can phone in our room?" Once I swallowed, I pitched my voice up and added a Josie-like "Oh my God."

Carl didn't snicker. Didn't smile. He was too busy looking constipated and shaking his head.

Through another mouthful, I said, "What's a matter now?"

"I don't even know when my own granddaughter was born."

"So? Sometimes I can't remember when I was born."

"You were born on October twelfth." He looked across the way at Josie, who'd parked herself at the front desk. "A peepaw should know more about his grandbaby, shouldn't he?"

He rolled his napkin and tossed it on the table, determined. I sat back and glanced at Josie again, who was now resting her forehead in the center of the desk pad. When she sat up, she had a wild look in her eyes that I knew all too well.

"Oh no," I muttered.

"What?" Carl asked, twisting in his seat.

Josie rose, using the desk for balance. The

automatic doors swung open as she stepped forward, then her wobble abruptly turned to a sprint. She ran outside, rounded the building, and stopped at the bushes right outside the window where we sat. For a second, she looked at her reflection with confusion, as if it weren't her own.

"What's she doing?" Carl asked.

Before I could answer, Josie bent over and vomited all over a well-trimmed boxwood. Carl reflexively turned away, while I gawked.

"Oh my word, is she sick?" he asked in disbelief. "Duffy, tell me what's happening. I can't look."

"She's . . ." I pressed my finger to the glass.

"She's what?"

Anderson sauntered to our table, unaware, holding a salt-shaker. "For you, Duffy."

Carl turned to him. "She's sick."

"Who?" Anderson said, looking over his shoulder into the dining hall, turning slowly, taking count.

"No, no," Carl said, waving for his attention, which came only after Anderson had made a full circle.

"Her." Carl flipped his thumb to Josie, or rather to where Josie should've been. But she'd gone; I'd watched her go. She'd run from the mess, right out the white picket

fence, past Centennial's painted sign, and taken a left, probably to the corner of Saint Michael's and Border Lane, which then led to the rest of the world.

"Where'd she go?" Carl asked.

"No idea," I said. But I did. I knew exactly where, and, worse than that, I knew why.

10

So. We no longer had to hide the child, and I no longer had to find her a fix. It should've been a relief, but instead it had me anxious. It felt like the day had flatlined now that my biggest worry was tonight's dinner menu.

Anderson, at Carl's insistence, jogged out front to take a look in all directions for our missing ward. Meanwhile, Carl went on and on about Josie's disappearance, and in between yammering, he held his hand over his mouth. There came a point when that's all I saw: a wrinkled, veiny, shaking hand.

We were too old for this.

Turns out, all that business about hanging around kids to stay young was a bunch of bologna; Josie had done nothing but wear us the hell out. Yet right this moment, I wanted nothing more than to drag her ass straight back here so Carl would start acting like himself again. It was a real predicament, one that had me wringing my own wrinkled, veiny, shaking hands.

"I give up, guys," Anderson declared, trotting back inside to the dining hall. "She's probably running an errand."

"She was sick," Carl reiterated for the umpteenth time, "and she already ran all her errands earlier."

Anderson positioned Carl's walker, then pushed the table back so I could stand. "Carl, I know this is hard to believe, but Walmart doesn't have everything."

"Can't you drive around and look for her?"

"Sorry, boss. Not in the job description. Anyway, I've got to help Luann give a few showers and start dinner."

"But she's missing."

Anderson smiled at this, as if it were a joke. Worse, as if he were the only one in on it. "Let's wait twenty-four hours before we file a police report, okay? In the meantime, you should go to Name That Tune. Sherri's deejaying." He put a hand over one ear and used the other to swipe at the air in a strange circular motion. Looked like a seizure, which faded into disappointment as he glanced between us. "No good?"

Carl turned to me now, pleading.

"She'll be back," Anderson said with unfounded authority. "Plus, you guys need to stop acting like she's not old enough to come and go like she wants."

I rapped my knuckles on the table, nursing the beginnings of a new plan. It didn't have a middle or an end, per se, but it had a good start. "Carl and I are going to take a walk out front."

"None of the nurses are outside," Anderson said.

"We'll stay in the yard."

"Not going to happen. You know Sharon's rules. You want to wander around, you need one of us or a visitor to keep you company, and, well . . . we're all busy right now."

"It's fenced," I said.

"Insurance," he replied simply.

This time, I banged the table hard. "Damn it, Anderson."

He scoffed, flippant on the surface, but his voice sounded wounded. "Seriously. What's up with you today, Duf?"

Carl interrupted. "I can't take this anymore. I'm going to my room."

I glanced at him. His pleading had morphed into something I didn't quite understand but tried my best to decipher. I decided he wanted us to regroup. "Yes," I said slowly, "to our room. Good idea."

We started off. Anderson crossed his arms, offering no more help. "You two are acting strange."

"We're going to play gin rummy," I yelled over my shoulder. "Don't bother us."

"Don't worry," he said. "I've got better things to do."

I sidled up to Carl's deliberate stride. We turned the corner into the hallway, and Nora, who was parked at the far end with her rolling cart, raised her clipboard at us before getting back to it.

"So, what do you want to do?" I whispered.

Carl stopped and faced me. "What do I want to do? Same thing as this morning. I want to give Josie a place to lay her head. I want to share a meal with her. I want to pass down some old stories and a few of my things. I want . . ." He exhaled a sad little breath. "I want to put things right. But without her here, I can't, can I? So . . . so I'm just going to lie down until she gets back."

He turned to move, but I put a hand on his walker. "You're joking, right? You already had a nap today."

He closed his eyes, meditating. When he reopened them, he said, "Just until she gets back. She must've . . . needed a little walk. Some fresh air."

I held fast to his walker. First I'd lied to

128

him about Josie, and now he was lying to himself. Damn girl had caused an epidemic. But it seemed fixable, if only we dealt in reality going forward. I said, "And what if she doesn't ever come back?"

"Then I'm not getting up," he said, his voice resonating. We shared a long minute of silence, and, during it, Luann passed by with a bathing kit and disappeared into Wayne Tisdale's room. Anderson soon followed, acting like he didn't see us.

"Carl," I said once Wayne's door had shut, "it's been a day, I'll give you that, but we aren't the kind to just lie down and die."

"Maybe you aren't."

"*We* aren't. We've talked about this. Carpe diem, etcetera, etcetera."

"What am I supposed to *carpe*, exactly?"

"This." I swung my finger around like a whirlybird. "You know what happens if you start lying all day in your bed. You might as well get on the bus to Simmons."

"Maybe that's where I belong."

My blood ran cold at his sincerity. In the crisp, clear second that followed, I realized Carl would much rather starve himself than shoot himself, and Simmons was the one place that would allow him to do it.

"You don't know what you're saying," I said finally.

"Duffy, look at me."

I gave him a sideways glance, hoping to touch him up like you would a bad photograph, but there was still too much fidelity. What I'd seen in his hand was everywhere now — in his hunchback, his bald crown, his cataracts. There wasn't an inch of him that wasn't dying. You could even see it as he turned his back and hobbled into our room.

"Carl," I called after him.

The bedroom door slammed shut.

I swallowed and glanced around, feeling like he'd abandoned me in our foxhole. Same as all my other comrades in arms. Nora had left her station. Luann and Anderson were busy sponging Wayne down. Shawn had Name That Tune underway in the atrium. It was also Saturday, meaning that the receptionist was gone, along with the custodian.

I stood in that empty hall with the slow realization of how very alone I was, and it frightened me. Centennial didn't hand out many moments like this, if ever, and in ancient times — before I started wearing Velcro shoes — this sort of solitude would've gotten me in trouble. When left unsupervised, I tended to seize the day in all the wrong ways. And that predisposition was still in my blood, because in the vacuum of this space all I could think about was taking it upon myself to fetch Josie. Which meant going to Hang Overs, the closest bar.

Sure, I understood for my part, entering that sort of venue was like playing with a dead snake that could still bite. And, yes, I recognized Sharon required us to stay put or stay at Simmons. But I'd once been sly, quick, and careful, and though that was eons ago, in my mind nothing had changed.

I tottered down the hall, peeked around the corner. Charles was parked next to the plaid living room couch, asleep. Ragtime blues filtered out of the atrium, along with voices jockeying for the win.

After checking over my shoulder, I snuck into the foyer and stood on top of the pad that magically opened the front doors. The ease of it felt like a go-ahead. A breeze rustled my thin hair; the sun warmed my face. I closed my eyes to it and let the last of my misgivings melt off until there was nothing left but a why-not-go-ahead-and-jump tickle in my toes.

There you go, skydiving again, I thought. Then with a little smile on my lips, I took a step, then a few more, until Centennial's doors whispered shut behind me.

11

Jesus Christ, it was hot. Maybe not at first, as I made my way past the rocking chairs, down the curb, and along Centennial's white picket fence, but once I hit the big welcome sign, it felt like I'd taken a left into the center of a potbellied stove.

By the time I passed Centennial's property line, I was a mess of expletives and heavy breathing. It felt like my lungs were collapsing, and it didn't help if I slowed, so I kept moving, thinking maybe I'd just forgotten what it felt like to truly work out.

I trudged along the road's shoulder, stomping in the overgrown buffalo grass. The blades folded underfoot with a crunch, the sun bore down, and sweat soaked my shirt. It all reminded me of pushing my mama's mower across her uphill acre in the dead of summer, after which I'd reward myself with a cold, frosty beer. Or two. Or twenty.

God, I needed a ride.

To this end, I raised my hitchhiking thumb as I walked, but the gesture soon turned into this unrecognizable half-mast appeal. Not that it mattered. The Saturday traffic was sparse and, worse, indifferent.

A dozen cars blew by without even slowing, and next came a one-ton dually, ginning up a swoop of wind big enough to give me a nudge. I stumbled, catching myself a few steps later. When I straightened up with my middle finger raised, I hadn't meant it for Centennial. But I'd gotten spun around, and there she was, at most fifty yards from where I stood.

Fifty measly yards.

I slowly lowered my hand. It didn't make sense. When had I gotten so old that this distance was tantamount to running a marathon? My boyhood hadn't been that long ago, had it?

I stood still, thinking up my earliest childhood memory: a trip to the city. It came to me in tiny bits — my pudgy fingers holding my father's hand, a passing car with whitewall tires, Cormac skipping beside me, his shoelaces untied. These bits didn't make a whole, but they were so faultless and real they might as well have happened yesterday. It *was* yesterday, in a way, and after a bullwhip snap of time, here I was today, physically unable to walk to the Saint Michael's traffic light, which blinked in the distance from yellow to red.

This adventure had been dressed up fancy when I'd walked out the door, clearly. Lipstick, hair done, the whole nine yards. Out in the sunlight, though, she looked like a real son of a bitch. And suddenly I preferred not to take her out. Not for Josie, not even for Carl. Nothing was worth dropping dead here, in the weedy no-man's-land between an assisted living facility and a mobile home community, *alone.*

So I'd go home. No problem. I'd slip back inside before anyone noticed, and it'd be like this never happened. All I had to do now was survive the trek back, which rolled out from under my toes in an endless line, looking . . . impossible, actually.

Deadly.

A minivan swept by. An old blue Lincoln followed, kicking up soot. I flapped my hand to clear the air, then froze. The old Lincoln had slowed and pulled over to the shoulder, with a single brake light shining and the motor idling. Almost like it wanted to give me a ride. And then it started backing up.

The relief of it almost knocked me down. To stay upright, I leaned heavily on the car once it parked, and made my way to the passenger side. Through the back window, which was jammed with a collection of big-eyed stuffed animals, the driver's outline belonged to a linebacker. But the window went down to reveal a cherub-faced Samoan lady — middle-aged, peasant dress, big honking jewelry.

She leaned over the middle console, her smile cut off at the corners by her cheeks. "You look like you could use a lift."

"Boy, I could kiss you," I said, opening the door without any further invitation.

Because the car rode low, it took a while to get situated. I'd forgotten the work that went into getting into a sedan. I dropped onto the faded, garish pillow-top seat and stayed where I landed, even though my bottom hung halfway off. Once I slammed the door, it shoved my ass over anyway, and more urgent was my shirt, which had ridden up to expose my hairless, wrinkled, bulging belly.

She offered her hand. "My name is Tiana."

I shook it with my left, since it was closer and less trouble to produce. "Duffy."

"Duffy," she repeated, testing the name out. "You were in my horoscope today."

I paused my blind search for the seat belt.

Of course an odd duck had picked me up. Who else would pull over for a fella like me? "You don't say. What was I doing there?"

"Existing. It told me to direct my attention to things I usually overlook." She squared herself with the steering wheel. "So where to?"

The question was innocent enough, but it caused a sudden, raw wave of dread. I'd charged a hill and then sat down halfway up, and now I had a chauffeured ride in either direction. Which meant she was either a blessing from God or an offer from the devil, and I stared, trying to decide which.

"Have you forgotten?" Her brow knitted. She produced a cell phone from the depths of her cleavage. "Do you have someone we could call?"

"I haven't forgotten," I said, defensive. "I was heading to . . . Well, have you ever heard of Hang Overs?"

"The bar *right* there?" she said, hitching her thumb behind her.

"That's the one," I said. "I was on my way there, and then I changed my mind, and now . . ."

She offered me a sly look. "Are you a Capricorn? Because today, it said to lean into your intuition to find the right answer."

I stared at her again. The gears in my brain

had gotten stuck. "I'm a Libra," I managed.

"I knew it," she said, scanning through her phone. "It says, 'Positive thinking will not get you to your next destination.' Does that sound right?"

"They all sound right," I said, looking to Centennial's wooden sign right outside the windshield.

Caring for Seniors Since 1994, it said. Welcome Home.

"It also says to tend to your body." She reached across me, taking the liberty of strapping me in. "So? What's going to be your next destination?"

It was funny how quickly my view of things could change, now that I had a comfortable seat and a little bit of air-conditioning. From this point of view, it seemed possible that I'd cried uncle too soon. I had speed on my side again, and maybe even the zodiac. Plus, things were just now starting to get fun.

"To Hang Overs," I said with confidence.

"You got it. I'm running to the craft store, but it's only a minute away." She put the car in drive and made a quick U-turn. "We'll have you there in no time."

"Right," I agreed from my spot in the passenger seat — the one place where I could do nothing but ride along. I felt exempt, absolved, content even.

While Tiana merged, she rolled up my window, which flooded the inside of the car with her perfume. I don't know if it was my conscience or my imagination, but it smelled the same as Alice's — rose water with honey undertones and a hint of balsam. I tried to ignore it, but even when I didn't breathe through my nose, I still had the taste in my mouth. It's like Alice was everywhere, but at the same time, nowhere close, and she was getting farther away every second.

The thought of her almost led me to change my mind again. But then we stopped at the Saint Michael's red light, waiting to take a right onto Border Lane. Outside my window, Centennial's signage had been replaced with Hang Overs', and the moment I laid eyes on it, my mouth went dry enough to spin cotton.

This was the worst best idea I'd ever had.

Tiana dialed down the air-conditioning. "Do you live around here?"

"Yes," I said, my voice thin.

"Moburbia?" she asked, referring to the mobile home park.

I wanted to tell her the truth, but the words wouldn't form. In the end, I could manage only a nod.

"Do you not have a car?"

138

A headshake this time.

She looked back to the road, saying nothing. She'd already done her good deed for the day by picking me up once. No need to do it twice.

When we pulled up to Hang Overs, I yanked at the door handle before we'd even stopped. I wanted out, if nothing else so I could breathe. But the door didn't budge. I tried again.

"It only works from the outside," Tiana said, parking. She left the car running, opened her door and let loose the fumes, then made a slow loop around the rear.

I sat back, drumming my fingers, staring out the windshield. *I'm at Hang Overs,* I thought coolly, looking at the building. Then again, with less control: *Holy shit. I'm at Hang Overs.*

It didn't seem real, mostly because in over forty years, the place hadn't changed. The oversize wooden shack still looked like a rundown bait-and-tackle shop, and, like always, the gravel lot had only a handful of cars. Just like that, I'd slipped back into my old life, and it didn't feel so wrong. In fact, it felt almost right.

"Here we are," Tiana announced, swinging my door open. "Are you sure you're all right? I mean, you seem . . . Are you all right?"

"You're an angel," I said, before endeavoring to get out.

She helped heave-ho me to my feet. "Don't forget to take good care of yourself."

"That's what I'm aiming to do," I said in lieu of a proper farewell while making my way to the front door. The excitement of it all had obliterated my manners. I couldn't believe I was here, when this morning I'd aspired to nothing more than breaking Reginald's winning streak at Name That Tune so I could rub it in anytime I passed his dining table.

A prickle crawled up my hand as I placed it on the well-worn handle. The low buzz of music filtered through the door, and I started to salivate. That was how fast my instincts returned.

I wanted a drink.

The to-do with Josie and Carl didn't matter. The fact that this might jeopardize my residence at the only decent senior living facility within a hundred miles didn't matter. Going AWOL on Anderson and Nora didn't matter. Even Alice didn't matter.

Nothing mattered besides vodka, tequila, rum, whiskey, brandy, and gin.

You know, the good stuff.
The hard stuff.

You know, the good stuff.
The hard stuff.

12

"Damnation, that door's heavy," I declared once I'd wrestled it open and stepped inside.

An emaciated, bearded man at the bar glanced at me with disinterest before returning to his glass. A pair of morose flannel-clad men playing cards in the corner did the same. Only a craggy middle-aged blonde perked up at my entrance, just as the door shut behind me, taking with it all of the sunlight.

I lumbered to the bar, trying to catch up with the scene. Nothing about it looked right. Back in the day, those of us who gathered at Hang Overs were a decent breed: working alcoholics. We'd come with our ties loosened or our hard hats under our arms, and we'd drink until our eyes crossed and we found ourselves singing "The Holy Ground" at the tops of our lungs even though we remembered only every third word. We'd flirt, we'd laugh, we'd

142

cheer for whatever ball game played on the TV screen, and then we'd pay our cut-rate bills and head home to sleep it off and do it again.

At least that's what I remembered.

It's possible, of course, that during my time off, I'd romanticized things a little. Or a lot. Because the patrons here looked unemployed and miserable, the song screaming on the stereo didn't even have a chorus, and the two TVs were airing *Wheel of Fortune* — on mute.

"What can I get you?" the bartender asked, monotone, drying her hands on the rear of her pants. She wore a sweatshirt with the hood up and cinched tight around her petite face, like she'd come in from the cold. Her demeanor hollered that she had no intention of chitchatting. Yet another disappointment logged. I frowned and read down the line of bottles but got sidetracked by Pat Sajak's face on the center TV.

"Isn't there a game on?" I said.

She gave her gum a slow chew before finding the remote and flipping it to baseball, though I couldn't see the team names or the score unless they were spoon-fed. "Better?" she asked.

"Sure," I said, then waggled my head to amend my answer. "What about the music?

143

This place allergic to Merle Haggard?"

Another chew of the gum — I was pushing it, I could tell — but she fished out her pocket phone and somehow changed the tunes with it. To my great pleasure, she picked Willie Nelson, though the bar still had something missing, and whatever it was put a damper on the blood hammering through my veins. I looked over my shoulder to figure out what else needed fixing, only be to be greeted by the blondie, who had notably forgotten to put on her bra this morning.

With her titties pointing at me, she flashed a phony sultry smile that framed one dead tooth. "You want to buy me a drink?"

"No, thank you. I just —"

She pulled a barstool near my rear end and gave me a tiny shove to sit down, which did the trick. "I'll have whatever you're having. You like sangria?"

"God, no," I said defensively. "I'm a whiskey man."

"Oh yeah?" The barkeep nodded in approval and pointed behind her. "What kind?"

So we were going to talk, I guess. About alcohol. It wouldn't be my first pick, but I'd work with whatever she gave me. Shrugging, I examined the wall again. Some labels looked familiar; some looked upside down even though they were right-side up. It was distracting. Dizzying. "I don't know. Single malt."

"With ice?"

I rubbed my hands together. Warmed them. Recalled that I hated cold whiskey. "Neat, usually."

"Top-shelf?"

I shook my head. "Rotgut," I said, by which I meant anything Canadian. I never treated myself when drinking; didn't deserve it. In fact, right now I didn't even deserve a sangria, seeing how I'd shirked the one and only responsibility I'd had in coming here. I glanced over my shoulder again, this time for Josie.

"Say, you haven't seen —" I stopped short as I turned back, because before me sat a lowball glass with a few fingers of the greatest fermented drink ever made. The sickly orange glow from the lighting above didn't do it any favors, and I could smell the ethanol — whatever she'd poured was cheap — but my stomach still bottomed out like when I had my first kiss in the back alley behind the dime store. Same dry-throat want. Same shake in my voice. "I didn't order that."

She poured another and slid it to the

blonde, who ran off with it in a hurry. "Not what I heard."

"Get your ears checked then," I said, hand on the glass to push it away. But for some reason, I couldn't make myself do it. Something about the way it fit into my palm.

"That'll be twenty-two dollars."

I snorted.

"I have rules here to keep the bums out. If you come in, you order. If you skip the bill, I call the cops." She wiped the counter, adding casually, "You want to open a tab?"

I cleared my throat, hopeful she was joking. But she looked as serious as the business end of a .45, which didn't bode well. Mainly because it had suddenly come to my attention that I'd walked in the door without one red cent.

"Look, I . . ." I cleared my throat again. The salivating had come back tenfold, now that I had a drink in my hand. I swallowed my spit three or four times before saying, "I'm just looking for a girl."

The emaciated man, who was building a tower with peanuts, piped up. "Aren't we all?"

The bartender smirked, while one of the flannel men waved in her direction for another round. She reached underneath the counter and produced a few shot glasses, setting them down heavily. "When you find her, maybe she can treat."

"Maybe so, if your two-bit whiskey didn't cost a day's wage," I snapped back, picking up the drink to return it, but instead it crept closer to my lips. I don't know how — maybe it was a reflex — but it crept close enough that I could've thrown it back. And part of me wanted to, yet a bigger part didn't, because despite now having the right music and a ball game and the blondie and some banter, I realized only one piece could actually make things feel complete: my disease.

Officially disgusted, I set the drink down. Pushed it away. I'd come for the girl; I'd come for a good reason. And I had this fuzzy notion that I'd ignored something important here, overlooked something obvious. I swiveled my stool to face the card-playing men. Their table had a tiny forest of beer bottles in the center, and on the outskirts they'd dealt cards for three players.

And their plus-one appeared as if on cue, exiting the women's restroom. She stopped midstride at the end of the short hallway when she saw me, looking about half as big as before. Too young, too small, too drunk.

One of the men beckoned. "Come on,

beautiful. I ordered us some more drinks."
He winked at his friend, though it lacked
playfulness.

"What are you doing here?" Josie asked.

The men turned to me. I motioned to her,
but the gesture fell away when her eyes
landed on my drink.

"Oh, look at you." She came closer, taking measured steps, careful to walk a straight
line. "Centennial doesn't do field trips here
too, does it?"

"No, I —"

"How did you get here? You didn't walk,
did you? I mean, you couldn't have.
You're . . . you're . . ."

"I'm what?"

"One hundred." She turned to the bartender. "He shouldn't be here. He's, like . . .
ancient. He lives in a nursing home —"

"Assisted living."

"I mean, he's a total liability. He could
keel over right here." Her dilated eyes were
on me, green and glassy. In them, I saw
myself looking like fifty measly yards of bad
road.

I said, "For your information, I came for
you. To bring you back home."

The corner of Josie's mouth ticked up.
"You mean *nursing* home."

I grimaced, which apparently amused her.

148

She tossed her head back and made a sound meant to be a laugh, but it came out so undone it sounded like a sob. It took me aback. I shifted uncomfortably in my seat, waiting for it to end. In this state, she was going to be hard to get outside, let alone into Centennial.

When she finally dipped her chin and met my eyes, her brow furrowed. "What's going on with you, old man? You're sweating."

I touched my forehead, surprised to find it wet. "Nothing. I'm fine —"

"You don't look fine."

My ticker skipped a couple of beats as she said this, and I coughed to get it back on track. The dull, searing pain that followed was probably psychosomatic, after all her talk of me dying here and now, and I refused to let it get to me. Instead, I wanted it to get to her. Guilt could be a powerful tool.

I squared my shoulders, even though it hurt. "Maybe I'm not fine. Maybe coming here to save you is killing me."

"Save me?" She clicked her tongue in disapproval. "Bad choice, old man. Bad choice."

I mopped my brow with a paper cocktail napkin, trying to think of a better angle, during which time she managed to grab my drink. "Hold on now —" I said.

But before I finished my warning, she consumed every last drop of whiskey with the quickest flick of her wrist. Her tiny Adam's apple bobbed up, then down, and just like that — gone.

I gawked at the empty glass she set down, disbelieving, before yelling, "Goddammit, Josie." How the hell were we going to get out of here now that I had a bill? I swiveled on the bartender and spat, "We're not paying for that."

One of the flannel men stood, his chair clattering back. The other rose too, slowly.

I didn't care, though. I was already walking the last mile of my mortality. What could they do to me? "Come on, Josie, let's go."

She didn't move. The men drew closer, grew bigger. One of them peered down and said, "You need to apologize to these two ladies."

"For what?" I blustered, pointing at the barkeep. "She's a crook." My finger swung to Josie. "And she's —"

"With us," one of the men said, looking like a rottweiler that'd jump me. He softened when he addressed the bartender. "We'll get the drink" — his eyes landed hard on me again — "as soon as he leaves."

"You got it," the bartender said, half paying attention, typing away at her phone.

Willie Nelson's "Whiskey River" ended abruptly, replaced by that terrible music from before. The bartender looked at me, gave her gum one final, definitive chew, then held her contraption up. "And if you come back, I'm calling the cops."

Josie folded her arms and stared, her eyelids looking too heavy to keep drawn. Her new friends flanked her. The emaciated man's three-peanut tower toppled, and he looked at all of us with his empty eyes. This is what my adventure had come to. Josie and this crew telling me to go home, instead of the other way around.

Well, screw them, I thought. *Who has time for this.*

With a huff, I slid off the barstool with as much grace as my body would allow, which wasn't much at all, before adding a bow. "I'm sincerely sorry," I said to the floor, then straightened up to address the crowd, "that you're all pieces of shit."

With that, I made my way to the door, though I couldn't help but look back once before leaving. Josie met my gaze. The man to her right eyed her bare shoulder, while the man to her left put his hand on the small of her back and gave her a push toward their table. And though I'd just as soon bite a bug than care, it made me wish I had more for those deadbeats than a single useless bullet in my pocket.

Josie raised a few fingers as a farewell, almost like somewhere deep she was sad to see me go, but then she turned around and wobbled away. With this, I blasted through the exit and stepped into much-needed fresh air.

I couldn't breathe. A vise had my rib cage tweaked tight. I was mad at Josie, furious at myself.

Eventually, all this anger rendered down into shame, burning so hot I wanted to bolt from my own skin. Peel it off like a coat. I kept reminding myself I hadn't taken a drink. I'd run to the edge of the cliff, curled my toes over the edge but backed away, and now here I was on the right side of Hang Overs' door, sober as the day I was born. All faculties intact.

With them, I took stock of my surroundings and realized I was standing next to an old pay phone, and, better yet, some saint had left behind a hackneyed quarter for a chump like me.

The vise relaxed a hair.

I peeked up to the sky, in case my direct line to God hadn't been cut, and thanked him. Even I knew enough to realize pay phones were prehistoric. The next miracle would be if it worked. I lifted the sticky handset from the cradle, licked my lips, and inserted the quarter.

At the sound of a dial tone, my skin cooled.

"That a boy," I whispered, my hand hovering over the number pad. Etched into the metal casing — below the stated rates but above the fossilized mint gum stuck to the casing — were the words *FUCK YOU.*

Get in line, I thought, and then dialed the only number I had memorized besides 911 and my own.

13

Two rings in and I had myself a sweet, oblivious "Hello."

"Hiya, Alice," I said, trying to keep my voice steady. "It's Duffy. I need you to do me a big, big favor, and I need you to do it for me now, if you don't mind. Get Anderson from the kitchen and bring him to the phone, would you?"

"Why? Are you okay? Did you fall in your room?"

"No, Alice, nothing like that."

"I'm happy to come across the hall if you need help."

"No, that's not a good idea."

"Oh my. That was presumptuous of me. You might not be decent."

"It's not that, Alice. I'm decent —"

"I've embarrassed myself, haven't I?"

"Never mind that. Can you please hurry?"

"Of course, but you've got me worrying about you."

"Don't," I said firmly.

"You're going to wait on the line, right? Or should I send him to your room?"

My goodness, the pair of us was not equipped to handle a pseudo-emergency. "Bring him to the phone. And whatever you do, don't hang it up. Set it to the side until he gets there."

"Okay. Give me a moment."

Indiscriminate clanking followed. Alice's fading voice repeated my directions as she exited the room. I waited. And waited. And waited some more. I should've expected as much, seeing how she moved about as fast as me.

A wooden bench skirted the same wall as the pay phone, close enough for me to sit and still hold the receiver against my face. I collapsed onto it, leaning my head up against Hang Overs' splintery, sun-bleached exterior, wondering if Josie was the kind of girl who had some snap in her garters when she had to fend for herself.

If I set the phone down and scooted to the opposite edge of the bench, I'd be able to peek past the bright neon beer signs in the window and find out. But to what end? Her knight in shining armor wasn't me. Couldn't be. I'd been banned from the bar at eighty-eight for disturbing the peace —

and, more importantly, she didn't want to be saved. At least not today. That'd have to wait until she hit rock bottom.

As I settled into this fact, some unreckonable amount of time passed. Who knows how long. I never wore a watch anymore; Centennial kept my time in meals.

Finally, Anderson's voice boomed on the line. "Duffy?"

At the same instant, a digitalized woman spoke. *"One minute remaining."*

"Anderson, God am I glad —"

"What's the matter, man? It's almost dinnertime. Are you having a wheelchair kind of day? I'll have Nora bring one by —"

"No, listen . . . Have you seen Carl lately?" The question was meant to help me attack this problem indirectly, spare myself some disgrace, although really it was only wasting time.

He paused. "I thought you guys were playing gin rummy in your room."

"He was . . . is. He is. I mean, might be."

"I'm confused." Fear crept into Anderson's voice. It belonged there, but for reasons he had yet to understand.

"What I mean to say is Carl's fine. Probably. I'm fine too. It's just that —"

"Enough. Why are we on the phone? I've

got Salisbury steak in the oven. I'm coming over."

"Don't —"

The phone clanked again. Alice picked it up. "Duffy? Are you there?"

"Thirty seconds remaining."

"Christ, Alice! Get Anderson back on."

"What's happening?"

I yelled from the depths of my diaphragm, "Get him back on, damn it!" I'd never spoken to her like that, not ever. Alice was delicate, proper, and I was hollering at her like she was a deckhand on a garbage barge.

She offered a wilting "All right, Duffy, I'm going," breaking my heart all the while. Apologies would have to wait, though.

Anderson came back to the phone seconds later. "*Where* are you?"

"I'm at Hang Overs."

"What? How?"

"I'll explain later, but I need you to come get me, and I need you to do me the favor of not telling anyone I was gone."

"Are you kidding me?"

"Before dinner would be best."

"Duffy, this is crazy —"

"Do you know where it is? Right on Border Lane."

"Yes, but —"

"Good, come now."

"I've only got my motorcycle —"

The phone cut off with a definitive click.

Still, I yelled into it, "And, Anderson, don't tell anyone, you hear? If Sharon finds out . . . Anderson? Do you hear me?"

I sat there with that sticky receiver in my hand until the off-hook tone burned a hole through my eardrum. Instead of standing to hang it up, I merely let it go. I had nothing left in me — not a damn thing more — to do anything else besides sit and wait. Anderson would come for me; I knew it. He'd charge hell with a pitcher of water for me.

The phone was still swinging when his motorcycle peeled into the gravel parking lot. He unsaddled in one fluid motion and ran to the bench where I sat. Kneeling, he grabbed my wrist and attempted to take my pulse, all while the dust from his arrival settled in the background.

I stared at him as he stared at his watch, grateful but also irritated. I wanted to get home without any fanfare. So what if I had an irregular heartbeat or the blood pressure of a man who'd been shot in the carotid artery? If I'd wanted an ambulance, I'd have called one.

When he readjusted his grip on my wrist, I snatched my hand back. "I'm fine. Let's just go."

He looked at me. Really looked at me. Then he asked, "Did you leave to find Josie?"

I didn't dither. "No." The truth would've begged too many questions, and at least a handful of them would've cornered me into a lie. Figured I'd save us both the time, seeing how we didn't have any.

Anderson accepted my answer with a nod, but it triggered a different concern. He narrowed his eyes. "What's your name?"

"The hell, Anderson. I'm fine."

He sat back on his heels. "Do you know the year?"

"Stop that. I'm not dying, I'm not disoriented, and I'm not a dementia-wandering fool."

He stood, pulled a phone from his pocket, and began to dial.

"My name is Duffy Sinclair," I blurted, "and I'm an alcoholic."

He stopped punching numbers. The phone dropped to his side.

"And as far as the year, it's been thirteen since my last drink." My heart went still after this confession. I hadn't said those words since my last AA meeting; hadn't needed to. "I know how I got here and how to get home, but I can't make it myself." I swallowed, adding miserably, "I need you to

159

take me home."

Anderson glanced over his shoulder at his motorcycle. He then joined me on the bench, with his sinewy arms resting on his knees and his phone sandwiched between his clasped hands.

In his silence, I said, "You know Sharon doesn't keep wanderers at Centennial. If anyone finds out . . ."

He didn't respond.

"I can get on that thing," I promised. "It's a short ride, and I've told you before I had a license back in Nam. Recon patrol team. Third battalion, twenty-second division, infantry. Used to drive 175-cc bikes through the rice paddies . . . Well, never mind. But still, I can do it. I've done it before. All I have to do is sit, anyhow. I can sit. I practice that every day."

The quiet coming from him was an intense sort of silent treatment. He toggled his phone on and off, on and off, watching it as if it could produce an answer, like a Magic 8 Ball.

I poked at his attention. "What kind of bike do you have there? It looks . . . foreign."

"Kawasaki," he said absently.

"Japanese," I ventured. "Well, it's a good thing I wasn't in World War One or Two, because I might not be able to board it due

160

to philosophical differences. But as it were, they were rather neutral during the —"

"My dad's a drunk." His dark eyes met mine.

My countenance fell. I sat back. "Oh."

"I used to pick him up from places like this all the time." He turned and gave the bar a once-over. "I've picked him up from here before, actually."

"Oh," I said again, for lack of anything better.

He drew a breath, looking away. "This is so messed-up."

"It is, and I'm sorry. But if I didn't call you —"

He turned back to me, angry. "Then what?"

I swallowed and thought of my legless years, when I'd catch a ride home by relying on the girl of the week, or a taxi, or public transportation, or, on occasion, myself. But none of that was a possibility now. Not without the ability to walk, or pay, or drive. For me, it was Anderson or nothing.

"If you hadn't come, then . . . I would have rotted here, I guess," I said.

"Son of a bitch," he muttered, standing abruptly and walking away, then shaking his head and coming back. "You know what? I don't even talk to my dad anymore because of this bullshit. He'd say: 'Come and get me or I'll go to jail,' 'Come and get me or your mom will kick me out,' 'Come and get me or I'll *die.*' "

"Anderson —"

He walked away again, then stopped and turned, hands on hips, looking at everything but me, and then, with as much abruptness, he marched back and thrust out his hand in my direction.

I regarded it, motionless.

He shook it at me. "Do you want to go home or what?"

I offered a meek nod. He grasped me around the elbow, like he always did, and pulled.

Once he had me upright, his grip tightened. "I'm only doing this once, and never again. Got it? I learned my lesson the hard way with my dad. He's . . . He's —"

"I know what he is," I said. I knew better than anyone. I could close my eyes and see him with exacting detail. No matter our differences, deep down people like us were all the same. We could only serve one of two masters: our addiction or ourselves. We earned our ticket to perdition this way and spent the rest of our lives looking to exchange it.

"Come on," Anderson said, tipping his head.

On my first step, my knee gave. He caught me and, from then on, served as the human crutch. A few yards from the bike, my other knee gave, meaning my feet were about as useful as hooves on ice. But Anderson took on the remainder of my weight with nary a grunt. Occasionally, I'd give a leg a weak kick forward. He kept encouraging me, saying I could do it, telling me we were almost there, but really it should have been the other way around, seeing how he was all but carrying me. For shame, but I had been taken home from a bar like this before, with puke on my shirt and blood on my knuckles.

We stopped at the rear of the bike — a glossy electric blue thing, with angles like a fighter jet and a slanted back seat only a little thicker than floss. Beads of sweat pooled along Anderson's hairline. My own dripped from my fingertips.

He inched me toward the back tire, until my shins touched the tread. Stationary, I could lock my knees at least, but the prospect of getting on the bike seemed impossible.

"I can't," I stammered.

"You don't have to." He gently nudged my feet wider apart with the toe of his shoe.

163

"On three, okay? One, two —" And with a single hitch in his breath, he lifted me up over the tire and onto the seat. The seamlessness had to be a product of deadlifting Charles on a daily basis, that fat bastard. Or maybe it was because of Anderson's loafing father, but I hoped not.

He never let me go, switching his grip as he rounded the bike, until finally he stood in front, stabilizing me by holding my upper arms. "See. Hard part's done. How are you? Okay?"

"Humiliated."

"Hold my shoulder here . . . Good. Now lean on my back while I get on . . . Yeah, like that. One, two —"

And then somehow we were both seated, ready to go. He started the engine, and its whine reminded me nothing of the rumble from my motorcycle days. I held loosely to Anderson's shoulders, leaning in only enough to keep myself from falling off. It was a sad attempt to maintain what was left of my dignity.

"Hey, Duf," he called.

"What?"

"You're going to want to hold on tighter."

"I am?" I asked, trying to sound casual.

"This isn't some tiddler. It's going to make the last bike you were on seem like a tricycle." The engine revved with a high-pitched whirr.

I swallowed but leaned in only a hair more. Anderson was more realistic. He grabbed my hands and hugged them around his chest, forcing me to bend so far that I had no choice but to put my cheek between his shoulder blades.

I said into his back, "God help me, if I manage to fall off holding on like this, go ahead and leave me for dead."

His reluctant laugh rattled through him, straight to my skull. We pulled out slow, never going much faster than thirty miles per hour once we hit the road. To me, however, it felt like riding lightning. The wind blew with enough speed that it didn't seem to have a direction; the trees blurred into a streak of green.

I was young again, weightless, immortal. I closed my eyes and guzzled in the free-falling feeling of being alive, thinking I was leaving the last of my problems in our growing shadow. But this spark only hung on until we hit the first stoplight, where I stretched from my hunch and peered back.

Behind us, I saw Josie standing on Hang Overs' porch, a speck in the distance, watching us go, and I thought I caught her calling my name just loud enough to be heard over that goddamn rice-burning motor.

I thought, but I wasn't sure, and that's why I turned away as the light turned green.

14

The ride flew by as fast as the last eighty-eight years. Before I'd caught my breath, Anderson had turned down the back alley to park in Centennial's rear. While he fetched a wheelchair, he left me on the bike, downwind of the Dumpster, my weight supported by an inadequate-looking kickstand. I held on like I was waiting in a rodeo bucking chute, pondering the upshot of letting go and falling to my death instead of going inside and dealing with whatever might come.

Anderson returned to load me up like the handicapped man I was. The vinyl upholstery of the wheelchair squeaked as I sat, giving me some unexpected comfort. The safety of Centennial was only a few wheel revolutions away. There, no one, not even myself, depended on me. Such was the beauty of assisted living.

The thought of Josie still being outside

the bubble haunted me, but I held the real frightening bit far away where I couldn't consider it — the fact that I was the one who'd left her there.

Instead, I focused on expressing my first official, comprehensible, overdue "Thank you."

"Save it. First, let's make sure I don't get canned and you don't get . . ." Anderson hunched, flipping down the foot pedestals, then came face-to-face with me, hands on either armrest. "You better pray my Salisbury steak isn't on fire."

Before I could respond, we were off, rounding the front of the building.

"This is what's going to happen: We're going to say you fell, out in the yard." He tipped the chair back to get the midget wheels over the curb. "You were out here waiting for Josie." The suggestion lacked anxiety on his part, but mine crawled up the sides of my neck.

"Then you fell off the curb over there" — he pointed — "where no one could see you even if they were looking out the window or walking in the front door, and I found you when I came out back for a smoke."

I twisted in my seat, drilling him with a look. "You smoke?"

He shrugged.

"That'll kill you young, you know?"

This amused him. "Little secret, man, that's my plan."

I turned back around, thinking of the gauntlet I'd sent my own body through. Drugs during my bell-bottom years, promiscuous sex from the moment I enlisted to the day I couldn't get it up anymore, and a half century's worth of alcohol. Here I was anyhow, wringing my eighties bone-dry. "Well, your plan sucks."

He stopped short of the front door, our reflections shimmering off the tinted glass. He straightened his shirt, his shoulders.

"What about the phone call I made?" I said, smoothing my windblown hair. "How should we explain —"

The doors whooshed open. I would've screamed if my throat hadn't constricted. Carl stood at the threshold, with Alice at his side. The rest of Centennial milled nervously behind them. Everyone looked to us, wide-eyed, even Charles. Valencia went to the trouble of standing, but no one spoke.

As I looked back, my heart tanned the inside of my rib cage. They knew. Every single one of them. Damn the phone call. It was the death of my alibi. The death of me. Sharon had probably already speed-dialed Simmons. And they knew that too. That's why they were all here, to say their early goodbyes.

Carl drew his walker closer, but I didn't meet his eyes. I was too shocked. Too ashamed. Me getting the boot turned both of our futures black. He put a hand on my shoulder, gave it a feeble squeeze.

I turned to the knit of his sweater — which smelled of his stale bed — and said, "I'm so sorry."

Reginald spoke up from the living room couch. "You should be. We thought you were Sharon when those doors opened. Now we have to sit around here and wait for her some more."

I threw him a terror-stricken look. This was all happening too fast. "Sharon's *already* on her way?"

He shrugged. "I'm sure. This is when she usually comes."

The reeling in my mind stopped. I could feel my face go blank.

Reginald scoffed. "It's a Saturday, you big dope. What did you think? We're waiting here for *you*?"

I took the crowd in again — including Carl this time, who didn't look happy, necessarily, but he'd clearly brushed his hair — and a slow smile crept across my face. Of course. Saturday night. Sharon's favorite time for a bunk inspection, because she liked to see what the week did to us. That's why everyone was gathered here, looking like nervous Nellies. They were worried about Sharon, not me.

I barked out a laugh. Followed it up with a no-holds-barred whoop. Carl dressed me down with a frown, but I was so relieved I didn't care. I'd been saved. This wasn't the end. I grinned and mindlessly nodded — at him, at everyone — but when I came across Mrs. Zimmerman, she threw me a piercing look that slapped the smile right off my face.

This time last month, she'd had a spell during dinner right in front Sharon — threw a fork when she couldn't find her words — and the very next day she had her thirty-day notice. A Saturday night visit, just like this one, had done her in.

Tonight, her eyes were clear and sharp. She knew where she was, when she was, *who* she was. She knew I was crowing about my Simmons rain check right in front of her, like an asshole. Everyone did; they all looked rightfully appalled.

"It's fine," Mrs. Zimmerman declared. "Let's not get out of sorts right now. We need to look snappy for . . . for . . ." She couldn't force Sharon's name out — I think because it was like poison, not because

171

she'd forgotten it, but it was hard to tell.

"You're right," Valencia said to rescue her, patting the empty spot between her and Sherri Linley. "I say you should come sit down here so Sharon can see us having a nice chat."

Mrs. Zimmerman nodded and sank into the couch as she was told, but in doing so, she relinquished the last of her moxie. Once the cushion had all but swallowed her, she moaned, "Oh, what am I going to do?"

Sherri Linley wrapped an arm around her shoulder. "Look to the Lord and his strength, Agnes."

Carl fished a tissue from within his sleeve, and it was passed to her via the bucket brigade. I sat there, wretched and useless.

Nora appeared. She offered Anderson a questioning look, but didn't press him in front of us. She rounded my wheelchair and grabbed the handles. "I'll take it from here."

Reginald shouted from the background, "Where have you two been anyway? Dinner's not going to serve itself, you know."

Alice shushed him over her shoulder.

"I had a little spill is all," I yelled to the crowd, as if they cared. Anderson stopped midstride on his way to the kitchen. I thought he might turn and help me in my lie, but after a beat he kept walking toward the smell of charred meat.

"Pardon us," Nora said, parting Alice and Carl by wheeling me between them.

When she turned toward the rooms, I panicked. Mrs. Zimmerman was right. I didn't need to lie down at a time like this. I needed to be spry and upright, the vision of health. Sharon meant to look each of us in the eye tonight, glance down at a file noting our independence or lack thereof, and decide how much trouble we were worth.

"Where are we going?" I blustered. "I'm hungry." Carl followed us as we made our way to the room. "Turn me around right now."

"Mr. Duffy," Nora reprimanded, "we're gonna take a look at you before you go rolling around here like nothing happened."

"Nothing did happen." I pointed to my roommate as a distraction, since he was an easy target. "*He* needs a once-over. He slept all day."

Carl balked. "I did not."

"You did."

"I rested."

"Like an invalid."

He pointed back. "You're the one in a wheelchair."

"Boys!" Nora yelled. She drew a frustrated breath. We'd stopped outside our room, and she looked into it and back at us. "I'm about to strangle you both with my prayer cloth. We do not have time for this. Sharon'll be here any moment. Now, Mr. Duffy, did you hurt anything? Are you having any pain?"

"One." I looked to Carl. "It's in my ass."

She pursed her lips. Carl, however, fought a creeping smile that warmed me. For a fleeting moment, a millisecond really, he was the Carl from the days of yore. From this morning, actually.

Nora crossed her arms.

I sighed. "My legs are just tired, and I'm thirsty. Maybe a little light-headed too, but nothing a good meal won't fix. My knee gave out, that's all. Nothing new. No need for a write-up. Anderson found me in short order. Did you know he smokes?"

She drew a penlight from the pocket of her scrubs and flashed it in my eyes. I looked directly at the beam without shame. My pupils were not dilated; this much I knew. Thank God I hadn't had a drink. Next came a pulse check, and I allowed this without complaint as well, practically willing my heart to sing whatever song she wanted to hear. When she'd finished making certain that I was alive and kicking, same as always, she leaned against the doorframe and took a hard look at me.

"Do we need to order you a walker?"

I peeked at Carl, stooped over his. "Hell, no."

"It beats lying in the front lawn," Carl said without any insecurity.

Nora shook her head. "I'm putting in the paperwork just in case. Now, do you need to use the restroom?"

"Jesus." I looked away from them, disinclined to answer, but truth was, I did, and worse than that, I needed her help.

"Mr. Carl, you been a blessing, but excuse us," she said. She read me well, because she was a damn fine nurse. My beautiful, lovely, hard-nosed Nora.

"I'll save you a seat." Carl gave me a meaningful look. We needed to talk.

I nodded.

He left.

Meanwhile, Nora pushed me into the bathroom, while I repeated for good measure, "I fell, is all. Nothing to worry about," to which she replied, "Mm-hmm, now let's see if you need any help getting your pants down."

Dinner was no longer Salisbury steak, like the schedule said, but instead breakfast, and eggs in the evening had created quite a stir. This — on top of me supposedly falling, news of that permit, and Sharon coming for a visit — made for some rare energy. The room buzzed with it.

I insisted Nora let me move from the wheelchair to the dining room chair. She argued, but I did it anyway, swallowing a shriek of pain. Once situated, there was nothing more for her to do but leave me to it. I made her take the wheelchair with her too. I didn't need it parked within a million miles of me.

Carl grabbed his napkin and set it on his lap, smoothing it over a few times to flatten the creases. I rearranged my silverware. Never before had we been uncomfortable in our silence, not even the first day we met.

He cleared his throat and spoke low. "What really happened to you?"

I weighed the truth and settled on punting. "Let's talk about it later, if you don't mind."

"I do mind. You discussed it with Alice already, didn't you?" He raised his chin, challenging me to lie. "She came and found me after your phone call . . . crying."

I cringed, glanced over at Alice's table, and caught her eyes on me. She swiveled back to her plate and started a conversation with Mrs. Zimmerman, who returned the favor by mouth-breathing. Once, Alice peeked back, lashes fluttering. I raised my hand, hoping to offer my apology and thanks, but she turned away too soon.

"Well?" Carl said.

I gave up my view of Alice to look at him. "Did either of you tell anyone else about the phone call?"

After a too-long pause, he said, "Alice told Valencia."

I nodded. To be expected. And safe enough.

"And I mentioned it to Charles."

"Jesus. Why'd you go and do a thing like that?"

Carl pointed a fork at me. "Because you were missing and I was worried."

"Haven't you ever heard the saying that two can keep a secret only if . . ." I looked over at Charles as he inched a glass to his lips, which were puckered and ready about ten minutes too soon. "Now I have to go over there and add some salt to his soup."

"Stop it. You would've done the same for me."

I swallowed and looked down at my plate. He was right. I would have sent out an all-points bulletin and rallied a search party to overturn tables and ransack closets to find him.

"And besides," he said, his fork drooping,

"I put a lid on it when the news started spreading that Sharon was coming. Sherri Linley invited everyone to a prayer circle to help get ready." He leaned over his plate, his sweater picking up crumbs from the top of his toast. "And we all think Sharon's coming specifically to see about Charles. Before you came back, Shawn announced that he's adding an extra exercise class next week and encouraged us all to come, since this is officially a no-lift facility. Have you ever heard of such a thing?"

I grunted. I'd read the fine print. Never worried much about it, because it seemed a subjective, rarely enforced rule. What was the difference between assisting someone up and lifting them up? Though upon reflection, there was a big difference when it came to Charles. Probably when it came to me too. It sounded like Sharon was coming from all directions — you couldn't be too frail, too forgetful, or too fat.

Carl looked me over, concerned and thinking the same thing. "Did you really fall outside?"

"I don't know. Did you really stay in bed all day?" I shot back, like it was a competition for the most unfit.

"I'll have you know that I got up because Alice needed me, and I thought maybe

178

you'd gone to find . . ." Torment flitted across his face, followed by the kind of hope that came along with dreaming too big. "Please tell me. Did you?"

The truth built up behind my lips and, at first, came out like a whistle between my teeth, until finally I confessed. "I did."

"Cripes," he breathed. "And?"

I closed my eyes to gather my thoughts, and there Josie stood behind my lids, loose-limbed and slurring, surrounded by round-ers who'd stick her in either a gutter or a cheap motel. When I came to, I was so ashamed that I answered, "No luck."

Carl blinked, and then a slow slump took over his body, like someone had removed his batteries. At the same time, Valencia — from a table over — announced to the room, "Sharon's here. Look alive, people."

And though I know Carl heard her just fine, he did no such thing.

179

15

Whenever Sharon Smallwood came, she strutted around the place like she owned it, which she did, but still. I hated her visits. And not only because of the power she held over my living situation. It was also because she disguised her fiscal agenda with genuine concern. That and she had a lateral incisor that pointed straight out. She went to great lengths to keep from smiling due to this, which you can imagine was quite a chore, and it made her face look like the navel end of a rotting orange.

Carl would often remind me that I couldn't fault her for her face, but I contended I'd rather have her incisor take aim at me due to an honest-to-goodness smile than have to look at that pucker. And here she was now, parading around the dining room in a navy pantsuit, her cheeks pulled tight by her tiny trap.

"Now's not the time to be pulling this

afternoon's white-flag stunt again," I hissed at Carl. "Bright eyes. You know the drill."

He pushed his uneaten food away. "I think I'm done."

Sharon's gaze swept over us, and I imagined her take on the room as something like a plan position indicator — the sonar sweep marking all those who were uneconomical, high-maintenance insurance liabilities. For now, we were two dull dots on the screen with barely audible beeps. Off the radar. Barely.

I discreetly slid Carl's plate back in front of him. "If today's proved anything, it's that you need to handle adversity a little bit better."

He shoved it away again. "I don't feel like eating."

I thrust it back and murmured, "Then move it all around and make it look like you're eating, but stop being so *goddamn dense.*"

His eyes widened at the accusation, and he gave the plate an angry push, and in doing so, tipped over a full glass of water in my direction. I couldn't move fast enough. The puddle rushed down the main thoroughfare of the table straight into my lap, leaving a scattered trail of square ice cubes in its wake.

Oh, how I wanted to stand and throw out a few curse words from my arsenal, but I didn't. I couldn't. Only three tables over, Sharon stood above a group of ladies, showing off a carpet square.

"For the new room," I overheard her say. "It's Berber."

As quietly and calmly as possible, I collected the four napkins at my disposal and dabbed at my pants, though evaporation would've been more effective. Carl, motionless and unapologetic, watched. I hassled with it long enough for the water around my rear to warm so that it didn't feel like I was sitting on a cast-iron commode in the middle of winter.

"This is not what I had in mind when you said you'd save me a seat." I tossed the damp napkins on the table and leveled my gaze. We'd officially had our first physical altercation. It seemed silly; it seemed serious.

Carl said, "You called me dense."

I hitched my head to Sharon. "Well."

He trained his curled pointer in my general direction. "You're the one who's thick. Do you realize all I've lost in one day?"

"Yesterday you didn't have a daughter or a granddaughter, as far as I could tell, and tonight you still don't. So when I do the math, it sounds like you've broken even." It was low, even for me, but I was officially beside myself.

"They were my dying wish," Carl said through gritted teeth. He tapped his temple with his finger. "If you don't understand that, you're missing something up there." Then his heart. "Or here."

I balked. "Oh, am I?"

"Let me mourn my losses in peace, Duffy, or so help me."

I snorted, leaned in close, and pointed to my pecker, which was the size of a walnut now, thanks to him. "And you're missing something down here if you insist on rolling over like you are."

He balked this time. "Oh, am I?"

"Grow some balls and stop acting like this. While you were busy mourning today, someone risked their life searching for your granddaughter. And that same someone is also trying to keep you from joining Charles and Mrs. Zimmerman in that hellhole they call a home. And what do you do in return? You don't even have the decency to say 'I'm sorry' or 'Thank you' or 'Excuse me for being an asshole.' So . . . so . . . so go ahead. Make your bed, I guess." I crossed my arms. "But know you're going to sleep there alone."

"Fine by me." Carl raised his shaking hand into the air and waved it.

"The hell are you doing?"

"Excuse me," he called. "Duffy needs some help over here."

My eyes went wide. That son of a bitch. How could he? Sharon turned to us with an arched brow. I could feel us growing brighter, beeping louder. She took a step in our direction and, in doing so, managed to knock me into next week. I saw myself in a different bed, eyes tracking a roach crawling in the corner of a different room, my unanswered call light for the nurse shining bright over my head, a fabric sheet hanging from the ceiling, separating me from someone other than Carl.

This is why I didn't notice that an unfamiliar man had entered the dining hall. He seemed to come from nowhere, though more than likely, he had arrived through the front door. His presence had brought an abrupt interruption to every conversation in the room, including, after a time, the one going on in my head.

"Hello?" he called. He stood with fists to his hips, legs spread wide.

No one answered. Carl, who still had his hand in the air, lowered it slowly.

The man eyed the room, taking a few self-assured steps forward.

Sharon intercepted him a foot away from us. "Can I help you?"

He took Sharon in, tip to toe, as if she were a thing to want. This tempered her cinched lips.

"I'm looking for Josie," he said.

Carl drew a sharp breath, which sounded like a squeak. All of my adrenaline rerouted from the man sitting across from me to the man standing in front.

"We don't have a resident here by that name," Sharon said.

"She's not a resident." He wiped the corners of his mouth and looked around before offering a toothy store-bought smile. "Definitely not a resident. I came because I got this weird phone call from here, and I thought . . ." He cast a glance at the ladies' table and shrugged. "I don't know. Maybe she came here to visit someone?"

Lord help me, I thought. *What have I done?*

Sharon spread her arms to the room. "If so, she's not here anymore."

He hitched his head at the nearest table, which happen to be ours. "Any of you know her?"

Carl's mouth opened, then closed. I swallowed hard.

Reginald, from across the room, spoke up.

185

"Who are you?"

Again with the smile. "I'm Bates."

Reginald nodded, as if this answer were satisfactory. "She's gone, but I think she's supposed to be back tomorrow."

Damn Reginald. I balled my fist up and pretended he was in it.

"Really?" Bates said, interested.

The kitchen door groaned, and Anderson appeared, holding a tray topped with twenty bowls of sugar-free ice cream. He halted at the scene: We were all motionless, eyes locked on this stranger.

Sharon clapped. "Well, there you go. It seems you've missed your friend. You're welcome back anytime if you'd like to join her, though. Who is it that she's seeing?"

She'd directed this question to Bates, but Reginald answered. "She's Carl's grand-daughter."

My fingernails left marks in my palm as I pulverized Reginald's brain in my hand.

Sharon pivoted to our table. "How nice."

Bates followed suit with traces of sarcasm. "That *is* nice. Which one of you is Carl?"

I locked eyes with him, while Carl looked the other way. The words *I am* danced at the tip of my tongue, but before I could open my mouth, Anderson swooped in, set-ting his tray heavily on the corner of our table. The bowls clattered against each other.

"Sharon, do you want to help pass out dessert? That way you can visit with everyone. I'll see this gentleman out."

The suggestion sounded benign enough, but the way Anderson held himself while balancing the tray with a single finger, the way the sinew in his free forearm tensed and rippled, the way his eyes blazed, it said all sorts of other things.

Sharon looked between us, her pucker returning to its former glory, and rapped the table with her knuckles. "Very good."

After the exchange of duties, Anderson stepped in front of Bates to lead him out. Bates took one more look at me and followed. Once I heard the suck of air as the automatic doors opened and closed, I let out a lungful of my own.

Carl looked at me, wide-eyed. Our melee from minutes ago had disappeared into the ether, gone as if it had never happened — at least for now. "Who was that?" he asked.

"That," I said, with a for-sure feeling in my bones, "looks like a sucker-punching kitchen cabinet."

16

Eventually, everyone abandoned their emptied ice-cream bowls and lumbered off to bed with overly enthusiastic good nights as they passed Sharon, who eyed me from behind the front desk while conferencing with the nurses before the shift change.

Alice loitered, standing at the edge of the television room, wringing her hands. The glow of the nightly news reflected off her face — a soft blue hue, almost as becoming as candlelight.

Carl and I had yet to rise, even as dusk overtook the sky, even as Anderson bused the last of the plates off our table. I didn't get up because I couldn't. Carl didn't because he wouldn't. Sharon kept glancing our way. Once, Nora did too, and it seemed a foregone conclusion that they were talking about me. Their unheard words rattled inside my head. *Does Duffy require an inordinate amount of your time?* A pause before an answer, followed by the truth: *Yes.*

Alice approached with a tin box in her manicured hand. "Care for a game of dominos?"

Carl shook his head, but I nudged the chair across from me with my toe and mouthed a *Thank you.* Dominos was a thinking man's game, a social venture, a good reason to be sitting there. She took a seat and handed each of us seven blocks, then laid a double six in the center of the table and looked up at me.

I set a tile down. "I'm sorry about earlier."

She picked up the tile and handed it back. "Play is clockwise."

Carl didn't take the cue. He was too busy stewing, staring past us with his lower jaw jutted out.

"Carl," I snapped.

Alice touched my wrist with her fingertips, her skin barely skimming mine, and this curbed my temper. She said, "Carl? Do you care to play?"

His stare shifted to his dealt hand. He played a tile ass-backward on the open end before returning to his faraway place. He'd been doing that all day, and I wondered where he went. There were so many possibilities, considering, but I imagined him flogging himself by reliving his sins. He was probably standing on his stoop at the moment, checking his shirt for makeup residue, before stepping inside a still house, where no children would ever run or laugh or be.

Alice cleared her throat and spun Carl's domino around to make the match. "Duffy? Do *you* care to play?"

I shook Carl's imagined past life off and tried to refocus on the reality of my own. I said, "Alice . . ."

"Hmm?" she said, sorting her hand.

"I didn't mean to speak to you over the phone like I did earlier. It's just that the circumstances . . . There's no excuse, actually. I'm sorry, is all. Sorrier than you'll know."

She didn't answer during my drawn-out breath — the one I took in hopes she'd fill the space with forgiveness — so I went on. "And thank you for not mentioning the call to everyone. That saved me some trouble."

In the absence of yet another response, I dared to look at her. She sat ramrod-straight, with her chin raised and a domino pinched tight between her fingers. Her dusty pink nail polish matched her blouse. Her hair matched the lace collar. She was beautiful, even at her age. It moved me.

She turned the domino over in her hand a few times, then set it on the table and massaged her swollen knuckles. "I'd like to know what all the fuss was about. Where were you?"

Carl shifted, tuning in.

My mouth went suddenly dry. I smacked my lips together a few times, sounding too much like Reginald, but at least it kept me from having to respond.

"Answer her," Carl demanded.

After wasting some time swallowing air, I broke. "I followed Josie."

Alice shot me a look. "Why? Where?"

Carl turned to face me completely, his eyes sharp and accusing now.

Admitting where the chase took me was too much. I played my tile — a blank. "I caught up with her, but . . ." A shrug. "I don't think she's coming back."

"You *saw* her?" Carl said too loud, slapping his palm on the table and shaking our boneyard.

I shushed him and peeked at the ladies still chitchatting at the front desk. Sharon looked only half-engaged with their conversation; her eyes kept cutting to our table. Our game needed to grow a little faster if it was going to be believed. I took the liberty of playing a tile for Carl even though it wasn't his turn. He raised his eyebrows, waiting for an answer.

191

I said, "I saw her, and the fact is that girl has her own plans, and they don't include us."

"I don't believe it. What did she say? How did she sound?" Carl said.

"She sounded . . . busy. She said she might not have time to come back."

"No," Carl said, still doubtful.

"And it's a good thing she's not here," I added quickly. "Think about it, with that Bates character and all —"

"I don't know about your Bates theory either."

Alice asked, "What theory?"

"It's your turn," I said, reminding her to keep us moving.

Carl said, "He thinks Bates is responsible for Josie's black eye."

"You think that man *hit* her?" Alice's dainty voice made the accusation sound unreal, as if these sorts of things didn't happen. I was grateful for this, to know that a lady like her could live an entire life nearly to the end without ever having to meet the backhand of a man. I was also shamed by this, knowing I'd yelled at her earlier like a backhanding man.

Alice grimaced and shook her head, playing another double.

"He seems like the type," I said. "The way

he came in. The way he talked. And that black eye. Josie is awfully vague about it. How does a kitchen cabinet even . . ." I swung my hand around a few times to simulate possible scenarios, dodging my head, looking like a jackass while doing so.

Carl put a stop to the show. "So you think he's a boyfriend?"

"Could be."

"Maybe he's her father," Alice said.

"He's too young for that, don't you think?"

"Uncle?" Carl guessed.

Silence followed. We were grasping. Our ability to measure age had been hampered by our own.

Alice finally said, "She's such a pretty girl. A smart girl. Why would she stand for it?"

Neither of us answered. We were too culpable. Before Josie's birth, he'd started the legacy of failed male role models, and I'd propagated it only hours ago. I hung my head while he slid a tile into place.

"If Josie comes back tomorrow, I'd like to talk to her," Alice said.

"I hope she doesn't come back." The words left my mouth before I'd had a decent think on them. I meant them. I did. Josie had turned my peaceful existence into a sideshow. But to say my wish out loud had been thoughtless. Carl stared at me, wounded to the core. Alice looked confused at best, appalled at worst.

I tried to qualify the statement. "I just mean, for her safety. I hope she stays away for her own good. Bates will be back tomorrow, believe you me, and I don't want her here."

"Well, I hope she comes," Alice said. "That way I can chat with her, and if that Bates fellow shows up, we can hide her. Couldn't we?" She looked between us, and our faces prompted her to ask, "What's the matter?"

Carl spoke up. "We could hide her."

Alice nodded, assured. "I think so too. And if she comes, we'll make sure to treat her like a lady all day. We'll show her what it's like to be respected, and maybe then" — her voice grew wistful — "maybe she won't allow anyone like that fellow to lay a hand on her again."

It was so innocent, so naive, and I was disgraced by it. I couldn't look Alice in the eye. I'd called Josie a piece of shit to her face. I'd left her there alone with those men while she was drunker than a fiddler's bitch. In my own way, I'd let her know I thought she deserved whatever she got. What had become of me? What kind of man did those things to a woman? To a child? Not me.

Not me.

I cleared my throat a couple of times, hoping to stave off the panic rising up through my gut.

"Are you all right?" Alice asked.

"Fine," I tried to say, but the word came out too loud and strangled, drawing the attention of Sharon, and next, Nora. I might've been able to wave them away if it weren't for this morning's incident with the eggs, or this evening's incident with the fall. My gasping didn't help either; the vise from this afternoon clutched at my chest again, fortified by shame and guilt and remorse — an astute conscience, really — and it kept me from drawing a decent breath. As Sharon drew closer with businesslike efficiency, it made it even harder to take in air. She was like a night hag, stealing my oxygen from the inside out.

Nora's step picked up, and again, like the morning, before I knew it, someone had my arms raised high above my head. Sharon looked on, and even in my distress I saw her calculating.

By the time I'd settled, a tornado had blown through my carefully constructed self-reliant facade. Sharon had witnessed the entire mess, and Nora, who'd placed a

195

hand on my back during the frenzy, noticed how wet I was. My shirt had sponged up Carl's spill. She drew her hand away and gave me a sideways glance.

"It's not what you think. It's water, is all," I said.

Under her breath, she said, "I don't mind that you had a little accident. It happens, but I can't take care of you tonight. I'm already off the clock. Zula will give you a sponge bath before bed."

A little accident. This expression infuriated me. It should be reserved for toddlers and bumper cars.

"It's *water,*" I said again. "I'll get in my nightclothes, and that will be that."

"Can I do anything to help?" Sharon asked.

Nora said, "We'll need the wheelchair."

"It's water!" I yelled, desperate.

Carl finally spoke up, his voice small and uncertain. "It is."

But his help came too late. Sharon had left to fetch a wheelchair, and Nora had bid me a discreet, pitiful farewell before slipping away to alert Zula of the lovely job she'd inherited. Alice stood off to the side, biting her thumbnail. I mouthed the words *They're wrong* and *I'm sorry* to her a few times, but the end result made me look like

196

a lunatic. Once the task force arrived, Alice disappeared, along with Carl.

And so there I was, with Sharon and her snaggletooth, looking about as debilitated as any one man could. The shift to the wheelchair was awkward without Anderson, full of groans and missteps and a tragic failure to lock the wheels, and, my God, I was wet. Wetter than I'd imagined, since it'd gone warm so long ago. The drink had traveled down my hemlines to my cuffs, up my back to my collar, and they all thought it was piss. There wasn't a thing I could say to convince them otherwise.

Once I was loaded, Sharon excused herself to do some paperwork in her office. Like hell. She needed to write a short list, and I was on it.

Zula, a gentle nurse with skin so dark it looked a fantastic shade of purple, unlocked the wheels of the chair, and away we went. She and I didn't spend much time together, because she worked the night shift and I rarely needed her help, but we were fixing to become intimate.

"Mr. Sinclair, you need a bath?"

"No," I grunted.

"Ja, no," she chided. "I will give you a quick one, and you will be clean. You will sleep well."

"It's water," I whispered, defeated.

"It's only part water, Mr. Sinclair. You do not want to leave it on your skin. It stinks. A quick bath will help you be in a good mood tomorrow. Look good, feel good, Mr. Sinclair. Now, now."

So that's that. She helped me clean, which was a blur of slack skin, Ivory soap, unnecessary swearing, and embarrassment. We used the common hall bathroom, since Carl had already fallen asleep and Zula didn't want to wake him. She then helped me dress, wheeled me into the darkened room, turned down my sheets, and assisted me into bed. As she tucked me in like a small child, all I could see was the bright white of her eyes, like two distant lighthouses. When she turned away, I felt disoriented. Lost. I was a million miles out without an anchor.

"You sleep good, Mr. Sinclair," said her disembodied voice. "Tomorrow is a new day." The door closed with a subtle click.

Slowly, my vision sharpened in the dark. The room turned into a spiderweb of shadowy lines. The ceiling took shape, the recessed lighting, the tangent wall. Carl's steady, soft snore kept me company while I stared at the room's outlines, wondering what exactly I was going to do, now that I'd set my own house afire.

I focused on the drawn window — where all this started — and some things, though not all, became clear. With effort, I sat up, swung my legs over the bed, and walked to raise the blinds. Outside, the light coming from the waning moon sliced through the nearby trees. There wasn't much to see.

No matter, I thought.

I made certain the window was unlocked, sliding it open a few times to check my work. After one last test, I shut it and walked to the dresser, found Josie's order pad, and wrote: *RESERVATION FOR ONE.* Then I ripped it out, stuck it into the corner of the window, admired it, and lowered the blinds. Finally, I fluffed the pillow on my bed and turned to the recliner.

"It's you and me tonight," I said, falling into it.

It's here I would wait. For the sunrise. For a new day. For Josie.

17

It's a wonder how sleep is so different for everyone, even though it's as basic as breathing. At least breathing has some uniformity across the human race. In and out, over and over again, preferably in a timely manner.

Sleep, though, it's unpredictable. It comes in spurts, or not at all, or burdens you so heavily that you do it when you shouldn't. I've often wondered why this is. I wondered it as I sat in the recliner counting the mini-blind slats, which glowed a pasty white in the darkness. Why was it Carl could string together eight uninterrupted hours in a row after resting all day, while I struggled for two? What was his secret, and what did it mean for me that I couldn't get the recommended shut-eye? Were we allowed only so many waking hours here on Earth, and after they're used up, we're done? Your heart ticks only so many times, and then . . .

It was silly, really. Insomnia had a tendency to do this to me, and my only hope for nodding off was if I allowed all my wondering to be just that.

Eventually, I fell into a fitful sleep, in which I dreamed of Josie. She was a kid playing on the monkey bars, and she kept falling. I wanted to help, but I didn't, because my neck hurt. It was a strange excuse, and I was furious with myself for not being more useful. It was my dream, after all. Why couldn't I make it so that my neck didn't hurt? And then the next thing I know, I'm awake — for real, awake — and lo and behold, it's because my neck hurt, thanks to the goddamn chair I was sleeping in.

I squinted at the digital alarm clock on Carl's bedside table. It was almost two in the morning, and I'd slept for an hour and a half. Sighing, I looked back at the mini blinds to count slats again. I'd work out an average, since no two passes produced the same total. I started from the top and had made it to fifteen when they bowed out toward me, clinking together with a quiet noise. I sat straighter, wide-awake now, just as they settled back in line with the window. The silence that followed went on and on, and gradually the tension in my shoulders let out. I was hearing things. Dreaming it.

Then there the blinds went again, clanking softly. I struggled to my feet and ripped the lift cord with such force I half expected Carl to wake up with the racket. But he didn't stir.

I'm not sure what I hoped to see. A repeat of yesterday morning, I guess. But there was nothing outside. Not even the feral cat that would occasionally lurk around in search of a rodent. Not a squirrel, not an owl, not a cricket.

My adrenaline drained into disappointment. I let the blinds drop back down and turned the tilt wand so the wind wouldn't keep blowing them like sails. As I adjusted the slats to the perfect angle, an unhurried realization came to me: I hadn't left the window open. I'd unlocked it, yes, but I'd closed it tight.

I turned toward my bed.

Sure enough, there she was, strewn across my mattress, with my pillow sandwiching her face, with her long black hair spread about like a halo, with one arm hanging partway off, fingers dangling from her drooping wrist. Eyelids fluttering, lips parted, chest rising and falling in a timely manner.

The sight gave me a hitch in my rib.

I shuffled forward and then turned in a tight circle, because I wasn't sure what to do with myself. I was thrilled to get my wish, but now what? I thought of waking Carl so he could share in the joy, but he slept as peacefully as she. I stepped closer and brushed a stray strand of hair off her forehead, careful not to touch the spreading bruise around her eye. At this vicinity, I could smell the tang of alcohol seeping from her skin. She didn't stir at my touch, and it occurred to me that she'd passed out here.

Centennial had officially become a flop-house.

It stood to reason. I'd left her in a state, and she'd arrived accordingly.

I moved her hand back onto the bed, across her stomach, and pulled up the covers she'd kicked down by her feet. As I tucked them under her chin, she sucked in a greedy breath and turned, her eyes flickering open for a millisecond. I froze, with my hands hovering over her like a blessing, and waited for her to relax again. But instead, in a drunken way, she fought to stay with it, and somehow her green eyes were on me — shining copper in the dark.

"Go back to sleep," I whispered. "You're safe."

There, a corner of a smile — so small I

wouldn't have seen it if I weren't so close. But it was there, genuine and easy. "You . . . you came for me." Her lids, too heavy now, closed again, and that tiny smile dropped away into nothing. Into sleep.

I didn't move. I couldn't; my legs were shaking.

I never regretted not having children, or, better said: I never regretted not inflicting myself on a child. Children need too much love, and despite what everyone likes to say, love is not free. Love hurts. It's action, sacrifice, hard, costly, and I was . . . I am . . . a selfish man.

Josie lying here drunk was proof of that.

She twitched and repositioned her head and, at this angle, looked more helpless than ever. More innocent. Like a baby in a crib. I wondered if Carl had ever looked down at Kaiya like this, and if he had, how he'd managed to walk away. I didn't want to judge him. Who was I to do that? But, then again, seeing with my own eyes what he'd abandoned, how could I not?

"Damnation," I muttered, pacing to the window and back. This little girl needed us. If what I'd done for her today begot gratitude, then by God, she was worse off than I'd imagined. Alice was right. Josie needed to understand that her self-worth didn't come in a bottle or from a bastard like Bates. It grew from inside and had to be watered right. And here we were, a house full of gardeners. Carl, Alice, Anderson. And me: Duffy William Sinclair.

Josie needed me.

Not since my brother, Cormac, had I borne a weight like that. And though I'd beaten Carl over the head all day long with the fact Josie had to go, as I stared down at this drunken barfly, this sleeping beauty, all I could think was: *Hide her. Save her. Keep her.*

I made my way around the room, using the bed as a guide. Zula had parked the wheelchair at the end of the dresser. I backed it up to our door, so that the handlebars pressed against the cheap laminate, and locked the brakes.

Then I sat in it.

I figured I wasn't going to sleep anyhow, and we couldn't risk Nora bursting in, like she did whenever we didn't answer her good mornings. I would be a human doorstop — a crude solution, but a solution nonetheless.

After settling into the wheelchair, I crossed my arms. Surprisingly, I didn't count ceiling tiles or mini-blind slats. I didn't wonder about the meaning of life or the lack thereof.

I just sat there, listening to the soft hum of Josie's breathing and the deep draw of Carl's, more content in the moment than I'd been in a long, long time.

```
┌─────────────────────────────────────────────┐
│                                             │
│        THE CENTENNIAL SCHEDULE              │
│          August 27 — Sunday                 │
│                                             │
│   8:00  Breakfast                           │
│   9:30  Arts and Crafts, Atrium             │
│  12:00  Lunch                               │
│   3:00  Current Events, TV Room             │
│   5:00  Dinner                              │
│   6:00  Campfire Sing-Along, Living Room    │
│                                             │
└─────────────────────────────────────────────┘
```

18

The knocking didn't wake me. Neither did
Nora's yelling. I finally came to when she
tried to open the door and the wheelchair
skidded an inch. Carl sat up at about the
same time, while Josie stayed dead to the
world.

"Mr. Duffy," Nora called, a panic edging
her voice. "Is that you there? Are you all
right?"

"I'm fine," I said, but had to clear my
throat and try again to make it sound believ-
able. "Fine."

Through the crack she said, "What's in
front of the door?"

"Just me sitting here in this wheelchair," I
yelled over my shoulder, "while Carl gets
going. Don't come in. He's bare-assed as a
baby." I pointed frantically to my bed.

Carl looked to it and back at me, confused
at first.

She's back, I mouthed.

208

His eyes widened. He threw off his covers — a smile stretching clear across his face — and reached for his walker.

"Mr. Duffy, move, sir, so I can help Carl."

"He's doing fine today, Nora. Aren't you, Carl?"

"I am," he said, even though I could tell he was counting down. He did this sometimes when he hurt too much to stand.

I said, "We'll be down to breakfast in a minute."

"Mm-hmm. I know what kind of timetable you boys run on. Let me help. Open up."

Carl rose, grimacing, and made his way to Josie.

"Wake her," I whispered. "Make her hide under the bed."

"Mr. Duffy, did you hear me? Open up."

"Just a moment," I said. "I'm seeming to have a problem here. Like the brakes are on or something."

"Why are the brakes —"

"Hold on now, let me just see —"

"Stand up, Mr. Duffy. That'll help."

Carl poked Josie's back. In response, she moaned and blindly waved an arm at the nuisance.

"My knees," I called to Nora, "are rusty today." The wheelchair skidded with more oomph, like Nora'd put her hip into the job of opening the door.

Carl poked Josie again, this time hard enough to make a dent in her dreaming. She pushed up on her elbows, her one good eye open, and looked around as if she'd forgotten where she'd laid her head the night before. Then reality set in like a double shot of espresso.

"We're rising and shining," I yelled to Nora, but also to Josie, giving her a wild look.

Again the wheelchair skidded, leaving a gap wide enough for Nora to reach her arm in and flap it around. Josie recognized the threat immediately, ripped off the covers, and flew to her feet.

"Under the bed," Carl urged.

Josie's quick reflexes should have been to our benefit, but her body hadn't really caught up with her mind. When it did, her face got a look — the same kind she'd had right before she left her lunch in those boxwoods. She ran straight to the bathroom and fell to her knees, hugging the toilet riser with one arm and gripping the handicap bar with the other.

Carl made a move to help, but he was useless at this distance. "What's wrong with her?" he whispered. "Is she sick again?"

"Never mind now." I stood, took one

enormous step, and slammed the bathroom door shut right as Nora gave the bedroom door a final thrust with everything she had.

She tumbled inside with a wildness I wasn't used to seeing from her. "*What* is going on?"

"Nothing," I said.

"Nothing," Carl echoed.

"God bless." She straightened her scrubs with a quick snap of the shirttail.

"Sorry about that. I couldn't get up," I said.

"We're fine, though," Carl said. "How about you? Are you well this morning?"

She grimaced and moved the wheelchair out into the hallway. Meanwhile, Josie's dry-heaving filtered through in spurts. Nora marched back inside, and Carl, in a genius move, started to sing "Nobody Knows the Trouble I've Seen," at full volume. Nora watched him for a moment with arms crossed, her confusion teetering on amusement, and so I joined him. I sang the bass while he sang the tenor, and Nora, eventually, smiled.

At the end of the first verse, Carl bent down and grabbed my slippers, which was no small chore for him, and tossed them near my feet. I slid them on and made my way to the door, still humming the mightiest tune I could manage, having forgotten the words. Carl followed, filling in where he could.

Nora trailed us. "You boys aren't even dressed."

Carl raised his pointer into the air with a wiggle. "Pajama day."

I hooked arms with Nora for stabilization, moving her farther along, while confiding, "Everyone needs a pajama day once in a while." This, I knew, was something she wouldn't argue with, especially after yesterday.

We sidled up to Carl, who looked at me and snickered. God, it felt good to be back in his good graces and see him happy. It felt like a ray of sunshine I could stand in all day, the kind that would fry your skin without you even noticing. This third-degree burn would happen, too, because at some point today we'd have to contend with the puking alcoholic girl in our room.

But not now. Acting normal was the only strategy available to us. So right now, we'd go eat our breakfast, for this was our daily routine, our priority, our mundane existence.

19

We arrived at our table to find Alice and Valencia sitting at it, chatting away. Both were dressed up. Valencia had on her cheetah-print number, while Alice had on pearls and a cream-colored cardigan to match. I glanced at Carl as we approached, wondering how in the hell we could include enough subtext in our conversation to discuss our present predicament.

Alice smiled up at me as Nora went about arranging Carl in his chair. Her rose-colored lipstick had taken a wrong turn at the top of her lip, veering due north at the Cupid's bow before righting its course, but even still, I found her lovely because of the effort. I smiled back with an unaccountable amount of Mr. Magoo — my drawstring pants were askew, my white undershirt dingy, my hair pointing any direction but down. She would've had to be very much smitten to find a man like me endearing. Never mind the debacle from last night, which I'd almost managed to forget about until I sat down at the scene of the supposed crime. The memory made me want to crawl under the porch and stay put.

Carl said, "To what do we owe this pleasure?"

"Well, we talked at length last night," Alice said, "and we had some ideas about what to do when Josie comes today."

Carl's gaze flicked to me. "Oh?"

"*If* she comes today," I said.

"Of course. *If* she comes, but I think she will. She promised Carl."

Carl squared his shoulders at this.

Alice continued, "My daughter Sydney is coming to take me to the department store, and I'd asked Valencia if she wanted to join —"

"Which of course I do, because I need some new Isotoner slippers."

"And you love to shop," Alice added.

"I do. I love to shop. I said to Alice, 'Alice, I could die happy shopping.' "

"That sounds like a nice day for the two of you," I hedged.

Alice said, "Yes, well, we thought it'd be even nicer if Josie came along."

"Alice told me everything," Valencia said, conspiracy and thrill lacing each word.

"I'm sorry if I should've kept it to myself" — Alice looked between Carl and me — "but I thought there's no reason to go into battle alone."

Carl cleared his throat and readjusted in his chair. "What are we fighting, exactly?"

Alice said, "That man."

"Bates," Valencia clarified. "Once I heard about him, I said, 'We need to do something.' That's what I said."

I sat back. A profound silence settled on us. The mere mention of his name gave the air around us mass. Battling him sounded abstract, if not impossible.

"How are we fighting him, *exactly*?" I said.

Alice said, "To start, we're bringing Josie with us to the mall today."

I laughed.

She waited, unflustered and without reproach, until I was done. It left me, in the end, flustered and reproached. She had a knack for that: letting me be without letting me get away with it. I loved that about her.

I said, with some manners this time, "You're going to have to explain this warfare maneuver to me. I'm not familiar with it."

"Well, that's because you're not a woman," Valencia offered.

Alice said, "What she's trying to say is that some company for Josie might be just what

215

she needs. And maybe while she's with us, if that Bates man comes back, you can tell him that she's taken the bus to Mineral Ridge or something."

"Improving morale while misdirecting the enemy," I said, finally understanding. "I like it."

"Wait," Carl said. "You want to take her away to the mall?"

"Well . . . yes," Alice said.

"No. No, no." He crossed his arms. "I'm plenty of company."

A quiet moment dawdled between us. When it'd drawn out too long, Alice put a hand on Carl's armrest. "I know you are, Carl, I'm sorry. It was a silly idea."

I cleared my throat. "Carl, if you don't mind me saying, maybe you're not the right kind of company."

"Oh, go fly a kite. I'm great company."

"But you're not a woman," Valencia said.

"What's that got to do with it?"

Alice put her hand on my armrest now. "Nothing. Forget I mentioned it. It was a really silly idea that I didn't think through."

Valencia said, "But we talked all night long about —"

"Carl, I don't want to take any of your time away from her. It's so precious, I know. I wasn't thinking. Like a shopping trip with

216

us would cure anything." She put a few fingers to her mouth and shook her head. "It's stupid, really."

Carl nodded, satisfied. I, however, found his logic incredibly misguided. I understood that he wanted to keep Josie company every waking hour in an attempt to make up for a lifetime of neglect, but the circumstances didn't really lend themselves to him being so rigid. First, Alice and Valencia were right: Josie's self-worth was not made by man alone. A shopping trip was a humble start, yes, but it was something. Next, it wouldn't serve us well to have Josie here *all* day. It would look suspicious, her hanging about while Carl napped, or spent an hour in the crapper, like he sometimes did. And let's not mention that the girl had no clothes besides the ones on her back and a pair of Carl's shoes. What better place to fix that besides a mall?

"Are you sure you can't spare her? It makes a lot of sense," I said, steady and low. Surely he could work through the same rationale as me without any hand-holding.

He raised his chin, exposing his turkey neck, and fumbled for his fork. "She came to see me, and I want to see her, and that's pretty much all there is to it."

"But it's only a few hours —"

"Stop it," he said between gritted teeth. "I'm not letting her out of my sight again."

"I understand," Alice said.

"*I* don't," I said, disappointed to already be picking a fight with him this early in the morning, only minutes after we'd officially made up. But what choice did I have? I was brimming to call out the obvious, and even the lesser-known facts, like that Josie would need a drink at some point today. We couldn't keep her here if she went cold turkey. And though she seemed plenty industrious, she wouldn't be able to squeeze anything distilled out of Centennial unless Anderson was hiding some home brew behind the clapboards. The mall would be a better bet, and though it was risky to send her off — I understood at least this much of Carl's fear — it was a necessity.

Our breakfast appeared in front of us — oatmeal and berries, with tendrils of steam forcing us to back away from the bowls.

Anderson reached across to fill our coffee mugs. "How's the gang today?"

"Lovely," Alice said.

Anderson paused before pouring me coffee. "And how about you?"

"Better, thank you," I said without looking up. One problem at a time.

After he'd slipped away, Alice said, "You

know the other idea I had that wouldn't take away from your visit with Josie at all?"

Carl blew on the steaming, shaking spoonful hovering near his mouth. "Hmm?"

"What if we asked Anderson to take her out on a date?"

Valencia clapped once. "Matchmaking. My favorite."

This time, I couldn't abide the idea. "That won't work."

"Why not? They could go out after we're off to bed, after he's off work. Those young ones stay out all hours of the night. Remember those days, Duffy? We'd eat dinner at ten and go dancing at midnight." Alice's eyes sparkled as she said this, her cheeks ruddy. "Home in time to watch the sunrise. I met Arthur that way, at the Lancaster Dance Hall, and we got married three months later."

Oh, I did remember those days, at least the best I could, seeing how most nights I'd been under the table, and this was precisely why Alice's plan would never work. Josie was a drunk, and Anderson, understandably, didn't have the stomach for us.

"Anderson's a nice boy," Alice went on. "He would never, ever . . ." She fussed with her napkin. "He wouldn't lay a hand on her. He'd open her door, pay for her meal. He's

219

a gentleman."

"With too many tattoos," Valencia added. "He should get them all removed. Imagine what those will look like at our age. I told him that too. I did."

Alice said, "I'm sure Anderson wouldn't be opposed to taking out a pretty girl like her."

"Well, I like that better than the shopping trip," Carl said.

"Maybe he's going steady with someone," I said.

"I don't think they do that anymore," Valencia said.

Alice said, "I think it's worth a try, either way."

I looked across the room at Anderson. He stood several tables away, holding on to the backs of two adjacent chairs, entertaining a table full of residents with his morning jokes.

"I don't know," I said, though I did. We would be actuating a catastrophic train wreck.

While we all took a bite of breakfast, Josie came in the front door, like she had the day before. This time, she knew her destination. She rounded the corner, eyes on our table, and flashed us a crooked smile, partly forced, partly not. What warmth there was fell on me specifically, so much so that I put down my spoon and stared.

She'd showered; her hair lay long and damp against her back. Despite wearing the same thing as yesterday, she looked refreshed, new. I noticed things I hadn't seen before: a cluster of freckles on the bridge of her nose, purple stud earrings in the shape of stars, chipped nail polish, and a single yarn bracelet.

She grabbed a spare chair and brought it to the corner of our table, then sat in it with her legs folded up under her like a pretzel. "Hey, guys."

"Well, good morning," Alice said. "What a nice way to start the day. We were just talking about you."

Carl beamed and laid his open palm on the table, which Josie looked at without understanding.

I leaned in and whispered, "He wants to hold your hand."

"Oh." She took it, laughing uncomfortably and sitting upright equally so.

Anderson returned — drawn like a moth to a light — with a dish towel slung over his shoulder and a swagger in his step. "Early start, huh? Can I get you some breakfast?"

As Josie looked up, the rising sun breached the tree canopy just outside the window.

The light sliced through the pane and between us, blaring straight into Josie's face, making her squint. Making her glow.

Anderson leaned in closer to shade her, close enough he could probably smell the agave soap we use in our shower. So close, in fact, I could feel the unseen vibration between them. It was chockfull of want and need and hope, and it was dangerous.

"Want to go to the mall?" I blurted at Josie. "Alice, she can join you, can't she? What time are you leaving?"

Startled, Alice turned to me with a frozen smile. "I'm sorry?"

Carl, who looked like he'd been hit upside the head with a nine iron, tightened his grip around Josie's hand. "We have plans."

I said, "What time is the mall trip, though? Maybe Josie can squeeze it in."

Carl stared me down. Everyone else looked to Alice until she answered quietly, "We're leaving at ten."

"We'll be doing arts and crafts then, thank you." Carl's eyes didn't leave mine.

"I love the mall," Josie said brightly. She gave their intertwined hands a wiggle. "I could bring you something back."

He looked at her then, at the exact same time Anderson gave up on being the human parasol. Josie was left squinting in the light again. No way she could see Carl's face across from her, naked with desperation, eyes on bended knee.

I could, though, and it made me cringe when he said, "But everything I want is right here."

Josie smiled, blind but certain, and gently untangled their hands. "Don't worry, Peepaw. I promise to pick you out something good."

20

Well, I'd officially sealed my fate for the morning with that stunt. Carl ate the rest of his breakfast without acknowledging me, though no one noticed because of Josie. She'd once again captured Centennial's attention, with visitors stopping by to fawn over her and inquire about anything from her favorite color to her choice in lotion, because *My, isn't her skin phenomenal.*

Carl shooed people away the best he could, acting downright rude sometimes, all in the name of protecting his sacred time with Josie. When he finally scared everyone off besides the four of us sitting there, he made an eleventh-hour effort to reclaim the day.

"How's your sour stomach?" he asked. "Are you sure you're feeling well enough to go shopping?"

"I'm okay," she said. "Actually, I left yesterday to go to urgent care because I thought I needed some legit meds" — she snuck a glance at me and shrugged — "but after I waited *for . . . ever* to see the doctor, he ended up saying it was just a little twenty-four-hour bug."

Carl's shoulders drooped, while the ladies nodded — and this blind acceptance shone so warmly on Josie that she went on unnecessarily. "I bet I caught it on the flight down."

The group quieted, ready for the rest. I sat with my chin in my palm, my attention zeroed in on her across the table, so I could soak up the fib I felt coming.

And it was a whopper. Apparently, she was on break from the University of Minnesota, where she was an undeclared major. There, she worked as a bookstore barista and lived in a flat with a roommate who fostered dogs. Rufus was her favorite, a shih tzu that looked like an Ewok but sounded like a hound. In her spare time, she liked to bike, weather allowing. And she was twenty-two. Twenty-two years old. And what of this persistent sickness? The random puking? It was nothing more than a tagalong virus from the commercial airliner petri dish, which she had braved so she could come visit Peepaw, who looked on with misplaced pride. It's like he'd forgotten she came through our window without even a pair of shoes, only to run off a few hours later in a pair of his. He latched on to this reinvented version because it suited him better. Everything in her story was shameless. Easy.

Josie kept peeking at me while carrying on. I looked back, unwavering, blank-faced, wondering what part of the truth she'd borrowed from to spruce up. I couldn't help but wish the sparkling bits were real, even though I knew better; I'd written the book on how to fictionalize a life. When I'd sat at new bars with new sets of ears, I became a CPA, an engineer, a pilot, a butcher. I wrote poetry, sang music, hunted game in Africa. But no matter who I was on any given day, I'd have a drink in front of me, meant to celebrate a life that was treating me far better than I deserved.

The lies finally stopped once I stopped lying to myself, and that only happened when everyone else quit believing my bullshit. It makes it easier to see that you're knee-deep in it when no one's helping you shovel. And at the moment, I was the only one leaning on my spade.

"My goodness," Alice said, after Josie's story dead-ended into the present. "You're certainly a busy girl, but I'm so glad you've taken a break to visit. Young people nowadays don't always do that, and it's been a treat for all of us, this morning especially. I could probably sit here with you all day long." She smiled secretly at Josie, then lowered her voice. "But I shouldn't, because I have to go to the ladies' room before my daughter Sydney gets here."

"Me too," Valencia declared, standing. "Excuse us."

"Of course." I moved to rise, as etiquette required, though stopped way short of actually doing so. It amounted to leaning forward, really.

Carl stood up for real, with a long-suffering sigh, and looked gravely down at me. "I should probably go to the bathroom too, since they're starting to set up the arts and crafts."

Josie said, "Wow. There's a serious run on the can around here after breakfast."

Carl faced her, amused despite himself. He shook his head in wonder. "Gee whiz, you remind me of your grandmother." His smile took on two parts sad, one part happy, and, as a final farewell, he grabbed her hand, raised it to his lips, and gave it a quick kiss. "Come find me as soon as you're home."

Josie nodded, obviously stunned by the affection. When she got her hand back, she wiped it discreetly on her jean shorts, and, as Carl shuffled away, it looked like she was trying to decide what she really thought of him. In that moment, I envied him something fierce, for having the slightest chance of being forgiven for a lifetime's worth of sins. How come he could do that when I couldn't even figure how to make up for last night?

I shifted in my chair. Cleared my throat. "Are you okay?"

"Fine."

"Those men —"

"They were no one."

"Did they hurt you? Did they . . ."

"No."

"Your eye looks —"

"It's fine." She bit her lip, and after a moment said, "Thank you for the bed."

"Well." I scanned the room, embarrassed. The dining hall had emptied. Alice and Valencia stood in the living room, powdered and ready. Sydney, who looked like a younger, taller version of her mother, walked through the doors, and joyful greetings ensued, after which Alice waved cautiously at me from afar, warning they'd leave soon.

I had so little time and so much to say.

My next words ran together. "Do you

think you can get yourself right at the mall? Not so right that you don't know your own legs, mind you, but right enough to come back here and be normal for a while?"

She looked perplexed. "What do you mean?"

I paused, drumming my fingers, sorting out how to word what came next. I didn't have time to chip away. Speed-round interventions required a ramrod. I whispered, like this would soften the implication. "Josie, I'm a recovering alcoholic."

A cock of the head. "And?"

"And I know my kind when I see them."

She reared back. "I'm not an *alcoholic.*" She said the word as if her tongue was a virgin to it, as if the pronunciation was in question and the meaning opaque.

I leveled my gaze. "I saw you drinking, and I saw you puking. I know with your mother's death and that black eye that things lately haven't been —"

"You don't know anything about me."

"I don't," I agreed, "except for this one thing I'm certain."

She dipped her head back and feigned amusement. "Okay, I get it. You led a crappy life, and when you catch me unwinding one time you think I'm an addict like you."

"That's not the case."

Her defense grew a knife's edge. "Well, then check this out: You're dead wrong, and you shouldn't accuse people of that sort of stuff. It's, like, defamation or something."

"All right then," I said slowly. "Prove me wrong. Promise here and now to abstain while you're staying with us. Don't leave Alice's side while you're at the mall, and once you're back, don't go on any more *excursions.* It'll make things a whole lot easier, don't you think?"

She sat back, crossing her arms, and mouthed something.

"Did you say something?"

She raised her voice. "Yeah, I did. I said you're a batshit-crazy old man who needs to mind his own business."

"That aside," I said, "could you do it?"

She paused, her brow knitted, her mouth clamped shut to withhold the answer we already both knew. Valencia, from far away, looked at us and tapped on her bare wrist.

"Speak up," I said. "You know us old men. Our hearing isn't so good."

She played with the frayed edge of her shirt.

I cupped my ear. "I'm sorry?"

"Fuck you," she said finally, leaning forward to get in my face. I didn't flinch, though. I let the seething blow by; I was a stationary object in a wind tunnel, creating a disturbance. The anger wasn't meant for me, and I knew this.

She stood, saying it again with extra emphasis: "Fuck *you.*"

I sat back into my chair, satisfied. "I'll take that as a no."

"You're crazy."

"Yet you're the one who looks it," I said. "How about you sit back down so you don't make a spectacle."

She edged out a glance to the main area. Alice shot us a questioning look in the midst of chatting with Sydney.

I answered with a reassuring nod and said under my breath, "Sit on down, Josie."

Josie obeyed, her eyes never leaving mine.

"Let me tell you something," I said. "I don't think you're bad for being like you are. I was like you are. I still am. I'm offering my help because sometimes we need mending and sometimes we need somebody else to help us thread the needle."

She blinked.

"And, well, I want to help you do that. Please . . ." I felt like holding her hand like Carl had, but instead I held my own, as if in prayer. "*Please* let me help."

Sydney took a step toward us, smiling her mom's smile.

"Get a drink at the mall," I said, fast-talking. "Keep yourself calm enough to come back. We're going to figure this out together." Sydney appeared at the edge my periphery. I finished in a desperate breath, "You and me."

"If it isn't Mr. Duffy Sinclair himself," Sydney said. "And this must be Josie. My mom said you're tagging along. About ready to go?"

Josie drew a deep breath and said in the tiniest voice, "Yeah. Thanks for including me."

Sydney put her hand on the small of Josie's back when she stood — a motherly move, one done with grace and comfort. "You bet. Who doesn't like shopping?"

As they walked away, I remembered what should come along with an intervention. Stakes. An end to enabling. A bottom line. I shouted across the room, "So that you know, if you come back too late, the doors'll be locked."

They stopped and turned.

Sydney said, "Are you giving us a curfew?"

"Yes, ma'am, I am," I said, eyes on Josie only.

"We'll be home early." Sydney laughed, hooking arms with Josie to lead her on.

The waiting ladies brightened as the pair

drew closer, exuding the sort of cheer women have whenever they congregate. It made me think of my mother's cookie parties, her book club meetings, her Bible studies. It was a world I didn't understand, though I trusted the system well enough. I'd done the right thing to ensure that Josie exited those doors with them at her side. It just made me nervous, is all. It's like I'd pushed my baby bird out of the nest with a broken wing and hoped she could fly by drafting.

I walked slowly after them, making it to the door just in time to watch their car pull away. It was hotter than deep-fried hell outside, but I stood there for a while anyway, doing something just shy of praying for her safe return. She needed to come back for Carl's sake. For hers. For mine. I stayed until my worry wound up tight enough to choke me, which was about the same time I'd sweated through my shirt.

I entered Arts and Crafts late and took a seat next to Mrs. Zimmerman. When she offered me a paintbrush and scooted over her plate full of dolloped colors to share, I thought of apologizing to her for last night. But she met my eyes with an unblinking stare that meant only one thing, and so I said instead, "What are we making today?"

"Vases for Allen," she said, who I knew to be dead.

Shawn came to our table, placing an empty bottle in front of me. "Super glad you could join us. Hope it's no problemo, but all we have left is Chianti." He smiled wide. "Now that everyone has their bottle, the first thing we're going to do is take off the label. Like so. I find peeling from the corner works best."

I looked at mine and shook my head. God had a warped sense of humor, and I would laugh if I weren't crying inside. I pointed at Mrs. Zimmerman's cheap merlot and asked, "What kind of flowers will you put in that?"

"Daisies," she said.

"Daisies," I agreed, peeling away the label of mine before setting off to make it something beautiful.

234

21

After vase making, I wandered around — a man without a nation. There was no love to be had from anyone. Half of Centennial had left with family members for the day, and the rest wanted to disown me. The few remaining residents were playing cribbage in the dining room, and they paid me no mind, even though I loomed over their game for far too long hoping for an invitation. The entire morning gave me déjà vu.

During my very first day at Centennial, I questioned the wisdom of selling my condo and most of my earthly belongings. I'd packed with the help of a hired hand, and had set aside things like my blender and my encyclopedia set, my tuxedo, and a collection of forty-two baseball hats. Things I'd carted around for decades. Things that I liked to have *in the event of.*

They couldn't go with me because they wouldn't fit in the shared room I'd toured, but also because there was approximately zero chance of an *event of.* I was graduating from that portion of my life. Moving on. Trying on a new shell, like a crab. And so there I was, with one heavy-duty cardboard wardrobe box and a smaller one for the knickknacks that survived the purge, standing at the threshold of Centennial's foyer, not knowing a soul. Thinking that this shell wasn't much better than a stick in the eye.

I drifted around the place much like now — without purpose, forcing myself to make eye contact with whoever I passed, commenting on nonsense like the weather and the calendar, while otherwise wishing there was a tenth-floor window I could jump out of.

And then I met Carl. Carl, with his photos of his wife and his goofy snicker and his bottomless drawer of giveaways. God had looked down on me with pity and replaced my surrendered junk, which had kept me company for so long, with somebody to round me off. With my first honest-to-goodness friend. A friend who had recently tested our affiliation in every way. And now I wasn't sure what I thought about him.

I looked across the dining hall. For lunch, he'd parked himself by Clarence Riley and Sherri Linley. Sherri was probably busy reciting the Old Testament to him or something. He didn't look much happier than me, checking his watch all the time and whatnot, but at least he wasn't alone. I poked at my grilled chicken sandwich and stared out the window, waiting for our girl.

Despite how this morning had gone, she hadn't managed to scare me off. It'd been a long time since a woman told me to go fuck myself, but I still knew how to carry on notwithstanding. She was stuck with me, whether she wanted to be or not.

If Carl had sat with me, maybe we would've talked about it. Maybe I would've told him about the hill we needed to climb with his granddaughter. But he wasn't having me, and because I was an immature old gaffer, this meant I wasn't having him either.

I pushed my plate away and settled in to watch the front drive until it produced the women. Then I smelled Anderson coming. A bird could have smelled him, between the woodsy musk and the soot from the flat-iron grill. I figured he'd come for my plate, so I pushed it farther to the table's edge without looking up. But then in addition to his aroma, I felt his presence. A hovering, close and confident.

I reluctantly turned toward it. "Yes?"

"Can I join you for a second?"

"I don't know if I can spare the space." I gestured to the three empty chairs. "But if you must."

He took the seat nearest me and went to the trouble of scooting it closer. "I have something for you."

"Are you serving me divorce papers after yesterday?"

"No."

"Are we going to talk about our feelings?"

"No," he said without pause, fishing in his apron pocket.

"Did Nora ask you anything last night?"

"No." He pulled out a piece of paper and unfolded it.

"How about Sharon? Did she say anything?"

He stopped.

"Go on."

"She made me explain why I had to throw away one hundred dollars' worth of meat."

"Of course she did. And what did you say?"

He folded the paper over his thumb so he could look past it at me. His jaw muscle pulsed before he spoke. "I told her you fell outside."

"Don't look so sad about it. That's better than the truth, right?"

"She asked me to document it, and then

238

she took your file home with her when she left."

I turned back to the window. "Well, isn't that some shit."

"Duffy, don't even think about it, man. I kept it really vague. Nora and I, we've got your back. We'll vouch for you."

"Why would you have my back after yesterday?" I asked the glass pane.

"Because I do. This place wouldn't be the same without you here. I mean, who would give me all my dating advice?"

I focused my attention on a squirrel gnawing on an acorn, trying my best not to be moved.

"Or who would tell me I have shit for brains whenever I can't answer some obscure 1950s trivia question?"

"*The Jack Benny Program* is not obscure."

He threw an arm over the back of my chair, prompting me to finally look at him. His tone evened out into something serious. "I brought you this."

I hesitantly took the paper and held it as far away as my arms could reach to read it. Even still, the printed words were blurred. I squinted. When the first line came into focus, I didn't have to read any more. The rest I had memorized.

"I hope you don't mind," he said.

I folded it back up. "I do not."

"I don't want to talk about yesterday, swear. All I wanted to do was give you that. It's something that's been lying around my place for —"

"Thank you."

He nodded and took me in for a long moment. "You hang in there. You got people here who care about you." He looked around, as if only now noticing Carl's absence. "Speaking of, where's —"

"Tomorrow's movie night. He's drumming up some votes to boot *12 Angry Men* out for *North by Northwest.*"

Anderson stood and said through a huge stretch, "Both good, but I heard the consensus was *Dancing with the Stars.*"

"Well." I looked up at him and shook the paper near my ear. "I'm sorry about yesterday. I was wrong to go, and I was wrong to put you in that position."

"Forget it."

"Number ten," I said simply.

"It's forgiven," he said.

When he left, I unfolded the sheet, pressed it to the table, and ironed it out with my palm. Then I closed my eyes and repeated every word, which had been seared into my brain like a ranch brand, starting with number one. *We admitted we were power-*

240

less over alcohol — that our lives had become unmanageable.

When I reopened my eyes, the light looked too bright, like a camera flash. Everything was stonewashed, even Sydney's car as it pulled through the porte cochere. I blinked a dozen times and turned to Carl, who met my gaze. *She's back,* we said to each other without a word. Even the doubt in the statement passed through the invisible string running taut between us. *Josie's back.*

The tinted rear windows of Sydney's sedan gave away nothing. It could've been empty, for all I knew. She walked around to the front passenger side and helped her mother out. Next came Valencia from the back, who put both feet outside before rising, one unhurried vertebra at a time.

My breath fogged the glass as I drew closer, and my heart two-stepped when something moved in the shadows of the rear seat: Josie. Or maybe it was just the play in the clouds sliding by the sun. Sydney snapped both doors shut before I could decide. She trotted ahead to catch up with the ladies, and Luann greeted them at the entrance. Meanwhile, I waited for Josie's head to pop up from the other side of the car.

But it never did.

Carl rose loudly from his chair. He took one searing look at me before grabbing his walker and hotfooting it out of the dining room. Sydney left just as fast. She was suddenly back at the driver's side, slipping behind the wheel, adjusting her rearview mirror, putting the car in drive. I wiped the fog away from the windowpane and it didn't come back. Not until she took a left out of the parking lot and disappeared.

22

Pacing at my age qualifies as self-harm, but this didn't stop me. I covered every corner of my room while despising myself for setting Josie on a course that didn't lead home, and I wore holes in the cheap linoleum, imagining where she had gone instead.

After more than a dozen laps, my legs burned and I had it in my head that she'd passed out somewhere alone. Or worse, with bad company. I finally stopped at the dresser, unreasonably winded and with an ache that went clear past my joints. I hated myself, and if I could've, I would've picked some other stationary object to lean on while catching my breath. That goddamn mirror wouldn't leave me alone.

So I focused instead on the corner of the dresser, where Carl kept an engraved gavel from his Knights of Columbus days. Next to it sat two wine bottles. The first was mine, decorated with geometric stripes, in gray, midnight blue, and yellow, with two white carnations popping through the throat. Really nice, if I did say so myself. The other was in its pristine original condition, save for the dog-eared label and the lack of contents. Shawn had gifted me the demo after noticing the attention I'd paid to the project. He'd thought perhaps I'd want to make another one on a rainy day.

I pivoted it around on the dresser's top so that it looked unmarred and, against my better judgment, popped the stained cork out to have a whiff. I wanted the tannins to dance across my nose — a quick tango, nothing like an actual drink, more like a nostalgic look at a picture — but there was nothing to smell. I shut my eyes and inhaled deeper, nearly plugging my nostril with it, and during my last draw, there it was: a hint of earthy, sweet ferment. My heart picked up speed, and the next logical step ensued. I turned the cork's maroon tip to face me and placed it on the tip of my tongue.

A rapping came at the door. "Duffy?"

Startled, I turned. The doorjamb framed Alice like a portrait. I corked the bottle and slid it back to the corner.

"You weren't at our current events discussion," she said without a trace of disdain. She didn't seem angry, even though I'd sent her to the mall with a puppy to watch and no leash.

"Oh, Alice." I hung my head. "I'm sorry."

"Don't be silly. You didn't miss anything, except Mrs. Zimmerman, bless her heart, was surprised to hear that Kennedy had died. After that, we discussed what to do about that renovation business, though we didn't come up with anything good."

"No, it's not that. It's that I should've told you."

"Told me what?"

"I had a feeling you'd lose Josie."

"I didn't lose her."

"I mean, that she'd lose you."

"She didn't lose me either."

I looked up. Alice stood perfectly still and serene, with her head cocked.

"But," I stammered, "where is she then?"

"The mall. She's getting a haircut. Sydney went back to pick her up. They should be here soon."

"A haircut?"

Alice gave me a sly smile. "A girl ready to change her hair is ready to change the world. I can't wait for you to see her. I bought her a new outfit, shoes and everything. I tried to talk her into this pretty, sheer blouse with a pink camisole underneath. It went with an adorable floral print

245

skirt, but I don't think it was her style. Oh, what am I saying? You don't care, but she picked —"

Alice didn't have a chance to finish. I wrapped her up in my arms, squeezing her close enough that the top of her head tucked right underneath my chin and her curls tickled my neck. She didn't return the gesture at first, probably because I'd scared her. But I didn't let go, and eventually her arms wrapped around my waist and squeezed me back. It'd been so long since I'd given or received a hug like this, and maybe it was the same for her, because we stood there for some time, not moving. Just the two of us existing in the space meant for one. The moment and the news she'd brought made me want to kiss her. And so I did. Right on top of her head.

Alice stepped back quick, smoothing her hair and checking her cardigan buttons.

I instantly regretted the impulse. "I'm sorry. It's just that I'm happy to hear Josie's coming back."

"Well, of course she is." Alice pulled her cardigan tighter. Her eyes flicked to the ceiling, the floor, the escape route map on the wall, anything but me. "We had a nice time."

I stepped aside, gesturing to the recliner. "Do you care for a seat? I'd love to hear about it."

She studied the chair before giving a quick nod. I scolded myself for coming on to her and took a spot on the edge of Carl's bed to wait it out. Maybe that's all it would take: time. I certainly wasn't going to outright address it.

"Well," she said, "we shopped, and had lunch at that Mexican restaurant, San Jose's. Sydney and Josie had margaritas, and after that, the makeover didn't stop with an outfit. Sydney talked Josie into a haircut, but then Valencia got too tired and we had to come back before it was done."

The tequila registered with me, but I pocketed it for later. "A makeover. Like in the movies?"

"Just a new outfit and a new hairdo, really. That was standard practice in our house every few months. My girls were spoiled, I suppose."

"Spoiled, but not rotten. Your girls are lovely, Alice."

"Thank you." Her clasped hands in her lap held all her focus, and she dropped her voice. "Josie told us about her mother."

I straightened. "What about her? What'd she say?"

"She passed away."

"Did Josie tell you how?"

"Some. Don't you know? I assumed you knew from Carl."

"I didn't press him," I said coolly. "What did you hear?"

The tension in Alice's shoulders shifted; it was no longer because of me. "She told us that her mother died two weeks ago. She wasn't really clear on how, but on the way home Sydney said it sounded like she'd been sick for a while, and Josie took care of her almost the whole time. Can you imagine, Duffy? A young girl like her doing that?" She focused on me, reverent almost. "It makes me think of my cousin Gordy. When his wife got her cancer diagnosis and it moved to her bones, he couldn't stand to care for her. He left it to the rest of us, and he was a grown man."

I said nothing.

She gave me a tight nod, sensing my discomfort. "I didn't know until today that Carl had lost his daughter, and I feel so terrible about it. We never acknowledged it like we've done with others. You know, in the blessing service when Pastor Jenkins comes or during Shabbat with Rabbi Weil. None of us even offered him any condolences, and I suspect he missed the funeral. Was it in Everton? Do you know?"

I shook my head.

"Can you imagine?" Alice said. "I'm sure the family was so shocked that they forgot to tell him, or maybe they were trying to keep it from him altogether. I hate when they do that, don't you? Trying to spare us by lying."

Again, I kept quiet.

She eyed the exit, and then me. "You know what I thought of? If Carl missed the funeral, we should put together a memorial. Maybe Josie would appreciate it too. We could talk to Shawn about arranging a trip to wherever she was buried . . . If you think Carl would want it, of course. You'd know better than anyone how he'd like to honor . . . My, I don't even know her name."

"Kaiya," I said, surprising myself. "Her name was Kaiya."

"That's beautiful," she said, then went quiet in appreciation or mourning, or both, neither of which I'd spent a moment on. The oversight got me feeling hotter than a burning stump.

Alice said finally, "If you wouldn't mind, ask Carl what he'd like to do. I overstepped things with the mall trip, and I don't want to do that again. It wasn't my intention."

"He's acting like a damn baby," I snapped.

Alice waited patiently for the rest. This was her way, to dangle a little grace out for me to leave or take.

"But I'll ask him tonight," I mumbled.

"Thank you." She tapped her thighs and used the armrest to stand. "I'm going to wait on the porch until the girls get back. I can't wait to see how the hairdo turned out." She hesitated. Her uneasiness had returned, and again I cursed myself.

She said, "I'll see you at dinner?"

"You know me. I don't miss a meal."

She nodded and made her way to the door.

"Alice," I said.

She turned, using the doorframe to pivot.

"I apologize for surprising you."

A half smile played across her face. "It's nothing."

I nodded. "All right then, well . . . all right."

Then she was gone, and I was alone, dwelling on Josie and wine and something that was nothing.

23

I stood at the mouth of the hallway, leaning up against the wall, peeking out into the main area. Josie had returned, and I knew this because the mob surrounding her wouldn't shut up about it. Carl sat on the nearest plaid couch, looking on with pride. I caught glimpses of her as the crowd milled.

First, I spotted her feet. Carl's orthopedics had been replaced with what looked to be a new pair of Chuck Taylors, which confused me profoundly. Chuck died in 1969 and, I thought, his shoes along with him.

Josie's hair, her trademark, had lost a foot of length and been curled, though the waves were already wilting. It would be stick-straight again by dinnertime; I knew this because the tails I chased back in Nam had the same hair, and no amount of time spent with a curling wand could change it. But I appreciated the attempt. She looked younger. More her age.

And her dress. It was candy apple red and sucking up almost all the light in the room. Thank goodness there was a jean jacket to temper it, but still, she managed to make the crowd look like the walking dead. And she made me look like an asshole, because outside of her fading black eye, how could the freckled, pink-cheeked angel standing there be an alcoholic? It seemed far-fetched. A figment of my imagination.

Anderson came to stand behind me, lingering over my shoulder. "Wow," he whispered.

I agreed but didn't say as much. We settled into a silence. I noticed Carl admiring a new picture frame on his lap, which must've been the gift she'd brought back for him. It looked to be the perfect size for the photo he'd torn up, meaning she hadn't bought him just any old thing. It was actually very thoughtful, if only he could still use it.

Charles drove his electric scooter into the crowd and parked near Josie. She bent down and listened intently to him. I cupped my ear, but to no avail.

"Man," Anderson said. "Chucky's pulling out the big guns."

"What's he saying?"

"He's telling her about his Silver Star."

I turned to Anderson in disbelief. "*He* got

a Silver Star?"

"Yeah. *You* didn't know that?"

"No."

"You're not paying attention then."

"What war?"

"Korea. Marines." He craned to see over me. I didn't break my stare with Anderson until he finally acknowledged it. "What? You want the details? Ask him yourself. He likes telling the story."

I looked back to Charles — narcoleptic, obese Charles — and marveled. No wonder he could hang out at the bulletin board, laughing without a care in the world. It's one thing for your life to taper down from nothing, quite another when you start with a Silver Star. And maybe that's why he slept so well too; he already had all his heroics out of the way. Nothing left to do but catch a nap. Though right now he was wide-awake, watching Josie spin at everyone's insistence like a tiny jewelry-box ballerina.

I drew a breath. "Should we help fawn?"

"No, man. I'd rather fawn when it can't get lost in the crowd."

"Oh, you're smooth."

"I learned from the best." He patted my shoulder. "I'll be in the kitchen if you need anything." He slipped past me, skirting the edge of the sitting room, and disappeared into the dining hall.

Somehow, along his way, he left a trail of energy that pointed right back to me. Josie ferreted it out. I straightened the moment her gaze landed on me, plastered on a huge-ass smile, and strode out of the shadows.

"A-hubba-hubba." My voice was too loud, my inflection too animated. Everyone turned. "All of you," I added, "look nice."

Valencia discounted the compliment with a wave of her hand. Reginald rolled his eyes.

"Did you have a good time?" I said.

Carl said protectively, "Josie and I are going to the room to look through some old picture books. She wants to know what I looked like when I was younger."

"Only difference is he's a few inches shorter now," I said, to no one's amusement.

Carl wrestled himself to a standing position and limped to his walker. "I even have a picture of your grandmother somewhere."

"You do?" Josie asked, her voice pitching up.

"Don't get too excited. It's just a wallet-size of a waitress holding a baby." The words came out cruel, like the woman had happened across his field of view at an inopportune time and the child had belonged to no one. They were cut sharp like that out of habit, and he realized it too late. He froze in place, like he might step in it again if he moved.

Josie bit down on her lip.

Alice offered, "Well, I know you have a really nice one of her grandmother on your mirror."

I demurred in the background, shaking my head. Alice swallowed the last word in some version of understanding.

"Come on, Carl," I said, putting my arm around him, hoping to jar him and give him a chance to redeem himself. "I'd like to see that picture you've gone to such trouble to save all these years."

Mrs. Zimmerman called from somewhere behind us. "Deirdre?"

She rounded the couch and pushed through the crowd, jabbing a skeletal hand between people to make her way. Her hair was disheveled, her gingham housedress stained. When she'd finally poked through the wall of bodies, she stopped dead in front of Josie. "Deirdre, darling."

They stood toe to toe, around the same height but mismatched in every other way. A long silence went by while they stared at each other.

The awkwardness spurred Carl out of his zombie state. "Mrs. Zimmerman, this isn't

Deirdre. This is Josie, my granddaughter."

Mrs. Zimmerman didn't acknowledge him. She grasped Josie's hands in hers and held them fast to her chest. "Deirdre, you've gotten to be such a lady. So beautiful. Isn't she, though?" she asked Charles, who nodded for lack of any better response.

"No," Carl said in frustration. "This isn't Deirdre."

Mrs. Zimmerman said, "Tell me, darling, do you remember what I used to sing when you were a little girl? To get you to fall asleep? You were such a fussy thing when you were a baby. I'd walk the halls and sing something. Do you remember what it was?"

Josie shook her head. "No, ma'am."

"Mama. Call me Mama, darling." She put her hands to Josie's cheeks and searched her face. By the looks of it, the disorder in her brain ran only so deep. I bet you could peel away Mrs. Zimmerman's exterior and find her hidden and shrinking somewhere inside, fighting like hell in a losing battle. Her disease didn't make a goddamn bit of sense to me.

"When did you get so formal with your own mama?" She glanced at us, embarrassed. "We haven't seen each other in a while."

Carl drew closer, angry now. "She's not

256

your —"

Josie held up a palm to him, never looking away from Mrs. Zimmerman. "I'm sorry, Mama. I don't remember the song."

Everyone quieted. Mrs. Zimmerman's nervous smile gained confidence, and she released Josie's face. The song started as a whisper, with a single flat note strung out between words. "Summertime, and the livin' is easy." It never changed tempo and remained off-key the entire time, but I recognized it well enough. I heard Ella Fitzgerald singing, not Mrs. Zimmerman, with Louis Armstrong's bright trumpet in the background. No one did George Gershwin's song justice like those two. No one.

"Oh, your daddy's rich, and your ma is good-lookin'. So hush, little baby, don't you cry," Mrs. Zimmerman finished, her voice faltering at the end.

Carl fell back onto the couch on the final note, Alice covered her mouth with a cupped hand, and Josie let out a huge held breath.

Mrs. Zimmerman, unaware that she'd picked off a scab, wrapped the girl in her arms and let out a joyful hoot. "Oh, it has been so long since I thought of that."

Josie buried her face in Mrs. Zimmerman's shoulder, hugging her back. "Mama."

257

Her voice broke. "Mom."

In the midst of this plea, Mrs. Zimmerman's happiness fell away. She held Josie at arm's length, her brow gathering into endless peaks. I could see her sense of things returning, by the way she looked at everyone around her. We flickered from strangers to friends and back again. It's when her scrutiny returned to Josie that her confusion warped into panic. She withdrew from the girl like you would a touched flame, and backed away shaking her head. She bumped into Reginald, then Valencia, and finally into Nora, who'd been watching all of this unfold from the outskirts, no doubt hoping it would have a more benign ending.

"Mrs. Zimmerman," Nora cooed gently, wrapping an arm around her, trying to lead her to safety.

"No," Mrs. Zimmerman yelled, jerking away. Nora gave her a little space, still whispering kindness, but Mrs. Zimmerman wasn't listening. She pointed at Josie accusingly, but also in triumph. "*You* are not my daughter."

We turned our gape to Josie, who looked back with her own building panic. It unhinged her a moment later, and, when it did, she ran, threading through us in a sprint to the hall, presumably to our room.

Carl attempted to stand, but he'd sat too deep in the couch to get up without some help.

"Duffy," Alice implored.

"I've got it," I said, giving chase, though I'd already used my best legs to walk a mile in my own room earlier. By the time I made it to our door, I found her holding the unadorned wine bottle to her lips.

The void of it hit her tongue. She shook it to try again.

"It's empty," I said, closing the door quietly behind me.

She looked at me as if this were my fault. Or, more accurately, she looked at me like I'd looked at her when she stole my glass of whiskey. To have that seething aimed at me, to be stabbed with it — it stole my breath, and I only regained it once she turned her attention back to the bottle.

"It was a craft," I said. "Vases." As if it mattered.

She growled in frustration — a low, guttural sound, like an animal. The noise built up while she raised the bottle high. She regarded me one last time before banging it with all of her tiny might against the dresser. A dent the size of a dime appeared in the soft pine.

"Calm down now."

She did it again, with great satisfaction, and the dent widened and deepened.

"Wait —"

Once more and the beveled edge of the dresser splintered.

I stepped forward to grab the bottle during the arc of her next swing. "Don't," I yelled. "You're going to break —"

It was then, with a flash of light and a deafening crack, that everything went black as space.

24

Luann's pasty face came into focus, floating over me like a crib mobile. Next, it was some guy named Glen, with his EMT ball cap and his oversize glasses and his annoying penchant for calling me "champ." The cramped interior of an ambulance appeared last.

Luann held my hand weakly. "Duffy, can you hear me?"

I tried to speak, but my tongue wouldn't cooperate, as if I'd had a stroke or something. The beeping of the heart monitor skyrocketed. After a few failed attempts at answering, I settled on nodding. Searing pain took over half my head. Felt like my skull had been pulled through a knot.

"We're on our way to Boones Memorial," Luann said. Her voice sounded both loud and soft, like she was yelling into a tunnel. "You fell and hit your head."

I closed my eyes and struggled into my

murky memory. The happenings of the previous two days filtered in through the fog. I reached to touch the injury, but it was hard to pinpoint, because the pain was a moving target. Before I made contact, Luann snatched my hand and held it down near my side.

"Hang tight, champ," Glen said, pressing a stethoscope to my chest. "Once they get you stitched up, you'll be good as new."

Please, I prayed, *let him be right.* Stitches meant surface wounds. It meant the damage went only a few layers deep. It meant the muffled siren fading in and out on its way around wasn't the Simmons anthem, playing just for me.

"Good as *new*?" Luann teased, speaking to Glen like I was knocked out cold. "This guy's eightysomething."

"Now see," Glen said, sounding casual too, "that's why I'm just a deliveryman."

Twelve stitches in all at the hairline above my right eye. After the doctor dressed it, he left me alone in the room with the promise it would heal up fine. I could hear the patient next to me through the baby blue curtain dividers. By the sound of his ongoing complaints, I diagnosed him with either severe indigestion or an ulcer. I could also

262

hear his concerned wife. Did he need a glass of water? Was he warm enough? Where were the doctors, and why did things take so long?

She annoyed the hell out of me with all her fussing. The curtain wall kept ballooning on my side every time she walked past on hers, and she did this a lot. I tried my best to tune it out, to ignore the encroachment on my already pitiful square footage, but then this man, the one who had probably eaten too much or worked too much or slept too little — there wasn't a damn thing wrong with him in my humble opinion — this man got visitors. A son, a daughter-in-law, and two small children who found a great game in poking the curtain and climbing underneath. My mood soured considerably at their arrival. When I'd had enough, I pressed my call button.

It took fifteen minutes, but a wisp of a nurse appeared. She stood at the computer and typed, her feathery fingers making no sound at all. "How are we doing?"

"I've been better." The family reunion next door had quieted, but I signaled toward it anyway and shook my head. "It's noisy."

"Welcome to the ER, Mr. Sinclair." She kept typing. "Transport should be here soon with your wheelchair. Luann has your discharge papers, and she's gone to find you a ride home."

I grunted and looked down at my hospital gown. I remember seeing my ruined shirt in the ambulance. By the looks of it, you would've thought I'd bled out. "I'm a mess," I muttered to myself.

The nurse glanced over her shoulder. "Could be worse. Heard you hit your head on a dresser before you hit the floor. You're lucky you didn't break any bones. That's what usually happens."

"Hips?"

"And wrists."

"We're that predictable?"

On her way out, she said, "There are always people like you who don't live by the rules."

Which was true enough, but when I imagined myself dropping lifeless to the ground in my room, my arms and legs falling at odd angles, bending but not breaking, this version of events seemed off. The nurse was right; I should've shattered something.

I weeded through the misconstruction, drawing myself back to the moments after Josie hit me upside the head. I'd managed to stand for a few dazed seconds, wondering what had happened, and then Josie caught me on the way down; I was sure of it. At some point, my head lay in her lap; I could feel the soft cotton of her new dress around my cheeks and saw red, be it her skirt or my blood. A drawer opened. A shout for help. Shoes. Many shoes, a surprising number, an odd number. I remember thinking someone must have only one leg.

He fell, she said.

Dial 9-1-1, someone yelled.

Jesus.

I've got them on the line.

Don't move him.

Hand her a towel.

Oh my God, I'm sorry, she whispered into my ear. *Please don't die. I'm sorry. I promise I'll never —*

"Duffy," Luann said, ripping the curtain wide and exposing the hospital thoroughfare, where an attendant milled in the linen closet and my twiggy nurse worshipped another computer kiosk. "Ready to go?"

I propped myself up on my elbows. "I haven't got my shoes or shirt."

She raised a pair of one-size-fits-all rubber-treaded yellow socks. "You can wear these and the hospital gown out. You're riding in a wheelchair anyhow."

"I can walk," I protested.

She uncovered my tucked-in toes while I adjusted the bed more upright. I wiggled my feet out of the way, making it impossible for her to dress me.

"Stop," she said, grabbing a wayward foot. "I *can* walk."

Her humor disappeared, and her grasp on my ankle tightened. "Duffy, you aren't walking. You fell two days in a row. This isn't negotiable. Not only does the hospital say you can't walk out of here, Sharon says it too. We've been short-staffed because of you twice now, so you're in a wheelchair for the next couple of days until we figure out why this keeps happening."

I huffed. Mandatory wheelchair time because of Centennial's bottom line. "You know what you can tell Sharon? You can tell her she can kiss my —"

The little girl from next door appeared, her pudgy hand gripping the gathered curtain, her uneven pigtails framing a chocolate-covered face. I choked on my unspoken word and offered Luann a compliant foot. Meanwhile, the girl looked at me with interest. She hid when I attempted a smile, then reappeared.

After a couple rounds of this, I spoke up. "Is your peepaw going to be all right?"

She scrunched up her face. "Who?"

"Your grandpa."

She nodded with exaggeration, all the way

266

up and all the way down.

"Well, that's good. Are you going to take good care of him?"

She nodded again and then hid and said through the curtain, "Are you going to be okay?"

Luann put on the last sock and straightened. "I'll be back. I'm going to find out why your wheelchair transport is taking so long. The taxi's waiting."

The child's mother's voice called, "Mary Lou, don't bother that man. Come here and sit on my lap and show Granddaddy your drawing." The curtain swelled as the girl ran off.

"She's fine. We're just talking," I said under my breath, to no one.

Sure, I could've yelled and had the little girl back to finish our chat, but I hadn't a clue what to tell her. Truth was, I wasn't all right. Not with Hang Overs and Simmons Home for the Aged calling my name in equal measure, not with Josie and Carl and Anderson and Alice disappointed with me for varying reasons, not considering my ride home was with a stranger in a taxi and the fact that I had no granddaughter to show me her lopsided one-eyed stick-figured version of me.

267

No, I wasn't all right. Not even close. My seams were coming undone, stitches or not.

25

By the time they loaded me into the taxi, it was midnight. Luann's shift had ended long ago, but she carried on notwithstanding. She had no choice, I suppose, because beyond getting me home, she needed to pick up her car and head home too.

As she made small talk with the taxi driver — he had been in the United States for fifteen years, the day's weather had been hot, and that smell (which was "interesting") was a combination of his dinner and the smoking passenger who rode before us — as they covered these bases and then some, I laid the good side of my head against the passenger window and let the glass cool my skin.

The town paced by in a stream of streetlights. We passed all my old romps. My old grocery store, my old gas station. We passed Century Bank, with its limp, oversize American flag hovering above the treetops, then

Frankie J's, which sold the best burgers man has ever known. We passed the Como Motel, which had two police cars parked alongside a man getting arrested.

Though I'd gone by these locales on a number of occasions, with Shawn driving me to Walmart or the movies or such, this was entirely different. It was the stars, the people gathering on the porches of restaurants, the headlights, the music piping through to our car during stops, the air, the moon, the locusts, the silence, the night.

It was the night.

I closed my eyes to it, and opened them only when the taxi's right turn signal sounded long enough that it had to be for one place.

Once parked in Centennial's drive, Luann paid the driver from her own wallet and asked him to wait while she fetched a wheelchair. He didn't speak to me in the interim. His eyes flashed in the rearview mirror a few times but otherwise stayed focused on the newspaper rolled up by the gearshift.

Luann arrived, loaded me up, and away he went. I felt nostalgic even to watch his shining taillights make their exit from our parking lot. He needed to tend to all the life after dark that I'd forgotten existed.

Luann had to manually unlock the front doors. At this hour, Centennial seemed like a sleeping giant who had swallowed a rotting meal. The main entrance buzzed with the low-wattage after-hour fluorescents. The place smelled strangely medicinal, something I noticed only now, having been gone for a while.

To my surprise, Anderson greeted us, sleepy-eyed and massaging one bicep. "Long day?"

"You have no idea," Luann said, marching behind the receptionist's desk to grab her things. She jammed her purse under her armpit. "Saline wash in the morning, new gauze, and" — she dug into her pocket — "this antibiotic once a day for a week, because — honestly, because I made them give it to him. The last thing we need to deal with is an infection."

"I got it," he assured her.

She called on her way out, "I better be getting overtime for this."

"Don't worry. You will." He locked the door behind her and turned to me, rubbing his eyes with the fat part of his palms. "How are you?"

"Shitty."

He sighed heavily and then came to stand next to my wheelchair.

271

"Did you stay to tuck me into bed?" I asked.

Anderson didn't answer. He stared into the darkened main area, where blankets were piled on the couch.

"Would you rather I tuck you . . ." I trailed off when the covers moved. "Is that —"

"Shh. She's sleeping," he whispered.

He pushed me forward, closer to the couch, where Josie lay curled up in a little ball, her knees nearly to her chin. The shadowy light draped over her like lace. Her new shoes sat on the floor beside her, right next to an empty bottle of scotch. Two glasses sat on the table, one still with a finger's worth of liquor.

"Anderson —" I started.

"Save it." He fell into the wingback chair next to mine, closed his eyes, and pinched his forehead like it might explode. His whisper turned heavy. "She's a drunk, isn't she?"

"I don't know." How uncertain I sounded about my uncertainty.

He sat forward, though I could hardly see him in the dull light. He was nothing at the moment but a bruised voice. "She was so worried about you, man. I mean, inconsolable. I wanted to take her to the hospital to be with you — that's what she really wanted

— but I couldn't, because I had to fill in for Luann. And then I thought, you know, after most everyone had gone to bed and Luann called to say you'd be fine, I thought we'd have a drink, relax, and wait for you to come home. Or maybe it was her idea. I don't remember. But I thought we'd get to know each other. And then . . ." He gestured to the bottle. "She wasn't sloppy about it, but she was persistent with the refills. Just like my dad. Exactly like him. She thought she was being sly, but I've seen those moves all my life. And then after a few, she was all over me, like, we probably could have had sex right here on this couch —"

I put my hand up. I didn't want to hear another word. "Don't tell me these things. This isn't just some random girl."

"Duffy." Anderson leaned in closer, his eyes ablaze. "I'm trying not to be just some random guy."

I lowered my hand. "You didn't —"

"Jesus, no. Of course not."

"Good."

He looked at me, waiting for the rest.

"She *is* a drunk," I said finally.

The tension drained from him. "I know."

"And she's more than that. She's Carl's, and she's being beaten by someone, and her mama just died."

He didn't respond.

"Josie's lost, Anderson."

Again, nothing.

I reiterated. "She's not just some girl."

"I *know.*"

I paused. A dull pain had slowly replaced the local anesthetic they'd pumped into my head. I gestured to it. "And this is her fault."

Anderson sat forward, his hands clasped in front of him. His silence indicated that he knew this as well, but, like me, he didn't know what to do about it. Turning her in would be the end of this; we were juggling a piece of glass that had splintered but not yet shattered. Pointing my finger at her would destroy what little trust she had in me, and to what end? I wasn't going to press charges. I wasn't going to stop my crusade on account of it either. If anything, over the past few hours I'd become more determined. I was her sponsor now, and I planned to serve her in good faith.

"It's late," I said. "Go home."

"What about her?" Anderson said softly, almost to himself. He regarded me. "I want to *help.*" His words went beyond tonight. They knocked on the door to where I'd already moved in, and I couldn't guarantee it was a safe place to be.

"Let me worry about her. You don't know

what you're getting into."

He raised his eyebrows and waited, prompting me to remember that he actually knew more than most. More than me, even; I'd only ever been on the broken end of this sort of arrangement.

"Call me a glutton for punishment," he said.

"You must be."

He scrubbed his face, frustrated. "What am I supposed to do with all this practice I have from battling my dad? Throw it away? Taking care of a drunk is one of my few talents."

"You have a lot more to offer than that."

"Like what? I barely graduated from high school because of that son of a bitch. I had to get a GED because I was too busy taking care of his shit. I had to" — he motioned to the darkened entrance of the kitchen — "work. And after all that, when I finally got the hell out of there, he was still an addict." He flung a pained glance at me. "I hate him, and I miss him. How messed-up is that?"

"It's not."

"It *is,* Duf. It's messed-up. He screwed me over. And, man, if you want to know how badly, how about this: Helping Josie feels like coming home, and I promised myself I'd never go back. But she's here, and I'm not leaving this time without having something to show for it."

We sat with this confession hanging in the air until I felt obligated to be the voice of reason. "This may not end any different."

He sat unnaturally still. "I know what I'm getting into."

I collapsed further into the wheelchair. "I want to help her too."

"All right."

"Okay then."

We sat in the darkness, mulling over our newfangled commitment to this girl. Paired with Alice's mission for her and Carl's absolute need for her, it had to be enough to shift the momentum. The lot of us were an immovable force.

Josie stirred as if she could sense this, unfurling like a stretching cat. Her eyelids fluttered open, and her gaze landed on Anderson. She gave him a suggestive, sleepy smile, her fingers playing on the space next to her. Anderson looked away from the invitation, like this was the only way he could turn it down, and faintly shook his head.

I cleared my throat and said her name. It came out with an endearment I didn't know I had in me. She sat straight up, surprised, gawking in my direction. I could only guess what she saw, with the bandages and the hospital gown and a long day weighing my shoulders down like a two-ton yoke. I concluded it must be pretty awful, by the look on her face.

"I'm fine," I said, hoping her dread would disappear.

And then it did, quite suddenly. Her face scrunched up, then melted into a mess, and before I could react, she had her arms around my neck and was sniveling into my hospital gown, saying, "You're alive, you're alive, you're alive."

I was so taken aback, the fact that the girl smelled like a distillery didn't even register. The fact that she was crying didn't either. I put a hand around her shoulder as she smeared untold amounts of snot on me, and it felt like the most natural thing in the world. "I'm alive," I confirmed.

She pulled away, wiping at her face before pointing at me in a drunken way. "You," she scolded. The words echoed. "You had me so worried."

Anderson stood. "Josie, keep it down, okay?"

Her finger swung to him, and she shook it a few times to punctuate unsaid words until finally blurting, "And you . . . You're so fucking hot I can't stand it."

"Shh," he said.

Her voice grew louder. She spread her arms, palms to the ceiling. "How am I supposed to be quiet? This is so great. We need to celebrate. Duffy didn't die."

Anderson turned to me. "She wasn't sloppy, I promise."

"I've seen worse." Truth was, I'd been worse. "Josie, sweetie, you need to keep it down. Remember, you're not supposed to be here."

"Oh, right. Shh." She pressed her pointer to her lips, though her volume didn't change. She took an errant step before regaining her balance and kneeling at my feet. "Did you see anything on the other side?"

"On the other side of what?"

"On the other side of this" — she twirled her finger around — "shithole. Did you see a bright white light? Did you see your mom?"

I put my hand on hers, ready to clear the air. But then her whispered pledge twinkled in the back of my mind: *Please don't die. I'm sorry. I promise I'll never* —

She meant it too. Addicts always mean this one thing. Even while drinking, we want to stop. Besides the booze, there was nothing more important to us than trying to be well

278

without it. It was a vicious cycle that had Josie stuck, and I resolved to give her a shove.

"I saw . . . things," I said.

She huffed, her wonder falling away to something else. She sat back on her heels and huffed again. "Your mom?"

"I think so, yes. I don't remember much. It's hazy."

"So when we die, it doesn't . . . end? I mean, if she was there, then it must mean . . . Is there a God?"

I swallowed a sharp breath.

The air-conditioning clicked on and droned.

She waited.

I readjusted and restarted. "It's *very* hazy, but one thing wasn't: I remember hearing you say you'd get sober if I came back. I heard your voice calling from far away. Did you say that? Was I dreaming it?"

She shook her head. "You heard me?"

"I did." I knew we'd have to have this conversation one more time in the morning when she had her wits about her, but for now I rode the momentum. "I came back because of that. No other reason."

She plopped an elbow on the coffee table for support, and it nudged the glass of unfinished scotch. She caught it, to keep it from tipping, and held fast. Her tongue appeared at the corner of her mouth.

Anderson knelt by her and slipped the cup from her fingers. "What do you say we call it a night?"

"How about you call it a night forever?" I said to her. "Keep your promise."

She looked at him, then me. Her voice was weak. "I hit you on the head."

"You did."

"And you died."

Anderson said, "But he didn't."

I said, "And now you have to make good on your pledge."

"Shit," she murmured.

"You can stay in the empty room here," Anderson said. "I have meds from my dad's last detox that'll make it easier. I'll be here in case anything happens, and I'll sit with you as much as I can. And Carl's here."

"And so am I," I said.

She looked at me now, the seriousness in her face swapped out for a slack smile. "I know *you'll* be around. You've been following me for days. At Walmart, at Hang Overs . . ."

Anderson shot me a look.

I shrugged. "What can I say?"

"You can say" — she lowered her voice — " 'Josie, I'm just acting like a dad since you don't have one.' "

Before I could respond, she stood, with the help of the table, rounded my wheelchair, and backed it up. "Which is why" — she steered me toward the hallway — "it's probably good you didn't die."

Anderson shadowed her nervously. "What are we doing?"

"Celebrating," she said. Then without any more warning, she took off with the wheelchair, so fast that my head lurched back.

"Careful," Anderson hissed behind us. And, "Quiet." And, "Shh." And a very desperate, "Slow down."

But we were moving, cutting left, right, swerving, fast as all get-out, with Josie's bare feet smacking the floor, her laugh echoing, and me holding on for dear life. I wanted to yell for her to stop, but that'd make even more noise. So I bit my tongue, clutched the armrests, and prayed for the drunk driver to park.

"Are you having fun yet?" she said, turning around at the dead end of the hallway, gearing up for one more round. And, God help me, when I looked down the drag, with Anderson standing in the middle, helpless to know how to stop her, I decided I kind of was.

She took off again, and I could feel myself

281

grinning while the tie strings at the neck of my hospital gown flapped behind me. We blew by Anderson, circled around, and swerved our way back to the dead end. There, she took a break, supporting herself with one side of my wheelchair. We were both breathing hard, looking at each other like we'd managed to rob a bank and outrun the police. It was a real nice moment, except for she probably wouldn't remember it. And that wiped my smile clean off.

Anderson caught up and angrily unlocked the spare bedroom's door. It creaked open into darkness. He turned to me. "This is not a joke."

The last shivers from our commotion dissipated into silence, making even our breathing sound too loud.

"I know," I said. "I'm sorry."

"Me too," Josie giggled.

He grimaced, shaking his head, and reached around the wall for the light switch. The bulb flickered on, lighting up the sparse furniture that'd been left behind: a bed with a stained mattress, a dinged-up nightstand, and an antique armchair, all pushed to the center in anticipation of the renovation. Josie peered in and back at us, her smile gone now too.

"It's only until you sober up," Anderson said.

Another glance inside. "But . . . but I don't know *how* to sober up."

I wheeled closer to reach her hand. When I grabbed it, she looked down at me. Her curls were gone, and her mascara was smudged, blood had dried on her dress, and her breath reeked of malted barley. All these imperfections, these festering wounds. Yet it didn't stop my heart from swelling so large that it might not have left room for anything else.

"Well" — I gave her fingers a squeeze — "lucky for you, I do."

THE CENTENNIAL SCHEDULE
August 28 — Monday

```
 8:00   Breakfast
 9:30   Bingo, Atrium
12:00   Lunch
 3:00   Soul Series: Mitzvos, Atrium
 5:00   Dinner
 6:00   Movie, TV Room
```

26

You'd think if you went to bed full of piss
and vinegar, you'd wake up just about the
same, but apparently get-up-and-go can
seep from your pores and evaporate like
sweat overnight, because, see, I woke up in
the morning drained and with a case of the
skull cramps.

Even my eyes hurt. Opening them put
undue strain on my newly sewn skin, so I
kept them closed, which was just as well,
because it gave me time to acclimate to the
slits of sun stamped across my face. Somebody had opened the blinds without my
permission.

"Carl," I said, my voice hoarse, "what time
is it?"

No one answered.

"Carl. Time."

Again, silence, the kind with a heaviness
that meant one of only two things: Either I
was alone, or Carl had died. I suppose this

would be a morbid thought for the average joe, but it was our reality every time we said good night.

I turned toward his bed. It was made with hospital corners and his faded orange afghan folded at the foot, like usual. I drew a breath of relief and squinted at his clock. A fuzzy glob of red double digits came into focus, which didn't seem right, but, sure enough, it was past ten in the morning.

I propped myself up, dazed. I hadn't slept in since moving to Centennial. The place shared the same schedule as army boot camp, and, like then, my body had become a finely tuned instrument, scheduled to the point I could predict what time I'd take a dump on any given day. To the minute. Hooah.

I rose with a groan and reminded myself that however bad I was feeling, Josie was sure to be feeling worse. Over the next twenty-four to thirty-six hours, she'd have the shakes, anxiety, and a pulse beating faster than a hummingbird's wing. I wished there were a way for me to take it on for her. But I couldn't, which was a blessing in disguise, since I was so lily-livered when it came to detoxing. If it were me trying to get clean, the moment I felt an unwarranted bead of sweat on my brow, I'd belly up to a convenience store check-out counter before the droplet had traveled so far as my temple. That's why it took me half a century to get my act together. No way Josie would share the same fate.

I swung my legs over the edge of the bed, bent on seeing her. Experience told me she'd be wide-awake, with a burr in her saddle and at least a week's worth of insomnia ahead. She'd be begging for solitude, company, and the gray area in between. I did gray well.

Before I slid off the bed, Nora skittered past the open door. I froze, thinking this would make me invisible, but she backpedaled and came inside.

"Mr. Duffy, you're up." She drew close and examined my head, humming a few descending notes. "Lord, you've had a rough couple of days. How you feeling?"

I beamed, which hurt. "Never better."

"Mm-hmm. You should've seen the ruckus you caused up in here. Sirens and lights and . . ." She patted her scrub pockets. "Let's see. I have your antibiotic somewhere."

"Can it wait until after I use the john?" I moved to stand.

She stopped me with a hand on my shoulder and offered a gentle smile trapped at the corners with regret. "I'm gonna need to get the wheelchair."

I sat back, and we appraised each other. She waited for an outburst, and I waited for time to start spinning backward so that we wouldn't be here now, with my freedom fading every time I blinked.

"Is that really necessary when Sharon isn't around?" I said. If anyone would be willing to give me some leeway, it'd be Nora.

She dipped her chin and looked at me like I was brain-dead. "Now how many kids have I got, Mr. Duffy?"

"I've my wits, Nora, honest to God. I had a little trouble last night right when I came to, but —"

"How many?"

"Two."

"And how many people are paying my bills?"

After a pause, I said with less gusto, "One."

"Correct. And who is that *one* person?"

"You."

"Wrong, Mr. Duffy. It's Miss Sharon Smallwood. She is paying my bills. And that is why" — she pointed to my stitches — "we're gonna wash that with some saline, put on new gauze, and then we're gonna get you in a wheelchair, like she says. Any

288

questions?"

"No," I said, finding it hard to swallow. Every avenue of escape was escaping me. Even my Nora couldn't help.

And so my morning started with a wound redressing, an assisted trip to the toilet, and a chauffeured expedition out to the hallway, where Reginald stood perusing the bulletin board.

He looked over his shoulder and tipped his head to my borrowed set of wheels: Charles's old king-size wheelchair. "Have you got Medicare?"

"This is temporary," I grumbled, glancing down the hall to the spare room before Nora turned me in the opposite direction. As she pushed me past my door, I noticed a new laminate sign. It glowed neon yellow, with bold font and an unfortunate picture of a tumbling stick figure.

FALL RISK, it said.

Things were even worse than I thought.

"I can wheel myself," I snapped.

Nora pushed me merrily along. "Oh, fix your face, Mr. Duffy. I'm only helping you get there before tomorrow. You hungry? Anderson left your breakfast at the table."

She drove me past the atrium, where bingo was well underway. I spotted Carl hunched over his card, having a fine time.

Last night, I'd decided we wouldn't tell him anything about Josie, because over the next couple of days she'd be in a horn-tossing mood, and he couldn't handle that. But, boy, did I resent that decision right this moment.

Nora parked me at my table, where a bowl of fruit and two pieces of dry toast sat. "I've got some meds to reorder, but I'll check on you in ten minutes and move you to bingo if you want."

I leveled my gaze. "Aren't you going to stay and spoon-feed me?"

She grimaced. "I'll be back in ten minutes."

Anderson sauntered up, clutching a wet dishrag and wearing a clean apron over yesterday's clothes. "Nora, don't worry. I got him from here."

"You sure? He's special today," she warned.

"Which means I'm feeling great." I shook out my napkin with a loud snap.

"Yes, sir, you are," Nora said. She exchanged duties with Anderson by patting him on the back and wishing him luck, then walked off with hips swinging.

Anderson made certain she was out of earshot before he fell into the chair beside me.

290

I leaned in. From this distance, I could see the bags hanging heavy under his eyes. We were both in fine form. "How is she?" I asked.

"Asleep when I checked on her last, about thirty minutes ago."

"Asleep?"

"She's been in and out."

"How?"

He took a fork and stood it up on its prongs, focusing his entire attention on making it balance. "It was a late night."

"Sure, but once you're up, you're *up*. Whenever I woke up after a bender without a drink, I had to manually close my lids if I wanted shut-eye. Like this." I demonstrated, for effect.

Anderson shrugged. "I gave her some Valium."

"Do what?"

"It was my dad's. Don't worry."

"What do you mean, don't worry? You can't treat a drug addiction with more drugs."

"Duffy, it's how they do it now."

"It's how they do what? When you go cold turkey, it means you go in a room with a few glasses of water and a prayer, and you sweat it out until your liver has shrunk back to size and your brain's picked up the difference."

"No offense, but I've done this more recently than you, and this is pretty normal. I even have some Antabuse, but I haven't decided —"

"Anta-what?"

"It's a drug —"

"Oh, here we go again."

"A *pill*. An FDA-approved pill that makes alcohol . . . nasty."

"What the hell does that mean?"

"It makes you puke."

"That's the dumbest thing I ever heard. Wanna know why? Because booze does that all by itself."

"No. I mean it happens right away. It's a psychological deterrent or whatever. It's been around for a while. I'm surprised you —"

I waved my triangular piece of toast at him. This was his plan? She didn't need pills, she needed God. She needed twelve steps and a moral inventory and a sponsor.

Anderson's fork fell over, and he looked up from it with complete exhaustion. "What do you want? You want her crawling up the walls? Convulsing? Hallucinating? You want her to get so crazy or depressed that she leaves, or . . . or . . ."

I reared back, once I filled in the blank.

"No, that's not what I want."

"What do you want?"

"I want her to be well."

"Same here, Duf. So let's use whatever we have. I have Valium and Antabuse, and you have . . ." He met my gaze. "You have you, and since she's not due for what I've got for another two hours, why don't you give her some of that."

"Me?"

He produced a tiny key from his apron pocket and slid it across the table. "You."

I set down my toast, wiped my fingers on my pants, and picked up the key to study it. My hands were shaking.

"You gotta go now, though," he said, "while Nora's in the office and Luann and Shawn are in the atrium with everyone else."

"Right," I said, but didn't move.

"You need help getting down the hall or something?"

I gave him my full attention. "Keep that up and I'm going to cancel your birth certificate."

He smirked and set his head on the table in the nest of his arms. "Good, because I'm wiped."

I backed my chair up.

"Hey," he mumbled into the crook of his arm, "don't get spotted going in, lock the door while you're there, and look down the hall first before you blow out, because —"

"I know."

We both went quiet, thinking about all the things we'd like to keep: my home, his job. We'd accepted the bet late last night and were placing our wagers today. Loading up the middle of the table with everything we got.

He propped his chin up on his hands. "Just watch your back. I'll keep an eye out from here."

Alice's loud bingo call echoed in the dining hall. Her voice made my heart jump.

"Go," Anderson said.

So without any more time wasting, I went, wielding my chair like a pro, around the dining hall chairs, past the welcome desk, and down the hall, all while Shawn was in the atrium hollering behind me, "Okay, everyone, clear your cards, it's a new game."

27

Blasted. Dadgum. Piece-of-shit, stupid door. With its stupid city permit. And its stupid tiny keyhole. I hated it. If I had it my way, I'd kick it down and send it through a wood chipper. Turn it into pulp. Make it into toilet paper. And then I'd wipe my ass with it.

Five minutes I'd spent trying to unlock the goddamn thing without waking up Josie or getting caught, and all I'd been able to do was fine-tune my personal circle of hell. It'd have this door in it, and Charles's wheelchair, and probably Reginald standing around, smacking his lips.

If only my hands would stop shaking.

I kept overshooting the keyhole, then over-correcting, and in between each goof I'd check the empty hall with my lungs stop-pered. I hadn't felt this zipped-up since do-ing recon in Nam. Maybe because getting caught here had about the same consequences.

Which got me thinking: *Screw that.* Change of plans. I'd knock, and either Josie would wake up and let me in or I'd pound the door down. Whichever came first. So I rearranged in my chair to give the door a good thump, but just as I was fixing to make contact, it flung wide open all on its own.

Josie leaped back a foot; I leaped up the same distance.

"Christ almighty, I think I shit my pants," I said, only half joking. My blood beat against my stitches, making the skin beneath the bandage smolder with pain.

"You scared *me,*" she countered.

"I thought you were asleep. Jesus. You shouldn't surprise people like that."

"Neither should you."

"Well, at your age, you can handle a little —" I stopped midsentence once I realized how wrong I was. Clearly, Josie had one wheel down and the axle dragging.

She wore her same old ripped T-shirt and a pair of borrowed oversize scrub pants, which were cinched tight at her waist. Her hair topped her head in a tangle, and the night sweats had coated her in a layer of oil that reflected the hallway lights, shining brightest on her black eye. But it was the stuff beneath the surface that really looked broken-down, the bit she thought she was hiding but a guy like me could see plain as day. It was her soul that needed fixing. The rest was just dressing.

A swell of clapping worked its way down the hall from the atrium, relighting the fire under my ass. "Never mind," I said, shoving my wheelchair forward. "Get inside before someone sees us."

She stopped one wheel with the ball of her bare foot. "Why are you still in that chair?"

"Because some lunatic compromised my integrity to walk." I glanced down the hallway and back. "Now let's *get.*"

She didn't budge, and after a few seconds of her standing there in my way, I realized that I was actually in hers. It took me another few seconds to process where she might be going, and why she might be going there.

"Josie?" I said carefully.

She met my eyes, saying nothing and everything at the same time, and just like that, Charles's old, cumbersome, oversize wheelchair was no longer a tool of the devil. It was my best friend. I loved it. I wanted to keep it forever, mostly because it blocked the entire doorway, and short of Josie climbing over me, there was nowhere for her to go.

I said, "You don't want to do what you're fixing to do."

"I got somewhere to be." She gave the chair a nudge backward with her foot.

I held the wheels tight. "You don't even have shoes on."

"Nope." She stepped back and stood on her tiptoes, as if measuring to see if she could hurdle me. When she settled back on her heels, she said, "Do you mind?"

"Plus, think about it: You're already twelve hours clean."

"Go, me." She bent down, putting a hand on either armrest, and looked deep into my eyes. "Now move."

I stared back, knowing the want that was roaring through her. It didn't matter if you were a day or a decade out; it never changed. But sometimes you could get close enough to the light that turning away from it got harder to do. All she needed at the moment was to face in the right direction. And all I needed to do was make her.

We searched each other's eyes. Finally, I sighed and rolled back a smidge. Josie's shoulders ticked down, and she stepped away to wait for me — this decrepit old man — to get out of the way. When she did this,

I used all the force I could muster and bowled forward, ramming her. The footrests collided with her shins. The wheels took out a few of her toes.

"Mother-effer," she yelled, hopping backward on one foot.

I shoved ahead again, like a right tackle, driving her farther into the room, saying, "Oh dear. I'm sorry." Once fully inside, I reached around and slammed the door behind me, backed into it, and set both brakes in place.

Josie scowled, gripping her injured leg. "What the hell is wrong with you?"

"You're *not* leaving."

She threw her head back, exasperated, and after staring at the ceiling for a dozen rambling breaths, she rushed to the bed, launched herself facedown onto the pillow, and screamed at the top of her lungs. She tossed a few kicks in to boot.

I crossed my arms and waited. This was my very first experience with a tantrum from a child, and I was finding that it didn't move me in the least.

Eventually, she came up for air, all pink-faced and hoarse, with smeared tears and sweat and snot. "God, this sucks."

"Sobering up is a bitch," I agreed.

She wheeled on me, angry. "Life's a *bitch.*

It doesn't matter if you're clean or not . . . it sucks *ass*."

"My goodness," I said. "Your hissy fit certainly has a tail on it."

"Leave me alone then! Why do you even care what I do? What's it matter to you?"

"I care because I know you can get better. *Things* can get better."

"You're mental. You know that? Even if you fix me, how are you going to fix my shitty life? Huh? I got no car, no apartment, no *job.* I mean, maybe you could fix it all if you go back in time and make it so my mom didn't . . . Make it so she wasn't . . ."

She trailed off, her eyes welling, and the new tears that were coming weren't the tantrum kind. They were bona fide and earned — the sort that made it hard for me to swallow — and my normal move to run for cover had been compromised when I'd locked us both in this pocket-size room.

"I know she was sick," I offered weakly. "I'm sorry."

"She wasn't sick," Josie blubbered. "She was *dying.*"

"I'm sorry. Please . . . please don't . . . don't cry . . . Don't . . . don't do that."

"God. Do you think I *want* to cry?" she said, her voice full to the brim with the weeps. "I'm sick of it. I *hate* it."

300

She tipped her head back, like that would keep the waterworks from coming, and I held my breath for the same reason. We were so similar, she and I. Tarred with the same brush. We both waited for it to pass — me staring at her narrow little neck, her staring at the ceiling again. But her breakdown only got worse, with tears spilling over her cheeks while she choked on sobs.

"It's going to be okay," I said lamely.

"How? Look at me. I have nowhere else to go besides a fucking *nursing home* —"

"Assisted living," I corrected without thinking.

Her crying skidded to a stop, and she righted her head and looked at me, blinking. Next, a strangled laugh escaped out of her throat. "Are you kidding me right now?"

"Well . . . no, it's just that —"

This made her laugh outright. She struggled to get back, pressing her hand to her mouth, but it was like trying to stop a sneeze. The giggles came, and then they came some more, and damn it if they didn't come for me. We spent a moment in this space, where things were both funny and sad, where it hurt to laugh. Eventually, she buried her head in the pillow, and the jag petered out, but the residue remained, and we both settled into it, quiet and deter-

301

mined. No way we were going back to all that boo-hooing.

I slouched in my chair, prepared to keep my mouth shut until Anderson came and took my place. It was the gray company Josie needed anyhow: a body breathing in the room, to remind her she wasn't alone. I'd relied heavily on my dog when sobering up. He was a loyal mutt. Quiet. Calm. Patient. I channeled him the best I could.

After a while, Josie rested her cheek on the pillow. "Maybe," she said, "if I just got myself right like yesterday —"

"Not going to happen."

"Why not? I could really, *really* use a drink. One little drink."

"Me too."

As I straightened, she perked up, hopeful. Then I double-checked the brakes of my chair and said, "But the answer is still no. That stuff kills you, body and mind, and there are better ways to die."

A flash of anger crossed her face, then disgust — with me, with herself. She hid in the pillow again and moaned.

I talked over the noise. "You know, sometimes you take a left turn and get on this one broken-down road, and you keep on it because you think there aren't any exits. But they're there." When this didn't elicit a response, I added, "This here's one."

She mumbled, "This is the only road I've ever been on."

"That's bullshit," I said, though not unkindly. "Things don't go rotten unless they're good first. Otherwise, how would you know the difference?"

She rolled to her back and went quiet. I watched the hitch in her chest, knowing every pull of oxygen was washing her clean. Every sober breath, every sober tear, every sober word. That's all recovery was made of.

Her voice came out small and cautious. "The road was better before my mom got diagnosed."

"Cancer?" I asked carefully.

A pause. "MS."

I nodded and went quiet. We'd had a resident here named Patricia who suffered from that. She was younger than most of us, less gray hair, but she beat us out the door, because one day she up and went blind.

Josie set her mouth. "My mom was everything before she got sick. I mean, I don't even know how she did it all. When I was a kid, she had two jobs, back-to-back, and I know she was wiped, but she still made sure that we cooked breakfast and dinner together in between shifts. No matter what."

"Tell me what you girls made."

"Anything French. She was obsessed. Always made crazy meals that she couldn't pronounce." Her voice gained some strength. "There was this one time she got this idea that we should go to New Orleans, because it was the closest we could get to France on our budget, and it couldn't wait, because she actually had two days off. So we go. Right then. We pack our bags and get in the car, and I miss school, and it was unreal. I mean, the whole trip we ate our way through the city, and stayed up all night, and . . ." Josie paused and offered a timid shrug. "I don't know. We just did stuff."

I nodded. "That *stuff* is on a different highway, and I'm certain that's the road your mama would want you on."

Josie's lungs stuttered as she inhaled — those jagged hitches that come after crying. "How am I supposed to get there without her?"

"You just do."

"But why bother? I mean, if you're just going to die anyway . . . what's the point if it just *ends*?"

Of course, I didn't have a good answer. Dying didn't make much sense to me either.

304

It was the most unnatural natural thing every human on Earth would ever do. Somewhere deep, we all understood that things weren't meant to go like that. But they did, and even though I was closer to doing it than most, it didn't mean I understood it any better.

I shrugged. "You get to tell one story here, and you don't get a rewrite. So what do you want it to say?"

She wiped her nose with her forearm before throwing her arm onto her forehead. "Here lies a girl who went to college, and had a real job and a decent boyfriend."

"I have a feeling that's just the beginning."

She grimaced. "I wish. I wake up every day ready to *start,* and then . . . and then I don't, and I hate myself — you can't imagine how much I hate myself — and then the only option after that is more. More until I black out or don't care, all so I can wake up and promise it all over again and fail all over again and hate myself all over again." The next words came out as a whispered cry. "It never stops. I can't make it stop."

"It stopped twelve hours ago. If I had a chip, I'd give you one."

She moved the crook of her elbow to cover her eyes. Her fingers trembled.

I stood. Tested my knees. "Let me get you

some water."

"Okay," she whimpered, before stopping me with a "No, no, no. I'm so fucking thirsty, but if I drink anything I'm going to puke."

"I'll get some anyhow and put it by your bedside."

I made my way to the bathroom. With the wall between us, it felt as if I'd cut our umbilical cord. There was nothing stopping her from leaving now, yet I returned to find she hadn't moved, besides having rolled up her pant legs. Both shins were already bruising.

"I'm hot," she said.

I set the glass on the nightstand. "You're young. This flu part will only last a few days, and then . . ."

"Then?"

"Then . . . well, honestly, for a while, you'll feel like you've been eaten up and shit over a cliff."

She swallowed slowly, and I thought perhaps I should word it differently. Make it sound less daunting, even if it was the truth. Before I got a word out, though, her face twisted up funny and, without any more warning, she bent over the edge of the bed and spewed all over my Velcro shoes. I didn't have time to dodge it. In the seconds that followed, we both looked at the mess in awe. The splatter pattern had an extensive and impressive reach for a girl of her size and stature.

"Wow," I said at last, lifting a foot out of the puddle. "Glad that's out of your system."

She lay back down, tears peeking out of the corners of her closed eyes. I dimmed the bedside lamp and slipped off my sneakers. I'd wash them in the sink and find some towels for the floor. Maybe some air freshener too. But first, I wet a paper towel and brought it back, laying it across her hot forehead.

"I'm sorry," she whispered.

"You're all right," I said, thinking that she owed me nothing. Neither an apology nor a thank-you. Not a thing. I was simply here filling a big hole I'd dug long before she was born. An enormous pit. One that went to the center of the Earth.

28

Back in my room, I had time on my hands and a wild hair up my ass. I pulled my mama's old leather-bound Bible from the depths of my closet, dusted it off, and set about bookmarking something special for Josie. An alcoholic sweating out the devil often found God to be a useful fella, so I figured: What the hell. Trouble was, every time I read a few verses, I'd confuse myself by thinking too much and then I'd flip to the next page, hoping for better luck. All of Psalms had blown by this way, plus half of the New Testament, and now I wondered how my mama had made reading the good news look so goddamn easy.

I was fixing to give up, but when Carl came into the room, I doubled down instead. I wasn't ready to make nice with him. Not when this mess of his had only gotten bigger since the last time we spoke. Not when I couldn't tell him the half of it. He must've sensed my cold shoulder too, because without a word, he stopped in the short hallway of our room, slid his closet door open, and made a bunch of commotion, trying to reach for something.

Eventually, it got annoying enough that I clapped the Bible shut and said, "What are you doing?"

Carl pointed up at the far reaches. "There's a shoebox I'd like to get down. It has . . . that old picture I mentioned yesterday."

I gave him a flat stare and then opened the Bible back up and held it high. The shuffling and clattering started again in earnest. I drowned it out by attempting another round of Psalms. *Bow down Your ear, O Lord, hear me; For I am poor and needy. Preserve my life —*

Carl's face appeared above the binding. "I can't reach it." He blinked at me, all fish-eyed, then cringed at my head wound. "That looks awful."

"Yes, well."

He sniffed the air and cringed some more. "And you smell funny."

"Do I?" I said, turning the page, knowing full well I reeked of Lysol and vomit. "Must be from the hospital."

"You should ask for a bath."

I lowered the Bible with a sigh. "Can I help you?"

"Actually," he said, cheered by having worn me down, "would you? Josie left a note this morning saying she'll be back tomorrow, and I'd like to get that picture down so I can give it to her when she comes."

I shook my head in disappointment. Carl sure liked going around his ass to get to his elbow. Giving Josie pharmacy lapel pins and family photographs wasn't going to cut it. What he really owed her — what she really needed from him — was a *moment,* a big honest mess of hurting and healing, but it didn't look like he was going to jump through that fiery hoop on his own anytime soon. So I guess that left me with one choice: I had to push him through it, the closest hoop being Alice's memorial idea. That had *moment* material written all over it.

"A picture's nice, Carl," I said, "but why don't you take Josie to see her mother for real when she gets back instead."

He startled, a sudden fire in his eyes. "For the love of Pete, Duffy, are you being mean on purpose? She's *dead.*"

"I meant you should find out where she's buried or whatever, and you should go there together. In fact, we could all go."

He made a face. "That's an odd suggestion in lieu of getting a box down."

"You could do both, obviously. I was just saying —"

"I've never had a stomach for cemeteries. They get me all worked up."

"That's sort of the point."

"The point of what?" Carl shook his head, swiveled his walker around, thumping it forward, and started vainly reaching inside his closet again.

I watched him struggle, thinking he deserved it, right up until it looked like he might fall and hurt himself. That was the last thing we needed. "You know, you could ask Anderson for help."

"He's in a staff meeting with Sharon."

The remark, offhand as it was, caused a quick fear to rise up through my gut. Sharon, here on a Monday. Having a meeting. That wasn't like her at all. I looked down at the Bible in my lap, thinking without reading, *Oh, my God, deliver me from the hand of the wicked, from the unrighteous and cruel man.*

"Rats," Carl said. "Maybe I can stand on a chair. Do you think —"

Before he finished, Alice scrambled to our door, breathless, her typically well-coiffed curls a mess. "He's here!" She clutched the

311

exterior hallway railing and hung her head, greedy for oxygen. "He's here looking for her . . . That man . . . Bates."

The Bible tumbled from my lap as I stood, though I hardly knew why I was on my feet. It felt like I'd gotten punched in two different directions at the same time.

"He's bigger . . . than I . . . remember," Alice said.

"Crap on a cracker," Carl said. "He's here right now? Where?"

"In the . . . atrium." She could hardly get the words out.

"Catch your breath, Alice," I said. "You're pale." I went to her and placed a hand on her back while peering down the hallway for Nora or Luann. They were nowhere.

Carl came to us, flipped down his built-in walker seat, and eased her into it. Then he looked at me with surprising determination. "Well? What are we waiting for?"

"We're waiting until Alice is all right," I said, speaking like he was dim, which he was. Yet Alice looked offended by the suggestion. "What?" I said to her. "I'm not leaving you here like this."

She drew in a rattling, asthmatic breath. "I'm . . . fine."

"Do you need to use your call button?"

She gave me a cutting glare. I glanced at

312

Carl, who had hobbled to the wheelchair parked inside the room.

As he positioned it behind me, I said, "Now wait a second."

"I heard Sharon has new rules for you, so sit down." He squared his shoulders. "We're going to take care of this fellow."

I blinked at him, surprised, then stuttered out, "But your walker —"

He rattled the wheelchair's handlebars, impatient. "Let's scare him off for good. That way I can give Josie a picture *and* some good news when she gets back."

Alice nodded in agreement, looking at us like there were no other men for the job.

So I sat. I sat because of that — and because Carl had finally stopped carrying his brains in his back pocket.

"Be careful," Alice wheezed.

"We'll send Nora," I promised, reaching for her hand. "Are you sure you're okay?"

She gave my fingers a solid squeeze.

"Ready?" Carl said, shoulders back.

I readjusted in the chair. It felt like we were men of war, gearing up. Like men with a measurable amount of testosterone. I could feel it rushing through me. The hot burn in my cheeks. My pulse pounding in my ears. I pointed to the atrium, chin raised, and said, "Floor it, daddy-o."

29

We arrived like a fading storm, flustered and
wheezing. Bates sat in one of the occasional
chairs, his ankle on the opposite knee,
without a bother in the world besides chatting up Reginald, who sat across from him.
They watched with raised eyebrows as Carl
fell into the closest seat and I backed up the
wheelchair from the sofa table I'd bumped
into upon entering. It took a five-point turn
before I was forward-facing and respectable.

The atrium was empty besides the four of
us. A bank of windows with a French door
sandwiched in between made up the back
half of the room, and the late-afternoon sun
streamed through, lighting up streaks of
slow dust motes. It was an ambience made
for knitting or reading, not combat.

To keep the wind in my sails, I took a hard
look at Bates and imagined him at his worst:
fists balled tight and held high, eyes ablaze.
A man who would kick a sack of puppies.

Or Josie. Or her shriveled-up peepaw and his friend.

In truth, Bates looked docile, with a hint of the same toothy grin he flashed at our last meeting. He appeared to be in his early thirties, though really, who knows. The only thing I noted of real consequence was the tip of his nose. It had a convoluted road map of busted capillaries, intersecting, overpassing, interchanging, the kind that spread with drink.

He hitched his head in my direction. "Hey, Gramps. Reginald here told me you fell yesterday. You all right?"

"I didn't fall. I was practicing my head-butts," I said. A long time ago, this might've sounded intimidating, back when I had the bruteness to back up the bark.

Bates smirked. "Maybe that's where Josie gets her hard head."

I glanced at Carl, hoping he'd spearhead the conversation from here. Bates obviously assumed I was Josie's grandfather, and it seemed wise to clear up that much. I'd already lost track of which lies were where, and this seemed like an unnecessary one.

When Carl finally spoke, I wished he hadn't. "Have you come for dinner?"

Bates's smile faded. "Nice offer, but I'm actually hoping to snag Josie. Seen her?"

We shook our heads simultaneously.

"We haven't see her *today*," Reginald corrected.

Bates looked between us, throwing a thick arm over the back of the neighboring chair, thereby flashing a tattoo on his inner forearm of two poorly drawn toddlers: a boy and girl, faces bloated, eyes too far apart, foreheads cut short by unnaturally low hairlines. He noticed me gawping and mistook it for interest. "My kids," he said, admiring them. "This one here, his name's Brock, and that one's Brandy. They're five now. I only get to see them, like, twice a year, because my ex —"

"Can we help you?" I said.

He regarded me, all the endearment in his eyes snuffed out. "Because my ex — one day while I was working at our bar — packed every single belonging we had, including our kids, and moved to Iowa."

"Women," Reginald said accusingly.

Bates nodded. "Exactly."

"She's not here," I said.

"Yeah?" He looked around critically while sucking his tongue, then let it go with a cluck. "I think I'm pretty warm. She crank-called me from here two days ago."

"Don't know a thing about it."

"Yesterday she was a no-show for work,

316

and last night she calls me from here again, but this time she's actually on the line, and she sounds . . . tuned-up, if you know what I'm saying."

"Tuned-up?" Carl asked.

"She *was* worked up yesterday afternoon," Reginald said with entirely too much authority. "I think it has something to do with —"

"Shut up, Reginald," I bellowed.

The room stilled as my voice's echo tailed off. I pointed at Bates. "She's not here and she's not coming back, and so neither should you. How about I show you out."

Not a single one of his muscles twitched.

Reginald piped up again. "Carl told me she's in town the entire week."

I whipped my head toward him. "I'll show you out too, you big moron. This is none of your business."

Reginald stood, puffed up with righteousness. "I don't know what you're so sour about, but I'm not going to sit here and take this." He shot me the evil eye. I took it in stride, because he gave it to me on his way out.

I turned back to Bates. "I don't think you have any business here either."

Bates's voice remained calm, pragmatic. "Actually, I do, and you probably want to

317

help me out with it, if you don't want Josie arrested."

Carl finally unfurled himself from the couch. "Arrested?"

I blustered, because I'd had enough dancing around. "All right. Who the hell are you?"

"Me?" A thumb to the third button of his wrinkled shirt. "I'm Josie's" — his head teetered in consideration — "boss."

"You don't sound so certain."

His shrugged at my scowl. "You know how it goes."

"No, I don't know."

Carl asked, "What sort of trouble is she in?"

Bates uncrossed his legs and drew forward, acting as if we were confidants. *Careful, Duffy,* I thought. *He's slippery.* Yet I found myself mirroring him — bowing forward like I had the polar end of his magnet in my breast pocket. I wanted to hear what came next, not because I believed what he had to say but because I wanted so badly to disbelieve it.

He said, "So a few days ago, I lent her my truck so she could pick up her mom's . . . remains."

"Her mom's what?" I asked.

"Her ashes."

"Holy buckets," Carl murmured.

I must've looked surprised, because Bates zeroed in on me. "She told you how her mom finally kicked it, right? Choked on her own spit and caught pneumonia from it."

I swallowed hard, thinking of my own choking incident, of Josie's quick reaction, of the flash of horror in her eyes. How many times had she done something similar for her mom, before the last one that finally killed her? I peeked at Carl. Whatever imagined version of his daughter's death he'd come to terms with had been plowed over. He hugged himself tight.

"Shitty way to go," Bates said, picking something from his teeth and examining it. He flicked his finger and continued. "So. I lent her my truck, and the next thing I know, I get a call from code enforcement, because it's wrecked and abandoned at the corner of Old Farm Road and Sanger."

Carl interrupted. "Sanger?"

"Yes, *Sanger*. Do you need me to talk louder?" His annoyance eddied through the offer.

"No, I . . . Never mind."

"Right. So she just left my truck there. Ran off without her shoes, even. Took forty dollars and a Snickers out of my console too."

319

I raised a pointer to shake at him, to accuse him of fabrications, but instead it hovered in the air like a question mark. The empty space between it and Bates filled with an image: pink toenails, dirty bare feet, a half-eaten candy bar. I lowered my hand and sat very still.

Bates said, "And you know what else she forgot besides her shoes?"

I stared, dead-eyed, waiting.

"She forgot her mom."

It took some time for this to set in, and when it did, a rush of anger followed. "You still have Kaiya?" The name rolled off my tongue like I'd said it all my life, like she was mine. "Where is she?"

"In a box at my place."

I sat up. "You give her to us right now. We need to mourn her proper."

He snorted. "First of all, I don't know you. And secondly, Josie and I need to talk in person. There's a lot of shit involved with this. I had to tell the cops that my truck was stolen. No other way around it. My insurance lapsed, and she damaged a city sign and some property fencing. No way I'm paying for that. Plus, now I'm driving around a tiny bullshit Honda rental because of what she did to my truck."

"How much to fix it? Maybe we can come

to terms right now and you can give us what's ours."

"She totaled it." A pause. "It'll cost fifty grand to replace."

"Fifty?" I thought I had heard him wrong. His blank face indicated I hadn't. "What the hell kind of truck was it? That's obscene. We don't have that kind of money."

I shouldn't have admitted it out loud, but it was true. Between Medicare and Medicaid, a vet housing subsidy, and our retirement funds, we had just enough to pay the bills. Carl had about five more years where he could really afford this place. As for me, I had four, after which I hoped to die. At our ages, in our circumstances, every penny was rationed, though it was more like wagering. If we lived a day longer than planned, we were screwed.

Bates shrugged. "That's not what I heard. When Josie called last night, she promised she'd pay me back right now. Something about a diamond ring that you gave her."

Carl straightened. "What ring?"

"Haven't seen it yet, but I have high hopes that it's a big-ass one." Bates looked at me, a half smile playing across his face.

I eyed Carl. I had only a college ring — a bulky gold thing, dented and dull. Worthless. But Carl, he still had Jenny's engage-

321

ment ring. It was an heirloom. He kept it in an old shoe-polish tin in the dresser. And it was big enough.

"You did give her a ring, right?" Bates asked. When neither of us answered, his grin gained symmetry. "I have a feeling there's two of us looking for her now." He massaged his palm while he thought. "So are we still claiming that she's missing and never coming back?"

"Yes," I answered flatly.

A moment of silence followed, stretching to an unbearable length. This wasn't going at all like I'd imagined.

Bates leaned back, casual-like. "Listen, I'm willing to accept the ring for the damage as long as it covers the cost, and I won't mention Josie to the cops, but I have to see her. She and I . . . She helps me hold down the bar, okay? Plus, she's been shacking up at my place. Her crap's still there, and I know she doesn't want to do me like my ex. So let's put our heads together and find her. How hard could that be? She doesn't even have any shoes. If we're having trouble, maybe we'll ask management to take a look around —"

"Please," Carl blurted. "That's not necessary. She's supposed to be back tomorrow. She left me a note."

"Shut up," I howled at him. At both of them, really. I couldn't stand Bates's fast-talking, because that's what it had to be. None of this seemed right. And then there was Carl, sinking our mission while we were still docked. In the hallway, he'd acted like he was game for a duel with the devil himself, rattling my wheelchair's handlebars and whatnot, except his nerve didn't last but five minutes. We'd come to chase Bates out, and instead he'd managed to trap us in our own home.

I pointed at him, desperate. "Have you ever hit her? Maybe we should call the cops on *you.*"

He slapped his legs and stood. "Okay, I think I've had enough of this."

"Good. Me too," I said. "Why don't you get the hell out of here and never come back."

He froze just shy of the atrium's exit and turned.

I craned my neck so I could look him in the eye. "Do we understand one another?"

He sneered at me, like I was an infant making a threat. "I know she's here somewhere, so it's guaranteed I'll be back. And, like I said, her mom-in-a-box is mine until we work some stuff out." He took a step closer and peered down. There, in his eyes, was the blaze that had so far been dormant. "Do you understand *me*?"

"You can go fuck yourself," I spat, though the words were equivalent to an air punch. As the last syllable left my mouth, Sharon appeared at the doorway, buttoned up in another one of her dark pantsuits. She crossed her arms and leaned against the jamb like a schoolmarm.

Bates looked her over with that toothy smile again, pulled a business card from his back pocket, and pointed it at me. "If you see her, give me a call."

"You bet," I said, the middle finger heavy in my voice.

He set the card on the table, pressed it hard with his pointer, and said under his breath, "You don't want to mess with me, old man." With this, he patted me on the back and strutted out.

Sharon watched him go and then turned to me with weightiness in her tone. "I need to see you in my office." She glanced at Carl with marginal concern. "Are you feeling all right?"

He nodded and struggled to stand.

I said to him, "Where are you going?"

"To check my dresser drawer and get my walker." He made his way by, clutching on to everything in reach: the chair, the table, my arm.

Sharon acted unconcerned that he might kill himself, and I didn't have the heart to tell him that half of his trip wasn't necessary. I already knew what he'd find. The lying and stealing was part of our disease on a cellular level. The shoe-polish tin would be empty. Jenny's ring would be gone.

Sharon said, "Are you available to talk now?"

I drew a jagged breath.

"Excellent," she said, rounding my wheelchair and giving it a push. "We've got business to discuss."

30

Sharon parked me in her office and shut the door, cutting off the purr of conversation coming from the main area. A chilly silence took over the windowless room, making it feel like we'd entered an alternate universe. I still had adrenaline pumping through my system, though dread was replacing it in short order. Nothing good came from seeing Sharon privately, yet here I was — in a wheelchair no less.

Sharon pushed me to her desk and sat, shuffling papers out of the way. Behind her sat a filing cabinet, above which hung a clock and a corkboard. I hadn't laid eyes on the board since my first week here, but there we all were, in alphabetical order — the residents of this home, mouth-breathing and fazed by a camera flash we should've seen coming. At the time, I thought it a nice way to remember names. Since Sharon had arrived, though, she seemed to be using it as a progress chart. Three pictures in the lineup had gone missing.

"If you'll give me a second here." She swiveled her chair to the filing cabinet and pulled open the middle drawer, dancing her fingers over the tabbed folders.

Meanwhile, I leaned over her desk to have a look at the oversize papers she'd uncovered. Instantly, I realized they were the plans for the renovated room, but before I could get a good look at them, she topped them with a manila folder. Then with practiced efficiency, she pulled a form from a desktop organizer and presented it to me with a flourish, along with her typical pucker.

"We need to talk."

"Oh?" My voice failed me on this single syllable. I hunched over the sheet but couldn't focus on the words. I could see it already: hallways full of shuffling people silently pleading for it to end. I'd walk around the same way. Vacant. Empty. Ready.

"So let's start here." She tapped her polished nail on the form. "Your fee structure needs to be adjusted."

"It does?" How pleased I sounded.

"It's going to be higher," she warned.

I blinked hard a few times and drew closer to the document. The header came into focus. CONTINENCE CARE, it said.

I sat up, affronted. "I'm sorry. I don't understand."

"We have different care levels, Mr. Sinclair, and sometimes you graduate from one to another, and when you do, you have to pay for the additional attention."

"I'm not incontinent, though."

She drew a patient breath and waited. *We* waited. Neither of us seemed willing to budge as the clock's second hand ticked away. Some indeterminate amount of time passed, during which I tried to convince myself this was at least better than what I'd imagined a minute ago. I should be grateful and placating and slink out of here pretending that I couldn't hold my bladder; that was easier than defending myself.

I hunched over the form again and squinted at the fee adjustment. "Christ almighty. Four hundred dollars a month?"

A ballpoint pen appeared by the decimal. "This amount covers bed pads or diaper orders, whichever, and this here is for additional laundering and room cleaning as needed. We have a fixed price because —"

"I don't need a *diaper.*"

She flipped the form to face her, wrote something, and flipped it back. "We'll order you some pads then."

I crossed my arms and leaned back. *Placa-*

tion, I reminded myself. *I'm not getting kicked out. After that, nothing else matters.* "Is that all?"

She tapped at the signature line. "If you'll sign here."

Without looking, I wrote a careless loop for my first name and a squiggly line for my last, after which I accidently passed the pen back with a little too much oomph. It hit her square in the gut and landed on the floor.

She bent down to retrieve it and set it gently on the desktop. "We also need to talk about your behavior."

"I'm sorry," I muttered, gesturing weakly toward her general midsection.

"Reginald came in with some complaints about a recent outburst."

"You and I both know Reginald's an arrogant asshole, so . . ."

She puckered her lips. "And Luann talked with me today about your brashness last night."

I pointed to my head. "Am I not allowed to be *brash* when they're sewing me up?"

"It was afterward."

"She wasn't exactly full of the milk of human kindness either."

"My point is that not everyone appreciates how you speak to them, and this moment here, now, is a perfect example. You've been unusually agitated lately, and it seems to coincide with your recent spills. You've had some coordination issues, haven't you?"

I exhaled heavily. "I wouldn't call it that."

"We've scheduled you for a doctor's visit on" — she consulted the file, then her calendar — "tomorrow, actually. You'll get those stitches looked at, and you'll also have a general checkup. I know you don't have a lot of family, so I spoke to Luann to help guide us" — she waggled her finger at my chest and hers, as if we were a team — "on what questions we need to ask and what concerns we have."

"I appreciate it, but *I* don't have any concerns."

She leveled her gaze. "Luann suggested that you might want to inquire about the possibility of dementia."

I swallowed. "That sounds more like an allegation than a suggestion."

"Mr. Sinclair, it's a matter of being proactive, and if you do have it, there are treatments to delay symptoms. And if you don't, then great. But considering some indicators we've seen, it's not unreasonable to inquire. You've been disoriented and moody. Luann said she saw you today in the hallway acting paranoid. Let's also admit, a common symptom is a lack of emotional restraint, and about ten minutes ago you seemed to be telling that nice gentleman to go" — the next part she whispered — "fuck himself."

I snorted, on the cusp of telling her to do the same, after which I planned a postal moment, where I'd throw the paperwork and the paperweight and the paper tray across the room. I wanted to roar. To tear the board from the wall and everyone's faces off it as well. I very nearly wanted to strangle her. Emotional restraint be damned.

But instead, I looked back at her lifelessly. An outburst would be counterproductive. A defensive attitude would be misconstrued. I could go to the doctor and give some blood, answer a few questions, kick out my foot when he hit my knee with a hammer, couldn't I? There was no harm in it. If anything, it'd give me a chance to prove Sharon wrong, though it did feel like I was accepting a dare.

"You're right," I said carefully. "I'll ask the doctor about my symptoms."

"Good. I'm glad we agree. I know none of these changes are easy. As far as the diagnosis goes, well . . ."

"Well what?"

She spoke matter-of-factly. "We're not

equipped for memory care or dementia. It's our policy to make sure you receive the absolute best care available, even if it means it's not with us." She set my new form in the folder and swiveled to file it, leaving me staring at the renovation plans.

The aluminum file drawer slapped shut, and Sharon's clasped hands topped the blueprints. "Don't look so worried, Mr. Sinclair. We want you to be well, and we're taking the first steps toward that. Now, is there anything else?"

I swallowed. Tapped my wheelchair's arms. "I don't think this is necessary." My voice had gone thick.

"I'll be here tomorrow afternoon, and we can review your doctor's recommendation and make a decision then." Her tone had finality to it.

We looked at each other. The longer we sat, the harder it became for me to draw a decent breath. I was slowly suffocating under a dog pile of problems. When I thought of them all at once, my heart smarted. I rubbed the edge of my rib cage to ease the pain.

"Very well then." She rose and moved the wheelchair so she could open the door, then pushed me into the main area. "Dinner should be ready in about fifteen minutes."

Alice, who sat on the couch with a paper-back, spun around and stared. I hadn't seen her since we'd abandoned her in the hallway. She seemed pale but otherwise put-together as usual. She shut the book and smoothed her hair.

Sharon parked me next to her. "Mrs. Roda, would you care to take this fine gentleman to dinner?"

"I would," she said softly, never breaking away from my gaze.

Once Sharon walked off, I looked up to the ceiling and said wearily, "Alice, the walls are coming down."

She reached out and clasped my hand. I topped it with my other. We had so much to cover. I needed to tell her about our colossal failure with Bates and the truth about Josie. We needed to talk about the renovation in real terms, without any pretending, and what it meant for me. For all of us. She probably knew if Carl had indeed lost his wife's ring, and how he was holding up with the news. But instead of speaking, because I'd had far too much of it in the past few hours, I asked her, without saying a word, how she was. She understood, nodded, and asked me the same, in the same manner. I gave her fingers a squeeze. And this was how we sat, sharing our life force while time slowly drowned us, spending what little we had left waiting for supper.

31

Anderson served spaghetti. He wore a sauce-splattered apron and pushed around the meal cart like a zombie. Our steaming, heaping plates were waiting for us when we arrived.

Carl was late. Valencia got held up at Sherri Linley's table, talking about her granddaughter, and incidentally sat down to eat. And so here we were: Alice at my right elbow, twirling her fork in overcooked noodles, and me, slurping them up in such a way that they slapped my face on the way in.

We had yet to speak, but I planned on telling her everything, starting with Josie. The girl was our most pressing issue, and I was tired of the circumstances making it look as if my brain had gone as soft as a plate of mashed potatoes. I just wasn't sure where to begin the story or which direction it should go.

While eating, I mulled over a decent prologue that might offer some perspective. For some reason, the day I enlisted came to mind — the same day I slunk behind my Ford Escort with two six-packs of beer and drove an hour to the place where we'd buried my brother. I'm not sure why I went. It's not like it had been something I was aching to do, or something I did often or ever. In fact, I had a date that night with a blue-eyed birdie whose trucking daddy was never home and whose mama worked nights. A gal who was sure to invite me in. But instead, I found myself sitting cross-legged at Cormac's grave marker with empty beer bottles lined up like infantry-men. I didn't come to cry or pray or think. No, I just hummed a tuneless song and drank for a few hours while the sun set behind a great big cluster of bur oaks.

I often drank alone before then, but that day was the first time I felt a real sense of contentment in doing so. And then what? I made certain to be content like that from then on, and it avalanched, like it does, and now here we were with Josie in a similar squall, purging in our spare room while her boss, or whatever he was, held her mother's cremated remains as ransom.

Somehow this order of events felt right

for the retelling. I'd start way, way back and then leapfrog forward.

Alice motioned to the corner of her mouth. "You have something there."

I wiped my face with the back of my hand. "Better?"

She nodded. Pushed some noodles around. "If you don't mind me asking, how did it go with that Bates character?"

"Alice," I said in the way of an apology, "we made it worse."

After a silence that sounded an awful lot like disappointment, she said, "How?"

When I looked her way to answer, my ticker missed a beat. She was close enough for me to count her smile lines and poach what little oxygen lay between us. "Vietnam," I said in a breathless exhale.

"Excuse me?"

Good God. I wanted her help, but I also wanted her to find me worthy of it. "The Vietnam War," I stuttered. "What were you doing during all that?"

"Well . . . I . . . Why do you ask?"

I shrugged and stuttered out the beginning of a few words. When she realized how much I was struggling, she set out to rescue me.

"Let's see." She looked up to the ceiling, like the answer hung from it. "During most of it, Arthur and I were married, and I was working as the receptionist at his dental office." Her gaze leveled out. "Then I had Sydney and stayed home. We lived in that neighborhood near the airport. Shady Grove. You know the one?"

I nodded.

"Well, we lived under the flight line since before the war, and it was never busy back then, you know, a town this size. But it got busy, didn't it? With them bringing home the bodies of all those servicemen. 1968 was the worst. All that air traffic noise would wake Sydney up during her nap. To this day, jet engines make me prayerful." She smoothed out her napkin and offered a fragile smile that tangled up my stomach. "What were you doing back then?"

Worshipping nothing but church keys and choppers, I thought miserably. It was shameful in comparison. Best I decided to skip that part altogether and get straight to it. "Josie's here."

"Josie?" She looked into the milling dining room.

Damn a cast line that couldn't be reeled back. "She's hiding." Damn everything.

Alice's hand went to her heart. "Hiding?"

I nodded before shaking my head and nodding once more.

"I don't understand."

"She's sick."

"Is it that flu?"

"Flulike."

"Why is she hiding?"

"Well." I ran a hand through what little hair I had and caught a glimpse of Carl making his way between tables. How wrong this was all going.

"Listen," I urged in a whisper, "let's not tell Carl yet."

"Tell him what, Duffy? I'm awfully confused."

"With the ring and all —"

"What ring?"

"Christ, never mind." I refocused my attention on the spaghetti as Carl drew his walker to the closest open seat at our table. I didn't look up from my plate until he made a very intentional show of clearing his throat.

"I have good news." With chin raised, he slapped the table. When he lifted his hand, he left a Texas-size diamond ring rattling on the wood.

I drew close to inspect. "How in the world?" After two tries, I had it pinched and inches from my nose. I wasn't sure about the going rate on the diamond market, but it'd definitely do. "But I thought —"

"Bates lies. He probably lied about all of it." Luann swooped by as he said this, arranging him in his chair before floating away to the next task.

I said, "But . . ."

Alice held out her hand in silent request. I set the ring in her palm, confused.

Carl regarded his plate. "Boy, this looks good."

"What's this all about?" Alice asked.

He tucked his napkin into his shirt collar. "It was my wife's, and Bates *claimed* Josie stole it, and then he demanded we give it to him, because he also *claims* she wrecked his truck."

"There's more to that," I reminded him.

He grimaced.

Alice said, "My goodness. What happened? What did you say?"

"We didn't stand as firm as we could've," Carl said, "but we weren't armed with enough information to make it a fair fight. Next time we see him, we'll have the real facts. Josie can fill in the blanks for us. For crying out loud, we don't even know if the man owns a truck."

"Should you get the police involved?" Alice said.

Carl stopped cutting his spaghetti and flashed me a look. "No . . . no, I don't think that's a good idea. It's her word against his, and even though I believe her, how do we know they will? It's just a mess. He probably thinks we're easy targets because of our age. But we aren't, are we, Duffy?"

I couldn't answer because my brain was doing yet another playback: me rummaging through my mother's jewelry box for her wedding ring, me moving aside costume bracelets, clip-on earrings, and a broken rosary while she's in and out of consciousness and her hospice nurse is taking a smoke break on the front porch. Me waiting in line at the pawnshop: crumpled bills, taxi rides, amber shots, bare breasts, strobe lighting mixed with cigarette smoke, rounds of drinks, lap dances, and promises and blackouts and, finally, pocket lint.

This clutter — my insides — belonged to no one but me. A ring-stealing addict seeing another where there wasn't one.

"Are we, Duffy?" Carl asked a second time.

I wanted nothing more than for Josie to be a finer human being than me, but still I said, "Who else here has a diamond ring?"

They looked taken aback. Alice, who had slipped Jenny's ring onto her pinky to admire it, removed it and demurely slid it back to Carl. "I do."

"Where?"

"In my room."

"Where?"

She dithered. "I have a secret hiding spot."

"Where?"

"I'm not sure it'll be secret if I tell —"

"Check it."

"Now?"

"Now."

Carl said, "Wait a second here. What are you trying to say?"

I looked at Alice. "Anyone else you know keeps theirs around?"

"Valencia wears hers, and I'm not sure about the other ladies."

A degenerate like myself would pick people who trusted him. "Of everyone here, you're the most likely target."

Carl huffed and picked up his fork. "Target? Please. You're acting like Josie has a criminal record."

"Maybe she does."

He pointed his knife at me, his tone less dismissive. "Stop it. I don't like that kind of talk, especially about my granddaughter."

Alice looked down at her plate while twirling a ring on her left hand that wasn't there. Carl took a hearty bite and chewed it like it was steak, like he was the head of our patchwork family, and that was that.

But it wasn't.

I leaned close to Alice so our shoulders touched. "You want me to go with you to check?"

Carl shook his head. "What a crock."

She said, "Should I really be worried?"

I nodded, and this was enough.

She stood, folded her napkin, set it on the table, and backed my wheelchair away from the table. "I'm sorry, Carl, but . . . excuse us."

Carl stopped chewing. Alice drove me expertly through the table maze. Behind us, Carl's walker clattered; he aimed to catch up. Off we went without pause though, through the dining room, cutting the corner at the welcome desk, and down the hall.

Alice's hand shook as she reached for her doorknob. None of us locked up here; our last real incident of theft was when Mrs. Zimmerman pinched one of Valencia's wigs and wore it around until someone broke the news to her that it wasn't hers. Point being, we simply didn't worry about larceny.

Alice swung the door open, and a cloud of her rosewater perfume escaped. The room was the same shape and size as mine, though softened by its Queen Anne furniture. Valencia's side was busy, with a nightstand full of miniature curios and a bed full

343

of unnecessary bohemian pillows. Alice's side had pink floral prints, and on her lace-draped nightstand sat a tissue box and a faux oil lamp. She pushed me inside and shut the door.

"Don't laugh," she warned, opening her closet and bending down to retrieve a pair of cone-heeled pumps. From the toe box she produced a mass of toilet paper. I relaxed. It was a good hiding place. The shoe alone would have been sufficient. Hell, maybe even the closet door would've been enough.

As I thought this, Alice unraveled the toilet paper. There wasn't much of it, but it seemed an endless line. Like a magician's handkerchief, on and on it went.

As she struggled with the tissue, I wrestled too. *Let the ring be there,* I thought. *Let it be gone. Let Josie be redeemed. Let her be condemned. Let me be right. Let me be wrong. Let her be like me.*

I am a selfish man.

Alice's effort gained steam. I rolled closer, tracking her circular search. Round and round she went, retracing squares, probably no more than a dozen. Then, one by one they fell as Alice plucked them apart. The final sheet floated to the carpet, leaving tiny downy bits in her hand.

"Oh," she said. She sounded so wounded. "Oh dear."

The hurt reached her brimming eyes about the same time it did my heart. My next words came out as a croak. "She's here. Follow me."

32

It happened like this: First, I blew through the door on foot while Alice trailed me saying things like *Maybe it wasn't her. Maybe I misplaced it. Maybe, maybe, maybe.* But she went quiet once she made it inside the room and could hear Josie's voice coming from the back side of the bed, down near the floor. The song was quiet, and without melody. A hum. A moan. It stopped as soon as Alice shut the door.

"Who's there?" Josie called.

"Me," I said in the usual way, having not yet decided what approach would have the desired effect. It seemed acrimony and empathy were mutually exclusive, though I felt both. I crept closer to the bed and peered over the mattress. Josie sat with her legs hugged tight, knees under her chin, a gossip magazine and a bottle of water near her feet. It looked all too familiar to me: this bastard version of the fetal position to wait your detox out.

She looked up and moaned, "This day is taking forever."

From the corner of the room, Alice spoke up. "I'm here too."

Josie flinched at the sound of Alice's voice, banging an elbow on the bed frame. She then let loose a colorful string of obscenities while rising with all the grace of a newborn foal. "What are you doing here?"

Alice crossed her arms. "I suppose I can ask you the same question."

"I'm just . . ." Josie eyed me, desperate for support. There, behind the bloodshot was an unusual clarity.

"Bates came," I said simply.

Her lucid focus landed back on Alice for a beat. "Oh God."

"Do you have something to say for yourself?" I asked.

"No, I . . . uh . . . um . . . It's that . . ." She panted out the next few breaths, then strung a bunch of not-quite-inhales together. It seemed a good recipe for passing out. When her hands came flitting up to her heart and she looked at me wildly, I understood what was happening.

Alice's strong-arm routine disappeared. Her brow furrowed. "What is it, sweetheart? Are you okay?"

"No," Josie gasped.

Alice crossed the room in a few quick steps, considering, and placed a hand on Josie's back. A maternal move. Like a palm to a forehead or lips to a scraped knee. "Josie, sweetheart, we didn't mean to frighten you."

"She's fine," I said, almost bored. Apparently even if I picked empathy, it did not equal compassion. "She's detoxing and having herself a little panic attack."

Alice shot me a confused glance, then said to Josie, "Lie down here, honey."

As Alice guided Josie into the bed, I backed away and gratefully fell into the nearby seat. Being sedentary in a wheelchair seemed to propagate the need.

"Now, try to calm down." Once Alice arranged the pillow and blankets, she sat on the tiny ledge still available, grasped Josie's wrist with one hand, and consulted her wristwatch on the other. She counted wordlessly until finally saying, "Oh my. One hundred and thirty." She looked at me. "That's too fast."

I shrugged. "Sounds okay."

A knock came at the door.

Josie panted out: "I think I need an ambulance."

348

"Duffy?" Alice said, an octave higher than usual.

I grabbed both armrests and leaned back a bit. "It's totally normal for what she's got going on. Promise."

"It's not," Josie gasped, sitting up partway.

Another knock, this time harder.

"It is," I said. "You may be racing for a few minutes more, but it'll pass. Although you won't believe me until it's over, so . . ." I shrugged. "And, FYI, your resting heart rate should settle down in a month or so, depending on if you behave."

Alice's eyes bulged.

Before I could defend my very experienced position on this, the door swung open, revealing Carl, with his feet planted wide in the confines of his walker and his nostrils flaring. "*What* are you two up to?"

Josie released the fistful of shirt she held near her heart and turned in toward the pillow. "Oh God."

"Josie?" Carl faltered into the room, eyes wide. "What are you doing here?"

"Dying," she said.

Alice rubbed Josie's shoulder. "Honey, I'm right here. Deep breaths . . . Carl, get Nora."

"Don't," I said.

"What is wrong with you, Duffy? Can't you see she needs help?" Alice yelled, shrill

349

and dogged. "Carl, please go. Now."

"Of course," Carl said, frozen in a stance of action. "What should I tell her?"

Alice said, "Tell her Josie's in distress. Tell her she's —"

Finally, I stood. The blood in my cheeks rose with me. I hissed instead of yelled, only because our covert operation hadn't been completely compromised, though it was going down the shithole fast enough. "She's getting clean."

Everyone stopped moving, except for Josie, who rolled to her back and stared at the ceiling.

I went on. "She's almost a full twenty hours into her detox, and she may be feeling ill, but I swear to you, she's not dying. She's actually starting to live." I looked at Carl. "Close the door."

He stood there stupidly.

"Close. The. Door."

He shut it so softly it sounded like a kiss.

I said to Josie, "It's time to fess up."

"My heart," she whispered without the franticness from before.

"My head," I countered.

"Please don't make me. I don't want to."

"There is want and need, and this is the latter. This here" — I directed my pointer to the crowd in the room and then to her

— "is step numbers four and five of twelve."

She closed her eyes.

"Bates was here," I said again, figuring it would keep her from lying any more.

"Peepaw," she whispered.

Carl inched his walker forward. "Yes?"

"I . . . I guess I'm an alcoholic."

"Guess?" I said.

"I am." Her face flushed. "I am an alcoholic."

Alice's chest hitched with her next breath. Carl came to stand by my side, leaning against the chair for support.

"Tell them more," I said.

"There isn't more."

"Tell them about your mama."

"She's dead."

"And was there a funeral?"

"No," she cried.

"Why not?"

"Because."

"Because?"

She curled up. "I left her in the truck."

"How come?"

"I wrecked it and ran away."

No one so much as breathed. It was all true, every bit of it.

"How bad was the accident?" I asked.

"Bad."

"You have insurance?"

A miserable headshake.

"How do you plan on paying him back?"

No answer.

I lowered my voice. "Tell them about the ring."

"I have it here," Carl said, patting his breast pocket for reassurance.

Alice removed her hand slowly from Josie's shoulder and stood. She turned her back, took a few steps, and when the space between the two women grew large enough that they couldn't reach out and touch each other, Josie choked down a sob.

"I'm sorry, Alice," she said. "I don't know what I was thinking."

The desperation in her voice cut me straight to a hundred apologies I'd made in the name of Johnnie Walker and Jim Beam. I felt like falling to my knees with the weight of both our shame.

Alice inhaled deeply through her nose and out through her mouth, and then strode from the room, brushing past Anderson, who must've opened the door only seconds before without any of us noticing.

Josie covered her face with both hands. "Oh my God."

Anderson glanced down the hall before slipping in and shutting the door, then looked at me like I'd shot him.

I said, "Anderson, I'm sorry. We had to."

"How are we going to keep *this* on the down low?"

"We're fine," I said. "Aren't we?"

No one answered. They were both too busy paying mind to their toes, the corners of the room, the backs of their eyelids.

Anderson appraised us. "If any of you open your mouth about this, I'm getting fired." His voice frayed at the edges. "Do you get how serious —"

"We do. It's just that we had to take care of something that couldn't wait." I offered Carl my seat, since his legs had begun to shake. "But everyone's on board. No one's going to say a word. Are we?"

Carl shook his head, barely.

Josie rolled over into the real fetal position this time, her back to us.

I inched to the foot of the bed, like she'd spook if I moved too fast. "That was hard stuff you did just then. I'm proud of you. Really proud. We're going to get through this." I looked to Carl, hoping he'd take my cue and pile on some early accolades. Instead, he sat there staring at Josie like he didn't know her from Adam.

She muttered, "I want my Valium."

Anderson came to the bedside. "Sorry I'm late. Dinner went on forever, and then . . ."

"Give it to her," I said. "I think she missed it."

"Can you guys please just go?" she pleaded.

"We're going," I said. "But before we do, tell me where the ring is. I'll sort it out with Alice. She'll understand, and then we'll all come back to talk when you're feeling better."

"It's tied to my shoes," she said, curling up tighter. "The ones she bought me."

Carl stood on unsteady legs and headed for the door without a word. I bent to the shoes by the foot of the bed, squinting. Closer still, and there: a glint, a tiny sparkle, a chip of a diamond. The ring was looped a few times into the third lace, and instead of fussing with it — my arthritis would have made it a ten-minute affair — I picked up the entire sneaker.

Anderson emerged from the bathroom with a cupped hand and a glass of water.

"You'll stay with her for a bit?" I asked.

He nodded, walking forward, forcing me toward the door.

"I know this seems like it's not going good," I whispered as I went, "but really it's just going —"

The door slammed shut on me, the permit fluttering in my face.

I blinked at it, then whispered, "It's just going like it does."

33

Carl had parked himself in the recliner, focusing all of his energy on the blank wall across the way. I sat on the edge of my bed, fussing with the bright white shoestring.

Josie had taken off her sneakers without untying them, and I swear, she must've graduated from some advanced course in complex knots. As I worked those laces, it pained my knuckles, the tips of my fingers, basically every jointed appendage, but I was grateful for the distraction while waiting for Carl to ask a thread of questions that would end with: *Why didn't you tell me?*

Alice's ring shone, even in the dowdy lighting of our room, splattering flyspecks of twinkle across the walls. It was a very modest oval cut, a simple ring, and it would be mine to give, once I salvaged it through pain and patience.

And practicality. After a good five minutes, I cried uncle and walked to the bathroom to fetch my grooming scissors, which had suffered disuse since I gave up trying to tame my nose and ear hair. Why, I figured, stop something from growing when the rest of me was shrinking. Two quick snips released the ring, and it fell, pinging on the bathroom tile until coming to rest under the sink cabinet, right near the toe kick.

"Damn it." I placed a hand on the counter, bent gingerly, and grabbed blindly. My finger brushed metal, but when I straightened with my prize, I found myself holding a bullet instead of a ring. The wrong solution to my problem. It took me a moment to realize it must've fallen out of my pocket when I'd returned from Hang Overs and Nora had helped in the restroom. I hadn't missed it since, and I held it up near my cheek and looked in the mirror, trying to decide if I was glad to have it back.

Carl's voice came around the corner. "Maybe this wasn't such a good idea."

I shook off the freeze that had overtaken me and peeked around the corner. "Do what?"

His thousand-yard stare hadn't changed. "Inviting Josie to stay. Maybe we shouldn't have done it. Maybe we should . . . tell her it's time to go."

I set the bullet in the soap dish and

stepped out to face him completely. "Are you joking?"

His eyes flicked up. "No."

I tried to remain calm, but I could feel the red rising. "So you're telling me that now that your granddaughter truly needs your help, you're unwilling to give it?"

"No, I'm just saying . . ." He shrugged.

I shrugged too. "The past few days left me with the impression that there isn't a thing in this world more important to you than that little girl in there. Has that changed somehow in the last ten minutes?"

He looked away.

I shook my head in amazement. "You are a piece of work."

"Why?" He looked genuinely aggrieved. "What've I done wrong?"

"You haven't done anything, that's what."

"That's not true at all. I've given her a place to stay, haven't I? I'll happily give her some money too. Same as I did for Koko. And Kaiya, if she'd accepted it. It's not my fault that —"

What was kindling inside me set fire. His words had hardly traveled the distance between us, and somehow I stood before him with my shaking fist right under his nose and my hot breath blowing across his face. "What the hell is a matter with you?"

He backed into his chair as far as he could, to gain some space. "This has gotten out of hand, Duffy, that's all I'm saying. It's more than we talked about. And there's only so much we can do at our age, in our condition."

"Speak for yourself." I backed away from him, disgusted. "I'm not a yellow-bellied coward who runs for cover every time —"

"I'm not a coward."

"Oh, you are. I've seen you in action all week long, and I've seen Kaiya's birth certificate too, you bastard. You signed it and then you ran. You've run from every last mess you've made, because you're a chickenshit. This is *your* mess. *Your* fault. She's there, in that room, broken, because of *you*."

"How? I don't even really know her."

"That's why, you fool." I shook my head, amazed. "My God, have you never stood tall for anything?"

He slapped his hands on the chair and pushed himself up, saying, "I've stood for plenty."

But as he rose to his feet, something — or maybe nothing — tripped him up, and he was suddenly lurching toward me. Instinctually, I moved to catch him, and the next seconds blurred with a fall that went at a funeral's pace. His hands were on my shirt, grabbing at my sleeves, the elastic waistband of my pants. I was nothing more than wheeling arms and surprise. Knickknacks rattled on the dresser. My view changed from the mirror to the window to the ceiling.

To the floor.

I blinked at the dust bunnies underneath my bed. The tumble hadn't hurt during the haze of anger. It had almost felt out-of-body, even though I was definitely in-body now, lying as helpless as a turtle on its back. Carl lay next to me, on his stomach, one arm pinned under him by his own weight.

"Christ," I groaned, "you're a piece of shit."

"So are you," he said, letting out a labored grunt as he rolled over in a multistep effort.

I took inventory, wiggling my toes, my fingers, my nose — nothing broken, nothing harmed, except for *us,* but what did I care for that anymore? I didn't. He'd let me down too severely: today, yesterday, decades ago. Or maybe my expectations were too high. Whatever it was, it didn't matter. The damage was done. At the very most, I cared that neither of us had suffered any bodily harm that would land us in Simmons, but beyond that . . .

360

"You okay?" I said.

He took stock and croaked, "Yes."

"That's a shame." I coughed.

We lay shoulder to shoulder, every hitch in our breath broadcast by touch, his more erratic than mine. My heart stilled eventually, while his shuddering became a constant vibration that traveled the length of the inside of my arm, tickling my palm.

I turned my head. Carl lay, gawking at the ceiling, tearless, open-mouthed, completely overcome, a trickle of blood coming from his nose.

"Carl? Are you sure you're all right?"

In response, he met my gaze, blinked, then curled into the crook of my arm and wept.

34

It took an extreme level of cooperation, but after a half hour we managed to sit up. Standing would be an entirely different endeavor. For right now, we needed a break. Carl sat with his back to the dresser, wiping his eyes and nose. I leaned against the bed, dabbing at my stitches with the nearby comforter to make sure nothing had broken open. It hadn't, though the cut was angry as hell.

"Duffy," Carl said, "I'm sor—"

"Don't." I leaned my head back, exhausted. I didn't have the energy or will to pardon him. Not yet.

The sun through the window had dimmed; it must've been close to bedtime, in which case we needed to decide how to make our situation look totally normal, or close enough to it, before the nurse on duty stuck her head in to make sure all was well.

Carl held his call button to his lips,

contemplating. I analyzed the dresser's pulls, wondering if they could be used like a climbing wall.

Carl said, "We're going to have to sleep here."

I huffed. "Like the good old days."

"I slept on the floor for an entire year when I was a kid and my mother's sister came to live with us."

"I slept on worse during all of Vietnam."

Carl hummed in corroboration, and we sat in silence again for a while. Then he said, without anxiety or doubt, "I need to get Kaiya."

His hand went to his breast pocket, checking for Jenny's ring. It had survived there during his fall, and he fished it out. All these years of giving stuff away, and now it'd come time to do it with something that mattered. He looked wrecked by it, not that I blamed him entirely. The man would have to trade what was left of Jenny for what was left of Kaiya, and in the end he'd have nothing.

I offered the only relief I could think of: "If you aren't up to it, I can exchange the ring for you. Bates already thinks I'm you anyway."

He gathered himself with a few measured breaths. "No. I have to do it." Each word landed with a thump. His conviction surprised me. Maybe it surprised him too, because both of his eyebrows were riding his hairline when he looked to me and asked, "*How* do I do it?"

"Well . . . Josie could tell Bates she wants to meet for a swap, and we can go instead. Anderson can drive us. We'll convince Sharon by saying it's something important. Something she can't say no to, like . . ."

Carl tipped his head back against the dresser. "Like a funeral."

I blew out a defeated breath. "A funeral would do it."

The rest of him wilted against the dresser. "When? Tomorrow?"

Now it was me who slumped a bit. "No. Tomorrow I have an appointment for my stitches, and some other stuff."

"What other stuff?"

"Some tests."

"For what?"

I answered, though I couldn't hear myself. *Dementia.* Odd word, that one. Dementia. Dement. Demented. Out of one's mind. They were going to test my ability to be me.

Carl turned stoic.

"It's nothing," I said. "I'm not worried."

"No," he said. "Of course not."

"Sharon's making me go, but I'm fine."

"You are."

This sounded definitive, whether it was true or not, and so we busied ourselves by breathing for a while. We both felt the same way about this. We would rather die than lose our minds.

Finally, Carl said, "So Wednesday then."

"Wednesday," I agreed. "And we should meet Bates somewhere public. Like Walmart. I don't want him near Josie, so if she insists on coming, she's staying inside the bus."

"Anderson can be our muscle if we need it."

I grunted, annoyed with the truth: We were two grown men who needed a third to protect us.

Carl cut my gripe short by saying softly, "Maybe after, we could spread Kaiya's ashes." He nodded to himself, appearing content with the idea, behind the pain of it. "I know of a good place, and . . . I think . . . maybe Josie might've been thinking the same."

He sounded low as hell. I bent and put a hand on his shin. "Where's that?"

After a hard swallow, he said, "I wondered why Josie wrecked that truck in such an odd spot in Everton. Sanger and Old Farm Road. Who drives that way anymore since they built the interstate in '61?"

"No one, I'd guess. There's nothing worth seeing out there."

"Except for Sanger Overpass."

I made an unimpressed noise.

He grew quiet, then said, "That's actually where Koko and I liked to meet. We'd do a little . . . parking. And after . . . afterward we'd stand at that overpass and watch the night train go underneath." The hot shame in his voice turned into an ache. "She loved it. She always made me stay until the very last car passed."

I tried my best to imagine it: the monotony of a long train, the white noise, the wind. It did sound like the sort of thing that could keep your heart still.

Carl fiddled with his call button, his eyes on the same faraway place as mine. He said, "I only went back once after we stopped going, right before I came to live here, and do you know what I found? The initials 'K and K' scratched out on the center brace." He looked at me then, his eyes wide. "I know it could be anyone, but I can't help but think maybe Koko shared that spot with Kaiya, and maybe . . . maybe that's why Josie was out that way with her ashes."

As I considered how fitting it would be if he were right, the door creaked and Nora peered around the corner.

"Oh," she said, as if she'd walked in on us buck-ass naked. And then again, in surprise: "Oh, Lordy!"

I went to speak, but Carl interrupted. "I fell."

The same words tickled the back of my throat. I wished I'd gotten to them first, since my reputation was already sullied in that regard, but I wasn't going to fight him on who should be the martyr.

Nora swept the door open and knelt between us, torn as to who to help first. "You two all right?"

"Fine," Carl said. "Duffy tried to help, and I dragged him down too."

She eyed me, and I willed myself to look back, neutral as ever. She said accusingly, "Your wheelchair is in the hallway."

"Oh, good. You found it."

She examined the space she had to heave us to our feet and shook her head. "That Anderson has been missing all day, I swear. Wait here. I'm getting Zula."

I said, "We'll put our pickleball game on hold."

Not even a smile. Her white sneakers squeaked as she scampered off, and I considered another play besides trying to charm her. Our rapport had taken a hit over the past few days, and I didn't like it one bit.

Soon, the squeal of rubber on linoleum doubled, ending with a swell in our room. "Oh, Mr. Sinclair," Zula sang. "Again? This is not good."

This declaration was followed by a flurry of logistics. The women decided where to stand, where to hold, which direction to move, on what count to heave-ho. Afterward, they hovered over us, beads of sweat on their brows and strained smiles on their faces as we lay fat and sassy in our respective beds.

Zula dimmed the lights, promising to check on us.

Nora folded the sheet down at my breastbone and left her hand there to rest. "Mr. Duffy, what are we gonna do with you?"

I topped her hand. "I don't know if you realize how much I appreciate you."

She responded with a sad sigh. She thought she was losing me, one slow day at a time. Or maybe, in her book, it happened fast. Downhill and done. Her hand slipped out from underneath mine and she left, turning once to take us in before closing the door.

A minute passed and I said, "Carl?"

Nothing.

"Carl, you're not already asleep, are you?"

This time, a snore.

And so I clasped my hands on my chest, faced the ceiling, and did my damnedest to follow suit.

I woke up in the middle of the night like someone had tried to smother me. Breathing felt like sucking air through my teeth, even though my mouth hung wide open. It took me a solid five minutes to stop gasping.

That sort of thing had happened to me only ever once before, as a kid, on the night I'd sensed my brother had passed away. This time, it didn't feel like someone had died, necessarily, but it sure felt like someone had left. A looping image of Josie walking right out the door kept playing in my head.

So this is how I came to be in the hallway at three in the morning, when I should've been in bed. I wanted a gut check. I was fully aware that Zula could come around the corner at any moment. She liked to read a book at the reception desk if no one needed her, so I imagined her this way to make myself feel better. If she showed up, I planned to claim insomnia, restless legs, nightmares, and/or sleepwalking. Anything that would keep her from reporting that I'd become a sundowner.

The main hallway at this time of night reminded me of the red-eye flight I took to basic training, with its soft aisleway glow and that human hum, the quiet proof that there were lots and lots of inactive, captive people. I tiptoed to the spare room, hoping that hum wouldn't stop at Josie's door.

When I pressed my ear to the city permit to have a listen: nothing. So I tried the knob. The door creaked open with a haunting noise. My breathing started going like it did when I'd woken up.

"Josie?" I squinted into the darkness.

My name came back to me, but about a dozen octaves too deep.

I smacked the overhead light switch on. The fluorescent bulb flooded the room, and Anderson appeared with his eyes smashed shut to the brightness. He was lying on top of the covers, fully clothed, with Josie's head nestled on his broad chest and the rest of her holding him as if he were a ring buoy in rough seas. She wore only an oversize undershirt, and it had crept up far enough to expose her upper thighs. Drool pooled near her mouth.

I felt like I'd come upon them when I shouldn't have, and also in the nick of time. "What are you still doing here?"

"Shh. Turn off the light," Anderson whispered.

"And the door's unlocked." I paced, then stopped where I had started, and asked one more time, "What are you still doing here?"

"Resting," he murmured.

"It's three in the morning."

"Huh?" Anderson propped himself up and squinted at his wristwatch. "Shit."

Josie stirred before cuddling into the new arrangement.

I took a moment to look at her, to appreciate the fact that she was still here. As I watched her sleep, the stranglehold in my shoulders let out. I'd never been happier to be wrong. "How is she?" I asked.

"Okay," he said, peeling her arm away from him, and next, her sweaty leg. Her eyes fluttered. He whispered to her, "I gotta go home and shower. I'll be back."

She unfurled enough to release him. He slid out from under her, stood, adjusted a fading erection, and slipped on his shoes near the bed. She rolled over, bringing the covers with her, to sleep some more. Anderson walked past me, flipped the light off, and held the door open for my exit.

I stood there, scolding him with a look.

"What? Nothing happened," he whispered.

"Well, no shit." I said. "Except that you are dumb as a box of rocks for staying here overnight."

"It was an accident."

I shook my head, but his hangdog expression softened me a bit. "There's still time to leave our mess to us and claim plausible deniability, you know? You don't have to" — I waved my hand — "get involved to the point that you can't walk away."

He glanced back at her.

"Anderson, look at me. This may not end any differently. Don't get in over your head."

He cupped my neck and steered me into the hallway. "It's a little too late for that, Duf."

"Maybe once you've gotten a cold shower" — I pointed at his pants — "you'll be thinking straight. Right now, you've got the sense God gave a goose."

"Maybe that's good. Geese mate for life."

I stared dumbly at him.

A crooked smile slid across his sleepy face, and he shrugged. "All I'm trying to do is the right thing, whatever the hell that is. Same as you, right?" When I didn't respond, he hit me softly in the upper arm. "Right?"

After a beat, I hit him back. And then, like he'd done so many times before, he laced his arm with mine and led me on. To my room. To my bed. To sleep.

THE CENTENNIAL SCHEDULE
August 29 — Tuesday

8:00   Breakfast
9:00   Cards, Atrium
10:00   Zimmerman Farewell, Foyer
12:00   Lunch
3:00   Happy Tails, Living Room
5:00   Dinner
6:00   Music Marathon Night, Living Room

35

I might've slept until noon if an ambulance siren hadn't woken me. It was a stationary whine, parked already, who knows for how long. It seeped into my dreams and came for Josie, then Carl. My eyes snapped open, and I sat straight up — my God, did that hurt — and called both of their names out loud.

"I'm here," Carl said quietly from the doorway.

He was hanging his head out in the hall, motionless, and I understood immediately by his *way* that the hoopla couldn't be for Josie. Whenever first responders came for a resident, the rest of us tended to drop whatever we were doing and stand along the hallways or at our doors — not as lookie-loos, but as well-wishers — though more times than not, wishing wasn't going to cut it.

I slid to the edge of the bed, aiming to

join him in standing guard, but hesitated. "It's not Alice, is it?" I had to know now, before getting up, because I'd lose my legs depending on the answer.

He looked at me and grimaced. "No."

"Who then?"

He shook his head and turned back, making me worry next for Valencia. I sucked in a deep breath, locked it down, then trudged through my knee pain to stand beside him.

At the mouth of the hall, a policewoman stood with a plainclothes gentleman and a medic, talking. There was no urgency, no rush. I put my hand on Carl's shoulder and squeezed, because we'd both seen this enough to know what it meant.

When they finally started moving, it looked like they were headed straight for us. They drew closer and closer and closer, until I was pert near ready to pinch myself, to make sure they weren't coming to bag me up. But then they went next door, into Charles and Clarence's room, shutting themselves in.

Their murmuring voices carried through our walls. I strained to listen in but heard only the drone of the television playing *I Love Lucy*. It was all Charles ever watched, and it had an unmistakable laugh track. I always bitched, because the speakers were against our wall and his hee-hawing constantly echoed in our room.

I said, "Is it —"

"I don't know. I haven't seen either of them this morning."

I shook my head. You'd think this sort of thing happened often enough we'd be used to it. That we'd expect it, even. But every time was a surprise. A reminder. I said, almost to myself, "I bet Sharon's happy."

"Happy is overstating it."

"She's definitely not sad." I leaned against the doorjamb, taking in the rooms across the hall, landing last on Josie's. "Wonder how motivated she gets when a room is halfway to empty?"

Carl grimaced. On paper, everyone was fair game — we all had at least seventy years under our belt and reason enough to quit this place — but Carl had a walker and I had a wheelchair. He tended to give up too easy, and I tended to fight too much. We were in the front of the line together, though I had him by a few falls, a bad bladder, and maybe a pinch of dementia.

I said, "If I don't die here, will you please kill me?"

"Ditto," he said, then paused thoughtfully. "Though we probably shouldn't do that if we want to meet up in heaven."

"Ha," I said. "Do you really want to hang out with me for eternity?"

He met my eyes, no fooling, and nodded. "Don't you?"

After a long moment, I nodded back, and the weight of it felt like a promise.

Anderson rounded the corner of the hall. Shawn followed, pushing Charles's empty wheelchair. I tried to figure what that meant — it was empty because Charles was getting either moved or *re*moved — but before I could work it all out, Shawn parked the chair in front of us.

"Howdy-ho. I know this isn't a good time . . ." He flipped his comb-over back into place, tucked his shirttail in. "But, Duffy, you have a doctor's appointment this morning."

"Oh no," I said, pleading for a pass. This was not the day to try and beat Sharon at her own game. "Can't we —"

He herded us into our room and shut the door. "We should've left five minutes ago." He swooped past, pointing to the banana hanging halfway out of his pocket. "Breakfast is taken care of, so all we have to do is get you dressed and in the van."

"Who is it?" Carl asked weakly. "Who . . ."

Shawn stopped mining for orthopedics in my closet and peeked out. His job as the life enhancement coordinator did not co-alesce well with days like this; he never could figure how to tone down his cheer-leader routine just right. He dived into the closet again before saying, "Charles."

"Son of a biscuit," Carl said, falling into the recliner.

I held my head in my hands for a moment of silence. I'd never liked Charles much, but now I suddenly wanted to do him dif-ferent. Now that it was too late. "What hap-pened?"

"Most likely" — Shawn held up Josie's shoe, perplexed for a fleeting moment, then went back in and reemerged with a pair of mine — "natural causes."

Translation: old age. It was a stupid ques-tion anyway. I sat at the edge of the bed, thinking Josie was right. There seemed very little point to all this if it was just going to end like it did.

"I guess we're making yet another memory board." Carl sighed.

"You betcha." Shawn's smile tightened as he pulled pants and a pair of socks from the dresser. "But not today."

I dropped my pajama drawers and stepped out of them, thinking a man shouldn't have to wait to be remembered. "Why not?"

"Because everyone's busy," he snapped,

before beaming again like a nut. "Happy Tails is bringing some dogs by this afternoon, and this morning . . ." He trailed off while helping me into my trousers, then straightened and dusted his hands. "We're seeing Mrs. Zimmerman off."

"You're kidding. *Today* is her last day?"

"Yepperoo. Her family is moving her to a facility that's better suited."

"Skilled nursing," Carl said like a curse.

"Jesus," I said. "It's like the reaping."

Shawn sighed, losing the facade enough to make you think he might be human. "I admit, not everything is going our way. But when that happens, I try to think about the things that aren't so bad. Like, did I hear right that Josie is coming to visit again today?"

Carl's eyes cut to me. "Yes, if she's feeling up to it."

"See?" Shawn looked plumb tickled again. "There you go. We have Happy Tails and Josie today, and tomorrow we have a magician coming."

Carl frowned. "We have a funeral to go to tomorrow."

Shawn paused in putting my shoes on. "I don't think it'll be organized that fast, Carl. They just called Charles's family thirty minutes ago, and he hasn't even left the building."

Carl opened his mouth, but it looked like he couldn't get the words out.

I intervened. "It's not for Charles. It's for Carl's daughter, Kaiya."

With my foot in hand, Shawn turned to Carl with a gape. "I had no idea. When did she pass?"

"Last week," Carl said.

"I'm so sorry. You should've told me. I'll make sure everything gets arranged. What time do you need me to take you?"

"Midmorning," I said quickly, "but Carl was hoping Anderson could bring us. He knew her . . . very well."

Shawn's brow furrowed as he thought, and then he began nodding. "Okay. All right. I'll talk to Sharon. I could cover lunch for Anderson."

"Thank you," Carl said.

"You betcha." Shawn tightened the Velcro on each shoe and patted the tops of them. "You're going to have to say your goodbyes to Mrs. Zimmerman on the way out."

He popped up and placed Carl's walker at his toes and the wheelchair near mine. When he had ferried us out of the room, he paused to flip down the chair's footrests, and I reached out to Charles's closed door and put my palm to it. Carl did too.

381

There was a subtle shift in the air then, a slow rising tide of quiet, and I couldn't help but think Charles was there, watching us, in the body from his youth, wearing the uniform from his glory days. It seemed silly, since I didn't know about all this kingdom come business, but the feeling was real enough to hang my hat on. And it had me wondering if Cormac was around right now, or my uncle, or my parents. It had me wondering what I had to do in order to hang around after the fact too. Because I'd made a pact with Carl just this morning I intended to keep.

Shawn broke the silence by whistling a cheerful tune. He pushed me toward Mrs. Zimmerman's farewell in the foyer, and Carl followed. The send-off consisted of a homemade banner, a crowd of balding heads, a few family members, and Valencia, waving a blue pompom without any fanfare. Her eyebrows were drawn on sad.

Shawn urged Carl to inch along the outskirts toward the door, warning of how little precious time we had. We stopped at the very end of the human corridor as Mrs. Zimmerman made her way out of the mouth of it. She paused, looking equally perplexed and pleased by the outpouring. The automatic door whooshed open at her arrival.

She turned and looked me directly in the eye. "Bye, Andy."

"Goodbye, dear Mrs. Zimmerman."

She smiled. "Call me Agnes."

"Goodbye, Agnes."

She walked out and stood under the porte cochere, scanning both directions, looking already lost. One of her family members, a tall man with a thick mustache, retrieved her and promised the car was being pulled around and everything would be just fine. Shawn pushed me past, toward Centennial's bus in the parking lot.

Carl stopped at the threshold, raising his hand in a motionless wave.

"Hold the fort down," I called. "And have Josie make that phone call about tomorrow's funeral. Don't forget."

"Yes, sir," he said.

The bus pulled out as they loaded Mrs. Zimmerman into the car, which was parked right behind the coroner's truck. I watched from the window, fogging the glass, until we turned a corner and they couldn't be seen anymore.

The doctor was brunette and built like an M48 Patton tank. She was middle-aged, professional, efficient, maneuvering the exam room on her rolling stool like there was no alternative mode of transportation. She smelled medicinal, though not entirely in a bad way. Her pressed white coat had her name embroidered in block letters above a winged, snake-wrapped staff.

I liked her style.

She either had a very good poker face or was not alarmed when she asked me to follow her penlight, or when she asked me to pronounce a few words, or when she stuck her fingers in the pit of my elbow and asked me to squeeze as hard as I could. No, she didn't even blink. She assessed my forehead with the same dispassionate manner, redressed it with competence, and rolled back to her computer for a few quick keystrokes.

"Now," she said, spinning to face me. "Have you noticed any signs that make you concerned about dementia?"

There that word was again. I glowered. "I'm here by decree."

The look on her face indicated she knew this already. "Would you be opposed to a quick cognitive test to give us a baseline?"

"If it means proving some people wrong, absolutely."

"Okay. Then why don't you tell me the month, day, and time?"

"August twenty-ninth. Tuesday. My appointment was at ten thirty, and" — I

384

leaned forward to see the clock — "it's eleven fifteen now."

"What floor of this building are you on?"

"Third."

"Great. Now, I'm going to give you a list of words, and I want you to hang on to them. I'll ask you to repeat them back to me in the same order in a moment. Ready?"

I nodded.

"Here they are: San Francisco, clouds, orange. Got it?"

"Yes. San Francisco, clouds, orange . . . you glad I remembered?"

She clipped her smile before it could be categorized as such. "Good. Now, would you mind writing me a sentence? Anything will do. Whatever comes to mind."

She held out a pen and my folded appointment slip. I took it, stilled my shaking hand and wrote, *I'm sorry to be wasting your time.*

She took it back, peering at it for longer than it took to read, then scribbled her own note and dangled it in front of me again. When I reached for it, she drew back. "Those words. Do you remember them?"

"San Francisco, clouds" — a pause thanks to the pressure — "orange."

"Excellent." She extended the note again. "Now read these instructions, and see if you can follow them."

Close your eyes for thirty seconds, it said. I did as directed, staring into the darkness while counting and thinking about how good it'd feel to tell Sharon to go jump in a lake. When I reopened my eyes, I found the doc with a pinched brow. She had the paper in her hand again, fetched quietly from my fingertips without notice. Had I read it right? Had I counted wrong?

"Can I see it again?" I asked.

Her mask returned. "How well do you sleep?"

I set my jaw. "Fine."

A nod. "Been depressed at all?"

"No."

"Have you felt unsteady lately?"

"No."

"Any trouble breathing? Chest pain?"

I paused. She'd tripped me up on my way to a clean bill of health. If I were honest, there were the twinges in my heart, especially during the bout at the bar and in Sharon's office. There were the breathing problems too, specifically at Walmart, during my fifty-yard walk, and last night at three a.m. But honesty didn't tell the whole truth, because it needed an asterisk. My symptoms had been caused by a girl who had climbed through my window a few days ago, and good luck treating that.

So I said, "Swear on my mother's grave, I've been feeling all right."

I couldn't tell if she believed me. Her best trait — this unreadable demeanor, this nonchalance — was losing its luster.

"So?" I prodded. "Did I pass my IQ test?"

She cocked her head. "Mr. Sinclair, the cognitive test I gave you is not in and of itself a diagnostic instrument for dementia. It's used as a benchmark for later, so let's hang on to it."

I crossed my arms and harrumphed.

"I suggest we schedule some imaging tests so we can get to the bottom of all the falls you've had lately. That worries me the most. I'm not thrilled about your blood pressure or your recent unsteadiness, so my priority is to rule out vascular issues before we pursue any other diagnosis."

I frowned. I wanted a written proclamation concerning my mental and physical vitality, a note that I could slap onto Sharon's desk whilst flipping her off. Instead the doctor had me worrying about brain fog and blood flow. And the way she spoke of them sounded concrete, which had me suddenly thinking of them as concrete. I saw myself as Sharon saw me, and after that I couldn't shake this feeling that my behavior over the past week *was* because of dementia, and that my heart *was* actually failing. Which meant all I had left to protect myself from Simmons were appearances.

"Am I stuck in this wheelchair?" I asked, panicked.

She clicked her pen. "You can graduate to a walker."

"You'll tell them that?"

"Yes." She pulled out a prescription pad and scribbled. "So I'll see you back here in a week for stitch removal. I'm prescribing you a beta-blocker to see if we can get that blood pressure under control, and you need to start taking it today. Next is something to help with urinary incontinence, which I see here has been a problem lately too."

Goddamn Sharon. "Thank you."

She ripped the sheet off and handed it to me. "Next week then."

"I wouldn't miss it."

She left with a two-fingered salute, a nurse returned with my check-out papers, and soon some nameless aide pushed me into the waiting room, where Shawn sat ignoring the *National Geographic* open in his lap in favor of his phone.

"You ready?" I said.

He tossed the magazine onto the neighboring seat. "Yessiree. How'd it go?"

"Swell." I rolled forward. "Let's get the hell out of here."

Shawn trotted around and pushed me out the door. While we waited for the elevator, I stared at the geometric patterns in the hallway carpet. A loud *ding* startled me out of the trance.

"Now to pet puppies," Shawn sang, pushing me in and pressing the lobby button. "Depending on traffic, we might even make it back for lunch. That way, you can sit across from your pals instead of my ugly mug."

"Shawn, don't sell yourself short. You're much hairier, but you're almost as pretty as —" I paused because Alice's smile flashed like a vision, but, more importantly, so did her ring.

It had completely slipped my mind and still sat on the bathroom floor, where I'd dropped it before the brawl. Or so I hoped. Good Lord, when did Dahlia come to vacuum and mop? Mondays, was it? No, that wasn't right. Tuesdays? No, no. Maybe it was the same day Jorge cut the grass, but what day was that?

I'd all-out forgotten.

The elevator stopped at the ground floor.

Shawn put a hand on my shoulder before exiting. "Were you going to say something?"

"Pretty as . . ." It had to be all the distractions. All the pressure. The disorder. This absentmindedness wasn't me at all. I was still normal. It was everything around me that wasn't.

He patted me reassuringly, and pushed me into the lobby and outside into the daylight. "Don't worry, Duffy. You're probably tired. You've had a rough couple days."

He didn't know the half of it. We hadn't even come close to the summit. Maybe we hadn't even started the climb.

Whistling, he parked me near the door for the bus's ramp and went to fire up the vehicle. Meanwhile, I closed my eyes to the sun and whispered, "San Francisco, clouds, orange," because, at the moment, there was simply nothing else to be done.

36

Shawn left me at the threshold of my room and ran off to tend to his business. I wheeled inside, right through a wall of bleach fumes. The beds were made, the dresser dusted, the mirror shone. Dahlia had come and gone. Her vacuum ran a few doors down — a muffled, revving hum interspersed with clacks whenever it sucked up something worth the noise. The sound reminded me of a mortar round — that's how much dread it produced in my sternum — so my first inclination was to avoid looking at the fallout. I pressed on past the bathroom, toward my bed, where a brand-new walker waited.

It had a gift bow and a note taped to the center brace bar. It wasn't as nice as Carl's. No tennis balls, no seat. I rose from the wheelchair, tested my stiff legs, and stood between the handlebars to see how it felt. The note, from Nora, said *Remember to count your blessings.*

"Jesus Christ," I said, though not in a manner she would approve of.

Nevertheless, it was hard not to admit that the walker lent a certain amount of security. With it, I walked to the bathroom, counted to ten to steel myself, and then looked down.

The ring wasn't there.

I moved the walker toward the toilet and managed to get on bended knee, groping blindly underneath the cabinet, near the toe kick. Nothing. Now I was on all fours, patting the ground wildly. Tiny cobwebs, a layer of cleaning chemicals, a pubic hair.

No ring. God almighty, there was no ring.

"Mr. Duffy!" came Nora's voice directly behind my ass. "What in the Lord's name?"

My startle turned into a clumsy ascent from all fours to my knees. By the time I managed to get an elbow on the counter, the surprise of her company had run its course.

"Have you fallen *again*?"

"No," I said to the commode. There was no room for me to turn around in this position. "I'm looking for a ring."

Her hand came under my armpit, and she grunted out the next words as she pulled up. "You mean the one in the soap dish?"

"Do what?" A hand on the toilet seat, a grasp of the shower curtain (causing a grommet to rip clean from its hook), a pull on an actual handicap grab bar, and, alas, I stood. Nora waited as I stared into the hollow of the plastic clamshell soap dish. Sure enough, there, next to a dehydrated sliver of bar soap and a single bullet, was Alice's ring.

I picked it up, slid it partway on my pinky, and worshipped it, speechless.

"Are you all right?"

I smiled and moved to exit. She stopped me with a flat hand to my chest and pointed at the walker.

"Oh, right." I fetched it with nary a grumble. What did I care? I had the ring. "This thing is grand." It sounded as if I really meant this, and maybe I did. I bustled past her.

She called after me. "Do you have any prescriptions from today that you need me to fill?"

"None," I called back. All of that could wait.

Right now, I needed to find Alice, and, as it turned out, I didn't even have to look for her. She was in the hallway, strolling while reading a tattered paperback romance from Centennial's library. I recognized the cover because Carl and I had poked fun of the bare-chested, long-haired man on the front. I stopped in her path and cleared my throat.

She lowered the book, then promptly hid it under her arm. "Hello there. It's good to see you standing. How was your appointment?"

"It was all right. How did everything go this morning?"

"To see two people out in one day . . ." She shook her head while Reginald stomped purposely by on the way to his room. The dining hall had begun to empty, and the milling crowd grew behind her, eddying in our direction.

I said, "Do you mind if we go somewhere more private to talk?"

She looked around. At Centennial, privacy was relative. "Where to?"

Somewhere in the recesses of my mind, this had become a romantic enterprise, painted with sharp, far-fetched strokes. There we were, standing in the shadowy canopy of a weeping willow during the edge of fall, a cool breeze so soft it tickled, the hills in the background unwinding into hay-fields, and me slipping the ring on her finger like a suitor would.

I snuck a glance at my ringed pinky finger. "How about the rocking chairs out front?"

She agreed with a dip of her head and

walked next to me, hands clasped tight. "So, there's a lot to cover, isn't there?"

"Some."

We walked past Shelly Lee, the receptionist at the front desk, a Mama Cass look-alike if you added twenty years and a can of hair spray. "Mr. Sinclair! Mrs. Roda! Where to?"

"Out front to rock," I said. "We aren't walking anywhere. Just wanted to get a bit of fresh air."

She waved us through, putting on the reading glasses that hung from her neck, while closing in on her computer screen. Alice snuck two peppermints from the candy dish, and we strolled to the chairs.

It had cooled some since my trek to Hang Overs, though summer still held tight. The trumpet vines creeping up the porte-cochere posts drooped on account of it. I motioned for Alice to sit first while I found a good spot for the walker. I also discreetly slipped off the ring, to hold it in my fist.

Once we'd settled into a rhythm, synchronizing our rocking, I said, "Alice, I need to tell you something."

"Tell me," she said, simply as that, and suddenly all my earlier fretting about how to approach this seemed silly. There was no need to start with Vietnam or Cormac.

Excuses, really. I needed only to state things as simply as she'd asked for them.

I swallowed once and began. "Josie and I, we're kind of the same."

"Are you? How's that?"

"Well, before I came here, I was an alcoholic who stole and lied, and did all sorts of other terrible things too."

Alice's tempo didn't change, though she was looking at me now. However much I didn't want to have to say these things, my need for her to know was that much more.

I continued. "For a long time, see, there wasn't a soul who called me on it. I hid it from my family, and everyone else I hitched my wagon to was the kind who had baggage or was baggage — people like Bates. So I went on being a sad human being for years and years until eventually I got too old for it." I put a hand on her forearm, prompting her to stop rocking. "Alice, I wasted all of my life. *All* of it. Decades gone because I was a damn drunk. I don't wish that on anyone: a life lived with nothing to show for it. Not a family, not a legacy, nothing."

"Duffy —"

"I want you to fight for Josie the same as you did before she wronged you. I don't want her to look back a half a century from now and mourn how little there is to see. I want you to forgive her."

"Duffy," she said again, softer this time, topping my hand. "I already have."

I huffed out a tiny smitten laugh. Of course. Of course she had.

"God, I love you." It came out as relief — my bared soul accepted. I should've been mortified by it all, but before I could retract the words, qualify them, amend them, I doubled down. "I love you more than you'll ever know."

With this, I opened up my fist like a blooming flower and raised my cupped hand so she could see.

When she reached for the ring, I recoiled a bit. I wanted to put it on her myself, and she sensed this and drew back as well.

"Duffy, I —"

"I just . . . I know it's not mine to give you, but —"

This time she grasped me. "I care for you, I do, very much, but you have to understand that I was married to Arthur for a very, very long time." I went to speak, but she interrupted. "Duffy . . ." We held each other's gaze, and then she let me go and plucked the ring quietly from my hand. "I can't. I promised him forever."

I wanted to speak, but it felt like my throat had been cut. I wouldn't take back my confession, not for the world, because it felt so good to be rid of it. But my adoration for Alice, my heart, I wanted it back, right up until she put her hands on either side of my cheeks.

"You are a good man," she said, each word standing on its own. "Whatever it is you're mourning from back when, don't. It brought you here, now, to do what you're doing, and what you're doing is honorable and right."

The preview of tears warmed the corners of my eyes. She held fast to my face.

"And as for us, we will keep each other company until there is no more company to be had. I'm certain Arthur wouldn't mind that one bit."

I could see the cataract in her eye, the delicate creases folding out from the corners of her lips. The worry in her brow. The contentment. Somehow, all this combined would have to hold me. At least for now. Her hand dropped away, and she sat back; we both did.

After watching traffic go by in the distance for some time, I asked, half joking, half not, "Do you think someday you'll ever let me steal a kiss?"

This made her smile, and she pushed back to start rocking again. Then without looking at me, she held out one of her candies like a carrot. I shook my head, because it felt like a tease, but then I grabbed it anyway and popped it in my mouth.

"It's sweet, isn't it?" she said absently.

I lodged it into the pocket of my cheek. "Like you."

She cocked her head and gave me a look.

"I'm never going to give up," I said.

"Of course not," she said. "And I wouldn't want you to."

37

Not long after Alice let me down easy, she declared the heat was getting to her and left me to rock alone. The wound from her rejection grew and faded in between breaths, making my heart beat funny. I was pretty sure I was going to die right there, a sad and lonely bachelor, but when God didn't put me down in a timely manner, I finally stood to stretch.

The new vantage point gave me pause; the world racing by me always did. There went a furniture delivery truck, followed by an SUV with a Bible verse shoe-polished on its back window. And there, behind that, a generic Honda sedan crawling down the road, driving so slow it caused traffic to skirt around and honk. I walked to the edge of the curb to see it better. Centennial's doors whistled open behind me.

The vehicle crept like it was on a hunt, and though the driver was nothing more than a dim outline behind tinted windows, the tinge in my back molars told me it had to be Bates. In a slow-motion moment, we met each other's shadowy squint.

"Mr. Sinclair!" Shelly Lee hollered from the open entry. "You promised me no walking."

"But . . ." I pointed to the car, which passed Centennial's property line and took off like someone had waved a checkered flag.

She beckoned me. "Come on in."

After one last look, I grabbed my walker and hightailed it past her. I needed to find Carl straightaway to see if he'd made tomorrow's arrangements like we had planned. If so, what the hell was Bates doing creeping around here? And if not, what the hell did Carl do all day long instead?

I rushed into the main area, thinking he'd be easy to locate, seeing how every resident had gathered there to wait for Happy Tails. It was by far the most popular event in any given month, but Carl was nowhere among the bunch. I ignored multiple reminders that the shindig would start in ten minutes' time, and left to check the television room, the atrium, our room, our bathroom: all empty. Next, I decided to risk going to Josie's, but I got no farther than a few steps in the hallway.

Reginald stood at Josie's door.

But of course that egg-sucking dog was actually a weasel. Stupid me should've done more to keep him busy, though I couldn't figure with what. Here he was now, fixing to sell me down the river, and here I was, fixing to swim upstream. Although . . . anyone watching us would've guessed we were both doing a whole lot of nothing besides standing there, still as stumps.

"What are you doing?" I called, my voice shaky and not sounding like my own.

He startled and turned, then became cross when he realized it was just me, and went back to it.

I drew carefully closer. "I wouldn't hang around there too much. Sharon might think you want your room done next."

He didn't budge.

"Happy Tails is here."

Still nothing, and I wondered what else I might try, but just then he snapped the city permit from the door, jammed it in his pocket, and walked casually toward me, like nothing was wrong. Even when he came within reaching distance, he still didn't look suspicious of me. Which made me suspicious of him.

"What are you up to?" I said.

402

He shrugged.

I looked him over accusingly. "Why do you need that permit? Are you giving Sharon a hand?"

"Yes, I'm giving Sharon a hand," he said, sarcasticlike. "You're a regular Ivy Leaguer, you know that?"

"Okay, then, what are you doing?"

He hitched up his pants and sniffed. "This is none of your business." Then he smiled proudly for using my own words against me, and strutted past, down the hall.

I blinked — trying to figure out who was running who around — then yelled after him, "If I find that on my door, I'm going to piss on yours."

He turned the corner, and once it hit me that the Josie jig was not actually up, I dogged it to her room and knocked nonstop until the door cracked open, then I slipped inside, shut it, locked it, and rested my forehead against the pressboard, breathing liked I'd just come up from a deep-sea dive. How much longer could we keep this going?

Josie said, "Nice entrance."

I pivoted my head enough to look at her. She'd showered and was wearing a Texas A&M sweatshirt, khaki shorts, and dollar-bin flip-flops. Both of Alice's girls were Ag-

403

gies, so I could only assume these hand-me-downs had been gifted by one of them. Much like alcoholism, sainthood seemed to be genetic.

"What are you doing here?" she said. "Peepaw just left to use the can, and I'm supposed to meet him in the main area in five. Is the hallway clear?"

"Bates is casing the joint."

She held steady for a moment, eyes locked with mine, then abruptly marched out of my sight line, forcing me to straighten up proper and turn around to see her. But once I did, the surrounding view didn't look right. The bed was covered with old shoe-boxes and yellowed stationery and *money.* Twenty-dollar bills were stacked in piles and resting in the hammocks of opened letters and peeking out of ripped envelopes. There had to be a few thousand dollars' worth, at least.

Speechless, I pointed at the shoeboxes, whose contents hadn't fooled me just once, but twice.

Josie didn't notice that I'd been struck stupid. She was too busy slapping cash piles angrily together and shoving them into an empty box. "Bates needs to get a life."

I made a worthless noise meant to be words.

She stopped housekeeping and looked up, then tracked my finger point to the bills in her hand. Flushed, she set them into the box and said quietly, "I was counting it, but I'm not keeping it, all right? He wants me to, but —"

"Is *this* why you didn't call Bates today?"

"What? No. We called him. He's supposed to meet us in the Walmart parking lot tomorrow. Everything's set. He even agreed to bring me my stuff."

I gathered my wits and faltered forward to the chair, grabbing an errant envelope from the cushion before I sat. "Then what the hell is he doing driving by?"

"How would I know?"

"Because you two were . . ." I waved the letter around. "What were you?"

"I don't know, okay? He was around." She started tidying up again, with even more determination than before.

"Around?"

"Yeah. *Around.* He was around when I needed a job, he was around when I needed a place to crash, or a ride. He was around —"

"When you needed a drink."

She stilled, breathless, and put her little fists to the mattress. Paper crumpled under her weight. "Yeah. Then too."

"Well," I said. "So what? Been there, done that with him, and never going back, right?"

"God no," she said, disgusted, then after a second, shook her head while fussing with the pillow. "I don't know what I was thinking, or how it even happened. One day, I'm working there, and the next he's asking me to move into the place he had with his ex and run their bar with him. I just went along with it. I never stopped any of it, because —"

"I get it. Drinking is better as a team sport." She looked relieved not to have to go on. I sat forward, zeroing in on her black eye, because it felt like we were finally in the space to talk about it. "When did he start throwing haymakers, though?"

The comment burned away her ease. After an incredulous huff, her hand came to her cheekbone. "You think *this* is from him?"

"You don't need some story about a cabinet, Josie. Not with me."

"This is from his truck's airbag." She gauged my disbelief. "I swear. That thing hit me in the face like —" A clap. "Right here." She ran the outer edge of her hand across her temple. "Knocked the shit out of me."

I drummed my fingers on the handlebars of the walker.

"I'm not making it up. I didn't tell you before because . . . well, hello? But I swear to God, it happened because I wrecked the truck" — the next part she struggled to stutter out — "because I was driving shitfaced."

How sober she sounded for once. How honest. Yet I still hesitated. I didn't want her excusing him by blaming herself; that'd be hanging the wrong man.

She stared hard at me, hands clenched to keep a tremor at bay. "Do I look like the type of person who would take that sort of shit from someone?"

I stared back, rewinding every moment we'd spent together. She was a hothead, like me. Name-calling and bottle-swinging. Fast-footed and sharp-tongued. The only conclusion I drew from this was that though she may have been a victim of many circumstances, this was not one of them. Thankfully. "No, no, you do not."

A barely there smirk played across her face. "That's right."

"But Bates looks like the kind of guy who would give it." This wiped the grin away. "Is he?"

She offered a tight shrug. "I've seen him throw down. I've seen him punch holes in walls. So, yeah, he gets amped, and he's probably amped right now. But I don't really blame him. I mean, I owe him a lot of money —"

"You owe him *nothing.*" I pointed the sharp edge of the envelope at her. "Carl is taking care of that truck, free and clear, so you can tell Bates to kiss your go-to-hell if he ever acts like you owe him anything. Do you understand me?"

She was full of air meant for arguing, but it went out of her in a puff. I nodded in approval, then realized I'd just about stabbed her to get my point across. To beg her pardon, I mumbled an apology and offered the envelope to her, but she didn't move to take it.

"Come on." I waggled it some. "Twenty bucks says there's twenty bucks in here."

She shook her head.

"What? Did you already go digging in this one too?"

"No."

I narrowed my eyes and flipped the envelope over, where the seal had already been broken. Inside, there was no money. No letter. Just an old black-and-white photo — the one Carl had been hunting for. I held it up, and a woman, pretty as pie supper, looked back at me with a glitter in her eye that matched Josie's. Even in gray scale,

Koko had a spark. Little Kaiya was a bundle of blankets, washed out against her mother's apron. But there they both were, preserved in a day that once was.

"Well, I'll be."

"I'm giving it back to him," Josie said. "Same with the cash."

I tore my eyes away from the picture to look at her.

She shrugged. "Him helping me pay for the truck is one thing, but this, it's like blood money. My mom never wanted it, so I don't either. And he can keep the picture to remember why."

Her voice sounded determined, but there was still a quiet question in it, asking me to weigh in. I looked down at the photo again — at that spark. I think Carl had meant to borrow from it, but he ended up stealing it instead. He took from Koko, and every generation after. And then he'd tried to replace it with Andrew Jackson, which was well wide of the mark. So maybe he didn't deserve any grace, after all that thieving, but still I said, "You're wrong."

Josie raised her chin — a little slip of a girl ready for a fight that didn't need fighting anymore.

I said, "Turning it away isn't carrying on your mama's legacy like you think, because that box of money right there, that *is* her legacy. By her hand, it's been saved . . . for you. Every time she sent a letter back, even if she didn't know it yet, she was giving you a gift. And Carl . . . well, giving is his nature, and maybe he's still working on perfecting it, but you should meet him where he is and take it how it comes."

Josie frowned, then hung her head to think on it.

Eventually, I said, "How about we do this: I'll do something special with this picture for Carl if you'll do something special with that money."

She hid behind the long apron of hair that had fallen across her face. "What should I do with it?"

"Get a piggy bank, first off. And then . . ." I paused.

She peeked up.

I wanted to list all the wonderful things that it would lead to, because here sat a girl who would go to college, have a real job and a decent boyfriend. Instead — since there still seemed a possibility to pull my chute at the end of this endless jump and land where I always wanted — I said, "You're going to have to find a new place to live."

A hush followed. Deep, digesting breaths.

She already knew this, but still.

I said, "We don't want to kick you out, but —"

"I know. I can't live at a . . . nursing home." She said that last bit as a joke and snuck a look at me to see if I'd caught it. Damn if I didn't smile. She poked the nearest box of money, her shoulders hiked up past her ears. "If you need me to, I could even go today."

"No. You should definitely stay tonight." It wasn't quite a thirty-day program, but it'd have to do.

She exhaled in relief. "Yeah. Definitely. One more day would be great."

We nodded at each other, committing to it. Then I went to sit next to her, to put my arm around her, and she let me. "We can make it another twenty-four hours without getting caught, can't we?" I said. "All we need to worry about at this point is getting your mama back from Bates without any injuries."

"Is that all?" she said, sarcastic, and we both went silent, listening to the purr of street traffic droning in the distance, punctuated only once by an engine's backfire.

They'd let loose nine puppies in the facility. They yipped behind the couches and underneath chairs. They peed and chewed and wagged. Shawn stood guard at the automatic front door so they couldn't escape, while the owner of Happy Tails, Tovah, chased them down whenever a resident wanted to snuggle.

Barkley, an elderly Labrador who'd been coming for years, rested near my feet. He'd raise his head up from his paws only when he wanted to yawn. Beyond him were more animals, including a poodle, a lapdog that might as well be a rat on steroids, and one very patient cat. Anarchy ruled.

Alice and Valencia sat on the couch together with a pup between them, tittering. The dog, still not completely steady on his legs, would wobble and fall whenever it tried to climb up Valencia's thigh. Carl sat in his walker's seat next to me, pointing out the errant runaways to Tovah.

All these high jinks, and I couldn't enjoy it. I spent my time checking the front door for Bates, and the hallway for Josie, who had planned on coming a few minutes behind me.

One of the pups — a shar-pei with a hippopotamus face and more rolls than you could count — sniffed around Barkley and, next, climbed on top of his back so he could reach my seat. Barkley let out a heavy sigh but didn't move. I gave the little guy a boost and fought the urge to smile while he crawled up my chest and touched his wet, cold nose to my neck. We had so many more important things to do than this, but these puppies. These damn puppies.

Anderson emerged from the hallway with Josie by his side.

I grasped my companion, whose dog tag said Sherpa, and tried to calm him into sitting on my lap while I motioned Josie over.

She cocked her head and offered me a smirk, a cold-sober smirk, and I knew what she was thinking. Happy Tails looked like a silly waste of time — Lord knows, that's what I thought at first — but the sentiment wouldn't last long. I held Sherpa up so that his soft, barreled belly replaced my face.

"Can hardly tell the difference," Anderson said as a puppy latched on to his shoelace and gave it a tug.

"Sic him," I urged. "Get 'em."

When the shoelace came undone, Alice yelled, "Good boy!"

And, in usual fashion, Anderson scooped the dog up and held him high above his head like a football and bellowed, "Who wants a puppy?"

A chorus of "I dos" filled the room.

Josie plopped down on the floor next to

Barkley. She scratched him on the head before sitting on her hands. The tremors were always a nuisance while you were climbing on the wagon.

"They'll go away," I said. "Maybe if you hold this guy?"

She considered him. "He does look like you."

"Attack," I said, releasing Sherpa, but instead of heading to Josie, he scampered toward the cat, then veered off behind the furniture.

"Some guard dog," I said.

Josie absently rubbed Barkley's head again. "So is this it? You all, like, sit around and pet some pets that aren't your pets?"

"I say it's wonderful. We don't have to feed them or bathe them or pick up their poo," Valencia said.

Alice added, "Especially after the day we've had."

And wasn't that the truth, with one resident sentenced to Simmons, another one to death. We counted on stuff like this to keep us afloat, and none of us took it for granted.

Barkley leaned into Josie, eventually setting his head in her lap. Valencia let out a hoot, because her puppy had finally scaled her leg and found something very interesting to smell in her armpit. Her laugh turned contagious, until everyone had it but Josie and me. Josie watched the routine with an observant smile; I returned to watching our backs.

"Help," Valencia giggled.

Josie leaned in to me and whispered, "This isn't bad."

I smiled and whispered back, "Welcome to Centennial."

She popped up to rescue the ladies from being licked to death. Meanwhile, I glanced over my shoulder at the front door, where Shawn stood like a lineman, poised to keep everyone from going out, though in my opinion, he should've been looking in an entirely different direction.

38

Josie noticed me jumping every time the front door whistled open and nagged me over the next few hours to relax. I returned the favor whenever her breathing started to look like desperation instead of an automatic body function. It took some time, but eventually my worry dissipated alongside the late afternoon. I stopped checking the door and peering out the window; Josie stopped having the shakes.

Happy Tails packed up, and Tovah said goodbye, but the aftereffects stayed. Pure joy bottled up to borrow from later. Bates became an addendum, moved to an unused corner of my brain to wait until tomorrow. And we only had one more night to worry about Josie being here. One more long night.

In the meantime, I took all that newfound energy to slip away before dinner. I snuck some tape, scissors, and a tacky album page from Shawn's crafting closet.

Back in the room, I located Carl's torn picture of Jenny. I had Koko and baby Kaiya in hand. The last bit was Carl, who waited in scraps in my cigar box. I pulled the walker up to the dresser, laid out all my parts, and went to it, piecing Carl back together like a jigsaw puzzle. At the end of it, I had all three girls behind the album sheet's plastic overlay, and then Carl, who looked fair to middling except for his missing left foot. If you weren't looking for it, you hardly noticed.

I trimmed the page and taped it to its rightful spot on the mirror, then backed up to admire it, pretty sure Carl would like it just fine. I thought it best if he used the frame Josie got him for a nice picture of the two of them, and I made a mental note to ask Anderson to snap one with his magical pocket phone.

By the time I left for dinner, I was practically skipping between the legs of my walker. Something told me this evening would be more than all right, and I was ready to take it in. Immortalize it. Wrap it up with ribbon before it had even come to a close.

There are only a handful of nights that are shelved in my memory bank as being perfect. There is the evening my father took

Cormac and me to a picture show, to see *The Wizard of Oz.* There is prom night, for the typical reason. There is one quiet night in Vietnam when the clear sky belied the war and gave me every constellation known to man. And then there was tonight at the dining room table, with Alice, to my right, talking about the beauty that comes from having pets in your family; Carl, to my left, arguing that they have no souls and therefore cannot go to heaven; and Valencia, in between, wearing a feather boa, jabbering on about a parakeet she once had. During all of this, Josie would catch my eye across the span of empty dishes and half-filled glassware, and we'd acknowledge a million things with one look. We'd made it to this point in earnest, and the dinner was nothing special all by itself, but considering everything leading up to it, it was something to behold.

It was Music Marathon Night too, meaning they put old tunes on the stereo and piped it through the main living room until eight o'clock. Cole Porter and Glenn Miller took turns filtering into our conversation. Anderson left the dirty dishes for later and joined us while the rest of the dining hall emptied. He straddled a backward chair, chin on the top rail, gazing at Josie.

418

"I say heaven is full of parakeets," Valencia said. "And monkeys probably too."

"What in the world are you guys talking about?" Anderson asked.

"Pet theology," I said, "which seems to be a combination of pseudoscience and blasphemy. Very interesting."

This elicited a group chuckle, and then everyone went quiet.

In time, Alice spoke up. "Anderson, would you tell us about this renovation? We've been talking about it all week long. When does it start, and how long is it supposed to last?"

He sighed. "Jackhammers come Monday morning, and . . ." A shrug. "Honestly, all I know is that it starts with that one room, and then as Sharon can afford it —"

"You mean as she gets rid of us," I said.

Alice clucked in criticism.

Anderson puffed out his cheeks, then let the air escape slow. "I don't know what to tell you. I'm probably out of a job when it's all done too."

"You could always work at Simmons," Alice said. "We could use you there."

My head snapped in her direction. "What do you mean, *we*? You're not going there." I pointed at Anderson. "And you, you'd be better off working at a dog pound."

419

"Duffy," Alice said evenly, strong and soft at the same time. "We can't pretend it's not happening, even if Reginald's right about it going slower than Sharon expects. We might as well . . . get ready."

I looked around as everyone nodded. Not one of them had war paint on, and a burning rose up from my belly. White flags were not my thing. Carl gave me a worried look, like maybe I'd forgotten our own preparations, our joint hustle to heaven. I hadn't; I just wasn't convinced I had to roll over to get there.

Anderson tipped his head to see me better and said, "I'm getting ready to go back to school once I get fired."

And wouldn't you know it: He'd turned the renovation into aspiration. That bastard. But good on him. At least we'd have one decent thing to show for it.

I nodded in approval. "I guess you'll have Sharon to thank for that."

He stifled a rascal smile and sat up straighter. "Speaking of, she gave us the go-ahead for tomorrow's funeral. So who's coming?"

"I say all of us," Valencia declared.

"If it's okay with everyone," Alice added.

"For sure," Josie said before anyone else could answer.

Hesitation crossed Carl's face, but he didn't protest. Neither did I. The Bates exchange would be dicey, but there was power in numbers, and they could keep Josie put while we took care of business.

Anderson said, "Where are we going after the pickup at Walmart?"

"Lunch?" Josie said.

We turned to her. She twirled a straw wrapper into a tight coil until it broke, then started to unfurl the remnants. "If it's cool with you guys, I'd like to grab a bite to eat and then head to this place called Sanger Overpass?" She tore the pieces until they were too small, then piled them into a tiny, neat hill. "That's where we . . . where my grandma is. Her ashes. I think Mom would like to be with her. There's this train; it runs every few hours, and in between one of them, we can . . ." She spread her hands, like letting a butterfly go. She followed this up with a half shrug. "I mean, since I can't take Mom to Paris, this is the next best thing, right?"

A hush fell across the table. Carl, with a loose fist to his sternum, looked to me. I nodded. He may not have known their birthdays, but knowing of this one hidden gem was worth more than all those sorts of facts and figures combined. There was redemption in it.

"It's perfect," I said.

"We can go to a French restaurant," Alice suggested.

Anderson rested his chin again. Beneath the table, Valencia tapped her feet to the music. It was one of my favorite tunes. Tommy Dorsey played a soft, sad trombone, but still he made you want to dance, preferably slow and all by your lonesome. "I'm Getting Sentimental Over You." The song belonged here, now, along with all my friends. I closed my eyes and soaked up the vibrato of the brass, the glowing notes, and officially shelved the evening along with the rest.

I don't know if it was the music or the late hour or what, but we should have seen him coming. We should have sensed him, even. But none of us did. We didn't hear the car pull up and park, or the door open, or his heavy footfalls across the room. Just like that, I open my eyes and Bates is looming over the table. A giant with a tiny toothpick sticking out of the corner of his mouth.

"Evening," he said.

Josie moved to stand, but Anderson put a hand on her shoulder and stood instead. "Visiting hours are over."

Bates made an I-don't-give-a-shit noise in his throat and pulled a chair up next to Alice, who made room for him with manners and fear. He sat with legs splayed and arms thrown over the neighboring chairs, and looked at Josie like she was the only one in the room.

"Hey, babe," he said flatly.

"What are you doing here? I told you over the phone —"

"I know we spoke, but that wasn't you talking." He hitched his head to me. "Grandpa over here has you all messed-up in the head. Why don't you come home tonight so we can relax and work everything out?"

The hair on the back of my neck prickled. He was used to getting his way, by making sure Josie felt wanted and wasted and willed. He'd come here to work her over.

Anderson pushed up his sleeves. "Josie isn't going anywhere."

Bates snorted. "Who are you?"

"A friend."

He switched the toothpick to the other side of his mouth. "Making friends already, Josie?"

"Just leave," she said. "Don't start trouble."

"I'm not here for trouble. I'm here for

you . . . babe." Again, the word was lifeless.

"I'm not your *babe.*"

"No?"

"You heard her," Alice said, each word like a wince. She went white when Bates shifted to see her better.

"Okay," I said, trying to move my chair back and stand. "That's enough."

Anderson didn't help me maneuver, and at first this agitated me, but then I was glad for it. I stood up all on my own, and even though my heart had begun to bite at the inside of my chest, I pulled my shoulders back so that I was nearly as tall as Anderson, who stood beside me.

"Let's save you the trip tomorrow morning. Do you have Kaiya?" I said.

Bates ignored me and leaned in, elbows on the table. "Josie, you got a shift tomorrow."

"I quit, Bates. I told you that."

"Really? You're just going to leave me like that?"

"You're a big boy."

He clamped his jaw down on the toothpick and stared. She stared right back. *Good girl,* I thought.

Behind me, Nora was running all over hell's half acre, passing out evening pills, and thankfully hadn't noticed the scene

424

brewing. But who knew how long that'd last, because beside me, Anderson's testosterone bubbled. He clenched his fist and rocked to his toes every few seconds. We had the makings of a good bar fight but lacked the bar. I hoped he understood this.

Anderson said to Bates, "Let me see you out."

Bates didn't move. "Can you afford to quit, Josie? I mean, what if that rock isn't enough for my truck? How are you going to pay your bail?"

"It'll cover the truck." Carl sat up. "I have it here."

"Hold on, though," I said. "First, where's Kaiya?"

"I threw the box in my garage," Bates said.

This disrespect to the body went against the older ladies' sensibilities for sure. They squirmed in their chairs away from Bates, who had again spread out to take up as much space as possible. Anderson looked on the verge of beating the ever-loving crap out of him right there.

Carl, in his quiet way, defused the situation. He pulled the ring from his shirt pocket, set it in the pit of his palm, and offered it to Bates like Eucharist. "Look."

Bates sat up to peer into Carl's cupped hand. Out of curiosity, Josie did too. The

425

overhead lights hit the rock just right, reflecting a beam back into both of their eyes.

"Oh my God," Josie breathed, looking up. "No way that truck is worth that."

Bates shot her a death glare. "I put a Hemi in it last year."

"It's ten years old," she shot back.

"So what? I bought it new." Bates pointed at the ring. "And for all I know, that's fake."

"It's not," Carl said quietly, folding his finger back over it, closing off the glare. "It was my grandmother's, my mother's, and then . . . my wife's."

I said, "Carl, maybe we should —"

"I don't care about the price. I want my daughter back." His voice broke. "You bring me my little girl tomorrow like we agreed. Do you understand? I've got to give her a place to rest."

Josie reached under the table and found my hand, squeezing it hard enough to turn the tips of my fingers purple.

Bates switched his toothpick over one more time. "Fine," he said finally, standing. "You bring that tomorrow, I'll bring the box, and we're done. But I'm not going to Walmart. I'm on the opposite side of town."

"The Sonic, then," I said. It came out as a cough, since my ticker was still acting up.

426

He gave me a cold stare. "You meet where I say, and I say we go to the place where Josie left my truck to rust. Just so you can see where the drunk-ass bitch wrecked it."

Before I even blinked at the name-calling, Anderson had a fistful of Bates's shirt in hand and their noses were tip to tip.

In the living room, Nora shifted, turned, tuned in.

Anderson logged the movement in his periphery, grimaced, and threw Bates back with a shove. "Get the hell out of here."

Bates took a few agile steps to regain his balance, his hands up like he meant no harm. But the look he laid on us said otherwise.

Anderson pressed forward toward the door, forcing Bates to walk backward as he said, "I'll bring your shit too, Josie. Save *you* the trip." He pointed past Anderson at her, and then me, baring his bleached teeth. Then without another word, he wheeled around and left. No one so much as breathed until a car door slammed and tires squealed.

Anderson walked back to our table, shoulders heaving, running both hands through his hair before stopping to hold his head like it might explode.

Josie stood and scanned the crowd. "I'm

sorry. This is all my fault."

"Don't worry, sweetheart," Alice said. "Sit back down. We're all okay."

She shook her head. "I . . . I've got to go —"

"Back to the room," I ordered. It was the only safe place for her to be. From Bates, sure, but mostly from herself.

"Let me go with you," Anderson said, reaching out, but once he heard the edge in his own voice — the rage that hadn't burned off yet — he stepped back and dropped his hand.

Nora arrived, cell phone ready. "Is everything straight? Do I need to call the cops?"

"No," I said. "It's all over now."

Alice swooped in. "He was a bully, Nora, but Anderson took care of him. You know what, though? I'd like my blood pressure taken, if it isn't too much trouble."

"For sure," Nora said. "You feeling all right?"

Alice frowned. "Precaution."

"Let me get my cuff." Nora trotted to the far reaches of the living room, where she'd parked her cart.

"Go now," Alice whispered to Josie.

So she did. She took off to the room, presumably to have a good cry. Anderson fell into a chair. Nora returned and took Alice's blood pressure, and next Valencia's, by request. They both asked questions about the circulatory system, the instruments used to measure it, all so interesting, all meant to keep Nora on task. Carl kept quiet while the Ink Spots crooned "If I Didn't Care" in the background.

When Nora took my pressure, she made some concerned clucks and took it twice. On the third attempt, she borrowed Anderson's watch. It didn't surprise me. I felt my heart beating all the way down my wrist, stabbing me under the clavicle, and, I reminded myself, keeping me alive. That's all I wanted out of it, nothing more, nothing Olympian, and so far, it was doing the job just fine.

"Any pain?" she asked.

Anderson peered over her, arms folded, brow knitted.

I saw in Nora's face that she meant to sideline me, and I had somewhere to be tomorrow. Somewhere I'd kill to go to. Plus, in lots of ways, my heart was working better than ever.

"No," I said with conviction and a smile. "None at all."

THE CENTENNIAL SCHEDULE
August 30 — Wednesday

8:00   Breakfast
9:00   Book Club, Atrium
12:00 Lunch
3:00   Magician, Living Room
5:00   Dinner
6:00   Trivia Social, Living Room

39

At the brink of waking, dreams feel real, concrete, and painted in the right colors. You exist there. So does everyone else. If it's a good dream, it's an all right place to be. For me, on this particular morning, I never wanted to leave.

I had some sense that the sun was up, that breakfast was being served, that time was a-wastin', but I couldn't get to the other side of consciousness. I understood that I lay in bed, but I believed my dream more.

I stood on Sanger Overpass, with the burnt oranges and peaches of dusk behind me and a skyway at my feet that looked as pretty as the old steel truss bridge in Tom Green County. Josie stood nearby, downwind, her hair dusting her shoulder and cheeks. We'd already released Kaiya's ashes. She'd made her way in loops, ribboning out and disappearing like the wind knew its purpose. Now we were quiet, content in her exit and waiting for the train — a rumble in the distance, like gravel filling an empty rain barrel, getting closer and louder until —

"Clarence Riley," Nora yelled in the hallway. "You gotta steer clear of my cart with that scooter. Lord, we need to get you lessons before you hurt somebody."

There the dream went, fading to black.

I opened my eyes, and the room corners that greeted me every morning looked more confining than usual. Carl had left the door wide open again, his passive-aggressive way of waking me. From the bustle in the hallway, I knew that breakfast had ended.

Clarence, riding atop Charles's old electric scooter, zoomed by. Sherri Linley followed. I could tell because of the constant whisper of her house shoes. She never picked up her feet.

She must've heard me too, specifically the "Jesus Christ" I uttered while sitting up, because she stopped and shuffled into the room. "Everything all right?"

God almighty. My legs, my hip, my head. And my heart. The sharpness from last night had subsided, evolved, mutated, and was now a dull ache with a wide footprint. Bearable but bothersome. "Fine, thank you. Saying my morning prayers, is all."

Her voice pitched up in disbelief. "You pray?"

I grimaced, manually placing each leg over the side of the bed. "Don't sound so surprised, Sherri. I come to Shabbat and chapel when we have them. You've seen me there."

"But I've never heard you pray."

"I've never heard you go to the restroom, but I suspect you do anyhow." She didn't act surprised by this stab, making me feel like the asshole I was. After rubbing my fists in my eyes and shaking off the last remaining sleep, I said, "I do it in my head mostly."

"Except today?"

I exhaled and took a break from trying to stand. "What is this, Sherri, the Inquisition?"

"I was only asking in case you'd like to pray together. It's been a long week, with Charles passing and Agnes leaving, and I heard you and Carl have a tough trip to make today. I've already prayed for you, but when two or three are gathered in His name, there He is also." She straightened her breakfast robe.

We appraised each other. The last time I prayed out loud was at my final AA meeting, and it wasn't the deep, honest moment it should've been. The Serenity Prayer always culminated AA's formal proceedings, and during it I remember having scooted out of my chair in the back so I could beat everyone to the coffee carafe. I stirred in cream and said whatever words didn't interfere with getting my caffeine fix. *God, grant me the serenity to accept* — sip — *I cannot change* — more sugar, stir — *courage to change* — sip — *the wisdom to know the difference.* Sip, sip, sip. *Amen.*

"Well," I said finally, "I guess there's no harm in it."

This pleased her, and she shambled forward, standing close enough to take my hand. Her fingers were warm, her touch gentle. She dipped her chin so that I was staring into the shiny, bald crown of her head. I closed my eyes dutifully and waited for whatever came next, peeking up when it took too long to get going.

Sherri's brow, folded into a dozen pleats, made praying look like hard work. I'd forgotten this part: the burden of collecting all your troubles and apologies and gratitude into one place. Maybe that's why I didn't do it often. But now, before I could help myself, there it all was. Everything in a moment. Forgiveness for me. Sobriety for Josie. Strength for Carl. A lucky break for Anderson. A chance with Alice. A raise for Nora. A new job for Luann. A heart for Sharon. And a new zip code for Bates. Better yet, a new continent.

"Do you want to speak first?" Sherri whispered.

I did but couldn't. There was too much. She'd tapped at a cracked dam and broken it. My heart swelled, burned even, like last night. "I'm saying them in my head."

She grimaced, frustrated by our backward progress. "Try."

Knowing she wouldn't let me go until I gave it a whirl, I decided on something benign and easy to put into words. The perfect wind from my dream. "I pray for good weather." It sounded like a petition from a child. A sturdy silence followed it until eventually Sherri realized I had nothing more to add.

She drew a deep breath and spoke collectively. "Lord, help us *weather* all things by aligning the desires of our hearts with yours. Make it so in your good time, in Jesus's name we pray —"

"Amen," I said, relieved. I couldn't handle the weight of it all anymore.

"I'm not done yet."

Anderson rounded the corner and stopped midstride. He wore a black suit, something

I wouldn't have guessed he even owned. It brought out the angles in his jawline and the broadness in his shoulders. The suit suited him.

"What are you guys doing?" he asked.

"We're praying," Sherri said.

"We *were* praying," I corrected, sliding my hand from hers and standing without any more premeditation. Felt like taking a round from a machine gun.

"It's about time you're up," Anderson said. "We've got to get moving. It's calling for rain this afternoon, so now lunch is at eleven, then the swap, then Sanger Overpass before the two o'clock train."

I looked at Sherri as if the weather were her fault, even though I knew it was mine. God owed me nothing, not even sunshine.

"You need help getting dressed?" He straightened his tie.

I hadn't pulled out my suit in years, and for whatever reason, I wanted to don it myself. "How much time do I have?"

"An hour or so."

This seemed like a reasonable allotment to get clothed. "I'm all right, but thank you."

Anderson nodded and placed my walker in front of me.

"Oh! One thing before you go," I said, remembering I had yet to give Nora my

436

prescriptions. I walked to the foot of my bed, where yesterday's pants hung, and fished in the pocket.

"I almost forgot something too," Anderson said. "Just so you know: Nora's coming today."

I paused with the slip in my hand. "Do what?"

"Sharon's orders. So I warned Nora that we have to stop by and pick up the remains from a relative on the way to the bridge. No big deal." He pulled the paper from my hands, peeked at it, and raised an eyebrow.

"It's for . . ." I didn't finish; there were too many things going around in my head. Mostly, I didn't like how the Bates exchange was fleshing out. A different location, compressed time, plus Nora. What could possibly go wrong?

Anderson slid the prescription into his jacket and clapped me on the back. "I'll get it taken care of." He hooked his arm for Sherri. "Shall we?"

She looked up at him, admiring. "You look handsome."

"Same with you," he said, walking her out.

After he shut the door behind him, I went to the window. Outside, the sky was cloudless but shaded in an inky blue that promised a toad choker. I mumbled, "God, if not the weather, then at least keep us safe today, okay?"

In response, nothing.

So I opened the window for him to hear me better, and the road noise spilled inside, churning around me, buzzing like an electric current. My heart rate picked up speed and became thin and biting at the edge of my chest. "God?" I yelled. "Keep us safe from Bates."

And still, nothing.

Damn that dead-air reply. All these years, and I still couldn't bear it. It's what drove me into the bathroom to gather my bullet in the soap dish. And it's why I walked back to my dresser and got out my gun. Because I didn't like His answer. If He wasn't going to promise to protect me and my friends, then I'd do it myself.

Loading the pistol proved a chore. My hands trembled. My fingers fumbled. But eventually, I won, snapped the chamber shut, and held it in my hand, like you do. I looked ridiculous in the mirror — maybe because I was eighty-eight with a beer belly and a swollen, stitched head and a damn walker. Or maybe it was because I had pajamas on, which was the only thing I could fix at the moment. So without think-ing much more about it, I set off to the rigorous job of putting on pants. There was no getting around without them. I had a pocket pistol to store, after all.

Carl wore his Sunday-go-to-meeting clothes: a button-down and a navy blazer. Alice had on a dark gray dress and held a purse to match, while Valencia had on a black number that reminded me of a kimono. On the couch, Anderson sat with ankle on knee and his suit jacket unbuttoned, looking even more James Bond than before. I couldn't look upon the lot of them without getting a twinge in my side. This felt like it might be our last great adventure together.

On the opposite side of the room, Josie sat in one of the wingback chairs and wore her red dress, cleaned and pressed, no bloodstains in sight. Her shoes had no laces, thanks to me. When she met my gaze, she smirked at my attire. My old suit didn't fit like it should — or, rather, at all. I'd grown too many inches out. So I'd settled on a pair of khakis and a black cardigan, which had some stretch and hung low enough to cover my pocket — which was just about all I could think about. Now that I was in public, packing heat seemed like overkill. I'd wanted to feel secure, but it actually caused more anxiety. Mostly because if I wasn't careful, the gun would clang against my walker when I walked.

"Are we ready?" Anderson asked.

Josie stood and led us out. A group loitered near the door to honor the mini funeral procession: Sherri, Clarence Riley, Reginald, Sharon even. They offered condolences to Josie and Carl as they passed.

On my way by Sharon, she held my hand longer than necessary. "We still need that follow-up meeting, don't we?"

I nodded to my walker. "Got an upgrade."

"I see. But we still have other issues to discuss."

Be nice, I thought, realizing most of my fight to stay at Centennial would be with myself. Sharon had me down but not out. I smiled big. "Will do, but you're also welcome to call my doctor. Tell her I said, 'San Francisco, clouds, orange.' Can you remember that?"

Sharon's brow gathered to match her pucker.

"Just do your best. She'll know what it means." I let go of her hand and moved on, feeling hopeful. I certainly wasn't going down easy. Once today was behind us, I planned on attending every workout and every sing-along, eating every vegetable, and taking every pill. When I got to Sherri in line, it was like she knew it too, because she gave me an extra blessing for a sound mind and a strong body. I thanked her with a sincere amen.

Next came Reginald, who smacked his lips together before mumbling, "Sorry for Carl's loss."

"Thank you."

He stopped me before I moved along. Stepped too close. "About yesterday . . ."

I raised an eyebrow at him.

"I'd appreciate it if you didn't mention it to anyone."

"No problem, seeing as how I don't know what you were doing, and it's none of my business anyway."

More lip smacking. I wanted to staple them shut to make it stop.

Finally, he leaned in close and spit-whispered, "Between you and me, I took off a few plug plates in my room yesterday."

I backed away, confused.

He exhaled impatiently and peeked at Sharon. She'd been pinned by Connie Salas, whose list of ailments had only just begun.

Reginald said, "I found old cloth wiring. Might even be knob and tube — really old — which means our half of the building isn't grounded. Needs to be addressed before Sharon starts spending money on curtains, if you get my drift. I called the city to make sure they knew."

I saw the usual gleam in his eye: him thinking he was smarter than a hooty owl. And for once, I had to give it to him. "Holy cow, Reginald. Does this mean what I think?"

"You're an idiot, so probably not." He pulled up his britches using both hands. Puffed out his chest. "It means if Sharon touches anything in this building besides the paint, she'll have to bring the whole building up to code, and I guarantee you it's cheaper to leave well enough alone. Unless, of course, she wants a —"

"Money pit," I finished, wanting to hug him. To give him a big sloppy kiss on his cheek. Raise him up on my shoulder and march him around. In the end, I collected myself enough to just offer my hand.

After I held it out for too long, like a chump, he gave in and shook it. And when we were at the tail end of that, I was moved to grab his wrist and raise it high like a boxing champion. I said loud enough for everyone to hear, "This is *the* man."

Reginald, once he got over the surprise of it, smiled wide, and for the first time ever, his eyes were shining and full of something other than shit.

40

I told everyone Reginald's news on the way to the restaurant, and it flipped their funeral moods upside down. And spirits lifted even more when we pulled into the cul-de-sac of François. It was one of the nicest places in Everton — the kind of restaurant with white tablecloths, waiters with bow ties, and mints presented on silver trays after the meal. None of us had ever been there, and we sure were excited. Seemed like outside of our pending exchange with Bates, this day was shaping up all right.

The valet waited outside the bus's bifold doors with his heels pressed together tight and his chin raised. The wind whipped at his hair; the storm was blowing in from the north. Alice flashed me a pretty smile as she stood. Nora strode down the aisle to straighten Carl's jacket, dust his shoulders, and help him up.

She turned, next, to me and ran a hand

over my cowlick with a sad sigh. "Mr. Carl should not be burying his baby, but you know what he told me last night? He said you're his rock. He said without you, he might not've made it to this day alive."

I blinked at her.

"Mm-hmm, you heard me. For once, you're not making trouble." She gave my arm a squeeze and a gentle push toward Anderson, who waited at the steps, hand out, beckoning.

When I reached the concrete, the valet offered a bow, and me not knowing what to do, I bowed right back. Anderson chuckled and swung open the glass doors. I drew a breath, stood off-center in my walker so the gun had some clearance, and made my way.

Inside, it was like English tea with the volume turned up only a little. Nora buzzed around us, pushing in our seats and tucking walkers away, but not before Anderson snapped some group photos, including one of Josie, Carl, and me. The excitement of it all. Here we were outside Centennial's walls for an unapproved, unmandated outing, living outside of the bulletin board frame. Anderson came as a friend. Nora didn't feel like our custodian. This was something special. Something different. Valencia was downright giddy.

"It's my treat today," Carl called out, satisfaction in his voice.

Josie sat next to me, leaning over my menu.

"It's in French," I complained.

"Duh, Duffy."

"How am I supposed to order?" I looked at the options cross-eyed.

"You can kind of recognize some of them. Pick one that looks like a French food you already know."

I pointed at one, putting emphasis on all the wrong letters. "*Souf*-flé?"

She snorted and studied her own menu for a minute.

"How are you feeling?" I asked, like I was only marginally interested in the answer.

She replied in the same manner. "My stomach is still off, and I'm, like, superanxious, but other than that" — she shrugged — "it's a normal day."

"Croissants," I said snapping my fingers. "Those are good."

She tried her best at not looking amused but couldn't hide the smile in her eyes. When it spread to her lips, she said, "My mom would've liked you."

"If she was anything like you, sweetheart, I'm sure I would have liked her too."

Valencia squealed at the other end of the

table. "What did I say? I said there'd be hors d'oeuvres! I did. Oh, what should we get?"

Josie peered up at the chandelier, then back to the menu. "She would have liked this place too. She could've ordered for us. She used to listen to these learn-to-speak French CDs in the car, just in case she ever got to Paris. I always thought they were dumb, but now . . ."

"Remember her like that," I offered.

Josie pressed her lips together. "Instead of dead?"

It was hard to come to terms with someone you loved dying, especially for people like me and Josie, who'd discovered it was easier to drink alcohol instead. But you had to look the loss in the eye, and if you were going to survive it, you had to believe that there were two different parts of every person: the stuff that ended up in the ground and the stuff that didn't.

It had never occurred to me so plainly than in that moment, and while something big and binding shifted deep inside me, I said, "She's looking down at you from heaven."

Josie nodded, pained and uncertain. I lifted the menu to hide the emotion building in my throat. Before I'd contained myself, a hovering person prompted me to peek over the edge of the linen paper. A waitress in a black apron and matching tie stood there, with an ironed napkin draped over her forearm and the heel of a wine bottle precariously balanced on top of it.

"Madame," she said, addressing Josie, "can I interest you in a glass of Château Haut-Brion, or maybe one of our whites?"

Josie looked from the wine, to her, and back.

"Our waters are fine, thank you," Anderson answered from across the table. "We won't be drinking today."

As suddenly as that bottle had appeared, it disappeared. I swallowed hard and stared at the unfamiliar words in front of me. Josie picked up her chilled water and sipped nervously.

Under the table, I found her hand. "I think I'm going to have the soup du jour."

"Me too," she said. "Me too."

I was drunk on cheese and bread and snails and duck. We'd eaten as if Anderson never fed us. The portions were tiny, but rich and beautiful. The chef had spread sauces over the meat like it was one of Shawn's painting projects. Between burps, I joked that I could feel my arteries closing up.

What time we didn't spend aahing over

the plates, Carl and Josie talked about Koko and Kaiya. They surprised each other by knowing the same things, like Koko loved variety shows and hated permanent hair dye, and Kaiya was born in the Year of the Tiger.

Josie and Carl's cheeks shaded pink the same way when they spoke. They also held themselves the same way when they listened — a pointer behind one earlobe, the rest of their fingers curled near their mouth. I think they sensed these reflections. Their bond across the table became real, taut as a hatband, passing straight through the middle of the table. The rest of us leaned back and tried not to disturb it.

Alice sat too far away for me to talk to. I tried, but it turned into a series of say-agains, so I resorted to winking whenever the moment seemed right. She'd smile back, making my heart bleed a little each time. Who would've thought it'd be so hard to steal a gal away from a dead man?

In time, the staff cleared our plates, replaced our napkins, and repositioned the dessert forks for the crème brûlée. I was damn near ready to explode. Heartburn had me clearing my throat often enough it'd become embarrassing, so I excused myself to the men's room.

Anderson rose and unfolded the walker in front of me. "You need help?"

"Why?" I whispered, drawing him close. "You want to hold my pecker?" After he gave the comment its due eye roll, I said, "No, but thank you. I need a little walk is all; I'm full as a tick. Go enjoy yourself. I've got it, promise."

And I did, for the most part. I made it all the way around the corner, as directed by the maître d', before having to stop, and it wasn't because my broken-down body failed me or anything as elderly as that. I stopped because of the bar. I had to. I'd never seen a more beautiful one in my life.

Hang Overs it was not. The liquors were backlit and sitting on glass shelves, glowing like angels. They weren't top-shelf; they were vintage. I came to the counter — a cold, veiny white marble with a bullnose edge, so as to not poke you when you bellied up. It had gold inlay that led to a matching bar sink, next to which sat a pile of bleached bar towels. A dozen taps lined up perfectly to list a bevy of imports, half of which I'd never heard of. And the glassware. A cup of every kind. Schooners, tumblers, shots, and snifters. None of them chipped. None of them spotted. They even had copper mugs for Moscow mules and pewter ones for mint juleps. It was a bar for the gods.

A tossed coaster arrived at my fingertips. "What can I get you?"

She had a warm smile, flawless skin, straight teeth, and auburn curls tumbling down her pressed shirt.

"What's your specialty?" I asked, rationalizing the question as curiosity and not a request.

"We have a few signature champagne cocktails." A drink menu arrived next to the coaster. "What are you in the mood for?"

The salivating began. I was Pavlov's dog. Before I responded — and I planned to with more harmless inquiries that would only lead to a tasting — a warmth grew near my shoulder. It spread until it became a presence, then more than this: a girl.

Josie leaned into the bar like me, so close our arms touched. The bartender had a second coaster in place before I'd drawn a breath. My heart leaped, for all the wrong reasons. Who liked drinking alone anyway?

Josie took the coaster and set it on its narrow edge.

"Can you imagine the sort of damage we could do here?" I asked.

"Totally."

I gestured to all that shone. "Look at it."

451

The bully inside of me had leaked out. *Stay. See. Partake with me.*

I could feel my push working too, but the truth was I didn't actually have to do much convincing. Alcoholics usually convince themselves.

She set her coaster down, like she might actually order, and said, "I thought you said there were better ways to die than this."

This flipped the switch, hearing my own words. "Josie," I stammered, shamed.

She looked up with these pleading green eyes. "Who's on duty watching me if it's not you?"

"I . . . It's me. I'm on duty. I'm here."

She stood very still, then abruptly stacked our coasters and pushed them off to the side. "Okay." She placed my walker and shifted me around by the arm. "Tomorrow, I'll try doing it all by myself."

"Me too."

We took a few steps, and Anderson skidded around the corner and stopped. One look at the backdrop and he had us pegged. "You two didn't have a —"

"Give me a break," I said.

Josie added, quieter and meeker, "No."

"Thank God. That would have been . . ." He put his hands on his hips and looked away, grimacing and shaking his head. When

452

he turned back to us, he looked decided about something. "Josie, I need you to know I slipped you Antabuse this morning. I'm sorry. I just . . . It's just . . . I knew today would be hard." He looked away again. "Shit. I feel like an asshole."

Josie let go of me and walked toward Anderson, stopping shy of passing him by. They stood shoulder to shoulder, facing opposite directions.

He studied her profile, practically begging for her to return his look. "I'm sorry. I should've asked you."

In response, she reached out with her pinky and linked it with his. Anderson glanced down at the small gesture before she slipped her hand away and walked on in a puff of red fabric.

He turned to me. "Shit. What did she mean by that?"

"She meant . . . thanks for being on duty. We're both glad, actually. But don't forget: You can't win her fight for her, so don't try." I sidled up to him, poked his foot with the walker. "What are you going to do when I'm not around to translate women for you?"

A tiny corner of a rueful smile. "I'll get a Ouija board."

"I'll be on call," I said. "Now help me

back to the table, would you? I want some dessert."

We exited into a premature night — an afternoon sky tinted a deep purple by low, dense clouds. The older women shrieked with surprise at the temperature. They clutched their cardigans and huddled while waiting for the bus to be pulled around.

For me, the chill was good. It knocked out my contentment and reset my worry. I checked my pocket and gave my sweater to Josie, so that the wind could stir all my senses that the butter and the heavy cream had dulled. The heart race I'd experienced earlier in my room had returned. The fear came back more sinister this time, strong enough that I tasted it at the edges of my tongue.

I yelled to no one in particular, "Should we wait for another day?"

Josie clutched my sweater tight around her. "Duffy, no," she called over the wind. "I want my mom back *today.*"

Everyone heard and nodded, reaffirming their commitment, all except for Anderson and Nora. They conferred with a look. If this trip were officially on Centennial's books, we'd be heading home, but if they tried that now, there'd be mutiny.

No one spoke while boarding. We didn't want to compete with the gale slapping at the windows. After a chorus of seat-belt clicks, Anderson pulled out. He drove with overt attention, hands at two and ten, eyes on the road. No lane changes without a blinker, no impatience at lights. But he was going fast. Faster than necessary. Maybe he thought he could beat the storm, though out my window a gust of wind ripped away the first few drops of rain.

He finally slowed down when he turned onto Sanger. The road went seldom used, and was full of potholes and empty gravel turn-offs. A few minutes in, Anderson came to a full stop at Old Farm Road, where deep tire tracks gouged out the dirt and a bent road sign lay fallen in the grass.

Bates was nowhere to be seen.

A soft patter of drizzle cut the hard-edged silence while we waited. Carl stretched his neck, looking out every window. I drummed my fingers to the beat: *Come on, bastard, come on.* The air in the bus wound tighter than a fiddler's string.

Then in the quiet, like a fire alarm, Anderson's cell phone rang.

I couldn't hear a word of the conversation while sitting in the last row, but next thing I knew, Anderson pulled out and floored it.

He flashed his eyes at me in the rearview mirror. The connection lasted all of a second, but I understood: Bates wasn't feeling cooperative.

"Slow down," Nora warned. "Better wet than dead."

My heart thrummed along with the engine.

Anderson leaned over to speak to Josie, prompting her to open the glove compartment. She pulled out a large first-aid kit, and from that she produced paramedic scissors, the kind with a funny angle in the shears and a relatively dull tip. Worthless for self-defense. My gun burned at my thigh.

We finally slowed, a feathery rain dusting the front windshield. The wipers squeaked as they skimmed the glass, leaving behind a clean sweep where the lattice girders of Sanger Overpass appeared. Anderson crept the bus to the middle of the bridge and stopped.

Carl grabbed the seat in front of him and pulled forward to look over it. "I don't see any —"

At that moment, headlights flashed behind us, brakes squeaked, and our vehicle bumped forward a foot. Everyone yelped in surprise. I shifted around to look out, and watched as a tiny bullshit Honda rental pulled back from our rear fender. Its headlights flashed in the cabin again and froze, painting streaks of humming light on the ceiling and warped shadows everywhere else.

"Duffy?" Anderson asked, squinting into the strobe.

"He's parked," I called before my throat closed up.

Anderson shook off his jacket, loosened his tie, and pocketed the scissors. "Nora, make sure everyone stays out of the rain. I'll take care of this."

"What's wrong with that fool?" Nora asked. "Is that who's dropping off —"

Anderson slammed his door shut. Valencia moved next to Nora, whispering some version of the story in her ear. Carl clambered beside me to watch from the rear windows.

Bates exited the rental car and pitched something over the bridge. On his way back, the men met in front of the headlights. They were mere outlines, rough drawings that spoke only in stance and stature. We heard nothing over the idling engines. When Bates's form spread, so did Anderson's. They stood with legs set apart, hands on hips, drawing closer and closer together until the inevitable was obvious.

Carl turned to me then, fire in his eyes, and pointed between us and the exit.

"Damn straight," I answered, because it was the only way any man worth his salt should, no matter his age.

41

We walked down the bus's aisle as casually as possible. Nora sat with her ear bent to Valencia, though she peeked up.

"Where do you think you're going?" She stood as Carl made it down the first step. "Nosiree. You need to stay inside the bus."

Valencia had trapped Nora in the window seat when she'd sat down, and she pretended to be helpful, trying to get out of the way, all the while making Nora's exit even more impossible.

Josie held the lever for the bus's door.

"Open it," I said.

"I should go. This is my mess."

"No, by golly," Carl said. "It's mine."

A moment passed, full of all the weighty things this meant. Next, a whoosh of pressure escaped as the doors sighed open.

Carl stepped onto the broken pavement, balancing himself with the side of the bus as he made his way to the back. I followed, watchful of my step. We moved into the misting rain and the flood of headlights, palms out. Bates and Anderson stood as silhouettes, coming into focus only after our angle changed. The lights played across their faces in angry ways.

Bates spotted us first and drew back from Anderson, waving his pointer. The motion was erratic. Drunk. "I'm helping Josie clear out her shit."

"Give it or I call the police," Anderson said.

"Call," he roared. "Let's tell them everything."

Stumbling, he walked to his car and dipped into his driver's seat, reemerging with a handful of clothes. He headed for the bridge railing, stepping backward a few times to regain his balance. Anderson grabbed his arm before he made it, and tried ripping a dress away. The rain had slicked the pavement, the fabric. Together, they edged dangerously close to the railing.

"Stop!" I yelled, my voice high-pitched and piercing.

Anderson stopped dead. So did Bates.

Then me too . . . once I realized I was holding out my gun.

Bates let the clothes drop to the ground. I trained the muzzle on him, more or less.

"What are you doing, old man?" he said.

Carl said, "Duffy, have you lost your mind?"

Anderson had his hands up, a pleading in his eyes for me to take it easy.

I tipped the gun to the car and back. My heartbeat had blended into a hum. "Get her stuff out. Set it on the ground. Kaiya too. Carefully."

"Are you going to shoot me if I don't?"

"Maybe." I aimed somewhere between his eyes, my finger on the trigger. I thought of Nam. I thought of the shooting range. I thought of my father with his arms wrapped around mine, helping me aim at a full soda pop sitting on a fence post. I could do it if I had to.

Water dripped from the muzzle of the gun. Beyond it, Bates blinked slowly. Then he stumbled to the car and dipped inside again, throwing clothes and shoes and a few books over his shoulder.

I readjusted my grip, willing my hands to stop shaking.

The final thing he pulled from the car was a box, which he held tight to. "Where's the ring?"

"Drop it, and we'll talk," I said.

The box landed with a thud at his feet. His eyes flickered on mine, and then past me, above me, to the bus's back window. "Josie? I see you," he called. "I gave your dead mom back. Don't you want to come give me a kiss goodbye for old times' sake?"

I turned instinctually to see if she was there, forgetting the first rule of war: Disarm someone when they're distracted. Bates pounced before I knew what had happened. He had my wrist in his hand, his boozy breath in my face.

Anderson raced to us like he'd been shot out of a cannon. And then, somehow, Bates was mixing with him over the gun, and not me. Carl stood paralyzed in the commotion, without his walker. I shuffled around the perimeter, not knowing how to reenter the fray. All the effort left my heart red-hot under my ribs.

A big thunderclap boomed as the gun disappeared between their tangled bodies, then reappeared in joint possession: up in the air, next out toward the bus, then gone again.

Josie ran to us from the shadows, splashing in the collecting puddles. "Stop! Please!"

She was another distraction, this time for all of us. The interruption caused a standstill. A blank void. Afterward: a shot.

The dampness in the air swallowed up the sound; the clouds echoed the bang back.

462

I clutched my burning chest and backpedaled, looking up at Nora and Valencia pressed against the window's steamed glass. I backed all the way up to a metal girder and stopped there, searching my shirt for blood. In the background, feet shuffled: the fight going on without me.

Josie came to me, hands cupping my face. "Are you okay? Are you okay?"

Unable to speak, I pointed at my shirt pocket. She searched, fingers splayed, patting, looking, frantic. My shirt was white. Wet but white.

She undid a couple of buttons, exposing my skin's pastiness, then turned me around, checked my back, the length of my arms. "Your legs? Did you get hit in a leg?"

I shook my head, for they were solid and trouble-free aside from my arthritic knees.

Her hands came to my face again. "Duffy, I think you're okay." She looked up at me with such relief in her eyes, then checked me again, this time with more composure. "I don't see any —"

Another crack in the air, bone on bone this time. Anderson stood twisted in a follow-through from a well-thrown uppercut. The gun lay on the ground, and before the next punch, he kicked it toward Carl, who bent down slowly — so damn slowly — to retrieve it.

Bates, staggering, put his hands up in submission. Anderson stood there, heaving, contemplating, then came at Bates again with a straight punch to the nose. It sent him to the ground, surprised and bloody.

Pain ran all the way to my fingertips, but I put my arm around Josie's shoulder. She turned into me as if *I* could protect her. As if I had the same strength as the two men fighting. As if I had more. She held her fist to the exact spot I figured I'd taken one for the team. Heat radiated from that node, spreading like slow-moving lava. I reminded myself that I was unscathed and looked down at my spotless shirt for assurance.

"Stand up," Anderson said, kicking at Bates until he obeyed. "Get the hell out of here."

Bates spat a dollop of blood onto the pavement. "The ring," he said, heaving. "Give me the ring, or this doesn't end."

Carl had the gun aimed at Bates. He'd gone white, but his expression gave away nothing else. He fumbled in his shirt pocket with his spare hand, fetched the ring, and held it straight out. The stance strained his muscles; both arms shook. Bates closed in, skittish, with the gun right in front of him and the man who had kicked his ass right behind him.

When he got close enough, he reached for it.

Carl drew it away, like he'd changed his mind. "If I let you have this" — he hugged the ring closer to his body — "then you don't come near my granddaughter or Centennial again."

"Whatever," Bates said, hand out.

"Or I'll report it stolen and I'll call in your bar for serving underage girls."

"Yeah, yeah."

Carl's eyes opened with cold-steel confidence. "And I will haunt you when I'm dead."

"Got it," Bates said, slower this time.

Carl nodded, satisfied, gave the ring a kiss goodbye, and set it gently in Bates's palm.

Immediately, Anderson started shoving Bates toward his running car, and slammed the door on him before he was all the way inside. The wipers threw aside water, and Bates laid on the horn. The car lurched onto the road.

When it inched past us, Bates hung his head out and yelled, "Die like your fucking mom, Josie."

I held the girl tighter.

She wrestled away and leaned into the wind, fists tight at her sides, and screamed,

465

"I'm going to live like her, asshole!"

The wheels kicked up mud, but once they gained purchase, Bates faded away at warp speed. No one dared move until distance shrank his taillights into pinpricks.

Finally, Josie spoke, her voice tiny and amazed. "He's gone."

Carl flipped the gun cylinder out like an old pro to unload the extra ammo, but there wasn't any. The only slug had been swallowed up by the sky, and good riddance. We didn't need it anymore.

Carl closed the weapon back up and tucked it into the front of his elastic waistband, the corners of his lips teasing into a satisfied smile; he'd bluffed and won.

"Is everyone okay?" Anderson bellowed.

A stream of answers followed. *Yes. Good. Fine. Alive.*

Nora emerged from the bus with Carl's walker. Valencia appeared too, gripping Alice's elbow. The rain came down harder now, dropping heavily onto Alice's looping salon-set curls.

Anderson strode to me, adrenaline still oozing from him. "Are you sure you're okay?"

I motioned to his split lip. "Better than you."

He wiped the blood away with the back of

466

his hand.

"You did good, kid," I said.

He relaxed into a swell of pride while I coughed. My breath had yet to catch up with me, or maybe it was the other way around. Before I decided, a train horn sounded in the faraway distance.

Anderson flicked his wrist to check his watch. "Shit. Train's coming."

The women picked up speed, heading toward the center of the bridge. Carl stood near the box, holding a black urn like it was a baby. Josie sprinted to his side, taking it out of his hands so he could walk. They came forward together, and it was a sight. A beautiful, sorrowful sight, which managed to take my breath away and give it right back to me.

Anderson and I trailed the crew, steering clear of their whipping skirts and hair until they turned upwind. Josie stopped at the railing, and we surrounded her, tight as a hug.

"What do I do before I let her go?" she asked.

"Say a prayer," Carl said.

Josie looked to me, *me,* and so I spoke, almost reflexively. The Serenity Prayer poured from my mouth — from my soul — in its entirety, and not just the most familiar first four lines. My voice carried with the storm, reaching past the faraway thrum of the coming train. It held strong even as my insides crackled. At the end of it, I drew a ragged breath as Josie uncapped the urn.

It didn't happen like in my dream. The weather wouldn't let it. Josie didn't even have to turn the urn upside down. She merely tipped it, and the gale reached in and pulled Kaiya out. She vanished upon exit. No long goodbye, no time for tears. Probably the departure she would've preferred after spending too many years here, disappearing.

A collective exhale followed the final speck of dust, except from me. I couldn't breathe. My chest pained me again, sharp and telling. It turned my vision red at the corners and seared me from the inside out. I staggered, though this time no girder caught my backpedal.

When I fell, I landed hard but didn't feel it. The group turned to me in surprise and, next, descended like a tidal wave. My name came in a chorus without harmony. *Duffy. Duffy. Duffy.*

It occurred to me briefly that I was having a heart attack. Past the pain, the realization was an afterthought, as if I were thinking of how tall I was or when my birthday was.

October twelfth. Sometimes on Columbus Day. But not always. Not this year.

I took stock of the faces looking down at me. Anderson's disappeared. Josie's came close, her skin damp, her hair plastered against her neck.

She shook me by the shoulders. "Duffy, don't. Don't you dare."

I'm fine, I wanted to say. *Fine.* But I couldn't find my voice.

"Stay here," she pleaded. "Stay with me, Duffy."

Beneath the ache that radiated the surface of me, I thought quite rationally, *But I haven't left. See. I'm right here. I've made good choices.*

The best.

Warm fingers took the hand that didn't throb, and I could tell by the frailty of the hold that it was Alice. Next, her lips warmed my palm, and then she pressed it flush against her cheek and held it there. I wanted to say, *You finally wised up and gave me my kiss,* but the words wouldn't come, so I tried instead to stroke her face. A callback from the olden times, from *my* times. A curled pointer across the apple of her cheek. I felt my fingers reaching, reaching, and wondered if she felt them too.

The measured rhythm of a train sounded

against the railroad ties.

Josie sat up, revealing Nora in my frame. She had her ear to my rib cage, her skin beautiful and dark against mine. Above her, Anderson hovered, blocking the rain, holding the paddles of a defibrillator. She looked up to him with a garbled command, and he handed off something, which she shoved inside my cheek. Aspirin. The cherry pill dissolved on contact, sweet and bitter all at once.

Those scissors appeared — the useless ones — and cut through the buttoned portion of my shirt as if it were tracing paper.

I'm dying. Again, it came as an afterthought. A matter of fact. It didn't produce the fear I'd expected, maybe because I always knew it would happen. It happens to everyone. My dread whenever I thought of this moment had been that I'd go slow and alone, but here I was with everyone I could ever wish for and it was coming at me faster than I could even process.

Charging, he said.

The pounding of the train echoed underneath us, rattling the metal webbing of the bridge.

I'm calling 9-1-1, she said.

Duffy, they all said. *Duffy. Duffy. Duffy. Clear.*

They backed away, all but Carl. He stood tall at my feet, chin raised, distributing his jowl so that he appeared years younger. That handsome devil. I think I looked him in the eye. I wasn't sure what I could and couldn't do anymore, but I willed him to absorb my forgiveness. My apology. I'd judged him this week, because he was human and broken like me. Like all of us. We were cut from the same woven fabric, with weft and warp.

He gave me a nod. A see-you-soon. Permission.

The concrete vibrated.

I drew a starved breath after the shock, then drowned in what wouldn't leave my lungs. Nora and Anderson worked in unison on my behalf, compressing, charging, breathing, clearing. I did my part too, with whatever I had left, but only for their sake. Not for mine.

Godammit, Duffy, Anderson yelled.

Valencia held Carl. Alice held Josie.

I could see them all.

Then suddenly, the pain fell away and I see myself.

It's what you've heard. It's that and more. It's colors you've never seen before and every joyful moment of your life wrapped up into a ball that shines brighter than the sun. There is light at the end of the tunnel, like they say, but it's not really light, it's love.

Past the storm clouds, there's the moon — I know because I can see it too — and past that, there's the universe, and afterward, there's forever. Imagine it going on and on and on. There's Charles. There's Kaiya, with Jenny and her son. There's my ma and pa. My uncle.

There's Cormac.

He's motioning for me to hurry up. He's not a boy anymore; he's a man, a young man, and so am I. Even so, he's still him; I'm still me.

There are angels too.

There is a God.

Carl turns his walker around, folds the seat down, and sits. His arms are draped over the handles, his head hung. Anderson pounds the pavement, opening the skin on every knuckle. He stops when the blood smears on his white button-down, and then he stands, takes Josie from Alice's arms, and holds her to his chest. I love him for that.

I love them all.

Nora starts singing a hymn that's joined in by a thousand voices. Josie peeks from within Anderson's grip, looking up to the downpour, crying for the first time today.

The train horn thunders.

I want to hold her too. Tell her not to worry. Tell her I'm here. But, most of all, I want to tell her the one thing she needs to know, and it is this: Rest assured, there is more to come. There never was and never will be any such thing as THE END.

THE CENTENNIAL SCHEDULE
August 31 — Thursday

8:00   Breakfast

9:00   Resident General Meeting,
       Living Room

10:00 Crossword Puzzles, Atrium

12:00 Lunch

3:00   Matinee Movie, TV Room

5:00   Dinner

6:00   Monthly Birthday Celebration,
       Dining Room

ACKNOWLEDGMENTS

First, thank *you*. This book started out mine, and now it's yours, which is how I always wanted it to be.

Thanks then to Penguin/Berkley, for making it so. Especially Kate Seaver, my editor, for her vision, kindness, and energy. To the team behind the scenes, including Sarah Blumenstock, Craig Burke, Diana Franco, Jeanne-Marie Hudson, Jin Yu, and Elisha Katz. And to Berkley's editor in chief, Claire Zion.

Thank you to my agent, Jeff Kleinman, for plucking me from the slush and patiently refining my work. On a bigger scale, to the entire crew at Folio Literary, including Melissa Sarver White, who has seen to it that these words are translated.

Thanks to DFW Writers' Workshop, the best writing community in the world — which is what happens when you combine talent, generosity, and magic.

Of course I'm indebted to my early readers and cheerleaders, my authors-in-arms: A. Lee Martinez and Rosemary Clement, my mentors. J. B. Sanders, Jr., my sage. Melissa Lenhardt, who cut the jungle ahead of me and continues to share the path. Brian Tracey, who dreams big and makes me do the same. Leslie Lutz, whose words and work make mine better. Melissa DeCarlo, who, in times of need, supplies insights and Ryan Gosling GIFs. Lauren Allbright, my ride or die, who talks to me daily about faith, family, and writing, in no particular order. And to John Bartell, who is the most heartless, hilarious beta reader alive. Sir, they say you should write for an audience of one, and I'm sorry to report that you're it.

Thank you to my pals on the ground of everyday life: all of my Greek Κουμπάροι, my Prairie Creek peeps, and my lifelong friends.

Finally, I'd like to thank my family. I've saved them for last because I know out of everyone, they're guaranteed to read until the bitter end. So a million thanks to the Fosseys, Greens, and Karants for all of the support. And to Marilyn and David Martin, my folks, for basically everything. If you see any wisdom or witticisms in this book, it's courtesy of them.

Thanks also to my kiddos — Tasia, George, Athena, and Frank. Those four little humans spin my world, and I love them big. And above all, to Matt, my better half, who never doubted that this journey would lead here. He's handsome and smart and the best kind of enabler. You were right, babe. Dreams are different than goals. Now come on over here so I can give you a kiss.

ABOUT THE AUTHOR

Brooke Fossey was once an aerospace engineer with a secret clearance before she traded it all in for motherhood and writing. She's a past president and an honorary lifetime member of DFW Writers Workshop. Her work can be found in numerous publications, including *Ruminate Magazine* and *SmokeLong Quarterly.* When she's not writing, you can find her in Dallas, Texas with her husband, four kids, and their dog Rufus. She still occasionally does math.

The employees of Thorndike Press hope you have enjoyed this Large Print book. All our Thorndike, Wheeler, and Kennebec Large Print titles are designed for easy reading, and all our books are made to last. Other Thorndike Press Large Print books are available at your library, through selected bookstores, or directly from us.

For information about titles, please call:
(800) 223-1244

or visit our website at:
gale.com/thorndike

To share your comments, please write:
Publisher
Thorndike Press
10 Water St., Suite 310
Waterville, ME 04901